LIVING DOLLS
AND OTHER WOMEN

GUERNICA WORLD EDITIONS 30

Living Dolls and Other Women

S. Montana Katz

GUERNICA
World
EDITIONS

TORONTO—CHICAGO—BUFFALO—LANCASTER (U.K.)
2021

Michael Mirolla, general editor
Julie Roorda, editor
Cover design: Allen Jomoc Jr.
Interior layout: Jill Ronsley, suneditwrite.com
Guernica Editions Inc.
287 Templemead Drive, Hamilton (ON), Canada L8W 2W4
2250 Military Road, Tonawanda, N.Y. 14150-6000 U.S.A.
www.guernicaeditions.com

Distributors:
Independent Publishers Group (IPG)
600 North Pulaski Road, Chicago IL 60624
University of Toronto Press Distribution,
5201 Dufferin Street, Toronto (ON), Canada M3H 5T8
Gazelle Book Services, White Cross Mills
High Town, Lancaster LA1 4XS U.K.

First edition.
Printed in Canada.

Legal Deposit—First Quarter
Library of Congress Catalog Card Number: 2020951112
Library and Archives Canada Cataloguing in Publication
Title: Living dolls and other women / S. Montana Katz.
Names: Katz, Montana, author.
Series: Guernica world editions ; 30.
Description: Series statement: Guernica world editions ; 30
Identifiers: Canadiana (print) 20200404318 | Canadiana (ebook)
20200404326 | ISBN 9781771835572 (softcover) | ISBN
9781771835589 (EPUB) | ISBN 9781771835596 (Kindle)
Classification: LCC PS3611.A8458 L58 2021 | DDC 813/.6—dc23

Chapter One:

THE CRIME OF THE SCENE

THE ERRIGON GALLERY IS LIT brightly on the darkening SoHo streets. It is opening night of a show of one of the hottest up-and-coming New York painters. In contrast to their brash and brightness, the paintings are hung with surprising reserve. As if to emphasize the point, the reception tables covered with manicured food, forest green, bound brochures, and elegantly printed price lists are decked in linens and outfittings in the staid, muted colors of eggplant, tomato soup, and egg yolk. It is only early evening, but people are already milling around, clustering at either side of the bar tables.

An elegantly dressed man in his early fifties flutters to and fro euphorically, dropping in on conversations and chuckling gaily. He is Frank Errigon, the gallery owner. His current show is launching with a bang. Both *The New York Times* and *The Village Voice* ran enthusiastic reviews which came out just this morning. In his left hand he is holding a small wad of gold embossed versions of the artist's statement, which also hangs poster size in black and white clean block lowercase print at the entrance, backed by a sampling of previous reviews of the artist's work. Frank Errigon hands these out selectively as he weaves his way through the space. He makes a mental note to expand his mailing list once again as he observes gleefully that all kinds of people turned out for the opening: local luminaries; the bridge, tunnel and expressway crowd; young professionals from the Upper West Side; a sprinkling of art historians from Columbia University; and it seems, the entire neighborhood of Tribeca.

The academics stand together, intently discussing university politics. They have the cheese platter and the scotch cornered, much to the chagrin of the bartender who was instructed to pour liquor sparingly. Three Lycra-clad women who appear to have had their lower ribs and backmost molars removed circle the artist and listen to a tale of his recent exploits on the chilly autumn beach in the Hamptons. A clique of six or so thirty-ish women and men hang on every nuance emanating from an older woman clad in an oversized black silk T-shirt, a long, irregular heavy gold chain, dungarees and Birkenstocks. She has a short, angular coif on her curly salt-and-pepper hair. Two suburban couples, standing in front of the centerpiece of the exhibit, a mural sized canvas, are discussing the traffic they encountered on their trip in to see the show. In the middle of their sarcastic yammering about the jams they expect to meet on the way out, Frank Errigon, polite but with an undercurrent of agitation, implores them to stand back and open up the space for others to observe the art.

Passers-by come in off the sidewalk to grab a snack and peek in on what is happening. Genuine viewers begin to peel off, leaving elated and impressed, as the evening wears on. An aerial shot from the thirty-foot ceiling of the reception is being videotaped by a New York University film student. The view resembles the weather show simulations of cloudy air disturbances over time. Snatches of the enlarged artist mission statement get caught in the camera's view, creating unintended near-poetic prose fragments which frame and provide virtual meaning for the movement segment on tape.

A young couple is arguing in the doorway alongside a large, explosive painting done in blinding tropical fruit colors, just as a middle aged woman and man emerge from the commotion and begin to find their way down the street. The man puts his coat over the shoulders of the woman. She shrugs it off, annoyed, and he barely catches it before it crumples to the ground.

In an agitated, fast paced voice, the woman begins to talk.

"It's a dark dusk, isn't it, Milton? And it's cold. Damp and cold. I knew we should have waited to have come on a clear, sunny day. I told you! But no, you said, we're set up to go, so let's go, you said. The coldest day so far. Now we're stuck walking from the gallery all the way in the dark, clear to Greene Street where you insisted we park." Her intonation indicates that she has started in the middle of a long paragraph which she has been reciting for years, if not decades.

"And with those headlines in the papers today! Did you see the picture on the cover of *The Post*? Disgusting.

"What was his name, the artist? *That* artist. Oh, yes. Swanson. Fred Swanson. Murdered in his apartment and cut into pieces. His own blood splattered on a work in progress!

"It was right around here, wasn't it? A block down that way, I think. I hate even to be near it. I'm really getting the chills now.

"Ach! Why do I ever listen to you? Let's get out of here." While she is talking at her husband, the woman is teetering east down Prince Street in her gold colored heels, black rayon pants and fur jacket.

The two of them are in their early sixties and have come to Manhattan specifically to attend the opening of the show, which they had read about in *New York Magazine*. The woman has a generous couple of layers of make up on her face which gives her pale skin a straw colored tinge, Fortunoff gold jewelry, and frosted, orange toned hair which is spray-held into frizzy curls on top of her head.

"Mabel, simmer down." He is wearing a navy blue overcoat, a hat, brown wool slacks and brown lace-up leather shoes with rubber cap galoshes pulled over them. "We're almost there. It's one block more and around the corner. Whoever went after Swanson is not interested in you. Or in me, for that matter. Looks like it was a drug vendetta, like everything else. Some cocaine debt thing. You remind me of the kids when they were young. Or even now that they're supposedly grown." Milton begins to lose his patience at the thought of the ever-mounting bills for his overgrown babies that he's still footing. Through his teeth he says caustically: "Just stop whining."

"You should have gone for the car while I waited."

"Oh, thanks. Maybe you'd like a chauffeur."

It is dark out, and together with the damp fall air, the dingy converted factory buildings sport a sinister look. Prince Street appears as though it hasn't been swept in weeks, if not decades, with clumps of cans, old half-decomposed soggy papers, spent condoms, cigarette butts, wrappers, and other assorted refuse lining the curb. A sludge-like dirt carpets the sidewalk. The parked cars are coated with a film of grime. Every inch of available curb space is filled, bumper-to-bumper. To a non-native, the dimly lit SoHo night streets look cold and menacing—not a bit chic.

Mabel and Milton pass a car that has a stationary triangle window smashed in. Mabel blanches angrily as they look at each other. They worry silently about their own car, as though to voice their fears would be to make them come true.

Anxious and disgruntled, as if the crime were her husband's fault, Mabel shuffles up ahead with her heels smacking the sidewalks with every step. When she reaches the corner of Greene Street, she looks back to Milton, three-quarters of a block behind, calls out a "let's go!" and pushes her way around the corner. Milton accelerates his pace, but before he can catch up with her he hears Mabel shrieking. Her voice pierces straight through the building which separates them.

"Ahh! Muggers! Milton! Muggers, mug-gers, MUGGERS!! MURDERERS! HELP, Milton!" While she screams, Mabel clacks all the way back to Milton and flies into his arms.

"Mabel, Mabel, calm down. Tell me what you saw," Milton says with a rapid cadence. And, then, with a claustrophobic tone, he says breathlessly: "Quick, let's get out of here!" Milton tries to pull Mabel in the opposite direction from their car, but she's so petrified that she's frozen in her tracks.

"Milton," she says, whispering into his coat lapels with a firm grip on them, burrowing her head as much as she can without crushing her curls. "There are thugs on Greene Street. A whole pack of them. In some kind of masks. I couldn't see what they were but all dressed like jungle militia. At least four of them. Four, large black men waiting for me. Let's go back to the gallery and call the police. Quick, the police, 9-1-1!"

"Mabel, are you sure?" Milton speaks as if he's just had a revelation. "Even if anyone was there"—he's reasoning to himself now—"with this racket they would have taken off. Maybe it was just shadows playing tricks on you. I didn't hear any footsteps, and they didn't come after you." Now gruff and impatient, he says with a growl: "Come on, let's get to the car and go home."

"No, No! I can't. I won't. Let's wait until they're caught."

In a huddle, Milton nudges Mabel in the direction of the car, hesitantly.

As the two of them make their way down the street, still in tight grip each other tightly, four women donning large doll masks of two versions of Barbie, a Cinderella and a Raggedy Ann are grouped in the middle of the block, out of sight around the corner. They are busy plastering some black and white posters onto the side of an old brick facade. The building had been turned into gallery and condo space. Now, it lies fallow as a result of the real estate crash in New York City. A couple of the pasters wear camouflage colored fatigues below their masks. The other two are wearing army khakis, one with a jacket with military decorations and the other with some kind of combat vest over the pants.

The street light near where they are working is out, so all four spend a good deal of time fumbling and bumping into one another.

"More paste this time, damn it, so we don't have to try to re-glue it once it's half up."

"Okay, okay. It is hard to tell where I've hit and where I've haven't in this light."

"Hey! Don't be so snooty. Sometimes I have to paint in light as bad as this."

"How many do we have up in this spot, Dolls?" the one in a fuchsia dress and yellow leggings under her army jacket asks as she steps back to count.

Just then, a pedestrian passes by on the other side of the street. She warily assesses the racket she hears, looks over, and sees the masked plasterers. Once she observes what is going on, her face relaxes and she shouts over while continuing on her path: "Hey, Living Dolls! Keep up the good work! Love ya."

"That's nice to hear."

"Yeah, but I think we could use a few more volunteers."

"And a few more bucks!" the one in the combat vest shouts.

"We've got enough posters in this spot, let's go over to Mercer Street now."

"Hey, Sandra, everything all set for the Halloween Gala? Karen really got an invite?"

"Sure did! The plans are as we discussed at the meeting, but you'll get a description and map by tomorrow."

As the Living Dolls chat frenetically, they scramble together their gear and trot off toward Houston Street.

At the same time, Mabel rounds the corner and exclaims, pointing her finger: "Look, Milton, here!"

"Mabel," he says indulgently as he plays the brave role, "there's nothing there, just an empty street, sweetheart." Milton then says in a solicitous tone: "It was probably just shadows playing games with your eyes. Let's get you home and into bed. We'll fall asleep watching *Kojak*."

"*Kojak*! Not tonight, not after this! I don't like *Kojak*. Milton, you know I don't." Mabel's voice has a pleading quality now and is significantly weaker than before.

"Quiet now, Mabel, save your energy. Look. See, here's our car. Its fine, not a scratch." Milton says this as much to reassure himself as his wife. He runs the palm of his hand along the side of the car gently, for extra measure.

After they drive off, the street is still and quiet with only two working street lamps casting a yellow pall over the newly laid, antiqued cobblestones. The four wet posters pulsing flush against the brick wall are there, waiting for daylight to break over them.

Chapter Two:

OUTSIDE

MARIA DARTS OUT OF HER office building in the same way that a mouse searches for its next safe spot. No farther than the lobby threshold, her right arm is already raised to flag a limo.

"Damn!" she exclaims into the thick autumn air as she sights an empty taxi sail past without seeing her emerge. "Why are there always cabs when I don't need one?"

In her late-thirties and a senior associate at the highly reputable law firm of Tasch, Highland and Moore, Maria has cultivated an image based on self-confidence and assurance. This persona is effective with her clients and appears to ooze from her every pore.

Before setting on her way, upstairs in her office suite, Maria gave her secretary instructions in painstaking detail concerning her whereabouts for the next couple of hours. She then repeated most of it to the receptionist in the outer office. Finally, she stopped in the front vestibule to carefully put together the contents of her briefcase and adjust her Diane B. business ensemble. Looking in the firm's entry mirror, placed to reflect the bold midtown skyline, Maria caught a glimpse of the mole on the right side of her neck, just an inch below her jawbone. She automatically rubbed her index finger over it, creating a familiar sore sensitivity. Her finger dropped as she remarked under her breath: "It's way past due to have this looked at. I've got to have Susie set up an appointment A.S.A.P." Maria was taking a pen and her appointment book to make a note to have her secretary call the doctor's office when she was interrupted by an abrupt greeting from one of the firm's senior partners.

"Logging in your hours, Maria?" He said sarcastically as he walked past without a pause for her to respond.

Maria watched him disappear into his office before moving away.

After standing at the elevator bank for a couple of minutes, Maria, becoming impatient, distracted herself temporarily by allowing her eyes to drift out the nineteenth floor hall window to the plaza below. She witnessed several people sitting on the well-maintained benches among the fall flowers and foliage, as if she were documenting their actions. They were engaged in ordinary activity, sipping coffee out of take-out paper cups, chatting and reading. Maria had a fleeting feeling of bewilderment over who such people could be, with so much time on their hands in the middle of the day. The elevator doors binged at her feet suddenly and with force. Maria scurried inside, forgetting her queries entirely the moment she stepped in. At the end of the long, slow ride down culminating with the heavy brass doors thrusting open, Maria burst out as though she was being ejected. She wanted to be off, on her ride downtown.

"Here I am," she bellows, waving her hand high in the air, knowing that the driver inside can't hear her.

"If there's heavy traffic, I'm sunk," Maria mutters to herself as the hired car pulls up to the curb and comes to a screeching halt.

Once inside the car, Maria tells the driver her destination and hands him a green company chit with the appropriate account numbers on it, filled in by her secretary. Then, as though no time had elapsed from desk to car, she immediately begins to sift through the file of her afternoon client.

The lurching stop and start of the traffic pattern down Fifth Avenue distracts her, and Maria looks up frequently to gauge their progress. From a distance the street has the look of the old subway tile mosaics, only without evident pattern. The thick emissions coming from the tailpipes serve to render the picture in antiqued sepia tintype, and the car fumes from the avenue are so strong that even the seasoned limo driver gags and begins to complain.

"Haven't seen air this bad since I visited my cousin in Pasadena. Used to be unusual here in the fall. Looks like we're going to have to get used to seeing it year round."

Uninterested, Maria closes the Plexiglas divider window between front and back in one liquid, wordless motion and flips to another section of her file.

As they cross Thirty-Ninth Street, Maria doesn't think of rolling up her window before she's covered with flecks of sand and dirt from the construction site there. As she dusts herself off, she notices that the wreckage is for new offices being built into a crack between two already existing buildings. The space is barely wide enough to allow one tall person to stretch both arms out in either direction. Maria wonders who would put up with what will turn out to be indecent office space at such enormous expense. A block down, she gets a sense of an answer as she is reminded how the neighborhood has boomed in the mid-eighties. She chugs past three gourmet food take-out establishments in a row and a chic restaurant with a Rosa Poreno marble façade and interior pastel frescos done in thick protruding plaster slabs.

A few intersections farther, in front of the old Altman's building, a punk skateboard artist is on the road weaving in and out of traffic, wreaking havoc. She has green spiked hair, cut-off jean shorts over black tights and a ripped, safety-pinned shirt which is fashioned to reveal multiple silver and gold rings which pierce the flesh running down her back. The girl also sports hot pink high tops and metal spiked leather bands on her wrists and ankles. Two cabs simultaneously lunge so treacherously close to her that they couldn't be mere miscalculations. The skateboarder gives them both the finger and a nasty grimace and carries on her way, managing to seem nonchalant and oblivious. When Maria's car wedges its way past her, the music blares so loudly out of the girl's headset that even Maria is jolted up from her files.

At the corner of Fifth Avenue and Nineteenth Street, Maria sees a group of kids on a school outing and thinks of her six-year-old daughter, Bessy. She has a pang of longing deep in the pit of her stomach. Maria came in late enough last night from work that Bessy was already fast asleep in her bed hugging her stuffed pig. She was tucked in by her father, Ben. Maria had to leave again this morning before Bessy had woken up.

A vision of Bessy at two and a half flashes across Maria's mind. She had just climbed her first tree. It was in Riverside Park in a bank of low, mock fruit trees in bloom. One had branches close to the ground, and Maria had helped the then timid Bessy hoist up to a limb six inches high. It is Bessy's expression of openness and delight that Maria sees now. The thrill was shared, lived by both of them, as if the mother-daughter pair was still fused not only in body but in spirit as well. Sheepishly, Maria recalls her feelings of unbounded love limited in fact by a growing impatience. She had already spent years as a full-time mom with Bessy's older brother, Ricky, and the weight of those years together with the added demands of a second child pulled Maria inwards where she felt a continuous need to escape. To do. To perform in other ways. To return to the successful professional adult life she had enjoyed unfettered by motherhood and a flagging marriage. In that moment in the park Maria had not yet decided to cut the maternal cord decisively and return to work, but she already longed to do so. Maria felt like a failure and a cad for this desire, and so hung for several months in a delicate balance of self-torturing ambivalence.

This morning, Maria had intended to set out a note for her kids at the breakfast counter, but she became so rattled by time that she rushed out in a frenzy. As a mixture of guilt and desire wash over her, she pulls out her appointment book. Opening to the current week with one hand, while taking out a pen, cap clenched between her teeth, with the other, Maria jots in the Saturday box, *take Bessy apple picking TODAY!*

Sunken into the Naugahyde seat of the limo, Maria lets her papers droop onto her lap. She feels despondency riding up into her body, as if her life were running past. A sense of her present rhythm extending forward and repeating endlessly into the future gives Maria vertigo. She tries desperately to remember the last time she relaxed, hung out with friends, or the last time she spent with Bessy when she could devote her full attention to their activity. She realizes that she's almost gotten used to the fact that, when she's home, she needs to be doing at least three things at once. That's one reason why she prefers office to home: much less conflict. No matter how rough a case she's on, it's a piece of cake compared with being home with two kids.

Maria rushes through her household operation for the billionth time, as the car jiggles on. She tries to figure out which chores she can cut down or out. She starts to mutter out loud with an increasingly frenetic tone.

"Maybe the kids don't need all those lessons. But they don't impact me, and they like to go. It's all the planning and organizing of our lives that I could do without. How to cut it down, though? Ben surely won't take it over. Of course not!" Frustration wells up as she envisions Ben, soft and passive, seated with the kids as if he were an active father.

"Why can't he do any of this? Well, he can, but he doesn't. Damn it, why does this have to be so complicated? Why does he have to jam everything up? Ben's like the copier at the office. The paper goes in but won't come out until it's withdrawn by the technician in torn, crumpled bits.

"He can manage his own affairs well enough. He can throw parties and play tennis. Used to be able to, that is. Now he just sits around, shooting accusatory looks at me when I walk in. And he's baffled as to why I don't want to see his face first thing when I come in the door every night. Hah!" Maria cuts herself off as though otherwise she might rupture her jugular.

Maria often has the urge to run away to a foreign country where her savings would sustain her for life. Sometimes she grabs her kids and runs in these fantasies, and occasionally she doesn't. Ben never figures either way in her dreams.

Feeling as though she might suffocate, Maria hastily stuffs her papers into her gold monogrammed briefcase. "Why am I sitting here reading these legal briefs: divorces, petty suits, even the Errigon case?" Maria says this to herself slowly, silently, and deliberately, low in her chest cavity. As a mindless distraction, she takes out a fresh pad of unruled paper and sets out to finally redo the home emergency telephone number list for Jackie and the kids. Her firm changed its phone system and numbers three weeks ago and Maria hasn't yet found a moment to create a new list to tape to the refrigerator. She opens a new, thick purple pen bought especially for the task and begins. As Maria is scribbling every name and number she can think of, she briefly lets her thoughts take her back in time to her college years.

"Oh, I'm not sure, but I think I'll major in poetry," Maria says in a wispy, breathful voice as she sits on the Smith College lawn under a flowering apple-blossom tree. She feels highly sophisticated in her black scoop neck leotard and patchwork, flair skirt. It is warm enough to be barefoot, and she is. Maria's minimalist leather strap sandals are sitting in a heap on the grass next to her notebooks and tasseled Afghani purse.

Maria, at eighteen, in 1970, has a beautiful, poured-on alabaster complexion, marred only by two tiny blue pouches, one under each eye. Maria takes these to be trophies from her studied, existential anguish. Her dark chestnut hair falls straight and smooth to just below her shoulders and she wears a flowered head band to hold her hair back.

"You can't, you beautiful idiot. English, perhaps, but there's no such thing as a poetry major," her friend Roberta says in a cheerful tone. Her demeanor is at odds with her visage, which often makes people do a double-take. Roberta can be seen, nine days out of ten, clad in black Danskin stretch pants and a long sleeved, black turtleneck shirt. As if her darkly olive toned skin were perpetually hiding.

"What's wrong with this place? Lots of colleges have a poetry major. Williams has one," Maria says looking straight on at Roberta with her clear, gray-green eyes.

"It doesn't really make any difference, does it? You know you'll breeze through the major requirements for philosophy and English, and then can concentrate on poetry. Of course," she continues with a bit of a devilish look on her face, "I can see that you're going to neglect the distribution requirements. Not least of which: science!"

"I can get out of a lot of that stuff. I'm working on my argument for it, but I want to present it at the last possible moment so there's not much they can do."

"I know, become a lawyer, you're a natural for it." With this Roberta shoots up and stands at mock attention.

Maria has to shield her eyes from the sun to look up at Roberta and respond: "Yeah, right. That'll be the day, and hell will freeze over and there'll be peace on earth, too."

List completed, Maria sits back in the seat of the cab, wondering fleetingly how she got from there to here. She instantly dismisses her sentiment by taking the offensive. "Just because I'm having lunch with Roberta doesn't mean I have to become all melancholy about the so-called good old days." At the same time, she's pleasantly distracted as the car reaches her destination and pulls over to the curb.

Maria anxiously steps out of the Black Pearl limo and into the heart of SoHo on Prince Street. She walks straight into the Prince Street Bar, through the double set of doors and peers around for her college chum whom she hasn't seen in almost a year. When she doesn't find her anywhere, Maria seats herself at one of the larger round tables for four.

"Ma'am," the voice of a waitress chimes, "you can't sit here, this table's reserved for three or more."

As Maria begins to respond, the waitress is already disappearing behind the swinging kitchen doors. Seeing this, Maria closes her mouth and makes no attempt to move.

"Maria! Sorry I'm late," Roberta says, approaching the table with an excited deadpan voice.

"Hello, 'Berta. You look great! I'm sorry, but just so you know, I can't stay long. I have to get to a client near here by four-thirty."

"No problem, Maria." Roberta relaxes into a chair opposite Maria, and grasps for a piece of bread from the basket in the center of the table. "So, what's up? I was surprised to hear from you. Any occasion? I mean, I'm happy to see you, but I know you, and your voice sounded suspicious."

"Right to the point, as usual, Roberta. It's true, I haven't quite admitted it explicitly until just now, but I think I've been going through an identity crisis of sorts. And you are the best person I can think of to turn to."

"Why, because I'm perpetually having one?" Roberta snorts these words out with a laugh. "I'm not sure if I should feel complimented."

A waitress comes over to the table to take their order, but Maria waves her away before she can ask, with a definitive: "Another minute, please." As if in the same thought, she continues: "No, really, Roberta, nothing seems to fit the picture in my life right now and you are the most intelligent friend I have. You always were."

"Thanks, but I think that's a sad comment on the circles you travel in. Got to get away from lawyers, Maria. I've always said so."

"Bullshit! You're the one who told me to go into law in the first place. I was thinking about that on my way over here. You were the one, my dear, who claimed I had a talent for it."

"Well, so what? I was right, but who said you'd love it? I only said you had the annoying habit of arguing everything. Anyway, I think the statute of limitations is up on this one, Maria."

"Don't make fun of me, Roberta." Maria looks on the verge of tears, with her eyes welling up and reddening.

"I'm sorry, kiddo. I shouldn't make fun. It's just that sometimes I'm jealous of how you knew early on to be practical. I see you as someone who made the right choices when you had the opportunity. Now, you have the bucks, the career, status, kids, great apartment. It looks like freedom to me. Looks like *a life*. Like, not that I regret any particular decision I've made, but you grew up and became real and I've stayed in some static, infantile, dependent and unformed world."

"And that's how *I* see it, but in reverse, 'Berta."

The waitress comes back, looking harassed and determined to get their orders this time. Both women simultaneously order the garden salad special and then laugh at their synchrony.

"I guess we're both pretty predictable, eh? Enough of this whining. I guess I've just got to reason my way through this. Tell me what's new with you."

"I want to hear more about you, but I will say that I have had a few breaks lately. I'm having a solo show in a new gallery in Philly coming up. I'll send you a card even though I know you can't get there. And, it looks like I might be made an offer from Cooper Union for a semi-permanent position. Part-time, of course, but I think I'll be able to begin to stop wondering each semester whether they'll ever let me teach again."

"Does that really pay the bills?"

"Has to," Roberta says while spitting an olive pit into her hand. She sops up some of the creamy garlic dressing with a piece of bread, and continues: "No benefits, of course. No health insurance or anything handy like that."

Having the urge to give Roberta money, and knowing it wouldn't be accepted, Maria changes the subject. "What about romance, 'Berta? Or sex, or something. What's doing?"

Roberta's face falls briefly until she can pull it back and under control, then the words rush out of her. "Maria, what I'm going through! Just when I thought I was off sex and certainly love for good—five years it's been—wham-o! I get a full blown adolescent-sized, hormone-roller-coaster of a crush on a colleague."

Roberta takes a bite of her bread, while Maria leans forward, closer to Roberta. "Who? Tell me! This sounds like fun. Why are you so embarrassed?"

"Because I did a long, slow motion free fall into what I'm scared to call love," Roberta says. "And, I'm afraid that I'll ultimately lose what has been a good friend in the process."

Thinking about the whole affair, Roberta continues: "I hope I'm not going to learn some kind of horrible lesson. You know, a thirty-eight-year-old body just isn't a twenty-two-year-old one. The packaging's not as attractive to these guys who can succeed with any age. I tried to say, well he'll have to be interested in *me*, the person inside, not just my body. I'm more interesting than some twenty-year-old. And he's got a forty-year-old body, too, so we'll be matched.

"But, no go. It doesn't work that way. I look at my flabby breasts and thighs and just sigh. So, I started going to the gym. Partly to run off steam, but mostly to try to firm up for the eventual moment. That was a whole humiliation in itself. After a moderate workout, I would feel like a bull in a bullfight after it's been stabbed several times, staggering, with blood flowing out of every orifice. Ha! I made some progress with this carcass, but still, it didn't help calm me down. On the contrary, to say the least. I mean, there I am in my studio, for weeks, with my body tingling. My whole *being* is supersensitive.

"One day, the handle of one of my paint brushes scrapes—gently, mind you—across my lips, and I practically have an orgasm on the spot. Rushes of fantasies come over me at the most inane moments. All of sudden, I get this sensation of my body on his, and I almost pass out. And this has gone on day after day, week after week.

21

"All the while, I've had a few meetings with him, some chance times we'd bump into each other on the street, and a few phone conversations. All bland, but friendly. I started to wonder if it was a two-way street. I thought he was just being subtle because he's married, and because he wasn't sure about me." Roberta cautions her next remark, trying to gauge Maria's response in advance: "I am sort of known as a lesbian." Maria's expression doesn't change, so she continues: "Not because of any specific relationship I've had, it just sort of evolved. And, I liked it and always sort of fantasized that if I ever did get involved again for the longer term it would be nice if it were with a woman."

Switching tones now and moving to the side as the waitress puts down her food with a scowl: "So here I am mooning—yes, really mooning—over a man. A married man. A married man with young children, no less. You know, I tried to downplay it while it was still a fantasy. I tried to joke to myself: 'Oh, I have a vaginal infection, that's what this is.' To no avail. I was quickly becoming dysfunctional. I would be trying to paint, trying to really focus on what I'm supposed to love doing, and all of a sudden, my body fills with blood, as if I am in the middle of the most delicious sex act, one I've never experienced in reality, mind you. My breasts pulse, my belly, my clitoris, practically buzz with over-stimulation, even the backs of my calves have become aroused."

"Roberta, stop, I'm going to pop out of my skin if you keep this up," Maria says, cutting in and turning slightly pink. "Tell me what happened, for god's sake!"

"I'm just trying to give you a picture of my state of mind, Maria. Before, that is, I screwed up my nerve to confront him. He did give me some encouragement. Not enough so that I became convinced he felt the same, mind you. But I did finally bring it up. I had to. After dreaming a thousand times over of how it would go, in the end I decided to be direct, not strategic. I just feel too old for silly games—he's either interested or not, I've said that over and over to myself, rationalizing.

"I started mildly, meekly commenting on the vibes between us. He claimed he didn't know what I was talking about. I should have stopped there. But I plodded on, determined, or hopeful, whichever. Well"—Roberta slaps her hand on the table as if in a drum roll—"what a thing adolescent puppy love is.

"The whole time on my way over to speak with him, I kept saying to myself: 'Better prepare yourself, kiddo, for the big letdown.'"

"'Berta! Tell me the punch line. Now!"

"Okay. Okay. It turns out, he's been dreaming of me too. For years! When I heard what he had to say, my whole body went up in flames. His too. The only thing is, he went dashing away pretty quickly. I think he was scared. It's not the same for me, I'm free. He has every second accounted for between his work, his kids, his wife. I know her, too. Or, I've met her a few times, anyway. I like her." Roberta's voice trails off.

"This is a mouthful, 'Berta."

"Yeah," Roberta says with a strange grimace, "not great, huh?"

"I don't know. Maybe it is."

"Maybe. All I know is that I'm still aching, literally, aching to be with him, and I haven't even touched him yet. I don't know if I ever will. I'm trying to give him some room to ponder without my calling him, but it's hard. Extremely."

The waitress comes to clear their plates, but Maria stops her. She turns back to Roberta. "Sounds like it's exciting at the very least, I don't have time to even notice anything like that."

"Sure you do, Maria. You just have to let yourself. Something simpler, though, I hope. How're the kids? I haven't seen them since they were knee high, as they say."

"I haven't either. Barely. That's part of the problem. I'm in complete overdrive with this job, and I'm never home. I've gone straight from a home-most-of-the-time-mommy to this. I mean, the job is great, I love it, usually." Anguish rises in Maria's throat as she speaks. "I love my kids, too. But right now they need me more than I can give and it's killing me inside. The longer it goes on, the more I want to avoid home altogether. And Bessy was only three when this started."

"Hardly a suckling, dependent babe, Maria. What are you kicking yourself now for? You know, of course, that you've been doing this for one reason or another at least as long as I've known you."

Maria laughs. "So, maybe I can blame this on you then."

"Seriously, kiddo, let's look at what's going on here. You've got two great kids, a promising career that's demanding right now. But, unless you decide otherwise, it's part of you. You can't just cut it off and go bake cookies and do laundry while your kids are in school all day."

"How promising, I don't know. I've advanced pretty far in the three years I'm back, but who's to say. I also sacrificed plenty for each minute notch of an advance. My kids have sacrificed a lot."

"But, they're in good shape, right? Happy? Have friends? Retract the happy, such a stupid expression. What kid is happy, whatever that means?"

"You know, it's not a matter of sitting on my tush waiting with bated breath to pick them up at school. It doesn't happen that way either. But, I leave before they do, usually in a frenzy of details, and come home after dinner, often after they're asleep. Then, when I am around they clamor to me."

"Quality time?" Roberta says lamely.

"What bullshit that is. What do you do, 'Berta, read *Parent Magazine* in your spare time? You know, Ricky seems okay, but he had me for five full years. Bessy, I'm not sure. She's beginning to have strange eyes, if you know what I mean."

"I don't."

"It's not concrete, at least to me. Just a sense I have. I keep trying to watch her, to figure it out. But, I'm not around enough to get a handle on it."

"What about a good child psychologist for her?"

"With an emphasis on good. Not so easy. But, also I'm not sure it's called for, she's only six. And, it's not like she's disturbed."

Changing the subject out of discomfort and shifting in her seat at the same time, Maria says: "And this is only part of the picture. I walk around with a huge ball of anxiety in my chest. A tightly, tightly wound ball. I can discern some of its strands, but they don't measure up to the whole." Maria begins to shred her napkin.

Roberta extends her hand over to Maria's to calm the activity as she speaks. "Maria, maybe *you* should speak to someone."

"I am. To you!"

"No, seriously. I'm beginning to sound like a walking advertisement for psychotherapy, but what's the big deal of going for some shrinkage? You can afford it." Roberta tries to keep the jealousy out of her voice. " Just to see if it's a help in sorting this stuff out."

"Come on, 'Berta, you know it's more of a commitment than that. You're in for two years before you even begin to assess, and by then they've got you pretty well hooked."

"Is this fear or experience talking, Maria?"

"Neither. Just common sense. Hey, enough of me, let's talk about the world, or art or something."

"Art is part of the world, Maria," Roberta says in mock indignation.

The waitress comes to the table and clears it while asking if they want dessert or coffee. Both women ask for coffee, and turn their conversation to other subjects.

Roberta and Maria are laughing convulsively over old college days when the waitress brings the check. Maria practically jumps out of her seat when she realizes how late it is.

"I've got to go! 'Berta, let me give you some money so I can fly out of here." As she blurts her words, Maria slaps some bills onto Roberta's napkin.

"Wait, let me walk out with you. I'll deliver you to your appointment."

"No, stay put. This was great, let's do this again. Soon!"

With these words, Maria is on her way out the door. She wants to walk the two blocks alone in order to collect herself and prepare for her meeting at the Errigon Gallery.

CHAPTER THREE:

INSIDE

MARIA IS DEEP IN THOUGHT as she walks along the spiffy low building façade of West Broadway in SoHo. She doesn't notice a ruddy well-dressed young man saying in an undertone: "Hey, can I walk with you, honey?" As he shifts his orange hair over his forehead, he bobs his middle finger vertically in the air, in and out of the circle he makes with the thumb and index finger of his other hand, darts his pointed tongue, and wiggles it suggestively in Maria's direction.

Maria moves on past piles of raw garbage barely bagged without seeing or smelling it, and past a black woman who looks sixty but is probably twenty-five, asleep on a sidewalk grating.

She pauses a few seconds to look at some abstract work in oils through a gallery window and notes a Tiffany lampshade in a display of the antique dealer next door. Inside, a dapper, middle aged man is tenderly exploring an antique lacquer box.

Maria proceeds at a good clip. She is busy wondering whether the real estate market could plunge low enough in SoHo for the artists who were forced out to the Greenpoint section of Brooklyn during the big boom years to return. Shakily, and a bit guiltily, Maria worries about what that might mean for the value of her still desirable co-op on the Upper West Side.

As she nears Frank Errigon's gallery, Maria focuses on the case. Generally, clients come to her office. In this instance, she's going to him because, on the telephone, Frank was making such a to-do about leaving his gallery to come up to midtown that Maria became exasperated. Maria is well aware that Frank is on the border of true phobic, and she doesn't want to be the one to push him over the edge. In the ordinary course of professional interaction, Maria is not usually cognizant of her client's idiosyncrasies, but in Frank's case they are impossible to ignore.

Maria arrives at the Errigon Gallery just a few minutes before their appointment, early, as is her habit. She pauses and takes a breath, touching her mole with her middle finger before entering through the formidable double doors hewn of rich mahogany and etched glass with brass fittings. This case is proving to be increasingly troublesome and Maria is beginning to feel burdened by its amorphous nature.

"Hello, Kim, how's it going? How's your coursework, still at it?" Maria says as she buzzes past the sleek reception area and on into Frank Errigon's private office.

By heritage, Kim is Hawaiian. She's the second generation to be born on the mainland. At five feet, two inches tall she manages to have a commanding presence partially due to her customary silence. She has a broad body and face, with dark eyes set wide apart, and thick, black hair cropped stylishly to just above her shoulders.

Kim barely has a chance to have her voice trail after Maria with a "Fine, thanks, Ms. Jacobs."

"Okay, Frank, what's today's emergency?" Maria says, more than asks, as she enters the room, closing the door behind her. She has a way of speaking that sounds intimate rather than abrasive.

"Ach, I just don't know what's going on. Everyone's talking about the Fred Swanson murder, it's got me unnerved. He was one of my discoveries, you know. Maybe his murder has to do with me. Or maybe it will!" Frank flaps his arms as he stands to greet Maria.

Always stylishly dressed and trim, which he feels is crucial to his business, Frank's wearing a tailor-made suit from London. His custom white shirt, which has a delicate pink cast, sets off his graying temples to good effect. Frank even wears his facial crease lines as though they are an asset. Today, however, his presence reeks of despair.

"The case is snowballing. Is there any chance we can wrap it up before Thanksgiving and before the holiday fervor begins? I'm seeing visions of plunging sales figures."

"Frank, stop," Maria says, cutting in. "The case is not exactly running away from us. And Fred Swanson's got nothing to do with it. Not to be too cynical, but his murder ought to help you sell off his stuff. Seems since the murder, the media's elevated him to the standing of somewhat of a legend. Let's get to work."

Usually a dignified man of incredible stage presence, Frank is often slumped and diminished in Maria's company. He believes that she holds all the cards and this places him in the awkward position of pleading.

"Those damn Living Dolls, how did they get it into their collective head to sue? Weren't the posters enough? They were for me all right! And why single me out? Why?"

"Because, if they're correct, you have the worst track record, Frank. That's why. Come on, I'm sure you don't want to pay my rates to cover old ground. What I need from you now are the figures we discussed last time. We'll see what we can do with them. Do you have them?"

"They're not good. Couldn't we just say I didn't keep records? I'm not required to, after all." Frank looks, tentatively, hopeful.

"But you did, and I know it. It's too late for that course of action. So, let me have a look to see what we can make out of them." Maria's voice is crisp. She's often tested in such a fashion by clients. She has never yet made the mistake of bending the law for one.

Frank goes sluggishly and reluctantly from the Noguchi coffee table, couch, and chair set they're sitting at, to his desk. Just as he's reaching for the file, the telephone buzzes and Frank jumps at the sound, startled. After a moment's pause, he pushes the intercom button.

"Kim, what? It better be important, you know what I'm doing in here, and you know me!" Frank snaps, and clearly regrets it a bit.

"Sorry, Mr. Errigon." Kim's voice comes coolly across the intercom. "But it's Dr. Rose on the phone and I thought you'd want to talk to him."

"Okay, good, transfer him to me." Frank utters the words as if he's in the midst of a *Star Trek* fantasy with Captain Kirk asking Scotty to beam him up.

As he's waiting, Frank says in a whisper with one hand cupped over the telephone receiver: "Sorry Maria, this'll just take a sec. It's one of the few clients who's remained loyal."

"Judging from your books, I'd say most have remained loyal. Maybe you lost a few on the fringes, but you're overreacting Frank, and that won't help our case." Maria forces herself not to become disgusted with Frank's histrionics.

"Howard, good to hear from you!" Back to reality, Frank is standing in a stiff and stooped position, talking much louder than usual, owing to his exaggerated and forced enthusiasm.

"The blue one you say? Couch size? I'm not sure which the blue one is. Would you like to come over and point it out? Messenger you a few slides? Right-o, they'll be in your hands in the morning. Goodbye, Howard."

Frank carefully puts the phone down, comes back to Maria, and slumps into one of the soft, cinnamon colored leather chairs. With his arms spread out along the outer rim he looks as though he's a propped up scarecrow, which is indeed how he feels.

"The *blue one*, he wants. What kind of a way is that to talk about a painting? A work of art? The blue one! I mean, I know this is a business, but I'm not selling paper clips, am I?" Frank's voice rises to a pitch and then drops low as he continues: "See what I have to put up with these days? Ach, where were we, Maria?"

"The file. You were about to hand me the file, Frank." With a touch of impatience and another of matter-of-factness, Maria gets up saying: "May I?" and walks across the room.

Feeling she needs to take command of the situation, she sits at Frank's Ruhlman desk.

Maria sinks easily into his Knoll, leather desk chair, and opens the file.

As Maria looks through the file, she's thinking about what a mistake it was to come downtown. She has to learn the lesson that on a client's turf, issues can become even more murky and complicated than they would otherwise. She resolves that next time they'll have to meet in her midtown office where Maria's authority is clear-cut. If she wants to have an excuse to meet with friends, she can do that on her own time, whenever that might be.

"So?" Frank demands anxiously.

"Well, I'll have to have some experts look at these figures, Frank, but you're correct, they don't look good. Why do you keep records of who sends in a portfolio?" Maria tries her best to un-crinkle her forehead, so as not to raise Frank's already agitated level of concern.

"I like to be able to look back and get a sense of my judgment. To see if I'm passing up people who exhibit well elsewhere, for example, and if I'm taking on too many flops. It's a way of assessing my instincts." Frank relaxes a bit, pondering his business and artistic acumen.

"And so many women sent in their work, almost three-to-one over men, and you took on close to none of them? Barely two percent of all your artists? Why?" Maria feels she's back to business herself, and on to something. A crack in the case, finally. Perhaps.

"It had absolutely nothing to do with their gender." Frank tenses again, and his body stiffens. "I don't even look at the bios before I review the art work. I just didn't like their work enough. None of it was as good as the stuff I did take. There's nothing I can do about that. I pick the artists strictly according to merit, it's as plain as that."

"And why, then, do you give the few female artists you take on such small commissions? Can you go over that for me again, Frank?" Maria tries to sound congenial so as not to scare Frank into lies.

"That's simple. It makes sense. The ones I took on were a greater risk to me, lower sales and all. So I think that it's only fair to share some of the burden with them."

"You can substantiate that, that the women have consistently lower sales than the male artists you exhibit?" Maria's tone has flattened considerably, and her hope is waning.

Frank starts to pick at the couch as he answers in what sounds like a low groan. "Look at page four there, Maria. No. I somehow couldn't prove it with the data I have."

"So, why do you think that?"

"I don't know, Maria." Frank's tone is despondent now. "It's obvious, that's all. If I like their work, I want to give them a shot. But they're less known, if at all. It's common sense. Everyone knows it. Ask anyone."

"I see. Let me change tacks for a moment," Maria says crisply, trying to be practical. "Is it really possible that in the ordinary course of events, the proportions of submissions could be weighted like this?" Maria is pointing at the file significantly now.

Frank flaps an arm and says: "Well, it was, wasn't it?"

"No, Frank, what I'm getting at here is whether the Living Dolls could have set you up." Maria has been percolating this thought for a few minutes. If she's right, she's still not sure what good it will do the case.

"Perhaps they stacked the deck by sending a lot of their work here? Perhaps, in disproportionate quantity than they would have were this case against you not in the offing."

"Nobody even knows who they are so it's impossible to say. All we have to go on are the damn posters that they've been plastering all over SoHo."

"Well, in court we'll find out." As she speaks, Maria sees Frank's eyes flash at the idea of legal proceedings, so she quickly adds: "If it gets that far. It's an angle we need to keep in mind. Not to mention that they have no interest in the case going to court, since then they'll have to reveal their identities. I wonder how long they think they can get away with anonymity."

Maria snaps herself back to the matter at hand. "Meanwhile, I'd like to see these figures plus another chart which breaks down submissions to your gallery by gender together with whether it was independent or by agent." Maria shuffles her papers and pads together, and slips them into her briefcase. Almost as an after-thought, she adds: "Oh, I'd also like a list with telephone numbers and addresses of the agents you deal with. Have Kim fax all of this to me by tomorrow, early."

Maria stands up, adjusts her outfit discreetly, and moves across the indigo and emerald Persian rug to shake Frank's hand.

"Goodbye, Frank," she says crisply. "I'll be in touch after I've had a close look at the facts. Sit tight and try not to overplay this. You are our weak link and I'm afraid you'll tip our hand."

She breezes out the door before Frank manages to respond.

"So long for now, Kim."

With this hasty exit, Maria is back out onto the busy gray streets of SoHo.

As if to replace Maria as she leaves the gallery, two women, arm-in-arm, enter. They look very much alike, except for their difference in age. One is dressed in a green hospital uniform and the older one in almost hippy style clothing replete with overalls from Sears. Both have curly, blond hair, one with gray strands woven in. The two of them are clearly enjoying each other's company. They move in unison throughout the gallery, stopping to pause and comment periodically.

"This is great, Mom. You should come rescue me from the bowels of Beth-Israel more often."

"Not on your life, sweetie. I didn't push you into and through a medical school so that we could blow it away on the streets of SoHo."

"Oh, so this is a once-in-a-lifetime spree, then?"

Becoming serious, Claire breaks their grasp and turns to her daughter. "Aviva, once you get through this, you will be almost home free. You can set your hours, do exciting research, relax on a regular basis. It'll be great. For now, you just have to plod on. I'm very proud of you." With this she kisses Aviva on the cheek and gives her a loving pat on the shoulder.

"I love you, Mom. I couldn't have done half of this without you."

"Let's not get maudlin now. Come, we were doing fine 'til I opened my big mouth."

"No, seriously, I know you made a lot of choices that cost you personally, just for me. I'm happy that one day I'm going to be able to pay you back. Materially, at least."

"How's that?" Claire says, chuckling.

Aviva taps her mother's cheek with a kiss, saying: "I'll support you, of course, you nut!"

"You'll do no such thing, my dear. You'll manage to rack up expenses on your own. I know you. Anyway, we're a team. What I did, I did for both of us. It wasn't ever you against me or you over me."

"Hey," Aviva almost shouts, changing the mood.

Kim looks up from her desk to see if there is anything that requires her attention.

"Let's go to Vinny's on Prince and have some of her mochaccinos," Aviva says, "like we used to early in the morning when you'd walk me to school."

"You've got to be joking, Aviva! Vinny closed shop *years* ago. Went back to Italy, in fact."

"So, come on, then, let's go the Cupping Room. I'm starved for one of their monster muffins."

"Good idea. Galleries like this depress me anyway."

They link arms again and scamper out and down the street like two schoolgirls playing hooky.

A few blocks from Errigon's, Maria decides to hunt down the most recent Living Dolls poster before heading back to her office. She turns the corner of West Broadway onto Prince Street, a likely location. Finding nothing on the first block, Maria goes straight past the now closed and empty artist hangout, FOOD, which sports a gigantic "For Rent" sign, and crosses the street. Wading through all the plastered show posters, store ads, and political notices, some partially scraped off or graffitied over, Maria determines that there's nothing on the next block either. She turns up Greene Street toward Houston. A third of the way up the block she passes an empty lot. Maria notes that the tree sized weeds reach to the second floor of the adjacent building.

"Tropics in New York," she muses as she continues on her search. All the old factory buildings there, many now turned into galleries and boutiques, provide ample space for plastering posters. But she finds none there either; having turned her head at the wrong moment, she walked right past the four freshly printed messages.

When Maria hits the blaring truck traffic of Houston Street and spies a few lone joggers atop the New York University gym across the street, she turns the corner discouraged. Before she can jump out of the way, a pack of panting leashed dogs almost tread over her. Their walker shoots a nasty look in her direction, as if to say she should have known to cross over, away from the beasts.

Absorbed in her pursuit, Maria walks past a battered white station wagon full of boxed merchandise in the back without noticing what is going on. The car rolls at a snail's pace hugging the littered, sooty sidewalk. There's a religious logo on the side of the car with a saying from scriptures. A middle aged man with weathered skin and wavy black hair that looks greased is driving with the curb side window rolled down. He is tailing a pubescent, dark skinned girl. The girl is carrying some school books and is advancing at a good clip. She appears unperturbed by the driver. As he pushes slowly on tracking the girl, he repeatedly hisses loudly out to her: "Come on, honey. Real quick, in and out. Just once, in and out."

When the man's voice reaches a rapid clip, the girl slowly turns her head towards the driver, and steps two paces closer to the car. She bares her braced, white teeth and slowly responds: "Open up so I can bite it off." The car immediately screeches away from the curb and speeds off down Houston Street and out of sight.

Almost ready to go back uptown, something about the diesel smell of the gas station at the corner causes Maria to remember a spot on the next street over that usually has signs pasted over it. She goes round the block onto Mercer, past the open commercial garage full of the smells and sounds of cars revving their engines.

There it is in clear black and white, like all of the previous posters. Maria stares at the poster and shakes her head. She thinks the Living Dolls have gone way too far with this one. A line about motherhood sticks in her throat until she lashes out: "Surely none of those damned artists work more than I do, and I have two beautiful kids."

Maria makes an about-face and briskly walks back down the block to find a cab. As she does so, she recognizes a new anxiety welling up in her. It is Frank's insanity about the Swanson murder. Maria tries to dismiss the feeling while speaking under her breath: "Ridiculous. How could there be a link to Frank? What would the reason be?" A sickly undercurrent, though, does not let her release the tension. While she's trying to push it out of her mind, she hails an eastbound checker cab on Houston Street. As her first foot is getting into the car and she gathers her skirt away from the door, Maria declares: "Fifty-sixth and Lex, please." She pulls her other leg in, and slams the door shut.

CHAPTER FOUR:

UPTOWN

SEVERAL DAYS LATER, MARIA SITS at her modern, cherry wood desk, wading through a stack of pink telephone message slips from clients and another stack from her kids.

"Bessy called: tell Ricky to stop being mean."

"Ricky called: tell Bessy to stop bugging me."

"Jackie called: help."

With a cup of coffee in one hand, she punches in her home number with the other. If Maria had ever managed to become a cigarette smoker, she'd be lighting one up as soon as she finishes pushing the buttons of her touch tone phone. She tried many times in college, but could never get beyond the initial coughing attack. Instead, Maria has her appointment book open. She's transferring in meetings her secretary has scheduled and crossing others out. She comes to the APPLE-PICKING WITH BESSY note and scratches it out heavily.

At the same time, in Maria's apartment, Jackie, the live-in college student who keeps the Jacobs' house from sinking into a morass, has just finished giving Maria's two children an after school snack. She has the appearance of a well-scrubbed Midwestern girl with straight, medium brown hair, light blue eyes, and preppie L.L. Bean style clothing.

"Bessy, Ricky, do you two realize how soon Halloween is? We'd better finish those costumes, what do you say?" Jackie's relieved to have an indoor activity on this clammy fall day.

"Mine first, it's almost done!" Bessy says while wiping peanut butter from her mouth and chin to her sleeve. "All we need to do is glue on the leaves."

"We also have to *make* the leaves, Bess," Jackie says, good naturedly. "I think we'd better use the green felt, not the construction paper."

"Mine only needs glitter, Jackie. Let's do it first," Ricky says plaintively as the ever-shunted first born.

"Let's take everything into the den and get set up," Jackie says. "I think we can work on both. I'll get the equipment and each of you bring in your costumes."

Just then the telephone rings. En route to scissors and glue, Jackie picks up the receiver.

"Jacobs residence."

"Hi, Jackie. It's me. What's going on?"

"Mostly the usual, a little worse," she says with an evident edge in her voice. "I'm sorry for all of the phone calls, but I just haven't managed to handle them today. It's a little better now that we've snacked and started on Halloween costumes again and for the final time. Before, everything I tried was falling apart and dissolved into continuous bickering. Do you want to talk to Ricky, or just let it lie? At the moment they're waiting for me to collect the sewing equipment, fairly calmly."

"No, let me talk to Bessy first. Try to get her without Ricky hearing, so he won't be breathing down her neck the whole time."

"Okay, hold on." With this the home receiver clunks down on a white laminate telephone table at one side of the kitchen.

Maria takes a deep breath, a gulp of her now tepid coffee, and glances at her other messages while she's waiting. She sorts them into calls she'll return today and those she won't.

"Mommy?" Bessy, an updated image of Maria, says in disbelief.

"Hi, pumpkin. What's going on baby?" Maria melts a bit, but her mind is also on her clients. She's very conscious of the time passing. This will not be a billable quarter of an hour.

"Mommy." At the sound of her mother's voice Bessy begins to whine and cry at the same time.

Hearing the pathetic gulping sounds, Maria gets an instant headache.

"Ricky wouldn't help me make fluffy pancakes and then he took his wood pigs out of my room even though I had them set up for a circus. Now he's in his room planning to blow me up. He said he's going to do it tonight when I'm sleeping. Tell him to stop, Mom. I'm scared. When will you be home?"

"Sweetie, you know that Daddy and I have to go to Daddy's office banquet. But I'll be home soon to change and we can talk about all of this then. You can help me get dressed, okay?"

"Okay, Mom. But tell Ricky now."

"Let me talk to him and I'll see what I can do. See you soon, Bessy."

Maria rubs her temples with her elbows planted on the desk, and has an urge to hang up the phone. Instead, she opens her appointment book and scribbles in on the Friday slot: leaf collecting in Central Park this weekend w/ Bessy & Ricky.

"Mom?" Ricky is nine and is beginning to go through an awkward stage. Somehow, in defiance of genetic theory, he has russet colored hair and freckles.

"Ricky, aren't you Bessy's big brother? That means you're supposed to help and protect her." Maria tries not to plead.

"But, Mom! She was stealing my stuff."

"Those pigs have been in her room for days, she's playing with them, not stealing. Why aren't you happy the pigs have company, considering you never pay any attention to them? Until now. Why?"

Maria's tapping a pen against the desk as she speaks.

"They're mine, Mom. When are you coming home?"

"I'll be home soon. In the meantime, please try to be nice. Put Jackie on the phone now, okay, sweetie?"

"Okay, Mom. Bye."

"Oh! Ricky! Are you still there?"

"Uh huh."

"Stop scaring your sister. Don't talk about blowing her up, she'll have nightmares. Cut it out for now and we'll talk about it later. So, let me talk to Jackie."

The phone clunks down again.

"Hi, Ms. Jacobs."

"Jackie, say 'Mrs.' You know I hate that 'Ms.' stuff. Listen, try to hang on until I get back. Maybe the costumes can wait. If you can make some half dollar pancakes with Bessy instead, I think that might calm everybody down. Even if it is almost time for dinner. I'm sure Ricky will want some if he doesn't have to do anything. Not too much syrup though or you'll have real live wires. See if they'll put jam on instead. See you later. I'm signing off, bye."

Jackie says goodbye and hangs up after she hears Maria's click. She sighs putting down the scissors she's still holding, and trots into the kitchen to assemble the ingredients before including Bessy in the production.

"Flour, baking powder, milk, eggs. What else? A little wheat germ, cinnamon, nutmeg. Oh, salt. Okay, ready. Bessy-o-Bessy! Want to make some pancakes with me? Bowls, spoons, measuring cups. All set."

As Jackie steps out into the apricot colored hall, everything seems a little too quiet. Jackie stops to listen and still hears nothing. She notices that darkness is seeping in the hall windows, the sun almost completely set. The seed of panic starts to well up in her throat as she moves towards the children's bedrooms. The Georgia O'Keeffe posters which line the wall never looked so sinister to her as they do now. Nor did it ever seem to her to take this long to make it down the hallway.

No sound emerges as she gets closer. Sweating, Jackie tries Bessy's door first, popping it open unannounced.

"Bessy! What are you doing, didn't you hear me?" Jackie's words blurt together like one long noise.

Bessy looks at Jackie from her seated position, curled up in the middle of the floor on her blue shag rug, book in hand.

Jackie is ashamed of herself now. "Did I really think that Ricky could blow Bessy up?" she wonders. "What is wrong with me today, anyway?"

"I'm making some pancakes, want to help?" Jackie tries to sound cheerful.

"You're just doing that because Mom said to," Bessy says in a calm, precocious voice.

"No. Uh, I want to. I heard you talking to Ricky about it and I got a craving for pancakes. Come, let's do it."

"Okay," Bessy says as she rises up while tossing her book open-faced onto the floor. She grabs the blond Barbie from the rug at her side. The doll is dressed in a pink fluff dress, and Bessy drags it with her out of the room and down the hall.

"You think you and Ricky could make peace long enough to give him some?"

"No, but you could give him some of *your* pancakes." Bessy's already halfway to the kitchen, and her voice trails behind.

Jackie catches up and says: "You know, I have an older brother too. Russell. I've told you about him. I read you a letter from him last week. Remember? I know that it's sometimes tough having a big brother." Very tough, Jackie thinks, as she remembers a few choice incidents.

Bessy has climbed up and seated herself on the white Corian counter next to the mixing bowl. All she says now is an absent-minded, "Uh-huh."

Jackie says: "But it's also nice to have Ricky to show you things, to talk to, and to play with. It's just not always easy. Bessy, you listening?"

"Can we mix up the batter now, Jackie?"

"Sure, sweetie." Jackie expels some air and tries not to sound exasperated.

"Let's take a look at the recipe."

Ricky, smelling the pancakes cooking, wanders into the kitchen just as the first batch is done. Jackie deals the pancakes out, and makes another round. While they are all three harmoniously munching on their pancakes slathered in butter and nutmeg and syrup, Maria is still wading through her return calls. She pauses for a moment after scrambling and sorting papers on her desk to buzz her secretary.

"Janet." Maria speaks firmly into the intercom. "Get me Mr. Walters on the phone, please. I can't find his number and you didn't put it down on his message sheet."

As she speaks, Maria notices that she has finally adopted a definitive speaking style, and it jars her fleetingly. When she was just starting out, she had a hard time establishing the proper lawyer-staff and lawyer-client hierarchies. She concentrated on adopting a gruff disposition with the staff and a firm, matter-of-fact tone with her clients. She learned quickly to turn a blind eye to the disappointment in her client's eyes when they found a young female as their lawyer.

"I'm sorry Mrs. Jacobs," returns Janet's disembodied voice ornamented with static. "I'll put you through right away."

Maria pushes down her talk button barely after Janet finished her sentence. "And Janet, see to it that you get the *McGeorge vs Nichols* file on my desk now too."

"Yes, Mrs. Jacobs."

After about thirty seconds, which seem an eternity to Maria, her office intercom buzzes and Janet's voice beams through: "Mr. Walters on the line."

"James, what can I do for you?" Maria says.

"I thought I'd check in and find out what's happened," James says anxiously. He sounds as though he's hanging on an edge somewhere in the Himalayas, rather than sitting plunk at his desk where he's in fact getting ready to pull out his John Glenn lunch box for a mid-afternoon snack.

"Not a whole lot. Cindy's attorney is stalling on the paper-work side. I warned you though that not much would happen before the first of next month. Is there any chance of a reconcili-ation in the offing?" Maria's hoping that this case will go away of its own volition.

After a pause and an almost audible throat constriction, James answers in a low whisper: "No. She's really dug her heels in. She's got herself convinced I'm the enemy." Then revving up to an angry pitch, James say: "It was that damned women's talk group she got roped into that started all the trouble."

Cutting him off as quickly as possible Maria responds: "Well, you never know, James, stranger things have happened. She might do a flip before all is said and done. I'll be in touch. Goodbye." She replaces the receiver before he can catch his breath. She hates divorce cases and doesn't handle them well. She has no patience for the kind of listening that is apparently required.

Maria hasn't hung up for more than ten seconds when her office intercom buzzes again and startles her.

"Yes, Janet?"

"Susan Lieberman on the line, she's been holding."

"Tell her that I can't take her call right now. I'll return it later." With that Maria clicks off the intercom.

Later that evening, Jackie is preparing to go to her karate class. She has fed the kids a macaroni-and-cheese dinner. Ben has come home and is comfortably ensconced in their impeccably renovated Upper West Side co-op. Reading *Time* magazine, which sports a cover photo of the slain Fred Swanson at work in his SoHo studio some years back, Ben has plopped himself on the couch in their Maurice Villency living room. Hanging above him is a bold paint-ing framed merely by painted wood boards nailed to the edges of the canvas. It's an early work of Roberta's they've owned for a decade. Ben and Maria have had several squabbles over replacing it with something more compatible with their current lifestyle. Maria knows that she won't prevail much longer on this score. She loves the painting dearly, mostly as a memento of the past.

Ben is almost softer than the stuffed upholstery, chubby around the edges. He runs an architecture firm in the West Village with two partners. When business is slow, he teaches a class in the architecture department at New York University to keep things moving. He has wavy, sand colored hair which he keeps cut close, and he wears well-tailored clothes that are on the sporty side. Ben's image of himself is a hip version of Ralph Lauren. Somewhere he knows that this idea doesn't conform too closely with reality.

Sitting, magazine in hand, Ben's mind wanders to the paucity of his family life. His kids are old enough to want to play without him, and he often has dinner alone after they go to sleep. He is hashing over and over seemingly endless permutations of these themes, when he recognizes that the dull ache in his right hip stems from the fact that his wallet is still in his back pocket. Ben reaches to scoop it out, and as he's doing so, remembers a card he stuffed into one of the slots months ago. He pulls out the card and stares at it. It reads:

Jean M. Hagedorn, Ph.D.
psychotherapy couples counseling
(212) 989-7010

A friend at work had passed it to him after Ben confided his troubles one day over coffee. Ben pauses, staring another minute, and then walks over to the kitchen telephone to call for an appointment. He punches in the number, gets one ring and hangs up. He hits the redial button, and forces himself to wait.

When Ben hears Jean Hagedorn's voice on her answering machine tape, he quivers, hangs up, and goes back to the couch, pondering the evening ahead. He'll put the kids to bed by himself again if Maria doesn't come home in time. He already canceled the baby-sitter for tonight because he can see that Maria has forgotten about his firm's shindig. He refuses to go through the humiliation of going alone this time.

The other wives, and the one husband even, of his colleagues in his architecture outfit always attend gaily, and look as if they're having a good time. Ben wonders why Maria can't muster any enthusiasm for his work. He takes it as a personal affront that she doesn't take him seriously. He is sure that she doesn't appreciate how hard he's worked to make the company take off and stay afloat through the crash in the housing market.

At the other end of the apartment, Jackie is going through her daily ritual. Every time she goes out, her issue is what she should wear. At the moment, she's tried on three different outfits and is on her fourth.

"Yes, oh, this looks fine, good enough," her running commentary goes, "but it's too loud. I don't feel like hearing any crap on the street for it. I guess I must be getting my period because I'm already seething just thinking about the stuff some creep is going to spew at me. I better go with the gray."

She takes off a turquoise dress and slips into some gray GAP slacks and a brown sweater. Annoyed at how plain she looks even though this is the objective, Jackie shoves her karate clothes roughly into a safari shoulder bag. She then tromps with too much determination out of her room toward the front door.

"Jack-ie! Are you going to karate again?" Bessy pleads as she darts out of her room and into the hall, landing at Jackie's side. She tugs on the corduroy fabric of Jackie's pants for emphasis. "Are you?"

"Yes, sweetie-pie. I'll see you in the morning." Jackie tries to sound calm and loving but her words have a sharp edge to them.

"Couldn't I wait up for you, just this once? Pl-ease, oh please!" Bessy jumps up and down, very excited.

At this, Jackie melts and kneels down to Bessy's level. Putting her arms around the girl she says: "Honey, you know that I go to my karate class every Tuesday and Thursday and that you never like it when I go. I wish you didn't mind so much. Maybe your mommy will come home soon."

"She won't! She won't, you know it."

"Well, sweetie, when I get home you'll be asleep already, but I'll come in and give you a big kiss, okay?"

This strikes the right chord and Bessy says, "Promise?" as she pushes Jackie towards the door.

Once on the street outside their apartment building, Jackie wonders whether she should go after all. She reasons that with winter approaching it gets dark so early that it's practically pitch black already.

As she passes a Citibank branch with a security guard posted outside, Jackie tells herself: "It'll be cold in the Y, and my knees still hurt from Tuesday's class. I could be studying instead, or at the movies. Well, no, not the movies, I guess. But studying, yes. I could use a jump on my math assignments this week." Out of the corner of her eye, Jackie notices that the guard has a revolver in hand, ready for use. She gets the chills and continues. "Maybe this is a waste of time anyway. Who knows if I'd ever have the nerve to use this stuff—if I ever learn it. And, even if I do, in this city, I'll just be shot down dead, pumped full of lead. Nobody messes with chopping and kicking anymore. I've got to find an easier way to fulfill the damn gym requirement. Maybe yoga's more my speed."

Jackie's litany takes her all the way to the subway station, two blocks north. She continues down the steps of the station where her mutterings carry her past the strong smell of urine. Her eyes are fixed on the dozen-odd smashed raw eggs which line the stairs and corridor. "A little early for these pranks, isn't it? I really should just pack it in and go home, who knows what's doing out here tonight."

On the platform, Jackie has made a habit of taking stock of who she's waiting with. As she takes in the station with a sweeping view, her eye catches some movement on the tracks. Jackie swivels her head to follow it, past a pile of litter, until she catches sight of a large rat slowly winding its way through the debris. The rodent wiggles over the rusted out subway rails, and under the lip of the platform, out of sight. The waiting area outlined in bright yellow stripes on the floor is covered in filth. Two modern and relatively new garbage cans are overflowing with newspapers, gum wads, spent Styrofoam cups, and what could only be described as muck. The overhead fluorescent lights buzz, and cast an unearthly green pall over the area. There's a man swathed in brown and blue rags sprawled across the only bench, and a municipal employee slowly moving cigarette butts and other trash from one spot to another with a broom. Jackie doesn't see him use the dust pan once, although he holds a firm grip on it with his left, gloved hand.

Near the maintenance worker is a teenage girl, burned by what must be one of the many tanning salons which have popped up all across the city. She looks as though she has poor balance and might fall over at any moment. Jackie can't make out if the girl is flying high on drugs or if she is ill. With her is a babbling toddler, seated obediently in a flimsy stroller. The girl is talking out loud, apparently to herself. At the other end of the station Jackie sees a pudgy, scruffy looking teenager with head phones on and Lou Reed's *New York* blasting out of them so loudly that everyone on both the up and downtown sides of the station can hear the lyrics distinctly. He's got greasy hair flung over his forehead covering an eye, a black leather vest with a Grateful Dead T-shirt emerging from its opening, jeans hanging low on his hips, and muscular forearms. Jackie glances down the platform, and up the long dark double flight of stairs to street level.

This bunch doesn't inspire Jackie's confidence; she's trying to restrain herself from bolting up the stairs, heading for home. Containing herself, she observes that one third of the lights on the platform are out, and distracts herself by counting the lights in the station. Simultaneously, in the back of her mind she's hoping for a full subway to carry her down to her Fourteenth Street stop.

Regressing, Jackie mutters aloud: "Maybe I shouldn't go after all. I'm tired, I lugged those kids around all day. I'll get my rape prevention training some other way. Maybe there's a video."

Jackie's tapping her feet and shifting her weight from one foot to the other. It's been eighteen minutes and no train.

"I should have brought something to read."

She paces a little, and now twenty-four minutes have passed. Just as she's wishing the homeless man would wake up so that she could sit down, Jackie notices a reasonably clean copy of the *New York Times Magazine* section from last Sunday's paper perched at the other end of the bench. She hasn't had a chance to read it, so she gingerly walks over and flips open the cover, hoping the pages aren't stuck together by somebody's snot.

The first page contains an ad, which Jackie studies, curious that there's no print, not even a brand name. Just a woman with velvet-smooth skin, that to look at is to want to touch. The photo provokes the desire to possess the model's implied moist sensuality. She is dressed in a low-cut formal black dress, heels, tulle sticking up fan-like on her well coifed head, estate jewelry, and what would be blood red lipstick and nail polish if it weren't a black-and-white photo. Jackie immediately starts to compare her own body parts with the model's.

She mutters: "Yeah, sure. If all I had to do all day was to pay attention to my body, I could look like that too." Knowing that this isn't true, Jackie immediately does a mental calculation of the calories she has consumed for the day so far. She fudges on the syrup.

The model is standing at the top of some steps looking down and at an angle to a tuxedoed man with wild, shoulder length hair at the bottom. Her back is to the reader, inviting one into her world, as if to say, "Follow, please." The building she's in is very old and clearly very elegant. The man, like the reader, is looking up at her, with no discernable expression on his face.

Jackie eventually becomes exasperated competing with the provocative backside of the model. She turns the page, where the secret is revealed. The next two pages, facing each other, are taken up completing the ad.

The woman, now inside a room lined with plush, satin pleated curtains, is on the left page, filling most of it. She's facing front this time with her head cocked back slightly, eyes closed and full lips parted. She is positioned in the classic pose symbolic of Madison Avenue female eroticism. The staging has the desired effect on Jackie who is, indeed, aroused. The woman's right, braceleted hand clenches a curtain, and her right arm juts out at a ninety degree angle from her body and forms a right angle itself at the elbow. The woman looks as if she's caught in a time-slice of orgasm. Her left arm is straight out away from her body with the left hand held now by the man who takes up the entire right page. He is nude, with bursting, smooth chest muscles, seen from the belly button up. He's biting that hand as if it were a ripe piece of corn on the cob. His expression is face front and brutal. Once Jackie takes in the whole scene she is simultaneously titillated and disgusted. She knows she is annoyed both because the ad had the intended effect on her and because she doesn't measure up to the erotic and beauty standards being presented in the photographs.

Not motivated to deal with the confusion the ad provokes, Jackie flips through the rest of the magazine until the train finally comes screeching into the station. She tidily plops the issue back onto its original spot, as if to rid herself of its contents and her quandary, and gets into one of the cars.

Because there hasn't been a train for so long, the subway is indeed well populated. At the next station stop, Jackie switches out of the first car she got into. A Hispanic man she initially sits down next to breathfully whispers an "Oh, mama" into her ear. On her first attempt to escape, he puts his hand on her thigh, near her knee, as if to detain her. Jackie stands up and walks over a spilling coke can, which has been rolling back and forth to the rhythms of the subway, to the other end of the car. She decides to get into the next car up at the next stop.

As she's waiting, Jackie feels herself perspire, and she curses the new trains that don't let you pass from one car to another on the inside. "What if I were really in trouble? I'd be totally trapped." As she begins to smell her own emerging fear odor, Jackie looks at the two-seater bench across from her. A large black woman, dressed in a flower-print dress, practical shoes, a hat and a brown jacket too thin for the weather, is reading a well-worn copy of the bible. Next to her, and wedged between her and the rail is a leather-jacketed man, tattoos running from each hand up his arm under his sleeves. He is asleep, snoring with his mouth slightly open revealing a large gold front tooth. Both of them have their feet planted on tattered remnants of the morning papers. At each stop, as passengers walk in and out of the door adjacent to the seat, fragments of newsprint waft out and onto the tracks.

To Jackie, it feels like it's taking forever to get to the next station. She watches her reflection in the car door window as if seeing a silent movie. The tunnel lights flash with approximate regularity through the window to create the effect of old black and white, silent filmstrips.

As she's stepping into the new car, Jackie notices that all the passengers are grouped at one end. At the other, there's a home-less woman with so many layers of encrusted dirt it's hard to tell where one begins and the other ends. Her stench is so strong that Jackie gags when she approaches her. The woman has open, oozing sores spread over her exposed calves. Her feet are covered with newspaper wrapped in plastic bags held up by putty colored rubber bands. The woman has a constant tubercular hack.

She takes up an entire length of the long, mid-car bench with her shopping bags full of used shopping bags and other assorted relics. The speckled linoleum floor of the car is chipped and blends with the bags and odd foot gear of the woman. Only the plastic bench is a shiny orange. It looks out of place in its surroundings. There is a dried coffee and milk colored splash on the wall and some of the windows behind the woman's head. The smell in the car is of burning diesel fuel, remnants of one of the many recent track fires. Jackie covers her mouth instinctively, wishing that she would learn to carry around the charcoal filter face mask she bought after the day she was trapped in the subway during an actual fire.

Taking in the too-familiar scene and feeling her anxiety level rise beyond the tolerable, Jackie rushes to another car farther up. As she finally sits down, she can still feel the warm breath on her ear and the handprint on her leg.

"Only two more stops," she says with a sigh as she slouches as much as possible into the unyielding plastic bench in an attempt to be as unobtrusive as she can.

CHAPTER FIVE:

DOWNTOWN

AT THE SAME TIME THAT Jackie finally emerges from her subway ride, Maria sinks into the soft seat of a Black Pearl limo and says, "Seventieth and Columbus, please."

The newly immigrated Russian driver tries to start up a conversation in his thickly accented broken English, but Maria cuts it off quickly. As usual, she has no energy, or desire, for chitchat with strangers. Her mind is on her destination, home, and the work she's taken with her in her briefcase.

At home, Ben has just tucked Ricky and Bessy into their beds, having read them another chapter of *Little House on the Prairie*. Ben stands staring at the city out of their oversized, thermopane living room windows. Out, across the park, and downtown.

He can see the Citicorp building with its illuminated top, the jewel-like Chrysler building, the Empire State building which has its orange and black Halloween colors on, and millions of little window and street lights glimmering into the dark night. It is this view that he thinks helps make all the aggravation and boredom of his life worth it. Ben is energized daily by catching sight of the city from such an advantageous angle. Watching Central Park change from summer to fall to winter moves Ben enormously, year after year after year. His kids have a good laugh over his sentimental tears. He is hoping for a lot of snow this season; that's when he finds the park is at its most beautiful. Ben steps over to their telescope and peers through it, out at the city. He turns it sideways and refocuses the lens, looking into a familiar apartment across the way. The woman is there, standing over her kitchen sink, dressed in a full slip with a robe draped over her. She looks worn out tonight and Ben feels the urge to call to her. Only once in all the years he's been glimpsing her has he seen the woman face to face on the street.

With the sound of two clicks of Maria's key in the lock, Ben is yanked back from his disembodied panoramic musings into the living room of their apartment at 9:13, which he reads on the digital display of their sound system.

"Hi, Benjamin. How're the kids? Asleep?" Maria says in one monotone breath more as a statement than a question. She has an innocent air, as if everything is as usual, so much so that Ben cannot determine if she is conscious of or oblivious to what she has missed this evening.

She's pulling off her puff hat and, at the same time, setting her briefcase on the side table in the front foyer. It is the sole function of the chrome and blue glass deco table to cradle Maria's briefcase and gym bag from late evening until no later than seven-twenty sharp in the morning.

"Just tucked them in a few minutes ago. You know what time they go to sleep, Maria. I feel like a broken record, but I'll say it once again. It would be nice if you could make a point of being home at least a few nights a week before they're in bed." Ben utters the words calmly as he eases himself from their oversized windows to the couch which he slides onto with not a little resignation.

"Ben! That's not fair." Maria's facial expression demonstrates that she is not yet fully out of her diplomatic office personality and is straddling the line over to her marital, home demeanor. There was a time, long ago, when the first exchange Maria and Ben had upon reuniting at the end of the work day was an embrace and long, slow, tongue on tongue kiss. "I'm usually home early. Very early. Tonight I just had a lot of work pile up and phone calls. All because I had to handle a crazed client with a very difficult case. I was home early yesterday."

"No, for the last three nights you've been at the office late, working on the Oliver case, I believe."

"Well, before that, I mean."

"That was Sunday, remember?" Ben quietly prods.

"I meant Friday, the before of work days. What about all of the nights you work late if you really want to get into it? Hmm?" Maria's voice has an edge of shrill desperation that she's trying to squelch.

"It was just a suggestion, Maria. Take it or leave it. The kids would like to have you around." Ben picks up on Maria's tone and this helps him keep an evenness to his voice. For added punch, he concludes softly with: "They miss you all day." He desperately wants her to feel consequences at a gut level.

Maria's words pop out before she can capture and re-modulate them: "They're in school all day!"

"They need you when they get home." Ben tosses his hand casually for emphasis. He likes playing Mr. Cool, it's something he can rarely manage. Ben wonders whether this ability stems from the fact that he doesn't care anymore.

"Jackie's here." Maria fidgets with some crackers and cheese on their butcher-block kitchen island. "That's why we put up with her. The kids love her." As she pops a cheese slice into her mouth, Maria reaches for a box of raisins and spills a clump out onto the counter.

"They also need their mother. They need you." Ben's has lost his resignation and is becoming increasingly fierce. If he had sharp teeth he'd be baring them now.

Almost up to a fight, Maria thinks better of it and flaps her arms. One hand lands on the counter with a small pound before she gathers up a bunch of raisins as she says: "It's not like they're suckling babies anymore, why can't they need you? You're their father. The kids have *two* parents, remember?"

"Because," Ben says, measuring the impact of his words slowly, "for better or worse, when they were small we trained them to need you. And so they do. It's not magic, Maria, it's how we raised them. Can't be undone now just because you want to."

Ben's attack is like a stab straight into Maria's stomach. She hurls a scowl drenched with venom, but had she had a few moments alone with his last statement she might be crying. Something she hasn't done in a long time. At the back of her mind, Maria tells herself to stop eating the cheese and raisins. Calculating, she figures that to make up for it, she won't be able to eat breakfast in the morning.

Maria lashes out. "It's fine for you to say so, seated so cushily in this apartment that I paid for significantly more than half of." She bites into a cracker topped with cheese and raisins smashed together.

Ben is becoming queasy watching Maria wolf down such unappetizing morsels as he says: "Not counting all the years you didn't make a single penny, of course." Ben is quick to respond as though the answer had been smoldering inside of him for some time.

"Well, that depends on how you count it, doesn't it? If you didn't have me around for those four years to take care of your children, do you really think you could have gotten so far? I, for one, seriously doubt it."

"*My* children?" Ben is incredulous.

Maria doesn't even hear Ben's remark; she's on a roll now. "And what you gained, I lost. If I'm not home every second now, maybe it's because I'm treading so hard to make up for those lost years.

"I'd be partner if we'd hired a nanny like everyone else in our situation. But no, you wouldn't hear of it. 'It's not good for the kids,' you'd say. And *this* is?

"You jerk, you don't even know what it's like trying to compete in a law firm. Let alone at one of the biggest and best in the country. I think you'd better just back off." Maria has to pull in the reins to come to a full stop. She could be off and going at a good clip all night long now that the floodgates have opened.

Ben's face gradually rises to a crimson color. He ponders whipping out the truth that at the diminished rank of senior associate, she'll never be in the running for partner. All he says is: "Let's hope this noble ambition of yours doesn't cost you the love of your children, not to mention mine." He desperately wishes she'd wise up on her own and see how twisted and out of shape her values have stretched.

With this last statement, Maria's shaking hands assemble crackers and cheese on a sandwich plate, and a Scotch glass with two and a half shots of White Label in it. She reaches into a cabinet and pulls out a container of chocolate chips. Maria munches a handful of the chips mixed with raisins while she dumps the remains of her cheese platter into the garbage. In her mind she repeats 'Enough! Stop!' over and over again.

Ben reads the despair on Maria's face and regrets his words. Knowing that the timing is off, he still can't hold himself back from bringing up the therapist.

"Maria," Ben says with a frog in his throat, "I think that it's time for us to go into therapy."

"Great," Maria says sarcastically, "after you." She bows, fanning out her right arm.

"No, I mean, together. We need to go to a couples' counselor."

Maria can't restrain her flabbergasted snicker. "Right, Ben. In my vast amounts of spare time, that's exactly what I'd like to do."

Maria picks up her glass of Scotch, and moves to the hall door, pushing it open with her free right hand. She feels a familiar and unwelcome heaviness in her belly and a sensation of rotting or composting inside of her. She runs a hand across her abdomen. Glancing briefly, furtively, in the mirror, Maria decides she'd better do her two hundred and fifty count sit-up regime before she confronts herself in the bath, as though her existence were defined by her abdominal measurements. A swell of anxiety surges through her, an increasingly frequent feeling. It causes a moment of panic during which Maria has the impulse to jump out of her own skin, to throw her body overboard. Essentially, to not have any physical extension, and, possibly, to not be at all.

Panic and exercises over, Maria decides to try a bath, one with bubbles. As the mound of pink froth rises up about the rim like a phalange of armor, Maria walks, half nude, to the hall to bring the cordless telephone into the bathroom with her. Once in the tub soaking, Maria sips her drink and feels better. She believes alcohol cuts through grease and undoes the effects of food over-consumption.

Ben gazes out the window again, but this time he takes in the view from the couch. He has lost interest even in the woman across the alleyway. For a few minutes it is completely silent in the apartment.

Once Maria feels that she's sufficiently numbed to some of the day's tension, she picks up the burgundy red phone and punches in Roberta's number. After five rings, Maria is just about to hang up, when a hello comes across the line.

"Roberta? It's me Maria. How are you?"

"Oh, Maria, how nice to hear your voice just now." Then, as if changing the subject: "Our lunch was really great. Let's make a habit out of meeting, why don't we?"

"'Berta," Maria says, "what's up? I know that tone."

Maria's words topple Roberta's barricades and she lets loose. "Maria, what an afternoon I've had. I just got back this instant. He called. He thought we could meet. I just can't believe it's happening like this, like in a sleuth movie, only the actors don't know the right lines.

"I never believed in that two pieces of one whole business. You know, like Cathy and Heathcliff. Like John and Yoko. But, now, I see it. It's just how I feel, and so does he. When we're not together, my body aches. It feels like I'm being ripped open from the inside. And when I'm holding him in my arms, I feel the tingling sensation of completion.

"Tell me, Maria, what do you think? I'm beginning to feel scared, I've never, never been like this before. Do you think it could be the raging hormones of menopause hurling me in their vise? Could this be real? Could this be love?"

"Hold on, Roberta. Hold on. Don't throw yourself on the moors just yet."

"No, Maria, please don't make a joke out of this."

"Well, tell me more then. I won't make fun, I swear. What's happened?"

"He called to say he'd like to meet. That he needs to be with me. But that was it, nothing specific. Nothing I could really hold on to. I think maybe she was around, so he had to be cryptic. We needed to meet somewhere anonymous, so we settled for the steps of St. Patrick's. You know, I was ready for my apartment, a hotel room, something with a bed, god damn it. I didn't think I could say it just like that over the phone. So I just agreed. A church. Banally poetic and bizarre.

"Anyway, we arranged for St. Patrick's since it's always crowded there. I got there first, of course. As I'm waiting, I should have brought a book or something, as I'm sitting there, my heart starts to pound. Then it started pounding hard, and fast. And stronger and stronger, until I could only take tiny, shallow breaths.

"Then, I'd been there ten minutes, it was actually just the time we were supposed to meet, but I started to feel like a fool. When it was two minutes late, I was sure he wasn't coming. I felt like the world stopped. My heart was going and I could see it through my shirt. I was thinking as I watched it beat thud, thud, thud, and the minutes tick, I'd brushed my teeth and wiped off my lipstick before leaving to meet him, I left my studio an hour early for it. The French expression for being stood up, *prendre un lapin*, take a rabbit, kept running through my head. Then, when I felt I couldn't hold out any longer, I decided, that, for sure, in ten minutes I'd leave. I'll go buy groceries, I resolved.

"I didn't hear or see any of the commotion on Fifth Avenue. Or rather, I did subliminally as a *Guernica* type of pastiche. But I was too busy trying to push my heart back into my chest cavity and fend off the waves of fantasy of kissing him, undressing him slowly. Then, suddenly, from behind, he appears and taps me on the shoulder."

After a pause, Maria says: "And, so? You were on the steps of the cathedral, then what?"

"We walked, we kissed, we fit together perfectly, like two clowns in love parading themselves in a schmaltz movie. I kept looking at him, trying to find some otherness. Something foreign. Anything that would break me out of this, but I couldn't find it."

"So, what's the plan? What do you do now?"

"I don't know. Wait until he can get away again, I suppose. It's not the worst thing for me that he has other commitments. I mean, I have a lot of work to do, and you know better than anyone what a private person I am."

"Other commitments, yes. But a *wife*, Roberta? Doesn't that bother you?"

"Maybe not. I'm not the jealous type. I think that I just have to try to remember that whatever is between them, or not, is their business, not mine. I don't want to know."

"I don't think that attitude will get you very far. You'll want to know and he'll want to tell. I think it's inevitable." Maria notices that her bath is getting cold, and turns on the hot water tap with her left foot as she hesitantly says: "'Berta, I need to ask you something."

"Shoot, what is it? Sounds like something heavy is coming."

"Maybe. It's about what you said when we met. About your reputation." Maria's voice trails off.

Roberta gathers instantly that, whatever it is, Maria can't voice it herself. After a minute to reflect, she hits on the theme: "You mean about my being gay, shall we say?"

"Yes."

Groping around for a handle on Maria's thoughts, Roberta starts to babble. "Funny it should come up at this point in our relationship, Maria. You know, there was a time at Smith I was really taken with you. I admired you so. I had ideas that our friendship could go beyond the bounds it had assumed."

"What happened?"

"How do you mean that? You were there!"

"But, I never knew." Maria's voice has a touch of wistfulness.

"I wasn't sure if you weren't interested and were being polite, or if you really didn't get it. I guess now I know. I had the sense, I remember, that you did know what I was getting at and couldn't, or wouldn't, I should say, deal with it."

"What's it like 'Berta?"

"Maria, give me a break here, please. Speak in whole, full sentences. What is *what* like?"

"To be interested in a woman."

"Hey, Maria, is something going on with you that I don't know about? This conversation seems just a tad uncharacteristic for Ms. Crisp, go-by-the-*New York Times* prescription plan efficiency here."

"Now it's my turn to be sensitive, please don't turn this into a joking fest. I just think about it sometimes, and wonder if maybe I've bedded with the wrong camp."

"I don't know, Maria. I have trouble with that kind of thinking. People are people. I have to operate that way. I mean, yes, sure women and men are socialized differently, and on a super macro level, they're different. But as individuals? I think that's another story."

"You're not answering my question!"

"No ... *I am.* I'm saying that I don't know if there's a difference to describe for you."

"Well," Maria says weakly, "you can't deny that there's a physical difference, can you?"

"I didn't think that you were talking about the act of sex itself."

"I'm not. Just the attraction part. It just seems that, for me, the consequences of the attraction would factor into the initial feeling." Maria becomes aware of a pulsation in the mole on her neck as she speaks.

"Look, I have an idea, Maria. Come with me, just to hang out. You'll see some aspects firsthand. Make up your own mind."

"Huh?"

"Oh—I mean, there's a great club for women—"

"Oh, no. No, Roberta, I don't think so."

"Why not? With a strictly tourist visa."

"No, I couldn't anyway. I have little enough time as it is than to go hanging around bars."

"Oh, please, Maria. Don't give me that crap."

"You'll have to excuse me, 'Berta. I don't know what I'm talking about here. I think I'm in overdrive on exhaustion. Maybe when I have caught up on sleep one day, I'll figure out what's going on in my pea brain."

"Yeah, right. If you have a pea brain, what do the rest of us have? Micro brains, maybe. You shouldn't let yourself even talk that way, it's counterproductive. You're going through some heavy stuff right now. That doesn't make you stupid, just makes you feel that way. Dulled, you know?"

"Maria, I hate to say this after such an intense conversation, but I should get off now."

"That's okay, 'Berta, me too. Let's get together again soon. I'll be wondering about you."

"Great, 'cause now I'll be wondering about you. Let me know when'll be good for you."

"I will. Talk to you soon. Bye."

"Bye, Maria."

Maria opens the drain to the tub, and remains watching the warm, soapy water slowly recede away from her body. As she sees her pubic hair ascend from behind the water, curiosity mixed with a surging inner sensation grabs hold of Maria. She reaches into one of the drawers in a small dresser perched near the tub and lifts out her magnifying mirror. She's never used it for anything other than suctioning it onto the medicine cabinet to tweeze her eyebrows. Now, as the last drops of water drain, Maria, feeling daring, thrusts the mirror between her legs as she slides her body into a reclined position. Legs spread, with her head crooked upwards and forward trying to see into the mirror, Maria awkwardly wedges her labia open with her other hand. Peering into the mirror, not knowing what she is looking for, Maria's neck begins to cramp and ache.

"What a throwback to the seventies I am," Maria mumbles trying to mask her embarrassment from herself. She catches herself, and takes a breath. "Don't do that to yourself, Maria, Roberta's right. Give yourself at least as much credit as you give your enemies."

She returns the mirror to its place in the drawer and hoists her body out of the tub. She feels heavier than usual, and clumsy. Maria is embarrassed by her own self and tries to squelch an inner feeling of turmoil. Once it has passed, she attempts to recapture the sensation in order to explore it. Too late.

"I need to start paying attention or I might find myself out on Broadway muttering with the best of them," Maria says under her breath. "My old technique of pretending I'm not a person in my own right's just not going to work any longer. I can see that much." After drying herself thoroughly, Maria goes through her four-step, anti-aging alpha-hydroxy Clinique facial routine. The process squelches all further thought. At the close of her night-time repertoire, she brushes her hair.

As Maria replaces her Kent, all natural bristle hair brush in the bathroom cabinet, Jackie enters the apartment. She looks tired and pale. She drops her bag at the entry and heads straight for the refrigerator. Door open, she hunts for some kind of snack that will satisfy her. Finding nothing, she munches on some blue corn chips while searching in the cabinet. Suddenly, she bends over the sink and spits out the chewed contents of her mouth.

"Agh! How did I buy unsalted again? They're disgusting!"

Jackie pours herself a glass of original flavor Tropicana orange juice and notices for the first time that Ben has fallen asleep on the couch. Jackie walks into the living room to turn out the lights over him. She mutters: "Exciting evening all around, huh?" and tromps straight to her room and flops down on her bed. The small room is only minimally furnished and is the least well-kept of the entire home.

Staring straight up at a crack in the ceiling, Jackie continues her query: "Was he flirting with me? Or maybe Norris had something in his eye and it wasn't a wink at all. I mean, he puts his arm around a lot of the girls, so that could've been meaningless too. Why did I run out so fast like my toes were on fire? Maybe he would've asked me out for a drink or something. Hah! Probably carrot juice, he looks so healthy."

"Jackie? You okay?" comes Maria's recuperated voice from the hallway.

Sitting up, Jackie answers a little embarrassed: "Maria? Hi. Yeah. Just kicking myself, but I'm fine."

"Didn't you get enough of that in karate class? What's up, can I help?" Maria's in Jackie's tiny room now and is making her way to the edge of the bed.

"Thanks, don't think so though. I just blew a great opportunity. But then again, I'm not sure. I think Norris, my karate instructor, was making eyes at me and all I could do was look the other way. I was nervous, I guess."

Maria laughs out loud, "I'm sorry, I don't mean to laugh. I'm not laughing at you, it just strikes me funny that a rape prevention teacher would be putting the moves on students. Shouldn't a woman be teaching that class?"

"Thanks, Maria. I can always count on you for the most perverse outlook." Jackie tosses her head in the direction of the living room. "Ben's asleep out there, by the way."

"I know, I was on my way to get him up and into bed. But, first, look at this." Maria wags two sheets of paper covered with large block letters and numbers.

"The phone list, finally?" Jackie says.

"Finally. I actually did it after this ridiculously long amount of time." Maria holds them up straight. "At least they're done. I'm going to hang them now, before they get shuffled back into my briefcase and hidden for a few more weeks." Maria moves towards the door as she adds: "See you in the morning. Goodnight." Maria briskly pats Jackie's leg as she rises to leave.

Jackie's "Goodnight" trails down the hallway after Maria.

CHAPTER SIX:

AROUND THE TOWN

E ARLY MORNING, AS MARIA IS about to leave the apartment, the phone rings out as if it were screaming.

"Damn, that's the ring of a client if I ever heard one," she says as she pulls off the glove she just put on and begins to unbutton her coat. She flops the glove, with its match, in the bowl of trick or treat candy set near the door for the night's events. Maria always gets fully dressed for the outdoors in her vestibule. Bessy teases her about this since she has a good sixteen flights of elevator ride before she gets to the building lobby which, starting in October, is consistently overheated.

Picking up the receiver, she already feels harassed. Maria yells to Jackie in the kitchen: "You should be getting this! Where's your 'Jacob's residence' when I need it?" She bumps into a large pumpkin on the counter waiting to be carved and then let's out a loud: "Shit! Who left this here?"

Jackie is making eggs and cinnamon toast and cocoa in the kitchen for the kids. A constant grumpy whine emanates from Bessy, who is emphatically demanding Lucky Charms instead, and Ricky, devilishly pounding on the counter, wants Fruit Loops with banana and apple sliced in. Jackie is calm this morning, and she calmly enunciates, "No. Come on guys, you had that stuff all last weekend while I was gone. And tonight you'll get plenty of treats on your Halloween circuit."

"Not from Ann!" Bessy screeches with a wild grin on her face.

"Just erasers from her. Let's not go to her door this time," Ricky says authoritatively.

"What do you expect from a dental hygienist, gumdrops?" Jackie says, and segues into her meal mode. "The eggs are almost done. You'll love them because I put a special secret sauce on them today. Wait and see."

Jackie quickly and surreptitiously slathers some mayo and ketchup on the fried eggs. Collectedness with the kids is Jackie's current method of revenge on Maria. She can see that it is having an effect today when she hears Maria slam down the receiver after carefully waiting to make sure the client had hung up. Maria picks up the receiver immediately, and punches in a number she knows by heart.

Bessy tries to interject herself into her mother's line of vision without moving her body by waving and saying: "Morning Mommy." After a pause, she repeats: "Mom?"

Maria is so focused on her course that she doesn't hear Bessy. After several seconds of listening to a taped message and beep, she speaks with the clear voice of someone leaving a message on a crackling tape. "Roberta, its Maria. Let's get together soon. Tonight after trick-or-treating would be good for me. Call me at the office when you can." She clicks off and hastily rebundles. Maria, before she gains awareness of her brusqueness, dashes out, tossing words behind her: "I'm off, see you tonight" from behind the closed door.

Under her breath, Bessy says: "Bye, Mom." Then she turns to Jackie and says, with her voice getting smaller, trailing off into space: "I wanted to tell her that Dad's numbers aren't on our new list."

Maria takes the subway to her office today. For some reason, she is in a furious and defiant mood. Maria storms to the station, past several kids on their way to school in full costume, and on past several incidents she doesn't even notice. A man in a shabby suit loitering outside the subway stop yells at her: "Oh, man-o-man, you can have my baby anytime. Can I walk with you, honey?" The man watches Maria dart obliviously past him and practically jump down all the steps at once into the subway. Out of sight, he calls after her with a bitter twinge: "In a hurry today, delicious?" In a louder voice, smacking his lips, he ends with: "That's okay, I'll catch up with you next time, cunt."

After school, Bessy and Ricky rush home with Jackie at a frenzied pace. Bessy is the most squirmy, with visions of bags of candy mixed with a tinge of trepidation.

"Jackie, Jackie," Bessy exclaims on the subway as she tugs on Jackie's sleeve. "Are we going to the Halloween party first?"

"We're going to eat a good, solid dinner early. Then you're each going to drink a large glass of milk. And, then it'll be time to change and go to the party."

"Who's taking us, you?" Ricky asks in a noncommittal tone, impossible to read.

"Yup. I get to go to the party, and your mom is going to take you around trick-or-treating."

"What if she's late? Will you take us?" Bessy sounds worried, as if the bags she had just conjured were vanishing before her eyes.

Their stop comes, and Jackie ushers the two kids out and up the narrow stairs to street level. On the way to their building, they pass by hordes of kids in full costume, already out making mischief. A shudder passes through Bessy as she recalls being pelted with raw eggs last year. And—she blocked this memory out until now—her near full bag was snatched forever from her hand by an older boy.

In another apartment, downtown, a member of the Living Dolls group is being unmasked by her own daughter. Sandra is going over some slides of her artwork at the kitchen counter while Leda and a friend are having a play date. Having made a wreck out of the tiny apartment and exhausted all other ideas, the kids decide to dress up in Sandra's clothes.

Decked out, the two enter the kitchen with a "Boo." Sandra nearly passes out, not from the surprise, but from the fact that her daughter has found her Barbie mask.

"Mom, I don't want to be a caterpillar anymore. I want to be a Barbie with a pink flowy gown, this mask you got for me is super!"

Trying to hold back from showing her anxiety, Sandra calmly says: "Hey, sweetie, we just finished your costume yesterday. Remember, we spent all day painting it? Next Halloween you can be a Barbie."

Sandra can't imagine how, after years of ingenious hiding, Leda managed to find the mask today. For a Halloween when Sandra happens to need it. A fantasy floats through her mind of Leda boasting of her mother's cool mask at school, and somebody there putting two and two together. Sandra is simultaneously trying to figure out how to obliterate it from the kids' memories.

"But I want to wear it this time! I'll be a caterpillar Barbie, how's that?"

"Leda, I didn't buy it for you. It's not my mask to lend you. It's Uncle Jeffrey's. He wanted to keep it here until tonight, then he's going to come get it and surprise your cousin Zoe. Sorry, honey. Your costume is better anyway. Why don't you two go check out your caterpillar get-up while I finish my work here? Then we'll bake muffins."

Deflated, Leda sighs an "Okay, Mom" and turns towards her room with a slumped posture. Her friend follows, imitating Leda's mood.

Reaching out, Sandra states crisply, knowing that she's succeeded: "Honey, give me the Barbie mask, I'll wrap it up for Jeffrey."

Later, as Bessy and Ricky are cavorting with their friends in the lobby of their building at the party, Maria struggles to get out of her office by the promised time. She packs her briefcase and nervously glances at the digital clock read out. The display tells her that it is near six o'clock, her deadline. A senior partner that Maria is working with on an involved and therefore rainmaker of a case knocks on her door. Ready to go, she calls out a hurried "come in."

"Oh, Dan, hello. I'm just on my way out, can it wait?" Maria surprises herself by her curt directness with someone who could change the course of her career effortlessly.

Clearly taken aback, the middle-aged lawyer responds: "Yes, sure, Maria. You off to a rush meeting I should know about?"

Not knowing what to say, Maria splutters out the truth: "Not quite. It's just that it's Halloween, and I promised my kids that I would take them out on the rounds this year. I swore on a stack of *Narnia* books." Maria's face molds into a grimace, trying to become an apologetic smile.

"Oh, well, by all means. Do what counts the most."

Maria detects what she surmises is an abundance of sarcasm in Dan's voice. She has a tactile impression of Dan's level of respect for her shrink in this exchange. In tandem, she feels her body cave in and curl into a stoop. Her mind feels muddied and frantic at once. As she's fleeing the suite of offices, clutching her briefcase, to finish her off, Maria senses the disapproving scorn of one of the female junior associates who is young and single. Maria breaks out in a sweat wondering if tonight has sealed her professional coffin.

As Maria barges into her apartment, panting, and just barely on time, Sandra kisses her caterpillar daughter goodbye to finish her trick-or-treating with her father on the narrow streets of the West Village. Having such a good time laughing en route to doorsteps with Leda, she lingered too long. Sandra has to hurry now to meet up with Karen and Claire for their protest at the First Annual SoHo Halloween Gala Fundraiser For The Arts. She charges home, gathers up her Barbie mask and a change of clothes and speeds over to Karen's on Prince Street to arrive, miraculously, only a few minutes late.

"Hi, Karen. Oh, you're dressed already, how efficient."

"Hey, Sandra, a bit out of breath, eh? Why don't you go change while we wait for Claire." Karen gestures towards a back room as she speaks.

When the three are decked out in ballroom costume dresses made with assorted military camouflage fabrics topped with sheer chiffon and their doll masks on top, they go over their plans one last time. The stocky Claire and skinny Sandra with her wispy and a bit unkempt hair look awkward in the attire. Karen looks like she belongs in the clothes.

"Look, the people at the door will be hired from some service. Chances are, they've never heard of the Living Dolls. They'll laugh at our funny costumes. Once we're in, it's all over. They won't be able to stop us. Claire, you have the inflatable bed pads?"

"You bet, printed and ready. These hoop skirts are at least good for concealing them if nothing else. I can't imagine wearing these things by choice!"

"You are, right now, you belle, you!" Sandra notes with a chuckle waving her hoop skirt gracefully through the air as she speaks mockingly.

As the three women approach the Green Room, a high-priced, over-decorated, and well booked SoHo restaurant where the gala is being held, they see throngs of costumed adults flooding into the building.

"It's like the topping on the cupcake that they dedicated this event to Swanson, isn't it?" Karen remarks bitterly.

"Okay, quiet now, Dolls. We're supposed to be undercover. No griping here, please. One, two, three, set! Let's go in. Hold your breath and look calm. No. No. Better breathe deeply to look calm, right? Karen, got your invitation ready?"

Karen thrusts out her costume jewelled hand, clasping a gold speckled and embossed card.

Climbing the stoop to the restaurant, Claire whispers: "Hold it, maybe we should hang back. Look who's standing at the door."

"No, we can't look suspicious in any way," Sandra says. "Let's continue. Try to relax."

They are greeted at the door by a tuxedoed woman who asks for their invitations. Karen hands hers over attached to a twenty dollar bill coyly sweeping her long, auburn hair over one shoulder while casually remarking: "We're a matched set, we travel everywhere together."

The woman lets them through without remark.

"Good work, Karen," Sandra says, pressing Karen's hand. "Typical that they can hire a woman to wear a man's suit and stand at the door, but they can only invite three female artists to the event."

"I bet they had no trouble inviting wealthy patrons of the arts, regardless of gender," Claire says.

The organizers have spared no expense in the preparations for the gala. Liquor and gorgeous appetizers float lavishly throughout the room. The decor has a dignified Halloween theme, and a podium is set up in the back center. Several prominent male New York artists and gallery owners are slated to speak. Virtually every guest is in costume. Everyone in the crowd seems to be having a riotously good time.

As the speeches begin, the three women confer and decide that it is time to split up and assume their positions.

"Now I see the flaw to our plans. Maneuvering in this crowd with these personalized jails called skirts isn't going to be simple."

"Claire, you're overly negative tonight, it's not like you. Just play the Southern Belle and titter your way through," Karen says fluttering a fan at her chin.

As each one arrives at her spot, there is little time to spare. Karen and Sandra position themselves at either side of the raised podium and Claire is out directly in front of it. Just as the third speaker is receiving a hearty round of applause, the three women signal to each other. They are each to time sixty seconds into the next speech, and release the self-inflating pads. It happens by chance that the fourth speaker is touting the art world as one of equality and diversity just when the time comes.

Up, into the air go six bed sized pads, each decorated from edge to edge with a black and white Living Dolls poster. Four of the posters were picked as the best of the Living Dolls series highlighting stunning statistics of discrimination in the art world, and two are specifically about the Halloween event itself.

With a few peals of nervous laughter coming from people dotted through the crowd, the audience and the speaker stand aghast, stark still long enough for the three women to quickly leave the building. They flee into the damp night air and head north out of SoHo, across Houston Street. The women are moving at a trot, laughing their way through several blocks, still in full costume, until they find themselves smack in the middle of the Greenwich Village Halloween Parade. The street is jammed with spectators on either side, and a thick, fat carpet of parade participants, which is slowly wiggling on its way. Part of the crowd moves with it, which gives the shape of the movement an overall symbiotic and sexual feel. Costumed and partying observers hang from windows, cheering. There is at least one costume for every female icon that exists, as well as floats and banners. A band is playing, which competes with multiple rhythms emerging from speaker systems perched on windowsills, directed outward. Mounted police officers are in evidence at the intersections.

The Living Dolls find they've been incorporated into the festivities alongside a contingent of Marilyn Monroes, made up to look like they had stepped out of the boxes of the Andy Warhol portrait. Feeling high, Karen waves her hands in the air, as if on a victory march. She twirls around in her large hoop skirt. The other two follow suit, swaying to the sounds of the parade. Several people simultaneously recognize that they are Living Dolls and cheer them on. Now full swing in the spirit of the parade, the three women are having a great time.

Having just come from working late at the Errigon Gallery, compiling ever more statistics at Maria's request, Kim stands at a street corner on the sidewalk watching the parade. The Living Dolls catch her eye and she follows them the length of a block admiringly. Kim doesn't feel disloyal in her momentary infatuation, since she doesn't believe there is any real threat to Frank Errigon from the Doll's activities. She hopes one day to feel as free as they look.

At home on the Upper West Side, Maria tucks her content but sugar-wired kids into bed, having read them a spooky Halloween story to cap the evening. She stares at them with affection. She feels trepidation as she wonders whether the emotions she is awakening to will drive the wedge deeper between herself and her children. She mutters in a worried tone: "I used to love them more than anything, and now I'm putting myself out there. People say you can't have happy kids without being satisfied yourself. I don't know about that, it seems like pop psychology didn't factor in the trade-offs of modern motherhood. Personal satisfaction is definitely one of the dreams deferred."

Maria hurriedly gets ready to go out, to make her date with Roberta. She notices how eager she is to get there, and her pulse rate surges consequentially. Amused at her adolescent behavior, she asks: "What am I doing, competing with Ricky to see who'll get to thirteen first?"

"Maria, I'm over here," Roberta waves from the bar of Amsterdam's, the latest hot spot in Maria's neighborhood. The restaurant is decorated simply, with lots of rough-hewn dark wood beams, and cheap, dark wood table and chair sets one would also find at an inexpensive Greek diner. The fare is equally basic, featuring plain, roasted chicken and mashed potatoes.

Maria makes her way over to Roberta and gives her a hug saying, "Come, let's get that table over there in the corner. At least it'll be semi-private in this crowd."

"There's no accounting for fad, is there, Maria?"

"Yes. Quite. I know what you mean, I don't get it either."

Laughing, Roberta says: "Right, but look, we're here too. Maybe everyone in the room is sitting here puzzled, saying the same thing!"

Once settled, having only had a minor skirmish with a man dressed in a wolf costume at the table next to them over chair space turf, the two look at each other and smile. They both eye his table, looking carefully over his companion, decked in Marie Antoinette style clothing and wig, with her breasts perched, asking to be called "boobs," atop what must be a heavily wired, push-up bra.

"So, how goes it, 'Berta?" Maria asks tapping the table lightly with her fingers.

Expelling a lot of air, puffing her lips, Roberta responds: "Ouf, I don't know. I'm confused."

"Great, that makes two of us!"

"You tell first then. What's up, Maria?"

After a pause in which Maria realizes that she's got nothing concrete to say, she offers: "No, you. I'm boring right now. No reportable material at the moment."

"If it were reportable, it would be boring. Tell me the stuff you're editing."

The earnestness in Roberta's voice somehow compels Maria to open up. "Well, I guess I just meant by that stuff's happening in my mind, but it's too fast. I can't clarify or even identify it yet. I keep getting this sensation of breaking loose, but I don't know from what or where to. It's vague."

Roberta laughs a cynical laugh. "What do you mean, you don't know from what? How about the confines of your life, Maria? I've never known anyone as regimented as you've become." Roberta takes a sip of her wine that's just arrived from the bar.

Maria, who's ordered a frozen Margarita, ignores her drink, as she becomes defensive. "'Berta, that's kids. Or, kids plus job, plus, plus. You just can't imagine how stuff piles up. Schedules. Schedules of schedules. And this is even with an au pair who does most of it. I don't have time to go buy the new stockings that I desperately need. It's just how it is till they grow up."

"Depends on how you do it, no? Couldn't you loosen up on family stuff a bit to make room for some individuality? It's what our country's based on after all."

"I have, I have. Just it's not what motherhood is based on. In this country, I might add. Individuality is still a male province."

"Doesn't have to be. I don't feel that way."

"Hey, look. This is something you can't know about unless you've been there. I can't even do my job to the extent I'm capable of under these conditions. They're always snickering behind my back because I pay some attention to commitments to my kids. And the irony is that I barely see them. I love them, yet I'm shunting them from my world, and then getting set back at work because of them. I'm beginning to feel so claustrophobic that I think I might actually stop breathing."

Maria's anxiety rises and envelops the table. The menus placed in front of each of them appear to shrink and cower. Roberta looks grave, and plays with her red, oversized paper napkin for a few moments of silence.

"But Maria, I don't think you can push away the fact that you need a change," Roberta says. "It seems like that's what you're telling yourself in a lot of ways. I mean, you don't want to crack any further, do you? You need to be calm enough to think this through. It doesn't sound like you can keep this up too much longer."

"I know," Maria says with a groan.

"Look, maybe a vacation would do the trick. To, sort of, have time to pause. Relax. Do nothing, you know. Don't travel, just plop yourself somewhere great. Seems like you need to provide space and time for yourself."

"Yes, but the amount of anxiety that would build in me because of time lost would negate the whole thing."

"Come on, Maria. That's horrible. A long weekend even. You could manage that." Then, responding to the waiter who had been standing patiently, ready to take their order, Roberta suggests mostly as a question: "We'll share an order of buffalo wings, corn bread, and a large house salad."

With no dissent or response of any kind coming from Maria, the waiter takes that to be the order and leaves silently to fill it.

As if nothing had intervened, Maria speaks: "Hah! I'd probably just spend the trip thinking about work, my kids, Ben. You know, not really resting or reflecting." Silently, Maria's relieved she skipped lunch today, so she'd be able to at least nibble with Roberta now.

"How are you and Ben, Maria? Do you two have fun together?"

Maria looks surprised by the question, as if she had never posed it herself.

Roberta takes Maria's silence as an answer, and says: "Well, no wonder then. Where's the joy, if you'll excuse the glib word, in your life? You've got all the hard choices and none of the reward. Of course you feel like you've got to bust out of jail to do anything at all!"

"Don't exaggerate, 'Berta. I'm hardly in jail." Maria's voice trails off, having weakened as she goes on.

"Look, Maria, I sort of know what you're going through." Roberta speaks with a hint of impatience at Maria's stonewall façade. "I mean, maybe part of it is our age, 'cause I'm having some similar feelings. I've joked to myself that it's midlife crisis."

"You mean your *Wuthering Heights* romance?"

"Well, sort of," Roberta says sheepishly, feeling guilty at having shifted the conversation onto herself.

"Tell me. Anything new?" Maria is only half interested, still caught up in her own dilemma.

Warming up to telling Maria about the recent developments, Roberta's voice becomes more animated. "Mostly, it's great. This is love, fast, real, love. I thought I knew about it before, but now I know how wrong I was. *You* were right about something, though, Maria."

"Don't sound so surprised, 'Berta. Occasionally I do have thoughts, you know."

"About jealousy. Seems to go along with the territory. Also something I've never experienced."

"What provoked it?"

"Well, foolish me. I kind of assumed, it's ridiculous when I think of it, I actually assumed that because I thought that we were falling madly in love, that his long, long term relationship with his wife was over."

"Uh-oh," Maria says as she stirs her margarita and takes a sip.

"You got it. He mentioned something in passing, I don't even remember what it was now. Anyway, in a split second it dawned on me that he was having sex with her. I couldn't even pause, I just shrieked out: 'You mean you're still fucking *her*?'"

"'Berta, 'Berta." Maria gestures with her hands. "Keep it down. The whole world is in here."

"I just couldn't contain myself. I was incredulous, shocked. I've never really believed in monogamy, and our situation is so screwed up. But I couldn't fathom getting into bed with someone else now. I can't fathom him doing it. I just saw her as a neuter mom."

"Oh, thanks, Roberta."

"*Her*, Maria, not you. I just kept bellowing: 'You're fucking *her*, you're *fucking* her?' I couldn't think of any other words. Like I just found out that all the laws of physics are false."

"So, getting past your eloquent declaration, what happened? What did he say?"

"It wasn't good. He got defensive at first, trying to say, what did I expect, he's been married to her forever, et cetera. You know, in the end I had to back off and swallow it. It's reality. It'll either change or it won't. Nothing much I can do about it except see how I feel about how he is when he's with me. See how we are together. So far, that's like a fantasy I wouldn't have known how to concoct."

"But, can you actually ignore it?"

"Yes, I think so. For the time being I can."

CHAPTER SEVEN:

AT HOME

"TODAY WE'RE GOING TO START off by looking at the classical elements of postmodernism. But first, a reminder: the midterm is upon us," Ben says to a classroom full of tired looking faces. "That means you had better get your questions in now. I'll leave a fifteen-minute period at the end for that. And, as a special bonus, today's material won't be on the exam."

A mixture of sighs of relief and hisses circulates around the classroom.

Ben shrugs his shoulders and grins. "Just shows you can't win. Can't please all the people all the time."

"Yeah, right. How about some of the people, some of the time? Anyhow, what he means is that he'll leave fifteen minutes out of his usual half an hour of overtime. Big deal. He thinks we've got nothing better to do than hang around here 'till nine-thirty every time. Guess he doesn't." Jeff lets out his remarks with a disgruntled air too loudly. Jeff has tousled blond hair, a studied rugged look, and sits in an intentionally sprawled, cocky pose. He's wearing torn blue jeans and well-worn sneakers, and is positioned next to Kim, as usual.

Kim is embarrassed by Jeff's remark, and barely moves, although she feels like she is squirming uncontrollably. She's mortified at the thought that Professor Jacobs may have heard. Sometimes Kim feels that she is the only one listening to Ben Jacobs. She likes him, and the material fascinates her. It's a great counterbalance to dealing with all of Frank's goings-on at the gallery. Ben is a methodical teacher and always lectures in the same manner. Today he is going to give a slide show at the end of the class, which is why Kim positioned herself at an aisle seat right next to the projector.

She had to go straight from work at the gallery to this course in comparative contemporary architecture at New York University. She barely had time to run the six long blocks between Errigon's and the school building. She spent the better part of the day trying to compile statistics for Maria that would put the Errigon Gallery in a favorable light. As she expected, her work was to no avail; the Living Dolls are not making frivolous claims. Kim rushed out of work feeling like the whole day had been a waste.

Kim and Jeff are sitting in the classroom in their plywood and metal school seats with Formica veneer, half desks that jut out on the right hand sides. Professor Jacobs is standing up at the front, sandwiched between the rust colored black boards and an old, beaten up dark brown table and chair. He has papers and books smeared across the surface of the table. A projector is set up at the back of the room with three full slide holder rings.

Every now and then Ben gets stuck in the middle of a word and needs to repeat the whole thing before he goes on. He gets frustrated when the words don't come out right. Ben doesn't pretend to be a good teacher, however, nor is he known for being one.

Over the years, Ben acquired several clients from having taught at New York University. Not his students necessarily, but they tell someone else about him, and so it goes. In this regard, Ben has had his eye on Kim mainly because her work puts her in constant proximity with the right sort of clientele. He made eye contact with her frequently at the beginning of the semester but then found himself worrying whether it was ethical behavior.

Now he barely looks at her. He currently settles for catching odd glimpses of her in class. He is pleased when he can sneak a peek out of the corner of his eye and see that she's paying attention. He is elated when she looks interested.

"Take a look at the side view of this work by Graves and tell me what it evokes for you," Ben, now at the back of the room, says as he clicks the viewer to the next slide. "That is, if you can see anything at all." Ben is constantly fighting with the department to buy a new screen because this one and only is so scratched. He might have prevailed had his temper not got in the way. As Ben pauses, he glimpses over to the wall clock and finds he has a disappointingly large amount of time to go.

"Susan, why don't you start off?"

Susan bolts straight up in her chair and begins. "Um. Well, I might be mistaken Professor Jacobs, but—"

"Don't be mistaken." Ben cuts her off. "Jeff, you give it a try."

As Jeff begins to stumble something out, Kim sits frozen in her chair. This is what she waits in terror of. She feels she has done a pretty good job of keeping a low profile in class. In fact, she has managed not to say anything at all unless it was to ask a question after class. And for those rare events, Kim waits until everybody else has gone. She is puzzled at her own behavior. Particularly since in class, and in the time between one class and the next, she has lots of questions and ideas.

Kim often ends up trying to discuss her ideas with Mr. Errigon. She feels she does all right even though he's in the business and this is only her first course. Kim enrolled because she decided that if she's going to be in the art world she ought to learn something about it. She started with Ben's course since she constantly hears people talking about the architectural quality of the paintings Errigon exhibits.

After class, once everyone has streamed out the door, Jeff runs through a variant of his routine, although Kim doesn't recognize it as such yet. As they leave the room, he tilts his head, taps Kim's elbow and says: "So, Kimmy, how about a cup of coffee or something before you reach your cubby hole and study your brains out for the exam? Waste of time, if you ask me."

"Why?" This last statement catches her attention.

"Because, darling, I'd like to be able to sit and stare at you a little longer. And this time it'll be face to face at least."

"No." Kim is giggling and blushing just a little. "I mean, why is it a waste of time to study?" She asks this in earnest and adds with pointed emphasis, "In your opinion, of course."

"Why, in my opinion, is it a waste?" Jeff responds as if embarking on a serious topic, but with a sly smile breaking out across his face. "Because you could be out with me instead. Movies, cafes, romance. Hitting this slide show doesn't hold a candle, no?" Jeff tries to take her hand while he is talking, but Kim subtly slips out of his grip. To conceal his disappointment, he pretends to need his hand to dust off his jacket.

"I happen to like the slide show. Nevertheless," she says. "Yes, okay," she concludes as if in summation, laughing.

"Yes? Yes, what? Excuse me, are you speaking in tongues?" As he says this, Jeff holds the door for Kim and they are hit with a rush of cold air, which reminds them just how overheated the building is. Before she can answer, the two are already out on the street and walking in the direction of Di Roberti's, an Italian cafe near Kim's apartment.

"Yes, let's go have a cup of coffee. I could use one of Lorenzo's double espressos before hitting the books."

In the cafe, Kim and Jeff are seated in one of the back booths, having been hit with a waft of dense cigarette and cigar smoke when they entered. They sit in silence a moment and marvel at the nineteen twenties' gold and sapphire blue tiles which decorate the walls. They look at pictures of Di Roberti's spanning six decades. It had the same furnishings throughout its history. Judging from the photos, the bakers have been making the same style pastries as well.

Without being aware, Kim sits at the side with her back to the door. This means that she is facing the mirrors which cover the back wall. As a rule, mirrors make her uncomfortable, and Kim definitely doesn't like to be forced to confront herself in public. At first, she squirms back and forth on her side of the booth to no avail. She has the look of a penguin waddling in place. She is well aware that her already flawed conversational abilities are only going to be further impaired by this. Just as she senses that the silence has become oppressive, the waitress comes to take their order. At this, both Jeff and Kim use the opportunity to become more animated as they strive for joviality.

"I'd like a steamed milk, an espresso, and an anisette toast," Kim says with a lilt to her voice.

"Hey, what happened to that double espresso you were talking about?" Jeff asks this almost seriously and then adds in his order: "A regular coffee and one of those chocolate rum ball things, please."

"Regular coffee?" the waitress asks with disdain in a heavy Sicilian accent, "You mean, *American* coffee?"

"Yeah," Jeff says hesitantly, feeling a little uneasy because of the waitress's tone.

"We don't make that here. Why don't you have a cappuccino?"

"Okay, good. Cappuccino," Jeff says quickly. After she leaves he remembers to add: "And the chocolate thing!" Then he turns to Kim and says with a sheepish look: "She does have a way of being intimidating, doesn't she? So I didn't know, big deal. Guess I never asked for that here."

"Guess not." Kim is embarrassed too and is still battling with her position in order to not catch glimpses of herself in the mirror. Most of the time Jeff, unknowingly, is blocking the path to her reflection. Kim tries to stay focused on Jeff's face.

"So, what are you going to do when the course is over?" Jeff asks trying to get them beyond the incident.

"Take another one, I suppose. Don't have to think about it just yet since we're only half way through the semester."

"Kim, is that really how you live your life," he says, still testy in spite of his efforts to squelch it, "a couple of months at a time? What about planning for the future and all that? I've got my next three years mapped out."

"Meanwhile, I have a job and you don't, so who's to say?" Kim says, also edgy, and surprises herself with her rudeness. Seeing that this outing is taking a bad turn, Kim is grateful when their order comes. They both use the interruption to start afresh one more time.

"You know," Jeff says, becoming serious, "what you should do is …"

Kim perks up with the tone in his voice; it sounds as though it is going to be significant. Jeff continues while diving a fork into the chocolate rum ball which sits on a white lace paper doily in front of him.

"Set up a quality kids' art center. A sophisticated one, not just one of those slapdash, sloppy operations you see all over. One for budding artists, I mean. You could mix up the media to keep them guessing, or maybe concentrate on whatever you're most interested in. If you specialize, you could get an edge that way. You're a natural for it: you're organized, caring, social, you work hard, and most important, you know how to be silent when necessary. That's crucial with a competitive business like that. The kids need to feel they run the show, and the parents also need to think that they have a big input. And, you're a minority, that'll be a plus.

"You can keep at your job at the gallery for a while to store away business information. Meanwhile, you can rack up a few more courses so that you'll know enough about art and have impressive credentials." Satisfaction emanates from Jeff's face with this pronouncement of advice. At this moment, he's feeling very warmly towards Kim.

Kim, on the other hand, is disappointed. Deflated, really. It's not how she sees herself. She's not even sure she likes kids, and hasn't been around them almost ever. She feels a yearning to do something more concretely expressive. Maybe paint, or become an architect like Jeff is planning to do. Kim listens to Jeff attentively anyway, for maybe he's right. It could be fun playing with paints and clay and stuff. But the responsibility of teaching and relating to not only one, but a whole group of children seems daunting and even oppressive. Not to be taken lightly.

Kim is silent at first, playing with her cookie, dunking it back and forth from milk to espresso. Then she responds slowly, not knowing how much of her aspirations and fears to let out. "Maybe. Sounds possible I guess, especially since I meet all kinds of people at Errigon's. That's not really what I envision though. Not that I have anything specific in mind. I mean, for now things are fine the way they are, I guess."

Kim isn't quite sure of what she has just said. She's feeling muddled. At that moment Jeff reaches down to scratch his ankle, opening up Kim's mirror view. She's horrified by this surprise glimpse of herself. She hadn't known how bad she looks. Kim resolves in one thought to learn how to do something more sophisticated with her makeup, to get a perm for her straight black hair, and to lose five pounds by Thanksgiving.

"But you can't just go on and on like this, can you?" Even Jeff knows that his paternalistic concern is pushing him over the line.

"Well, I think I'll take a film course next. Which reminds me, did you see the new Chabrol yet?" Kim looks cheerier as instantly as she switches the subject. "It's called *L'Enfer*, or 'Hell' in English, or something like that."

"No, want to go Friday?" Jeff jumps at the possibility being suggested.

"Uh-uh. I can't, but let's go the night of the exam, what do you say?"

"Sounds good," Jeff says, gathering some composure, and trying to conceal how pleased he is at any future arrangements to be with Kim. He feels almost giddy at the prospect. Maybe after the movie she'll finally sleep with him. Kim is speaking as Jeff is awash in musings of this delightful fantasy.

"Say," Kim blurts with a thud in her voice, "did you hear about the finger in SoHo yet?"

"I've heard of fingers and I've certainly given the finger driving on those horrible bumpy streets downtown." Jeff smirks wryly, amused by his wit.

"No, really, I saw it. You know the Living Dolls' posters I've been telling you about?"

Something in Kim's tone piques Jeff's interest. "Kim, I know about the posters, tell me already!"

"Well, I was on my way to work, walking down Prince Street when I saw a large crowd up ahead." Kim pauses to formulate her account and sips some milk from the top of her cup. "I was going to ignore it, cause you know how people are in New York. They'll crowd up just for the sake of it. And I saw it was a motley collection."

"Kimmy—get to the point! What finger?"

"I am. I am. Finally, I saw a police officer backing everyone away, putting up that yellow tape, you know? Then I noticed a couple of reporters and realized that they were standing at the spot of one of the recent posters. Another plainclothes officer was up on a ladder, dusting the side of the building for fingerprints. It was a whole operation. There were these officers arguing with a sanitation crew. They couldn't convince the street cleaning truck driver to shove off and stop splattering the area with wet garbage.

"Anyway, tacked up in a corner of the poster was a real, human finger. What looked like fake blood had dripped down onto the print and the sidewalk. It was awful, I got a stomach ache and had to sit still for a while when I got to the gallery.

"I didn't tell Errigon. I didn't want to be the one to cause him to fly off the handle."

"It's related to that murder, isn't it?" Jeff is casual and abstracted about the whole thing while Kim looks sickened just by recalling the incident.

"That's what people are saying, but who knows? Why do that on a Living Dolls poster?

"Oh yeah, there was a note with the finger. Written in green ink in sort of like a Gothic kind of print it just said 'pay attention.' That's all. And they say they found no clues, nothing. Not surprising, considering the conditions they're operating under."

"Hm. Who, I wonder. Is it a note for the Dolls or for the public? Maybe one of the Dolls did it."

"Oh, right. Now you sound like the paranoiac Frank Errigon," Kim says with a guffaw. "They've been at this poster thing for years. Why would they get violent all of a sudden? I mean, usually you know where a fringe group stands on that kind of stuff up front, don't you think?"

"Yeah, like the Earth Firsters."

Kim shifts in her seat and suddenly feels tired in spite of all the caffeine.

"Shall we go, you ready? I'd like to do some studying before I go to sleep."

Jeff is already flapping his fingers in the air while Kim finishes her sentence. "Oh waitress, the check please. This one's on me, Kim," he says as he plunks a ten dollar bill on top of the check before the waitress has fully released it onto their table.

"Oh, no you don't. You try this nonsense every time!" Kim is smiling as she slips a five into Jeff's hand.

"Kimmy, hey, come on. You know it's a man's place to pay. At least, every now and then. I wouldn't want to get regular about it. Just this once, tonight, it would make me feel better about keeping you from your studies."

"Nope. No sir. Sorry buddy." Now she's giggling out of nervousness. As she gets up, Kim reaches for her coat and puts it on in the aisle. When Kim puts her hands in the pockets to get her gloves she also finds the five-dollar bill.

"Jeff! Don't be ridiculous," Kim says with a slightly hoarse voice as she slaps the money onto his chest. Jeff makes no move for it, so it falls to the floor. Kim walks to the door, saying behind her: "Generous tip you're leaving there." Jeff scoops it up and gallops after Kim who has already said goodbye to Lorenzo behind the counter and is just beginning to tread the three steps up to the sidewalk of First Avenue.

Jeff walks her the four blocks to her apartment. Since she really does want to study, Kim tells him that he can't come up to hang out this time. Instead, they position themselves outside the dimly lit, dilapidated apartment building. As they stand talking, both of them are growing colder and colder. The two of them manage to come up with topic after topic which they feel compelled to discuss. Like magnets, they finally have to be almost pulled apart. It is over an hour and a half since their arrival at Kim's building when they actually say goodbye and Jeff starts the trek westward to his apartment.

For once he doesn't feel that she is rejecting him in sending him home. Jeff is sure he made progress tonight. He has visions of himself with Kim, slowly undressing her. He sees what he imagines her breasts to look and feel like, brown, round, and firm, with a brick red-brown center. Jeff tries to imagine the shape of her vulva and wonders about her pubic hair, is it straight or curled? As he feels himself enter her body, he begins to shiver with excitement. "Next time for sure," he says to himself as he turns the corner of Avenue A away from her building.

As Jeff utters those words, Kim climbs the last flight of cracked marble stairs to her apartment. She already has her keys out at the fourth floor and is now pointing a Medeco key into the top lock of her brown metal door. Her mind is debating how much work she can accomplish at this late hour when she is still weary from rushing around at the gallery all day.

"At least I don't need to be at Errigon's until ten tomorrow," she mutters as she wrestles with the bottom lock which is getting stickier and stickier every day. She resolves to buy some WD-40 tomorrow. Kim's apartment is considered to be a large studio because the kitchen is separate. Once inside, she follows a set routine: she flops her coat, bag, gloves and mail on the only chair in the one and only room, goes to the toilet to pee, washes up as if for bed and slips into some pajamas. Then she is set to think about what to do for the rest of the night.

CHAPTER EIGHT:

ASLEEP

"Eight, nine, ten," Kim whispers under her breath as she switches her stretch position from her right to her left Achilles' tendon. Because she only studied an hour the night before, Kim decided she could catch enough sleep to set her alarm for an early seven o'clock wake-up to jog before work.

"Six, seven, enough!" She grabs her keys and heads for the door dressed in turquoise sweats, a purple pouch waist belt, and Brooks running shoes. Kim has taut, lean muscles, the product of a strenuous exercise regimen coupled with a minimalist diet. She doesn't own a scale but can usually guess her weight accurately to within a quarter of a pound.

Out on her jog, Kim takes her well-worn course up Avenue A past the Odessa Coffee Shop where she is a breakfast regular, and on into Tompkins Square Park. Kim cuts across, diagonally down the middle of the park before she starts to circle around it for her five lap route.

She began this pattern to be able to run through the clusters of pigeons and squirrels eating the dry bread left for them by the early morning shift of waitresses at the Odessa. Now, however, she does it more to assess the events with the squatters. In the last few days, people have come to put tents up for the homeless.

An entire shantytown has been built in the park, replete with grills, animals, laundry lines, and banners. Everyone is tensely waiting for the police to try to take them down. Another riot is imminent.

"Morning, Kimmy. How many today?" A jogger blurts as he darts past her going in the opposite direction. Kim will have to answer on the next lap when they pass each other again.

Kim is in her own world as she treads around the park, trying to organize Jacobs' course in her head. It helps her focus on the important stuff to put all the pieces together and in perspective. Her mind wanders to the day Ben showed a slide of a building they had been discussing.

Instead of the usual documentary style, museum quality slides, this one was obviously a tourist item. It showed a blond woman in a skimpy bikini posing at the entrance to some monumental building, facing the camera with a big smile. Ben flashed the slide on for about thirty seconds. Then he said, chuckling: "Just making sure you're all awake out there," and went on with the class as if nothing had happened. Everyone tittered, some, mostly women, more nervously than others. Kim let out an odd little laugh too. Jeff guffawed out loud and this made Kim feel uneasy but not for any reason she could articulate.

A trim, white, middle-aged male jogger dressed in expensive sports clothes calls out to Kim, "Looking good, keep it up, sweetie!" The remark brings Kim's mind back to the present in an instant and she realizes that she's lost count of her laps. As she's trying to figure out how far she had run, Kim stumbles on a crack in the sidewalk but catches herself before she falls.

She collects herself, calculates her mileage, and continues on around the park. She runs through a clump of feeding pigeons, and watches them flutter away only to quickly swoop back to the pile of crumbs. As she jogs, Kim decides to try to clear her mind and relax for the remainder of the laps. Being one of those overcast days whose dim light sets off the intensity of colors in objects,

Kim notices the different hues of the brick and brownstone buildings that line the streets around the park.

On the north side of Tompkins Square, all of the buildings have been renovated with no expense spared, and the exteriors have been steam cleaned or recoated. This side exhibits the pristine brick reds, and brownstone pinks. On the east side of the park, the row of tenement houses has been left untouched and some of the buildings completely abandoned, save the occasional squatter, for seemingly decades. The interior of the park itself is a testament to the tension between the wealthy newcomers to the East Village, the Ukrainian population, and the Puerto Rican inhabitants. In the center of Tompkins Square there is a spanking new playground, painted in bright primaries with refurbished, green park benches all around it. The rest of the park lies in the same ruins it has been left to in the past.

Kim notices a group of five dark skinned boys, none older than nine, approach her. The kids are on their way to school, she thinks.

"Hey, mama, suck my dick!" one shouts at her with his hands cupped around his mouth like a megaphone.

"Ooh, ooh, look at those tits," croons a boy no more than seven years old.

As they come nearer, Kim sees that each kid has a stick in his hand and that they are holding them in a menacing grip. She is so shocked by the discrepancy she perceives between their age and their actions, that it doesn't occur to her to run away, and she continues on her course.

The boys surround Kim and begin swatting her lightly with their sticks, commenting on things that could be done with parts of her anatomy.

Kim feels like a trapped deer. In her fright, she looks around for help and feels a wave of relief when she sees two black men in white uniforms just up the block, a couple of yards in front of her. A few seconds later, the commotion arouses the men's curiosity.

They stop and turn around to see what's going on. When Kim sees them halt, she relaxes and figures that the game is up. The boys also take note, and for an instant freeze in their tracks and look scared.

All eyes are on the men as they take in the scene with a glance. The anticipation hangs heavily in the air around the boys and Kim while the men assess. It takes no more than half a minute for them to act. Sly smiles cross over their faces, and one winks in the direction of the boys. With that they turn around and walk on.

Kim makes use of the otherwise motionless moment to extricate herself from the circle the boys have formed. Kim flees faster than she's ever run before, clear to the outer southwest corner of the park and across the street. She feels suddenly and completely exhausted and decides to head back home for a quick shower, hopefully a hot one.

On her way back, Kim first stops at King's, an old, now shabby, luncheonette with forty-year-old lime green marbleized Formica. To save time, she buys a jumbo cup of coffee to go instead of brewing it at home, and a copy of the *New York Times*. A magazine rack hangs above the stacks of dailies on the right wall at the entrance to King's. Across from the rack is the cashier, surrounded by small candies and at least twelve varieties of chewing gum. Soft porn magazines are so prominently displayed that no one can miss them. They are so much a part of her everyday life that Kim registers the pictures of contorted nudies on this month's covers without even being consciously aware of it. All the dailies' headlines scream news of the finger found downtown. The bloody digit and the note are deftly photographed for several covers.

"Long time no see," says the overweight balding Ukrainian man who runs the place.

"Haven't been able to get up early enough to jog lately, Joe," she says as she hands him two dollar bills, still shaking. When he puts some change in her hand, Kim continues over her shoulder still a little out of breath: "Thanks, see you tomorrow, I hope."

Heading home, Kim, already angry that there probably won't be any hot water, ponders the decrepitude of her apartment building. She never knows what to expect. The boiler has been turned on and off repeatedly and sporadically over the last few weeks for repairs. The tenants' committee decided not to demand a new boiler from the landlord until they'd won an intercom system first.

Even this was a huge political battle. Kim recollects the last residents' meeting, with annoyance. She was expecting some unity against the landlord, and found only factions. The people in the front of the building can just stick their head out of the window to see who's ringing the bell. So they were not keen on the resolved priority ranking for repairs. People at the back have to walk down the stairs and then take a gamble with their lives because the front door is solid metal with no peep hole. The back side tenants won the vote at the last committee meeting mostly because intercoms have been legally required for years. The tenants thought they could get a New York City inspector out to fine the landlord until the violation is cleared. So far they have waited for months for an inspection to take place and the people with back apartments are becoming restless.

Ensconced in her own back-of-the-building apartment, Kim takes sips of her coffee while getting ready for work. From this point on, she has a set routine. She showers in her many times patched-over black and white tile, old New York bathroom after carrying her cup of coffee in with her. She sets the Styrofoam cup on the sink in reach of the copper and chlorine green stained tub-shower in case she wants a quick sip.

As she dries herself off, Kim switches on a battered, black pocket radio perched on a wooden dresser to listen to golden oldies, 'sixties music she's too young to remember, while she's debating what to wear. Unless it's one of those rare days after a clean-up, she has to rummage through the heap of clothes on the chair to find what she wants. Today, Kim slips on a purple top and skirt combination only to rip the whole thing right off. That outfit is replaced by a black sheath dress, black flats, and mauve pantyhose.

"Okay. Not bad. Not great, but it's good enough. Let's get going now." Kim often speaks in the third person about herself to herself. With this approval, she marches to the bathroom mirror and applies makeup. As she is putting on a mixture of brown and red lip gloss, which she always feels is her barrier against the world, she murmurs: "Good, this is so it won't be me in there at the gallery today at all. Camouflage."

Kim usually ends up with some combination of purple eyeliner, black mascara, and brown-pink flesh tone shadow that works as a concealer on her eyes. Just as often, she has first tried to apply some charcoal gray kohl to her lids, trying to imitate a smoky black and white Jacobi portrait she once saw of Lotte Lenya.

Since this is the day of her exam, Kim is nervous even though she has, by now, prepared quite thoroughly. At work, she can barely hold a thought, to the point that she comes frighteningly close to alienating a steady customer. If Frank had witnessed her demeanor, he might have fired her on the spot. Particularly now that he is constantly on the alert for ruination since the Living Dolls started to focus on him. Frank, however, is in his inner office talking on the telephone with Maria when Kim reaches the peak of her distraction.

"But, Frank, it's just not true. You have no evidence." Maria's voice is sharp.

"Of course I do. The posters are about me. So the finger is also. It's a direct threat. It could be a death threat! I need protection. Can't you get a court order or something?" Frank is whipping himself up into true histrionics.

"Stop, Frank, enough. The posters are not aimed only at you. Let's cull a little perspective here. We have no evidence that the finger has anything to do with the Living Dolls. They certainly haven't claimed that action."

"What, are we going to wait until they plead guilty to murder? That was a *real* finger, Maria. Wake up, we're talking big time. This is scary. When I no longer worry about my gallery, we *know* it must be serious."

Maria's mind wanders as Frank rants until it hits her that all of Frank's frenzy may be the result of guilt. She wonders if he's capable of tacking a human finger to a poster on Prince Street. On the very poster which he so fears. Frank has often struck her as seriously unbalanced, but Maria had more or less chalked it up to the kind of business he's in, the disparate worlds he has to straddle to keep afloat. She tries to picture Frank climbing up a ladder, finger, hammer, and nail in hand, in the dark of the night. She can't. Instead, she sees him constantly dusting off his latest suit, worrying that blood from the finger will soil it. Definitely not the sort of violent act she would expect to come from Frank.

"My head's on the block now for real. Aren't I entitled to some protection around here? Did I vote for Koch so that I have to spend my own money to hire private body guards to do the work of the city police? Come on, Maria, advise me! That's what I'm paying you for, isn't it?"

"Frank, right now you're paying me to listen to you vent your fears. Unreasonable fears. I think we should both direct our energies toward the real issues in this case." Maria is completely bored now, and thumbs through the file of her next client as she listens to Frank drone on. Maria flips open her appointment book and sees her note about the leaf collecting with the kids that she didn't do. She pens in a reminder to find out when Wollman Rink opens so that she can go ice skating with Bessy. Maria throws her head back for a few seconds and daydreams of going away for a lone weekend. "Maybe to Gurney's on Montauk?" Back to earth, with Frank's voice in her ear, she settles for trying to get to the gym more regularly. Maria makes a note of this in several spots in her book with many underlines and asterisks penned in red.

Eventually, Frank exhausts even himself. He remembers that he has pressing work concerning the next installation, and hangs up with a nervous twitch. Maria shakes her head into the telephone receiver and gets on with her day.

Later that evening, having barely escaped from the gallery with enough time, Kim finally arrives at the classroom to take the midterm. She's relieved just to have made it there. Seated at her desk, test in hand, she glances up from her exam paper to see Jeff tapping his pen against the faux wood Formica top desk. She can't decide if she sees frustration or boredom on his face. Kim decides it is the latter. This makes her feel ludicrous, taking such a long time structuring her essays before she actually starts to write.

Forty-five minutes early, two students hand in their exams. Kim sighs in exasperation and pushes on. She's scribbling furiously in a blue exam book, trying to describe how Frank Lloyd Wright's design for the Guggenheim was intended to be integrated into Central Park, not across the street. The essay is on the interplay between building composition and landscape architecture, and that's the only example she can think of. Kim's drawing a complete blank on the names of Barragan's work, so the fact that she can envision them in excruciating detail is useless to her at this moment. Annoyingly, her mind keeps wandering back to the day the class discussed these issues. She's unable to stop the flood of memory.

Kim had waited until after the class was over and Ben had answered all the other waiting students' questions. She and Ben began discussing a question she raised when he casually interjected: "Say, it's late, why don't we get out of this cold, empty building and finish our conversation over a drink? How about Lady Astor's over on Lafayette Street? We can talk undisturbed there. And, besides, they make the best Bloody Marys ever."

"Oh, no thanks. You're right, it is late. I shouldn't keep you," she said, stunned and at a loss for any other words. Kim tried to feel that Ben's offer was ordinary and above board.

"Keep me? It'll be a pleasure. Let's go." Ben nudged her elbow and steered her out the door. Kim felt flattered and kept silent.

A few other students get up and hand in their papers. This shakes Kim out of her remembrance and back to the essay at hand. When she finally finishes, she has filled three blue books and has answered an extra credit question. She is one of the last to finish. She neatly numbers the booklets and makes sure her name is clearly written on each one. As she slowly gets up, Kim sees Ben staring out at the space in front of him. She puts her exam down on the pile and says: "Goodbye, thanks." Ben doesn't respond or even register that he sees her at all.

Jeff is waiting outside with a cup of coffee in one hand and a Marlboro with smoke swirling from it in the other. His jeans are relatively new and untorn, and he is wearing a red and white checked shirt tucked in neatly, almost fastidiously. He has dark brown loafers which look a little too new and bright, and blindingly white socks. Jeff finished a half hour ago and doesn't think it went very well. As Kim approaches, a smile covers his face. He blurts: "Ready for the movies? Show time is in fifty-two minutes, let's get going!"

Kim's thoughts are still on the exam, so she is taken aback by Jeff's outburst. The fact is, she forgot all about their arrangement. "Huh? Um, hi, Jeff. What'd you think?"

"Of what?" Jeff says with a mockingly quizzical look on his face.

"Come on, don't joke. I worked hard in there."

"Oh, the exam. Who knows? It was okay I guess. Kind of silly questions though, don't you think? I always feel like I'm in a colony of ants in an exam room. All busily scurrying ink over their wide lined blue book pages." Jeff tries for his casual best.

"Let's get something to eat, I'm starved. Want to go to one of those Indian restaurants on East Sixth Street?"

Kim senses her own exhaustion now. She feels as if all the blood has drained out of her. She knows that she'd really prefer to go home alone with some pizza and watch a crummy *Godzilla* or some other 1950s B movie on television.

"Eat? How can you talk about food when we have a date for the movies? Didn't you eat anything before the test?" Jeff is genuinely crestfallen, seeing his date slip between his fingers like sand.

"I was at work, remember? I even sold one today!" She perks up a little thinking about this. "An expensive painting, ten minutes before closing. If she had deliberated any longer I would have been late for the exam."

"No wonder you think it was hard. If I were hungry and light headed, I might have too." Realizing that he had better change his tack if he wants to keep her company tonight, Jeff switches gears and tries for considerate now. He takes Kim's left arm and leads her around to the direction of Sixth Street. "Okay, let's get some nourishment into you."

After dinner, Jeff decides anxiously that this must be the night he's been waiting for. Kim has suggested that they go up to her apartment for coffee and dessert. They buy a bag of assorted cookies from Di Roberti's and take it back to her place to brew coffee. For different reasons, this time both of them have forgotten about their plan to go to the movies.

As she puts her top lock key in the apartment door, Kim remarks matter-of-factly: "You'll have to excuse the mess, I haven't paid attention to home maintenance since I started to review for the exam." She throws her keys on a stool near the door and they flop their coats and bags on top of them. Both plop onto her pull-out couch bed, which is out at the moment. She has only one other place to sit and that is the chair with all the clothes piled on it. When Kim realizes that they're both on the bed together, she shoots up and begins to chatter and make the coffee. Jeff has realized too.

As she fills the water kettle, Kim blurts: "So, what courses are you taking next semester, Jeff?"

"I don't know, I signed up for some stuff but I think I'll change it all around." He switches his position to rest the back of his head on his hands as he stretches out on the bed. Kim takes note of this and decides to fold up the couch as soon as possible. While Kim talks, Jeff peers out the window to the other apartments across the narrow brick alley below. He looks in on a woman nervously talking into a telephone receiver. The next apartment over is dark. Jeff can just make out the flashing red light of an answering machine. The pervasive blue light of a television blares through the darkness in the window two floors down, next to which Jeff can see teenagers practicing rap moves.

"To what? I thought you had things all figured out well into the next decade," she says as she nervously scoops coffee into the Melitta filter. She has one of those X-shaped glass flasks with a blond wooden handle around the center. She is just using up the last of her bleached filters.

Flora, Kim's older sister, had called her in a panic a few months back. Dioxin was the latest item on her research agenda. Kim was to stop using all bleached paper products instantly.

"But Flora, I can't get along without those things. What am I supposed to do?"

"Use dishtowels instead of paper towels. Use a washcloth instead of cotton balls. Buy unbleached coffee filters. D'Agostino has them. Buy recycled typing and Xerox paper for that office of yours. Use scrap paper for your class notes. Okay? And cotton flannel pads instead of Tampax, which might be killing you. I'll send you some pads if you can't find them."

"You're forgetting something aren't you?"

"Oh yeah, use a handkerchief from now on. Obviously, Kimmy."

"No, I meant toilet paper."

Kim realizes Jeff has been talking and she hasn't heard a word.

"Hey Kim, what's happening with that coffee? Almost all of the cookies are gone already."

"Sorry Jeff. It's dripping through now. Why don't you fold up the couch so we can sit more comfortably. And you can dump my books and stuff off the table and onto the floor so we can set our cups somewhere."

Deliberately ignoring the couch, Jeff clears the table by taking one book at a time and carrying it clear to the other side of the room. He looks as though he is moving in slow motion. When Kim brings the coffee pot over he is almost done and says: "I'll get the cups. You just sit down now."

Kim looks about uneasily but isn't sure if she has cause for alarm. She starts to fold up the couch and Jeff returns with the cups and a carton of milk and helps her position the seat cushions. That makes her feel better and a little guilty that she suspected anything at all.

As he's seating himself on the couch, Jeff speaks with a non-chalant air. "Kimmy, what do you think about doing a project together for the final paper for Jacobs? He said we ought to work in teams anyway. I think we would do well together."

As she crunches on a biscuit, Kim offers a cheery "maybe" and ponders the idea for a minute.

"What'll we cover, the architecture of New York Italian cafes? Perhaps a comparative study of Greek coffee shops versus Spanish diners?"

"Well, I was thinking maybe we could study Fuller's work together and come up with an interesting angle," Jeff says, sounding straight as an arrow.

"Not a bad idea." Kim's taking the proposal seriously now. "We really didn't spend enough time on him in class."

"Let's go to the library together tomorrow and look at slides. Maybe we'll come up with something. Deal?"

"Deal."

They both seem pleased with this plan. Happy so far with the course of events, Jeff moves closer to Kim. He leans his elbow on the back of the couch and positions his arm so that just his fingers are touching Kim, cupping her shoulder. Kim shifts her position as if she needs to in order to see him, and Jeff's arm falls with a thud on the couch behind her. He takes advantage of the situation and now places his hand on her hip.

"Jeff—"

"Shhh! Don't say anything Kimmy, let's just enjoy this moment."

"Huh? Jeff move your hand. Come on, stop joking. You know how I feel about all of this. Just let it lie, Jeff." Kim's voice mounts in anger.

"Kimmy, don't you see how great we could be? I know it. Just wait and find out." Jeff sounds casual but deliberate.

"Jeff, I told you the first time we went out together that I'm not interested in romance and I'm not interested in sex." Kim tries to keep her voice matter of fact. "You're just going to have to take my word for it. Don't pursue this any further."

"Not with just anyone. I understand that. But you and me together, we could have something special. Let me open up the bed and show you what I mean. Don't make such a big deal out of it. I know you're in for a terrific surprise. Come, Kim. Let me show you. It's time."

"Stop this right now, Jeff and forget about it." Kim tenses up now in frustrated anger.

"Kimmy, you're being foolish. Don't you realize that I can rape you if I want to anyway?" The words roll off Jeff's tongue like butter.

Kim keeps a poker face fixed on, and stands up saying, "Jeff, I'm leaving the apartment, I'll be away a little while and when I get back I expect you to be gone." She takes her keys and coat and leaves. She doesn't feel afraid, just annoyed.

At first she intends to circle the block, but then as Kim approaches her apartment building, she decides to walk down First Avenue a bit and then return. On her way up the block the second time she notices how dark the street is. One of the street lamps near her door is out.

As she gets closer, she takes her keys out. She hears some rustling behind her. Kim pivots her head back sharply and sees nothing but a still street. She turns her head face forward to proceed and hears the rustling again. This time she stops in her tracks, which she doesn't like to do so late at night on a small dark block. Kim surveys the scene. She can't see a soul. Lots of parked cars, some garbage fluttering around on the sidewalk. Windows lit up from the inside. She can still hear the rustling, and finally locates it. One of those flimsy plastic shopping bags with handles cut out from the produce grocery stands is caught high up on the branch of a tree flapping in the breeze.

CHAPTER NINE:

IN TRANSIT

"KIM, CAN YOU COME IN here a moment?" Frank Errigon says over the office intercom the next day in the gallery.

She comes through the door dressed in what Kim calls her "SoHo best."

"Yes, Mr. Errigon?" she queries in a slightly too cheery tone.

"We've been singled out in a poster again," Frank says, jumping right in. "We've got to start proving our case, we can't let them keep twisting the facts."

Frank is pacing back and forth, letting the jacket of his new Armani suit flap to and fro. He looks like a suave men's clothing ad gone haywire.

"The Living Dolls again?" Kim offers blandly.

Somehow Kim's interjection allows Frank to end his frenzy and take a seat behind his desk. Looking composed, he tries to strike a more dignified tone. "Yes, Kim, the Living Dolls. We must let them know we mean business. That we will not tolerate their slanderous posters. Not to mention all the violence. We need to direct all of our energies to this and get the job done. By this time next month, I don't even want to remember who they are."

"Mr. Errigon, may I ask you a question?"

"What is it?" Frank has the patronizing sound of a moody dentist who has just taken a course in doctor-patient relations.

"Well, I might be way off the mark but it seems to me that we need to reserve our energies for the next exhibit. Remember how difficult the installation is going to be? And of course, we also need a lot of time for our best clients. To make sure they keep coming in." Kim feels that she's speaking pretty boldly, but she has given the issue a fair amount of thought over the last several weeks.

Frank starts to fidget as he begins to see that this is another of Kim's convoluted speeches. Kim sees the impatience on his face and blurts: "Well, my question is, is this poster business actually hurting our sales? I mean, I haven't noticed any changes since the Living Dolls started their campaign against us."

With this, Frank bolts out of his seat, snapping: "And the lawsuit? The lawsuit, Kim? Did you forget about that already? And what about the murder, and the finger? Of course things have changed!"

"Just pursuing this a moment further, Mr. Errigon." Kim stands firm, ignoring the Fred Swanson issue which no one appears to think is tied in, and fighting the strong urge to back out of the whole topic. She's not sure why she is bothering, and wonders what it is to her even as she speaks.

"I mean, I know I don't understand anything about the law, but I'm not clear what they'll get even if they win. Are you?"

"Money—probably plenty. And they can plaster posters everywhere saying they won. They can humiliate me."

"Maybe you can settle out of court. Isn't that what everyone does these days? Maybe you can get them to stop their posters as part of the agreement."

As their dialogue continues, they are incessantly interrupted by both the telephone and Frank's hysterical digressions. Kim stands in the same place throughout, which means that sometimes she's been talking with Frank behind her or off to one side because of his erratic pacing. Kim's gradually becoming accustomed to this behavior of the last few months and made the practical decision not to let it get to her early on.

"Kim, thanks, but let's stop this chatter and get to work. Go out and copy down the poster exactly. It's on Mercer again between Houston and Prince. Oh, and there's another on Prince right near Nature's Foods. Go to that one, it's closer. Then come back and check our records and prove them wrong."

"I'll try, Mr. Errigon."

"Don't try, Kim. Do it, and the sooner the better."

"But the last one about you was correct."

"Go. This one is wrong. Completely wrong. And get the numbers Maria requested, we'll messenger the whole wad over today."

Walking down West Broadway with the sun glaring in her eyes, Kim realizes how happy she is to get out for some air. On the sidewalk she notices some scattered twenty dollar bills and feels a thud in her heart. As Kim stoops down to gather them, she sees that they are too small to be real and carries on her way, disappointed for a few seconds. As she makes a left onto Prince, she decides to buy a quarter pound of Frank Errigon's favorite lunch salad at Donald Sachs and a small size, eight grain baguette. Hopefully it will perk him up.

Once inside the upscale gourmet takeout food shop, Kim positions herself at the back of the line. She watches, as if through a microscope, the man two ahead of her eating out the entire plate of super chocolate chunk brownie samples. She ponders how ordinary looking he is with his dull brown sweater, wire-rim glasses, and unremarkable features. Not ugly at all, and nowhere near handsome either. After he pays for his order and takes his bag from the person behind the counter, he grasps for his white plastic coffee mug. He brought it in with him and had it perched on the counter with steam from the coffee inside flowing out the top. Kim follows his hand and glances at the mug. She notices its red print design which reads: DOLL HOUSE, N.Y.C. #1 Topless Bar.

Back outdoors once again, before she knows it, Kim is square in front of the new message. She is instantly relieved when she sees that nothing is nailed up to this one. Two identical posters are plastered side by side to a converted factory building. Clear in its solid black block print on white poster paper, they have only one sentence:

SOME GALLERIES EXHIBIT ALMOST NO WOMEN ARTISTS.

Below, a long list of gallery names follow with percentages next to the names, all in single digits, which Kim doesn't think it important to jot down. She wonders vaguely why Errigon couldn't have just told her what this one said, it's so simple. Kim knows she is doomed, there is no way she can prove them wrong this time either.

Farther downtown, south of the gallery, in the Living Dolls member Karen's apartment, the telephone has just rung enough for the answering machine to take the call. As the message begins to play, Karen grabs the receiver.

"Hello," she huffs, out of breath, having rushed up the stairs when she heard the rings.

"Hey, Karen, it's me Sandra, one of your comrades-in-costume. We did a pretty good job at the Halloween extravaganza, if you ask me."

"Yeah. People took note of that ridiculous prank."

"Stranger things have happened. I wonder if it made anyone think, or if it only had shock value."

"I don't know," Karen responds still catching her breath.

"I overheard a bunch of people talking about it the next day at Pearl Paint. It seemed to sort of rattle them."

"It seemed to rattle Claire. Did you catch the look in her eye?"

Sandra answers quickly: "I did. I didn't know what to make of it. Seems like she's been pretty distracted lately. Maybe she's working on one of her super-immense sculptures again. Those always take a lot out of her."

"You're right, she is, in fact. I went over to her studio the other day and got a glimpse of it. You have to hand it to her, when she does something, she does it all the way."

"And so do you. Speaking of which," Sandra deepens her tone for effect, "congratulations! I read the review of your show. Couldn't have been a better write-up."

"Thanks. I'm pretty happy about that. In fact, so much so, I can't concentrate. You think I need bad reviews to keep me going?"

"I hope not. But while you're loafing, could you call some of the Dolls about the location of our next meeting? It's going to be at Denny's office. And Claire told me she has a few new items for the agenda. Maybe you can talk to her too, since you're keeping track of that stuff?"

"Right-o. You know, Sandy, I should really get off now since I wasn't even in the door when you rang. Maybe we could get together, though, before the meeting and chat."

"Sounds good. I'll try to arrange for the child-care thing with Steve. See you soon."

"Bye."

Simultaneously, Claire's arm stretches across her long table for a tool. She's busy in her two-room studio in SoHo. It is actually a rent-controlled apartment that Claire began renting as studio space in the nineteen-seventies. Since then, the building population has changed, but, try as they might to oust Claire, they have failed miserably every time. Claire will never leave willingly. She has utilized every square inch to the maximum, from tools hanging from pegboards, to the built-in drying racks she installed. It is her haven. The walls are painted in a pale gray to offer the minimum of distraction, and the flooring is painted, wide wood board in one room and speckled linoleum in the other. Claire loses track of time while at work, her whole being absorbed in the pursuit of the manipulation of space. Currently, Claire is bent over, engrossed. She has the look of someone feverishly piecing together a two-thousand-piece jigsaw puzzle. While she is intent on her work, she doesn't hear the faint scratching noises which seem to be coming from inside the walls.

Claire pauses and looks upwards just as a louder rubbing sound comes from the alley. Distracted, she mutters, "Goddamn rats," and paces the length of the room. Claire thinks for a minute and decides to investigate the noise. She grabs a heavy chisel and a mallet and softly approaches the door jamb.

Peering through a crack in the door, at first Claire sees only a strip of color, cloth. Then, slowly, a slight young man comes into focus, dressed in brown and purple, entering from the window. She waits for the right moment, and then torpedoes into the adjacent room. She yells, pointing the chisel at the boy and brandishes the mallet. He freezes and looks as though he might pass out from the sight of Claire whirling towards him.

Claire pins him to the exposed brick wall and whispers, slowly, into his face: "The deal is, I didn't see you, and you didn't see what's in this room. To make sure you got it, I want to hear you repeat after me."

After letting the kid exit the way he came, Claire shakily tosses the kid's wallet on the table and takes a seat. She rests without moving for more than half an hour.

Her concentration broken, Claire rises from her chair and elects to clear her head with a walk. Outside it is a bleak, gray day. The sky has opened up to a slow drizzle, as if to rain fully would break the mood. Claire covers herself with a bright yellow plastic rain coat. Her feet slosh on the gray asphalt, kicking wet clumps of fall leaves. She is splashed more than once by an oncoming car hitting a puddle. Claire decides to surprise her daughter Aviva with a quick visit and then get back to her studio.

She pushes through the outer metal doors of the hospital and puts on a knowing demeanor in order to be able to sail past the attendant at the silver and blue Formica sign-in desk. She has a good notion of where Aviva is likely to be at this hour, and makes a beeline for that ward.

"Mom?" Aviva's tone has a tinge of horror. She is on duty, dressed in her green hospital uniform.

Claire kisses Aviva on the forehead. "Hi, sweetie. Good morning." Claire begins to take off her slicker, revealing her plaid work shirt and worn, blue denim coveralls.

Aviva tries to replace the slicker on her mother's shoulders as she speaks, her voice dropping to a whisper. "What are you doing here again, mom? Are you all right?"

"Sure. What do you mean, do I have to be sick to get in to this hospital to see my own daughter?" Claire shifts her weight from one foot to the other while talking.

"Don't take this the wrong way, Mom, but I'm really busy this morning and I can't stand here and talk with you. Tomorrow evening I'll be free and home. You want to call me then, or come over?" Aviva is feeling desperate. She can't be seen blabbing with her mother in the halls. She's barely scraping through the training as it is.

"No problem, Viv," Claire responds in a strained voice. "I'll catch you later. Gotta tell you what's doing with my work. I'm on to a new one. It's gigantic. I feel great about it. Maybe even my gallery can squeeze it in someday when it's done."

Cupping Claire's back with her right hand and forearm, Aviva leads her to the elevator bank. In an amused but bored voice, Aviva speaks as if chanting: "I heard about it yesterday, remember?" Clasping Claire's hands now, she says: "Make it easy for me to say goodbye, Mom." As they hug, Aviva pushes the button for a down elevator, and waits until Claire is ensconced inside it. Aviva pauses at the landing, pondering her mother's state of mind. "I don't see her for weeks, and now she's popping in on me practically daily. Something's up." She resolves to try to have a talk with her mother, face to face, over the weekend.

CHAPTER TEN:

AWAKE

"**A** FINGER. WHY A FINGER? WAS it from the right or the left hand, and what could that mean?" Maria is ensconced in her office with the early morning shift still on duty at the law firm. She came in to have some extra time to grapple with this new, macabre twist to the Errigon case. She is neck high in files. Susan Lieberman, however, has just caught up with her.

"Okay, put her through," Maria says, sighing. She knows this will be a tedious conversation at best, and wonders if she owes this courtesy just because they went through law school together.

"Maria? Long time no see or even hear. How're you doing? You're still working the early hours, I gather."

"Fine. Hello, Susan. I am exceedingly busy today and it's not even eight o'clock yet. Do you think we could chat another time?"

"No. I didn't call to chat. A few prominent attorneys from the metropolitan area are putting together a lawyers' association for women. Part of the purpose is to create clear and practical sexual harassment guidelines for firms, to help implement them, and to do some educational work in the area. I want you to come on board."

"Susan, you know very well that even if I weren't too busy, I'm not interested or even sympathetic with that stuff."

"I know. That's why I think it imperative that you join us."

"No thanks, Susan. I have to go now."

"Hold on. Just think about it for a second, look at yourself, you are a prime example. Senior associate, the subtle mommy track. Not partner as you deserve, nope. Just a permanently underpaid, overworked and lower status position, and no time to see those kids they're punishing you for being able to have.

"In fact, far less than ten percent of the nation's law partners are women! Doesn't that startle you? Only two women ever on the Supreme Court and the first wasn't appointed until 1981!"

"Enough, Susan. I don't have time for this now. Besides, you know I don't believe in making women into a special interest group. If they want to be treated equally, then they have to behave equally. Women need to take care of themselves and be team players instead of whining for preferential treatment every time one of them stubs her toe."

"It's too bad you're saying 'they,' Maria. You are one of those 'them,' you know. Talk about preferential treatment, did you hear about the party my firm had over Labor Day?"

Busy sorting through the papers on her desk and, making a mental note to put a stop to her bullshit about herself and independence before she starts to sound like Susan herself, Maria answers disinterestedly: "No, I happily did not."

"We—and I say that with much sorrow—had a wet T-shirt contest featuring our summer associates. Only the *female* associates, that is. I couldn't put a stop to it. And what do you know, we hired the winner. As one of my highly esteemed partners explained: 'She has the kind of body we'd like to see more of.' How does that grab you?"

"It doesn't. Good-bye, Susan." She hangs up the phone.

"I'll send you our brochure," Susan says into her receiver too late.

Uptown, in Maria's apartment her kids are both sitting over their hot five-grain cereal. Ben is also at the counter, scribbling notes into his leather bound pad which he carries around in his hip pocket.

"Hey, Dad, let's play tic-tac-toe," Bessy says as she watches her father absorbed in his writing.

"Not now, sweetie. Did you finish your cereal yet?" Ben asks out of one corner of his mouth as he continues on with his project.

"No, I'm full. I don't want anymore."

"Me too," Ricky says.

Ben looks up from his pad to peer into their bowls. "No dice, you two. Finish up, how else'll you make it through the day?"

Back to his notes, Ben is making a five-point outline, with the letters A through E in bold capitals breaking the page into sections. He's trying to put his reasoning in order, so that he can talk to Maria calmly about going to the marriage counselor. His past attempts have failed, he thinks, because each time he lost it, being overly invested. She's gone cool, and he's boiled. This time he'll have his crib sheet, and it'll be over the phone.

Once he is done plotting, Ben plays a game of tic-tac-toe each with Bessy and Ricky before Jackie takes them off to school. Ben waits until he hears the elevator door slam shut and then goes to punch Maria's office number into the telephone.

"Maria, please. This is Ben."

"Ms. Jacobs's office, can you hold?"

Ben squirms out a 'no' too late, he's already on hold. After a minute, Maria's secretary returns to Ben's line, and puts him through.

"Hello, Ben. How's your morning going so far? Kids off?"

"Hi, Maria. Listen, I know you don't have much time, so I'll come to the point right away." Ben knows he's already losing it. His palms are sweating. He balls up his outline, and pushes on.

"I've given this a great deal of thought, as you can imagine."

At that moment, Maria's office intercom buzzes. "Ben, wait, I'm sorry, I have to take this. Please hold a sec." Maria pushes down the intercom talk lever. "Yes, what is it?"

"The firm meeting is beginning, Ms. Jacobs."

"Thank you, I'll be right in." Maria pushes the hold button to get Ben back, and begins loading her briefcase for the meeting as she speaks, "Ben, you there?"

"Yes, Maria. What I am trying to say is—"

"Ben, listen. I have to go to a meeting, can this wait until tonight?"

An image of Maria coming in the door, late, beat from work flashes before his eyes. "No, Maria. It can't. This only needs to take thirty seconds, if you'll just let me finish my sentence." Ben's voice is uncharacteristically commanding, and he likes the feel of it.

Maria is temporarily startled, and she listens.

"We need to put ourselves on better footing, Maria. And I've come to the conclusion that we can't do that without the help of third party intervention, so to speak. That is, we need, I really think that we do, we need to go, together, to a marriage counselor."

Ben's words are entirely meaningless in Maria's ears. She is, at the moment, panicked about showing up to the meeting late. Instinctively, she acquiesces in order to get out the door and into the conference room. Maria doesn't have the feeling that her agreement will have any actual consequences.

At the meeting, Maria's mind keeps wandering to the Errigon case and the meaning of the tacked finger. She has to continuously monitor herself, to reel herself in, back to the discussions underway. Her hands are splayed on the table surface in front of her. She takes them both in in one gaze and stares at them. She then looks over each hand in turn, and then her eyes move, from right to left examining each finger individually. When she hits upon her left ring finger, dressed in her wedding ring set, her eyes go out of focus. Maria has a disorienting sensation pass through her, as if she had stared at her face in the mirror so long that her features detached and moved around.

Many images, some surreal and indiscernible, float across her mind. She feels her body become plastic and stretch into contorted forms like on a wad of Silly Putty. Maria tries, ineffectively, to pull herself together and reintegrate. A partial vision of herself and her sister as children is fixed at the back of her mind, and she cannot shoo it away. Maria feels woozy and only begins to refocus by noticing the unruliness of her fingernails. This distracts her back to the present as she resolves to stop tearing her cuticles apart and to make time for a quick manicure this evening.

CHAPTER ELEVEN:

IN DREAM

I N A DISGRUNTLED FASHION, MARIA prepares to go to her first counseling session with Ben. In her office, she ties up loose ends on the telephone while packing her briefcase. The therapist's office is only four blocks from hers. That had been one of the conditions that Maria laid down, that she could not take the time out for couples' therapy plus travel. It had to be conveniently located, and Ben had followed up on several recommendations before he found the right therapist in the right spot.

Out walking, propelled towards the address Ben had written on a slip of paper, Maria moves through the pedestrian traffic with a determined air even though her mind is so jumbled with cases that it is, effectively, empty. Upon entering the waiting area inside the suite of offices, Maria takes a dislike to the framed posters on the wall which she considers devoid of personality. As she sits, waiting for Ben, Maria tries to reconstruct how she ever agreed to this fiasco in the making.

Ben comes hurtling in just as the therapist enters the waiting area to introduce herself. Maria looks her up and down and doesn't like the choice of clothing on the therapist either.

The three of them make their way into the back office, and assume positions in the three separate seats, Maria and Ben both avoiding the couch.

The therapist leans down towards the floor to pick up a pad and pen while she says: "In the first session or two, I usually take notes to help me acquaint myself with new clients. Thereafter, I'll dispense with them, except in unusual circumstances in which I feel I could serve you better by jotting a few things down. My sessions are forty-five minutes long."

Changing her expression and position to give an appearance of receptivity, she says: "So, what brings you two here?"

There is a pause, in which Maria looks calm and contained as if she has no intention of speaking. Ben looks from the therapist to Maria and back, and then begins. "It was actually my idea that we do this, so I guess I should start. A friend had given me the name of a marriage counselor that I carried around for too long. I kept pondering it, and tried to indirectly hint to Maria about going. Finally, I just felt we had to do it, that I couldn't pussyfoot around anymore." Ben turns a magazine over between his hands, fidgeting as he speaks, rolling it up, fanning it out.

"I ... I guess I've been kind of lonely lately. Maria works around the clock, not that I blame her. I understand why she's doing it. She has to now. But, I watch the kids need her and not get her. I see myself want her and not get her. I don't mean sex here, I just mean companionship. Or both, I guess, to be honest. That's why we're here, right?"

After shifting positions so that he's got his elbows perched on his splayed knees, Ben continues. While he talks, he doesn't look directly at anyone. Occasionally, he looks into the face of the therapist. It is almost as if it is a Maria doll sitting in the corner, being talked about.

"Before we had kids, before we were so boringly settled in, really, we were deeply in love. I still get gooseflesh when I think back to those days. Maria was in law school, and then a young idealistic lawyer, and I, a fledgling architect. We went out, had great times with friends, made love wildly. I don't think I'm rewriting history, we felt we were made for each other. And then we had kids. Ever since, we've been way off kilter. Don't misunderstand, we both adore and love our kids enormously. And I've really tried to be a true father, not one of these absentee models that replicate themselves everywhere. I've definitely gone out on a limb that way, to be close to my kids and to help Maria. But for that, I suffered somewhat professionally. People still have a hard time respecting a man professionally if he's involved with his family. Maybe even more than a woman, since they expect her to be nurturing, even if she's also a professional of some kind. What do you say, Maria?"

Maria turns a hand palm up as she nods silently with an odd smile.

Ben continues on after glancing over at Maria. "So we have these two gorgeous kids. Maria did a great job when she was home with them, almost too great since she ran herself ragged for them. But then when Bessy, our youngest, was just under three, Maria felt she really had to get back some of her professional standing. I supported her and still do, one hundred percent. But of course, as anyone could predict, that's when everything came tumbling down around us. If we could steal a minute here or there before when the kids were miraculously asleep at the same time, and we didn't need to cover some planning for household strategy, after Maria went back to work, we had zip. Nada. No hope even, well into the future.

"Now we have a college student living with us, and so we have hope again. But little else, in practice. We seem mired down in schedules, tasks, and work. Neither of us even gets to relax with our kids. I see the au pair chuckling with them, and I feel surges of jealousy." Ben shifts to lean back in the soft chair, putting his arms on the rests. "I think," he says in a tone of thoughtful pronouncement, "that the problem is not only logistics. I feel like schedules and details have grown over everything else like ivy. One of the things that is covered, I feel, is me. It seems like half the time I'm invisible to Maria, or worse, an obstacle that's in the way. Like, just to bring out one small example—I don't want to be making accusations, but just to illustrate what I'm talking about—Maria replaced the old emergency telephone and information list we keep plastered to the refrigerator with an updated one. I wasn't even on it. Nowhere! Then, our daughter Bessy penciled me in. Now, I don't think that was intentional or malicious. It was worse. I didn't even come to mind for Maria. To say the very least, in other words, I think we're stuck in a rut. Maybe something that we could derail, if that's the right metaphor, in here."

Maria listens to Ben's words dispassionately, and doesn't make a move to take a turn now that Ben has stopped. Partly, she has no inclination to, and partly she is worn out from work and hunger. The therapist lets a couple of seconds pass before speaking. She gazes, without expression, from Ben, who looks exhausted after his speech, to Maria who appears inscrutable. "Maria, how do you feel about what Ben has said?"

Maria is surprised to be called upon so directly; it isn't her image of what transpires in therapy. She tries her best to use her authoritative office voice to say: "I don't know. I'll have to think it over." Only once the words are out of her mouth and gone, does Maria realize that she has said nothing of substance at all. She wonders for a while what she would have liked to say. Much of the session goes by, with only Ben and the therapist having an exchange.

In what she cannot believe could have been forty-five minutes, Maria realizes that Ben is getting up to leave. She shakes hands with the therapist, and follows Ben out to the lobby.

Ben talks to her without looking her in the eye. "Maria, you know, if we're to accomplish anything at all in there, you're going to have to talk to us. Participate."

"Are we going back, Ben? I thought we'd decide that *together*, tonight, or tomorrow."

"No, Maria. We've got to go back. Nothing can happen in one session."

"But maybe she's not the right person for us." Feeling like this discussion is happening too close to the therapist's office, Maria whispers.

"I think she seems fine. What's not to like? What's the problem?" Ben's words have a sharp, accusing tone.

Maria retreats, not having the desire to argue over something that seems insignificant. "Nothing. Fine. I've got to go. See you tonight."

Ben gives Maria a peck on the cheek, and they part, each to return to work.

Back in her office, Maria fends off two separate hysterical clients on the telephone, simultaneously. As she's getting off the line with one of them, a partner from her firm barges in on her.

"Maria." He begins to talk, heedless of the fact that she is speaking. "I need you in conference room B right away." With that he leaves, dropping a file in front of her, marked Confidential: eyes only.

Maria hustles to mollify the remaining client and hang up as quickly as possible. Having accomplished the feat, she rushes down the hall, and opens the conference room door to find a heated meeting with one of the firm's largest clients in full swing. She takes a seat at the oval table and tries to rapidly assimilate what is happening.

An hour and a half later, the crisis is averted and the meeting is over, in part owing to Maria's quick wit and diplomacy. The partner walks Maria out and, when they reach her office door, he taps her shoulder, exclaiming: "Thanks, Maria. I knew we needed a woman's touch in there. We might have lost them without your input."

Feeling empty, Maria returns to her desk to find whining messages from her kids. Maria drops the pink message slips as if they were hot and grabs her coat. Not knowing what she is doing, Maria finds herself briskly walking uptown on Madison Avenue. As she marches, her mind races as if her life is replaying itself before her eyes. She is jostled by women in long fur coats, block after block. Strollers push her out of the way, as do pedigree dogs in jewel-studded jackets. The Upper East Side culture is one she has never come to terms with, and she looks upon it with disapproval.

Now Maria's mind is in such a fog, that the crowds on the street feel like an affront. She has the bizarre sensation of the sidewalk giving way underneath her.

Maria appears at the entrance to the Carlyle Cafe and enters. As she cuts a path to a table, one of the well-heeled waiters asks another to go to Burger King on their break. Seated at a table and having a black coffee while she smells the tempting fragrance of fresh baked pastries, Maria takes in her surroundings. Amidst the plush decor, she finds herself next to a man and a woman decked out in modified punk attire of black leather, zippers, and safety pins. For lack of something to do with herself, she listens in on their conversation.

"And then you were the only one who understood what I was talking about. If we don't have purchase order numbers in those receipts—"

"They could go to the wrong store—"

"Right. That's right."

"He just doesn't get it, that it's important, and whatnot."

"Right. Right. And to make it worse, the client, this great, important, client changed her mind twenty-four times about the upholstery fabric."

"Yeah, once it was even after we'd cut the stuff."

"Right. And we had to change the trim each time, and the kind of wood. He let it go by though."

"Yeah. We messengered them how many samples?"

"I don't know, maybe hundreds even. And now no purchase order numbers."

Bored, and her mind alarmingly vague, Maria recognizes that she needs to get a handle on her life. Staring into the black coffee as if a tea leaf fortune might emerge, she tries to ponder her feelings. On uncertain ground, she doesn't know where to begin.

"Well, this is surely not a billable half-hour. Why don't I care? I need hours, productive hours on that sheet. I need my kids to stop bugging me. I need my clients to stop bugging me. I need."

With those last words, Maria is shocked into self-recognition. "*I* need," she repeats.

As if for the first time she becomes graphically aware of her own existence. No sooner does this happen than she resumes her normally hollow state. She's lost again, wondering whether she should order something to eat. Opting against food, Maria begins to finger the center bead of her necklace, gaining reassurance of her presence from it.

"What I *need* is a rest. Roberta is right. A vacation, maybe. Maybe alone. For a weekend, even. That ought to be possible. Yes. I'll check my calendar when I get back and do it." With resolve, Maria pays for her coffee and practically runs back to the office.

She picks up her phone in response to what seemed to be a blaring ring.

"Maria, hi, I'm glad I caught you."

"Roberta?"

"Yes, sorry to call you at the office. I'm sure you must be busy, but I wonder if we could talk. If not now, maybe we could make an appointment or something."

"'Berta, you sound so formal. What's up?"

"I'm sorry to call you with this, Maria, I feel like an overgrown teenager, but I've kind of surpassed my threshold for tolerance of anxiety."

"Stop apologizing. Tell me what's going on."

"I don't even know where to start, now that I've got you live on the wire."

After waiting through a pause, Maria encourages her. "'Berta, 'Berta, start anywhere. Just talk to me."

Roberta is fighting back gagging on the tears and phlegm that are washing down the back of her throat. She sniffles, blows her nose, then speaks. "I don't know. You know, I just have this dreadful feeling. I have this picture of myself looming over everyone, large and gawky. I see myself looking like Ethyl Eichelberger, but without any of his talent. Just ungainly.

"I think I've got to end this relationship before I let it consume me entirely. I feel physically sick half the time, I eat erratically, I don't sleep much. I'm ruining my life with it. He tells me all this awful stuff going on with his family break-up, and I react like it's happening to me. But then I feel doubly bound, because there's nothing I can do about it. Finally I understand how claustrophobics feel."

"This sounds dreadful and serious, Roberta, but I don't have a clue what you're talking about. Give me a hint here."

Pulling herself together slightly, Roberta's voice becomes a little clearer. "Well, you know, I told you how incredible I think he is. How incredible we are together. For the brief and few times we've been together I have visions dancing before my eyes of this great love stretching out into the forever. You know how frenzied and aggressive I am with my work, but when I'm with him I feel like I could lie in his arms for days on end. We talk, laugh even, and we have this incredible, explosive kind of sex that I can't reconstruct mentally afterwards it is so intense. So different. When we're not together, stupid as it sounds, I ache for him, my whole self does. I feel like he's become a right I'm entitled to. He feels the same way, breathes me with every breath, he says. And when we're together, I *know* that it's true. But when we're not, I'm sure he believes what he says, but it doesn't jive with his behavior.

"I mean, he told me he wants a divorce, that he's getting one. At first it freaked me out because he's got a whole family. I didn't want him to do something that big based on me. But he says it's been on his mind for a long time, long before me. So, okay. I stop trying to talk him out of it. So, he brings up divorce with his wife, takes her to a divorce mediator, a therapist really. He starts sleeping in a different room. And I begin to feel like our relationship all of a sudden has infinite possibilities. I find myself bouncing down the street. A little guiltily, though. But not too much, I mean, their bad marriage isn't my fault.

"But, then. Then, I become really sensitive when he says 'we' and means he and his wife when I thought he meant me. Then

I become frustrated because between his work and his kids, I get relegated to the late, *late* hours even for a telephone conversation. Late enough that normally I'd be asleep."

"Why?"

"He waits until after his wife is asleep. *She's* sleeping, and I'm not because otherwise it's nothing.

"She tells him she'll fight him till his death if he does this. That he's ruining everyone's life. He gets depressed and turns into jelly. And I start to feel invisible."

"Do you talk to him about this, 'Berta?"

"Yeah, sure. But it doesn't really get anywhere because he agrees with me. He agrees, when I explain it from my perspective, but I don't think that he actually gets it. I think he's too caught up in his guilt."

"Or maybe in his ambivalence?" Maria ventures.

"It's possible. I've discussed that with him too. He says no, but I'm not convinced. I don't really think he's ready for what he's doing. He hasn't thought it through."

"The problem really is that you swallowed the rhetoric, and you became ready for him to be free."

"Yup. I don't want to call it rhetoric just yet, but you're right. I made myself available and now feel like the door is slowly, mercilessly closing in my face."

"But 'Berta, your situations are entirely different. He has to do an awful lot of traumatic stuff to be available, you just needed to make a mental decision."

"Sure, that's true, Maria. I don't expect him to pack up and leave, abandon his kids, and so on. But I do expect a commitment to progress. Instead, I see only regress. She even asked him the other night to get back into their bed. I don't see why he has to tell me everything. That really gave me the jitters, like what was the context that made her think that was an appropriate request?

"Then I noticed that a long time had gone by since he had done anything at all about any of this. No more therapist, she didn't like that one. No more divorce, she didn't want one. Maybe a separation, he said. No phones or visits to me till after she's asleep. She, she, she! Now his wife is running my life too.

"I just can't take it like this. Walking around as if I'm a phantom. And then I get to hear all the bad stuff about her tantrums, about how his kids are getting affected. So I start to feel like, maybe I really am just chopped liver. A mere vehicle for whatever it is he's going through."

"Midlife crisis, maybe?" Maria tries to joke.

"Don't really think so, but I feel like I don't know anything anymore. I am distraught. It seems like this great love, this really deep inscrutable thing is fizzling down the toilet. And for bullshit."

"'Berta I understand how you feel, but breaking up a family isn't bullshit. It's serious and difficult. Maybe it's to his credit that he's doing it this way, rather than flying out in a huff. I hear that you feel like he's not recognizing the position you're in, but it seems you're doing a bit of the same."

Too deep into her own funk, Roberta can't consider Maria's caution seriously. She glances at a clock behind her and is startled by how late it is. She is about to be late for a Living Dolls meeting. "Maria! I didn't realize how late it is, I should let you go," she says frantically.

Maria laughs as she says: "Good timing, 'Berta. You mean, *you* need to go. Right?"

"Yeah, sorry, Maria, I do. After giving you a charley horse in the neck, I've got to run to a meeting."

"Okay, Roberta. So long. Let me know how it's going."

"Sure. See you soon. Let's get together for a movie, something good and distracting."

"With depth," Maria says. "I could go for that also right about now."

They hang up simultaneously, and Roberta rushes out the door.

Maria's telephone rings out again as soon as she hangs up with Roberta.

"Maria, we've got to talk." Frank Errigon's breathless, desperate voice resounds across the wire.

"Frank?"

"Maria, can you meet me somewhere? Anywhere. A cafe maybe, near your apartment on your way home?"

"Frank, it's late. Can you call me tomorrow in my office? I'll be in early. We'll set something up then." Maria moves to begin to hang up.

"No," Frank says with urgency. "No. Maria, now." He almost hisses the words.

"Frank, I can't go anywhere at this hour. Why don't you tell me what this is about." Maria rolls her eyes as she speaks.

"They found another finger, Maria. Number two!"

"On a poster, again?"

"Of course, note attached, written in blood. I'm out of my mind with fear. Maria, we need to do something."

Maria's thoughts churn at a rate faster than she can grasp them. She comes to two conclusions: first, after this exchange with Frank, Maria knows that he had nothing to do with the severed limbs; second, she knows that she has to seriously consider that the fingers do have something substantial to do with the Errigon case.

"Frank, do you have any idea why someone is doing this?"

"Why? Why? Of course, why! They're threats. Warnings. They're telling us that we have to cave in to their demands. The posters, the lawsuit. They weren't enough, weren't fast enough. Now they want results any way they can get them. Like Nazi Germany!"

"Frank, stop. That's ridiculous, the Nazi part. But, when you say 'they', you mean who?" Maria believes Frank to be completely off the wall, an hysteric not worth questioning, but she continues to have a lingering hope he'll come up with something useful. She figures that she'll go one more round, and then tackle the problem on her own.

"Are you kidding me, Maria? How did I get you? The Living Dolls, of course. Who else would it be? Who else would walk around in crazy masks tacking live fingers to those posters?"

"Are you saying that someone was caught in the act, Frank? When?"

"No. No. No. I'm just saying, of course it was them. Don't be a fool. Who else cares about those damned posters?"

"You."

After a pause, Frank stutters: "Are you accusing me? Because if you are—" His voice reaches a high pitch.

"Frank, enough! Of course not. I'm saying that the posters wouldn't be effective if nobody cared. You do, other gallery owners presumably do. Maybe some museum curators. Art critics have been leveled in some posters. It seems the whole of the New York art world has reason to be at least moderately interested in what the Living Dolls have to say."

"But it's all gibberish! They lie!"

"That's a tangent right now, Frank. We're talking about the fingers, and who could have placed them. You know what, Frank, I'm going to make some inquiries. You are right in that it is time to flush out the relationship between the fingers and your case. If any, mind you. I'll contact you when I learn something. Goodbye, Frank."

"Maria, wait, don't hang up just yet."

"Frank, I must. We'll talk soon."

After hanging up, Maria feels better. She knows now that she has to delve into this, and the sooner the better.

CHAPTER TWELVE:

AT MEALS

"**B**ESSY, THAT'S WONDERFUL! AFTER IT dries, let's hang it up so that everyone can see what you did," Sandra exclaims as she swoops down to Bessy's level at the elementary school desk covered with tempera paints. Teaching art is Sandra's paid gig; her own art work and Living Dolls work fit in around the edges of school hours.

Bessy glows as her demeanor transforms in response to the art teacher's words. She sits up straighter in her chair and appears to grow. All her energies used soaking up the praise, Bessy can only nod. Sandra gives her a pat on the shoulder saying: "Why don't you rest a minute and try another if you feel like it before it's time for recess?"

Suddenly, the teacher leaves the room with the children unattended. She rushes down the hall to the staff toilets. As she enters she covers her mouth with one hand and clutches her crotch with the other. Sandra barely makes it to the toilet bowl before vomit comes spewing out. When she's done heaving, she pees and splashes her face with cold water. "I've got to go get a test today. This can't go any further," she mutters as she exits the dull green, institutional bathroom.

Back in the art room, Sandra walks around, trying to block out the noise level created by the kids, looking on as she watches them busily painting and splashing colors across their tables, sometimes hitting the paper. She's concerned about Bessy, who she considers withdrawn. Too serious for her age, and maybe a little morbid. As Sandra circles around the room, the image of Bessy puffing up at her commendation saddens her and sends her mind wandering to the day she spoke to her mother, Maria, at parent-teacher day early in the fall.

"You have a very talented daughter, Maria," Sandra said bluntly while she was standing in front of the cork board with one of Bessy's creations pinned to it. "She's got a fantastic imagination," Sandra said into a void since she got no response the first round.

"Hmm? Yes," Maria replies, not looking in any specific direction.

"Bessy, I mean, she did this painting. Look at the shapes. I don't know how much was actually intentional, but this is quite a striking composition." Sandra's eyes look like they are trying to bore through Maria's skull, searching for signs of life, if not compassion.

Now they are both looking at Bessy's work. It's a picture of two girls, one significantly taller than the other, on either side of the page, facing away from each other, with gray-blue clouds in between. Sandra waits for some reaction from Maria, and searches her face.

Maria looks at the painting, but doesn't register its content. She remarks in passing: "She's a mature kid. Nice colors she chose. Great picture. Bessy's told me a lot about your class," she says, clearly embarking upon an inquisitive path. "Do you really have nude models?" Maria looks a little impatient now, almost as though she's in a rush.

"Yes. It is a great experience, the kids love it. A lot of good art work comes out of the days we have models. I'm lucky to be able to find people who will work within the school's minimalist budget." Sandra beams in self-congratulation.

"But, do you actually think that it's a good idea? Aren't the kids a little young for that? Don't you have to clear things like that with Mr. Calley?"

Her mood changes in a flash as Sandra realizes the intent of the questions. Testily, she says: "I guess you better take this up with Calley yourself," and then for Bessy's sake she awkwardly tries to temper the blow to end on an amicable note.

"I greatly enjoy watching Bessy develop her artistic talents in this class. And I think working in here gives her immense satisfaction." It comes out as if a robot had spoken even though Sandra is completely sincere in her words.

Maria is already halfway across the room by the time Sandra finishes speaking, and leaves without another word.

"Sandra! Sandra, come help me," a kid shouts from across the room. "I spilled all the brown paint. I need some more!"

Sandra goes over for the cleanup. Lately the smell of tempera has been making her stomach queasy. Even on cold days Sandra keeps the windows wide open. Usually the time flies by for her with this class, but Sandra's bodily sensations weigh on her, and she feels as though she has to drag herself from one spot to the next. She's glad that this is her last period for the day, and that it is almost over.

A few long minutes later, as Sandra swings the Morningside School door open to leave, she looks more like a student than one of the teachers. Clad in fuchsia colored high-tops, blue jeans and a green knit sweater with an orange scarf slung around her neck, she might have been sixteen just as easily as her actual thirty-eight years. Her cinnamon brown hair with blond highlights, cut in shoulder length soft curls, contributes to the look. Sandra is often heard saying that her life doesn't allow her to advance beyond teenage since she is constantly on the run.

Some days she goes from her studio, to school to teach, to pick up her daughter Leda, then home, and later to long Living Dolls meetings at night or to the private art classes that she gives for several groups of adults. Other days the elements switch around but essentially the day is at best just as harried. Not to mention she's got to fit in therapy once a week, shopping, cleaning, some cooking—although Steve does most of the food prep—and, some fun time with her daughter. It's not until Sandra creeps into bed at night that she allows herself to feel tired. Somehow, by morning, at seven o'clock, she's ready to bolt out of bed and start another discombobulated day. Oftentimes she feels she has to go on automatic pilot just to be able to do it all.

As she bounces down the steps of the school, Sandra chuckles to herself while nodding to Jim Brady, the high school history teacher. He and most of the other teachers on staff have the impression that Sandra leads the stereotypical life of a carefree artist. They imagine her rolling out of bed at ten, attending wine-cheese-and-grapes openings in the evening garbed in Isadora Duncan style gowns, and dabbling here and there on a canvas when the mood strikes. They resent her greatly.

Along the way to the Number One I.R.T. subway stop at One-hundred-and-tenth Street, Sandra decides to skip. She usually feels lighthearted on her way to get Leda. She misses her, but happily acknowledges that the days of her being with Leda all day, every day, are long over. Reflecting on this fact, Sandra fleetingly wonders if she's capable of commencing that cycle all over again. She flies by some kids playing hopscotch outside a once grand apartment building heavily decorated with gargoyles, goes on past the Whelan's drug store at the corner, down the subway steps, and into the station.

On the way down the outer flight of stairs, Sandra is accosted by three separate homeless people asking for money. As the third is telling Sandra to have a nice day, she overhears a kid behind her ask her mother why those people are so dirty.

"Because that's how they're supposed to be, sweetie," the woman answers.

"Why, Mommy?"

"Because, a long time ago they were bad and God punished them by making them crazy. If they had been good, they'd still be happy and clean now."

The girl is silent after the explanation. She simply turns her head around to look back at the threesome while being hustled into the cavernous station by her mother's firm tug on the hand.

Sandra shudders and starts to boil inside. She's deciding whether to say something to the mother and child. She calculates that the net result could be counterproductive. Reluctantly, she keeps on going through the turnstile, and in to wait for the train.

On the platform, Sandra is surrounded by teenagers with headphones, yelling to each other over the competing tapes. She glances over towards the newsstand to see that the dailies have yet another Brooklyn shooting splashed across their front pages. This time a nine-year-old was killed, caught in the line of fire, walking across the street on her way to school. She's touted as an honors student, liked by everyone.

Sandra looks down the platform and sees Scott, one of the gym instructors at Morningside. Before she can walk the other way, he sees her.

"Hey, Sandy, hi!" Scott bellows as he waves and barrels over in her direction, his musculature determining his duck-like gait.

"Hello, Scott. How's the soccer going?"

"Oh, okay. It's a little cold lately for that. We've been concentrating on indoor basketball and track for the past month. Are you free now? Want to go for coffee, or lunch if you haven't had any yet?" Scott's eyes are sparkling.

Before Sandra can answer, their train comes in to the station and both step aboard and sit together on one of the two-seaters at the end of the car next to the doors.

"Sorry, Scott. I can't." As Sandra responds, the subway screeches out of the station and the lights begin to flicker on and off.

"Oh, going to a museum or something, huh?" Scott says into the darkness.

Sandra doesn't answer.

"That's okay. Next time. Meanwhile, I have a new line of grass and coke if you're interested."

"You know I'm not, Scott." The lights come back on semi-permanently and Sandra continues: "Even if I was, you know I couldn't afford it on the Morningside part-time salary."

Sandra tries to make light of the subject. She can't decide if she should report him to somebody or not. If the school staff weren't so hostile towards her she probably would have done so long ago. But as things are, she doesn't think she'd be believed anyway. Since he, so far, won't deal to kids it doesn't seem as important.

"Ha! Yeah, you're right. But maybe some of your arty friends. Pass my name along, okay?"

"Ladies and gentlemen," they hear blare out of a megaphone originating from a man dressed in a clown suit at the opposite end of the car. He's carrying a paint can plastered with pictures of hungry children. He has a well-timed, between-station spiel that allows him to pass the can around for money before the next stop.

"He's a Moonie," Scott whispers to Sandra.

"I know," she answers, imitating Scott's tone.

Having collected all he'll get from the crowd in that car, the clown exits the car at the following stop and goes on to the next one.

While Scott yells over the sounds of the subway at Sandra about some school issue, her mind wanders until her eyes hit upon a subway poster cater-corner to her seat. After she reads the print, she takes it in with a silent smirk.

The poster is divided in two horizontally. The background of the top half is littered with weapons such as brass knuckles, spikes, clubs, pistols, and knives. Superimposed on this photograph, the print reads:

**KILLERS, MUGGERS, AND RAPISTS
HAVE THEIR WEAPONS.**

The bottom half features a picture of a telephone receiver stemmed by its curly black cord, with print that states:

NOW YOU HAVE YOURS
212 577-TIPS CRIME STOPPERS

Both photographs are in black and white, and all the print is blood red.

Sandra is more than ready to get out when the train haltingly pulls into the Fourteenth Street station. "Bye, Scott. See you next week at the faculty meeting," Sandra chirps, and she bounds out of the car before Scott can reply. Behind her she hears a cheery "So long" just before the door closes Scott in and chugs towards his destination in Brooklyn.

As Sandra climbs the outer subway stairs, she is buoyed as she realizes that Scott didn't get out with her yet again. The last time they rode the train together, Scott came along in spite of her strong, and almost harsh, protestation. It wasn't until they got to Leda's school that she managed to make it clear that she really would not permit him to greet Leda with her.

Unfortunately, the net result of that last skirmish was that by the time Sandra met Leda at her school for pick-up, having staved Scott off, she had a very perturbed expression and was aggravated for the first few minutes. Sandra didn't know it, but Leda came up with a personal interpretation of her mother's condition. Being accustomed to seeing her mother agitated around the edges, Leda was often worried about Sandra, especially in her absence.

"Sweetie, oh, I missed you, missed you, missed you!" Sandra exclaims as she rushes over to Leda and picks her up, hugging her.

"Hi, Mom." Leda gives her a big kiss and then makes it clear she wants to be put down before she is embarrassed any further in front of the other kids. Once back on her feet, Leda slyly peers around to assess the damage.

Leda sports a bizarre look today, wearing black jeans, a

red cotton turtle neck, and her mother's black lace undershirt squeezed on top. An awkward attempt at chic. In the morning before school, she also tried to pick her hair out and up in spikes. But, Leda being half white, does not have hair sufficiently capable of that, so it has the appearance of a messy bird nest.

"Ready to go?" Sandra asks beaming.

"Uh huh." Leda plays it cool.

"Have all your stuff?" Sandra glances about. "Didn't you bring the lunch box today?"

"No. Remember, that was yesterday. Dad put that pea soup stuff in the thermos."

"Okay, let's get going then. We have to pick up a few things on the way home." Sandra takes Leda's hand and they make their way towards the school gates. She tells herself not to forget the pregnancy home test kit.

"Not again, Mom!" Leda yanks her hand free and grimaces. "Where do we have to go this time? Can't we just go home?"

"You want to eat dinner, don't you, you goose? And I have to pick up some slides at Spectra on La Guardia Place." Sandra's trying to cover up her anxiousness with a cool veneer. She needs to get the errands done.

"That's far! Let's order Chinese for dinner. Or pizza. Please, Mom." Leda tugs on Sandra's hand.

Sandra looks down and sees a tired looking daughter. "Okay, honey. No food shopping. You look sleepy already. What'd you do in school that was so exhausting?"

"Nothing." Leda clams up.

"How was school today? Anything happen?" Sandra's hoping for an amicable conversation to lull them through their stops.

"It was okay." Leda knows what her mother is up to.

"Well, hmm. I can see you're not in the mood for chit-chat." Sandra also knows that Leda knows, so she just bites the bullet. "We still have to stop by Spectra, though. I need to work on the slides tonight."

"But it's not on the way! Let's go home." Leda's protests sound fierce.

"Would you like to sit down at Caffé Dante and rest for a while? You can have a hot chocolate or something," Sandra says, crouching down to her daughter's level to gauge her actual tiredness while they wait for the light to change at Sixth Avenue. She has a pang of guilt for bribing her daughter in that fashion.

"Oh goody good. Great idea, Mom. Let's go. I want one of those long cookies too, okay?" Leda adds as if she were bargaining on unsure ground.

Walking on Bleecker Street, they turn down MacDougal toward Houston. Leda sees some money lying on the sidewalk and, delighted, she squats in order to pick up one of the bills. Once in her hand, she sees that it is phony, printed on one side and too small to be real. As she flips it over to the other side, she sees a photo of the backside of a nude, dark haired woman wearing only black spike heels, sheer black stockings held up by her hands clothed in lacy, elbow length black gloves.

The woman is looking back over her shoulder, so her devilish facial expression can be seen. Then, in the top right corner, it says, "Adults Only." In the center of the paper is a starburst motif with print in the center of it, which reads:

Push … Push … Into my BUSH

Underneath in bold, large printing is the phone number:

970-BUSH.

Finally, at the bottom in small print, Leda reads:

No man has ever satisfied my sexual desire!
$3.50 per call

Leda quickly crumples the fake money and tosses it into the gutter before her mother can see it. She knows that Sandra would just make a big deal out of it.

The two of them walk another half a block in silence and find themselves in front of the café. As they enter Dante's, Sandra sees a few people she'd rather avoid, so they go over to the other side of the café, even though they will have to sit in the smoking section. "It's afternoon, so it won't be too crowded," Sandra rationalizes to herself about seating Leda in the smoke even though in fact it is rather full of people gesticulating with lit cigarettes in hand.

As always, there is a group of older Italian men sitting at the oval window table on the smoking side and a group of older Italian women sitting at the identical table on the non-smoking side. Both tables sport permanent "Reserved" signs, and members of both groups are puffing away on tobacco products. The men favor cigars, the women, Camel Lights. At the women's table they're discussing fund-raising figures for the local church festival and the men are trading calamari recipes as if they were state secrets.

Sandra asks the Maltese waitress to bring them a hot chocolate, an espresso and a sesame crescent. Leda is already busy playing with the sugar shaker and the ashtray. They are sitting underneath one end of the large mural of Venice, which covers an entire wall of the cafe.

"Break it in pieces, Mommy," Leda commands, looking at the cookie as their order comes.

Sandra cracks the long crescent shaped cookie dotted with sesame seeds into three segments and a lot of crumbs. Leda immediately pops one end of a piece into her cocoa and holds it there until it is soaked. Sandra sips her yellow foam laced espresso and wonders whether she is pregnant, knowing with virtual certainty that she is. She and Steve have been trying to conceive for over two years. She was just becoming used to the idea that it probably wouldn't happen. "I shouldn't be drinking this if I am," Sandra chastises herself, with only a tepid degree of conviction.

"Can you take the seeds off, Mom?" Leda asks as she pensively observes her cookie fragment turn cocoa brown.

"No, silly. There wouldn't be any cookie left if I did that."

As Sandra tenderly watches her daughter slurp the hot chocolate out of the cookie, she asks: "What do you think about going to that dance class with Jessica at the Joffrey?"

"I don't want to," Leda responds, her mouth already covered with chocolate and soggy cookie bits.

"Doesn't Jessica like it?"

"Yeah, but it's creepy," Leda says sloshing the second cookie fragment into her cup.

"Creepy?" Sandra's distressed now since she's trying to find a way to have more time to work. She decides not to push the topic now. Maybe she can build up to it a little differently later. Her bedtime story will have a dancer in it.

"Hey, Sandra!" a middle-aged, squat woman in brightly colored Guatemalan clothing blusters into the cafe and alights on Sandra and Leda.

The mother and daughter both pivot around simultaneously and Sandra hesitantly responds: "Claire, hi. Haven't seen you since Halloween, where've you been? How are you?"

"Oh, not too bad, really. Rolling with the punches, as they say and I try. You?"

"Good. Claire, this is my daughter, Leda," Sandra says with a broad smile, gesturing towards Leda who is too preoccupied to look up.

"Hello, Leda." Claire tries a hand signal to get Leda's attention, but to no avail. "Do you read me? Oh, well. We've become boring adults, I guess. Serves us right."

Sandra diverts the attention from Leda, observing Claire's package. "What's that you've got under your arm there? Looks intriguing." She gestures to the over-stuffed portfolio case Claire is wrestling with to keep the contents from spilling to the floor.

"More slides, more query letters, more stationery. More bullshit work. My gallery axed me. I'm on the sales round again."

"That's too bad, Claire. I'm sorry. You don't deserve it. You're one of the most innovative sculptors around. I always think of you when I need inspiration to continue painting."

"Wow! Don't say another thing. I want to bask in this moment. What words. Can I quote you on that in my sales pitch?" Claire smiles and laughs, as she remains standing in front of Sandra and Leda's table. Leda continues to appear oblivious to the adult conversation as she plays with the salt-and-pepper shakers. She's telling some horse story in which the utensils are the central characters.

There is an awkward moment of silence between the two women. Sandra begins to open her mouth to say that she and Leda must be going when Claire interjects: "Can you believe the coverage the Fred Swanson murder is getting? They have him practically elevated to a deity. You know if it was one of us, it wouldn't even make it into those inch length articles buried at the back. Not to mention the radio, television, every daily in the area, and a national magazine, no less. I mean, not that I condone his murder, but he was a nobody. At best, a mediocre painter. That's it."

Sandra can see that Claire is revving up to a frenzied pitch and doesn't interrupt although she wants to. Her voice markedly agitated, Claire continues: "It reminds me of the Central Park jogger thing. Which was awful of course, but we all came to know every minute detail. While at the same time, no one was interested in the equally brutal rape of the black woman in some projects in Brooklyn."

"I know." Sandra fidgets. She's heard Claire go on at great length about this discrepancy. She's groping for a way to cap the conversation without being rude.

"Disgusting!" Claire says, taking Sandra's assent as a signal to elaborate. "Only that was an issue of race, this one is race and gender, and class probably too. Swanson came from quite a pedigreed and moneyed empire.

"I'm thoroughly sick of it. We don't even pretend to have a meritocracy anymore."

Sandra is suddenly acutely aware that Leda is absorbing the diatribe, and begins to squirm. Having tried some eye movements and facial expressions to an oblivious Claire to get her to tone down her remarks, Sandra finally butts in. "Hey, Claire, you don't have to convince me. I agree, plus some. That's why our education efforts, so to speak, are so important. Right?"

"Right," Claire says. "It's also why I drummed it into my daughter's head that doing something practical, where she would have easy access to self-esteem, is the best thing she could do for herself. Miraculously, I succeeded!" Claire is suddenly radiant and upbeat. "She's a resident now at Beth Israel. Doing well too. She loves her work. She'll get respect, a sizeable income, and a flexible schedule. I keep telling her, no pediatrics. New parents bug you night and day, and she'll never pay off her student loans."

"That's great, Claire. Maybe I can go to her when she's set up. Her name's Aviva, isn't it?"

"Aviva Stern."

"Ah, she's got your last name. Leda has mine. It's nice isn't it?"

"Definitely. I knew I couldn't do it any other way. I loved my father, but it was bad enough I had to bear a man's name in a long, patriarchal line. It's time to put a stop to that shit." Claire glances at her watch. Alarmed, she exclaims: "Yikes, I've got to go. See you at the next meeting!" and rushes out the door as suddenly as she appeared.

"I want another cookie, Mom." Leda demands looking obstinate, like she has a trump card in her hand, having endured such a long, adults-only conversation.

"It's too close to dinner, sweetie. You know that." Sandra feels she is on weak ground since they have no dinner in the offing as yet.

"But look at all the cocoa I have left. I need one."

"I bet you could find a way to drink it without a cookie." Sandra knows she's on more secure footing now that Leda has started to plead.

"I don't want to, Mom!" Leda's swinging her feet wildly now and crumples her brow. She knows she's lost this skirmish.

"You know what, Leda, we've got to get going anyway. You sit here, I'm going to pay up at the counter." Sandra takes her wallet out of her purple knapsack with the Oberlin logo on the back and stands. "Be back in a sec. Hold tight."

When Sandra returns, she picks up one of the paper napkins off the table, wets a corner of it with her spit and wipes most of the mess off of Leda's face. She notices a lot of gook on her daughter's hands too but decides that can wait.

All of their errands finished and two blocks from their apartment, Sandra and Leda are eager to get home. Walking at a good clip, they whiz by acquaintances and neighbors with quick hellos and nods. The air is dampening as evening approaches, and the sidewalk is becoming wet and slippery. Sandra tries to keep a firm grip on Leda's hand so she won't trip in her fatigued clumsiness. In all the rush, somehow Sandra manages to watch a uniformed sanitation cop on foot patrol make a lewd face and slurping noise at a young woman who is walking past him. Just as the woman silently passes beyond the cop, he calls out after her.

"Hey, pussy, want to drink my milk?"

Sandra's blood is boiling already, but when she observes Leda taking in the scene, she loses it altogether and yells at the cop.

"Hey, you! Give me your badge number and name. That's conduct unbecoming of a city official, particularly one in uniform and on duty."

As Sandra approaches him, yanking Leda along with her by the hand, he covers his badge so she can't see the number.

"Go away, ugly dyke cunt or I'll write you every ticket in the book. And take your little half-breed rat with you."

In shock and horror, Sandra pulls Leda quickly down the block and away, yelling over her shoulder, "I'll report you, you bastard!"

In response, she and Leda hear a litany of grotesque, hysterical sentences hurled at them all the way down the block, including some obscene suggestions for what the cop would like to do with Leda.

"Two more flights," Leda announces with a little quiver as she and Sandra climb up carrying a box of slides, a Clear Blue Easy kit from the pharmacy, a pizza with mushrooms, seltzer, and a carton of milk, to their fifth-floor walk-up apartment on Downing Street in the West Village. Both of them are shaken from the confrontation outside. Sandra is frantically groping for a way to discuss the incident with Leda.

"Where's Dad? He should be home by now," Leda asks, looking about the dark apartment, and appearing calmer once inside her own home.

Sandra switches on the light in the front room revealing a panoply of colorful hanging objects, most of which are hung from the sleeping balcony in one corner of the room. The walls are painted with a muted gray-purple and there is a moss green rug on the floor. Steve and Sandra sleep on the balcony and Leda occupies a little room separated from the main room by a truncated hallway. Off the hall is one of those pink tile, rounded tub and squared off sink, 'forties style bathrooms that looks like it came directly from a movie set, except for its tiny size. Leda's room is painted in a cactus flower color and she has a fold-out futon bed which doubles as the chair. In her small room, Leda always has a painting easel out, her toy farm with all its animals and fence winding its way around the room, and a collection of building blocks of odd shapes and colors that Sandra had made for her sixth birthday.

The kitchen is off the front room on the opposite side from the bathroom. In spite of its size, they managed to fit everything

Steve needs to experiment with recipes. Even though he has a "lab" kitchen at Patisserie Lanciani on West Fourth Street to work out of, he often tests new concoctions at home. He even foists himself from the balcony, down the merciless, utterly vertical ladder, to the counter top at times when he is already in bed and half asleep.

Sandra installed a pop-up counter in the kitchen which is where they usually eat. For company they open up a table, which is tucked and folded off to one side in the entry hall. They place it awkwardly jutting out into the middle of the green rug and cover it with a taxi cab yellow cloth to hide the fact that it is only an old and battered, oversized card table bought at the flea market on Avenue of the Americas.

"He must be whipping up a double decker, vanilla and burgundy sauce crisp, or a dessert soufflé with candied fiddle-head ferns. You know how carried away he can get sometimes. He'll be home soon, I'm sure. Let's eat this pizza."

As they begin to make a dent in the large pizza pie and drink milk, Sandra distractedly gets out the phone book, flips to the blue pages and finds a number for the Department of Sanitation.

"What are you doing, Mom?" Leda asks with a mouthful of mushrooms and cheese in her mouth.

"I'm going to report that horrible man. Hopefully he'll be fired or at least harshly warned. Either way, he'll get the message that he can't behave in that fashion anymore." As she's explaining, Sandra already has the cordless phone cradled on her shoulder and is dialing the number.

"Hello? I want to file a complaint against one of the officers on foot patrol today."

Sandra chews some pizza crust while she waits on hold. Finally, she hears some fumbling on the other end.

"Lieutenant Saunders here. How can I help you?" A mature female voice comes across the wire.

"I'd like to file a complaint about the conduct of one of your officers."

"Who?"

"I don't know his name, he withheld it."

"Badge number?"

"He covered it up as I approached."

"Where did the incident occur?"

"On the corner of Bedford and Cornelia."

"At approximately what time, ma'am?"

"Around four o'clock."

"P.M.?"

"Yes"

"Okay, let me put you on hold while I determine who that was."

Sandra eats more pizza and smiles weakly at Leda, winking her right eye.

"Ma'am?" the lieutenant returns.

"I'm here."

"Okay, that was Officer Houd. We've had other complaints against him. Tell me what transpired." She had an encouraging amount of zeal in her voice now.

As Sandra retells the incident in graphic detail she wonders whether she should have done this when Leda wasn't there. Once was enough for her to hear it and Sandra is becoming agitated all over again. Simultaneously, Sandra worries about Leda's nutrition, that pizza is hardly an adequate dinner. She resolves to start cooking whole meals again, maybe even get into a modified macrobiotic program. When Sandra comes to the end of the story, the lieutenant tells Sandra that she'll also have to supply a written report. The sooner the better. An officer can be sent around to her home the following morning at eight to pick it up if that is convenient. Sandra agrees, hangs up, and finishes her slice of pizza in silence.

Later, in her apartment, Sandra waits to be set loose by Steve so that she can make the Dolls' meeting.

Agitated, she ponders out loud, pacing. "So, okay, I'm a horse at the start with a broken gate. Haven't I ever heard of babysitters? Why do I set myself up for this bullshit? This has really got to end."

As it happens, Steve doesn't turn his four-sided key in their Fichet lock until nine o'clock. Leda has just gone off to sleep although she tried her best in a variety of ways to stay up for him. Sandra is grumpy and annoyed because, as if she didn't go through enough today, in the morning she went to great pains to impress upon Steve that she needed at least half an hour in peace to prepare for her meeting tonight. Now she'll barely be able to dash out and get there almost on time.

"This changing of the guard is later then agreed upon, you realize," she snaps as he enters. Sandra is already pulling on her boots and stuffing papers frantically into a folder.

"It wasn't my fault. I could've been here an hour ago," he pleads with an impish look, covered from head to toe in splotches of flour and assorted food splatter remnants. He looks like an overgrown elf from the Keebler factory. Steve is on the tall side, handsome, and black. Although he looks athletic, in fact, it hardly ever occurs to him to work out. His hair is cut short, with just enough length to be able to pick it into a cylindrical shape, with a flat angled top. The haircut confirms Steve's already playful look and demeanor.

"I hung around near one of those posters to get the inside dope. I thought you'd want to know that they found a second finger. Tacked up to a poster, just like the first."

"Shit! What is going on here? Why did some New York psycho have to pick our posters?" Sandra slams the heel of a boot hard onto the floor, but keeps her tone down because of Leda.

"So you think it's unrelated to the Living Dolls activities? Just a nut?" Steve asks.

"I don't know what else to think. I mean, Frank Errigon's not going to go around tacking up bloody fingers out in the cold."

"You just never know who's going to crack, Sandra." Steve smiles slyly. "It could even be me. Who knows what could happen if a masterpiece of mine fell in the oven on a too-hot night of low sales?" Steve wiggles his fingers towards Sandra, gearing up to tickle her.

Sandra dodges, and remarks in a facetious tone. "Well, it was about to be me, you're so late tonight!"

"Now you can see I'm innocent. I was fact-finding for you."

"Yes, fact-finding for me for five minutes, and the other fifty-five of them you created." Sandra pauses to take in the ingredients on his pants and crack a smile. "What was it tonight, by the way?"

Given this slight avenue, Steve can't contain his latest invention any longer. "It's better than the traditional Prince Albert cake by a long shot. Wait till you try some. I'm going to try to duplicate the formula right now. By the time you get back, I should have it ready. It's incredible! Go, go, so I can get started." And with this he bundles Sandra and gets her out the door inside of a minute.

CHAPTER THIRTEEN:

UNDERGROUND

IRONICALLY, TONIGHT THE LIVING DOLLS hold their meetings in the business office of a successful male painter for whom Denise, a member of the group, works.

"Hi, Denny, where's everybody?" Sandra says as she comes bustling in, assuming she'd be last.

"Hopefully, we'll find out. Like a cappuccino? You look chilled around the edges. Today we have Sambuca to lace it with. Want a round? I'll make it." Denise gets up to open the cabinet and start up the Gaggia. She steps to one side of the cabinet in a showroom display pose so that Sandra can get a good view. In traditional Indian garb, Denise looks striking showing off the shiny new equipment.

"Wow! Where did that come from? What happened to the old Melitta drip? I'd gotten used to it."

"My boss-man decided to upgrade. Then, like all good members of the rich and famous, he got a super discount. One of his clients from Dean & Deluca gave it to him at cost. Not bad, hmm?"

"Shows how much I know, I didn't even think D & D sold big equipment like this. It has a steamer too, right?"

"Of course, dummy. Where've you been? To make the story even worse, when Garth at SoHo Wines heard about the gift, he sent over this jazzy bottle of Sambuca to go with it. Now how about that cap 'n 'Sambuca?"

Reclining into an Italian black leather chair, Sandra says: "Well, that's another sort of embarrassing situation we won't have to worry about ever needing to cope with, even when we do rise to the top of the female art ladder."

"The kitchen stool you mean," Denise says.

"Don't joke, Denise. Not about that." Shifting gears, Sandra remarks despondently: "I think I'm pregnant."

"Well, don't jump for joy, sweetie. Why do you look so glum? Haven't you been trying for this?"

"Yes, I guess so. But now that it's probably real, I can't remember why I wanted it." Sandra pauses for a moment. "Maybe I didn't really think it through before. Maybe I didn't have any reasons. I'm not sure." Her voice trails off.

Denise looks uncomfortable and says: "Well, you've got a choice, you're not stuck. You just have to decide. Leda's a great kid. If you're really unhappy, why not stop with her?" Denise's facial expression tells Sandra that she's sorry to have said anything that sounds like advice.

"I know. I'm feeling too worn out for this. Maybe I'm too busy; it seems like the whole thing could turn into a scheduling disaster. Maybe I'm just too old."

"Who's too old? No one here is older than me!" Claire booms coming through the door.

Denise pivots around to see who else is making noise at the entry door.

"Hi, Claire, Roberta. Come on in."

"Now that I'm here I can say that it's getting late and we can't stay all night again like we did the last time," Roberta says as she sinks into the velvet couch kicking off her pink and green cowboy boots. "Maybe we could start by reading our fan mail while the others trickle in."

"You make a sensational image on that couch. All the colors on you highlighting the soft gray velour couch," Claire says, seating herself, coat still on.

"That's not plain gray, you know. It's muted gray-purple. I'm intimate with that color. I stare at it on my walls. That is, when I have a chance to sit still at home." A cynical chuckle bubbles through the surface of Sandra's words.

Roberta is busy soaking up Claire's remark as complimentary. For emphasis, she strikes a stylized deco pose, tossing her black and blue hennaed hair into the air and behind the couch.

"I went to hear Cecil Taylor last night, so I'm pretty zonked. I hope we don't have anything too difficult to do tonight. He was fantastic, by the way. Really ingenious the way his sound envelopes you. His band, the audience, in one big floating capsule. I don't know how he does it."

"Doesn't really come across the same way on his recordings, does it?" Sandra says. "I bought two at the same time once and was disappointed. There's some element of his music that just doesn't get translated onto tape. Not to mention seeing him perform out on the street with Min Tanaka. No way even to describe that. Probably even videotape would be too flat. He played, they *both* moved. It was awesome! Any of you there? It was one of the most inspirational *and* confusing events of my life. I felt jumbled for weeks after."

Claire laughs. "Maybe it's all the smoke in the room. I don't know, try as I might to listen, his stuff just sounds like traffic noise to me. But then, I'm the type that likes nice, simple tunes set to a song that has a story or something."

"What kind of animal are you, Claire? A Long Island throwback from the forties?" Denise says jokingly, laced with a tinge of genuine intent.

Somehow the mood in the room is becoming uncharacteristically testy for one of the Living Dolls meetings. The crackle in the air is tangible to all.

"Just someone who cringes at the sight of a *Playboy* cover as going way too far, I guess," Claire says.

"*Playboy*? Don't tell me about *Playboy*. I still have the tape marks on my kitchen walls from the day I found Alvin's collection under the couch pillows. I was naive enough to put up a few centerfolds. I thought that it would embarrass him and show him how ridiculous the mags are." Denise notices that her flesh isn't getting goose bumps and prickling at this recollection, as it once did.

A couple of light titters go around the room, and Roberta says, chuckling: "So what happened, Denise, you set the whole pile of magazines on fire and burned the building down?"

"No, I was really stupid in those days. He liked them up, so did his friends. I was horrified. I was stunned. Frozen really. Fortunately, it was close enough to Super Bowl Sunday, the day I finally wised up at least enough to get rid of him. Not before he took a few serious swipes at me—like a few hundred thousand zillion or so other creeps do annually on that glorious day."

The room became pin-drop silent while Denise was talking and the level of bitterness mixed with fear rose in her voice to an emotional, if not audible, scream.

Claire ventures an, "I'm sorry, Denise," feeling pretty lame.

Denise's face changes from tortured to flip in a flash. She says in an almost sing-song tone: "Yeah, me too. So much for the good old days of so-called sexual liberation. May they get further and further away. After all these years, I did see the shithead at the Pineapple Gym on Houston Street. Just as I was about to sign up!"

"So that's how you ended up at the Joy of Movement?"

"Yup. That's it. He's still calling my moves. Pathetic. Luckily, I think Joy is a better place anyway. At least he's got me dancing again, modern this time. The teacher is fantastic." For emphasis,

Denise snaps the neckline of her Lycra leotard she has on under a lime green V-neck sweater.

Trying to deflect the conversation, Roberta says in a too shrill voice: "On to our fan mail?"

"Our work will seem like a breeze after this, Denise, I had no idea," Sandra says. "You know, they found another finger. Up on one of our posters."

"Yup. And it had a note too. Just like the first," Claire says. "Said something like 'I want action.' Maybe not exactly that. I remember it being general but threatening. I think that we should do something now. We might need protection."

"Wait, let's not get carried too far away here," Denise says. "Don't forget all the threatening mail we've gotten. Some of it chilled even my bones, but we never felt motivated to take precautions."

"But these aren't just words we're talking about now," Claire says. "Fingers! Real, human, severed, fingers. One by one. Do we want to wait for the whole hand? Or someone's head?"

"What can we do anyway, patrol our posters day and night? It's enough we have to create and plaster them," a young woman in the room contributes.

"Now notice, everyone," Claire states, talking over the chatter. "If ours were any other posters, not 'women's posters.' the media'd be all over this. But instead, nothing. Not more than a few tiny peeps."

"Oh, I don't agree, Claire." Roberta says. "There's been plenty of attention this time, for all the good it does. And with two fingers, I think the dailies will make a huge gory deal out of it."

"Which might not be so bad," Sandra says. "Maybe the racket will put a stop to whoever the perpetrator is."

"Okay, let's place bets," Claire says. "I'm going to call the papers right now and find out just how hopped up they are about this."

Claire stands, and goes over to the desk at the end of the room and sits down to dial 4-1-1 with pen in hand. She calls out: "Hey,

Denny, I like the groovy message pad here. It reminds me of my youth. It's psychedelic."

The rest of the Dolls decide to read the mail while Claire makes the telephone calls.

"You brought the mail, right Denise?" Roberta asks.

"There's not much today, just a few pieces," she says collecting herself. "Let's see. Let me dig it out of this endless pit of a pocketbook."

Denise is rummaging while a couple more of the group come in and take seats quietly. "Here they are: one, two," sucking in her breath while thumbing through the envelopes. "Six, seven, letters."

"Number one: Dear Living Dolls," Denise reads. "Keep up the good work. I'm with you. I work at a gallery on Spring Street and you're right, they are a bunch of pigs. Someday I might count the ways for you, but for now, here—" Denise draws a blue bank check out of the envelope. "Fifty dollars. That's great!"

"And coming from someone who probably couldn't afford that too easily."

"I wonder if her pigs are worse than mine," Roberta says.

"On to letter number two: 'To the Dolls, Have you fully considered the natural order of the universe? Boulder greater than stone, tree greater than shrub, God greater than man, man greater than woman, children, and animals. Read your Aristotle!' Oh, my, my, my. This one goes on for two pages and, let's face it, we all have the gist of what it says. Too bad he didn't enclose a leaflet about the second coming of Christ."

"Well, any response is a good response, right Dolls?" Karen says just entering the room. At the same time, Claire returns to her original seat.

"I personally could live without some responses," Sandra says.

Claire waits patiently for a few minutes for a break in the conversation. Finally, she says: "So, does anyone want to hear my report?"

Denise says jokingly: "Yes, tell us how we'll be splashed across every front page in the morning."

"No dice, Denise," Claire says in a somber tone with one hand on a hip. "Virtually no coverage planned. Perhaps a curt article here and there. Not newsworthy material. Its old stuff, evidently."

"Well, perhaps we should push on," one of the Dolls says. "If we need to pursue this, maybe we can worry about it another time."

"Yes," Sandra says. "Let's see if it'll blow over before we get too worked up."

Claire sits tight in her seat, mouth clamped. Denise picks up the bunch of letters and resumes where she left off.

"Quiet now, it's time for number three: 'Dear Living Dolls, As a fan of your work and a supporter of your goals I want you to consider the following question: Don't you think that your use of Barbie dolls and overt sexual innuendo belittles and undercuts your cause?'"

After a pause, Denise says: "It's signed: In earnest, a feminist who worries about portraying negative female images."

"Well, this one's a little too heavy for me tonight. I think she worries too much. Maybe she should contact The Feminists Fighting Pornography group. They'll give her an ear-full."

"I don't know, we've had this debate before, after all," Leigh says as she is taking off her coat. The large room is now filling up to almost crowded. Someone has brought a large jug of apple juice and little plastic cups which are being passed around the room in zigzag pattern.

"What are we supposed to do, walk around in men's suits, ties and all?" someone from the back calls out.

"Ah! The entrance of the floppy bow tie into the business and boys' clubs of the art world." Roberta poses in her signature salute.

"Seriously. Some of us have been concerned about our use of negative female images, as our admirer calls them. Why buy into fifties' aesthetics of female style, a decade that was not kind to women?" Claire says.

"On the other hand we don't want the feminist label stuck on to us, it's death!"

"But that's what we are," Claire says, "and I'm proud of it. I agree with this fan, I've been saying similar things for a long time."

"Yeah, but remember," Roberta says, "we don't want the good old boys to be able to peg us so neatly. Once they think they have our number, we'll be easy to ignore. And that's the real death. We've got to keep them guessing. Plus, wearing army fatigues with a mask on top is hardly equivalent to donning one of Barbie's frilly frou-frou dresses seriously. I mean, let's put this in a little perspective here."

"She's right," a woman standing off to the side concurs. "This is a strategic, and not a purely political, issue here."

"We've discussed this over and over and we have always concluded the same thing," Denise says testily. "So let's let it be for now. It's a late meeting and we're all pretty much here by now. Let's save the letters and ensuing debates for the end, if we have time. Otherwise I can go through them for checks and then pass them around. Okay?"

"Good, yes. We really have to get the next poster underway and discuss the Errigon suit," Sandra says.

"First things first, we need to get that poster plastered out there ASAP."

"Shouldn't we finally discuss retaining a permanent lawyer? I mean, Janice can't just keep doing the absolutely necessary papers piecemeal."

"Yeah, Sheila's right," Roberta says. "Plus, Errigon's got a great, tough lawyer. I ought to know, I went to college with her."

"You what!" Claire exclaims. "And this is the first we've heard of it? Are you nuts?"

"Hey, hey, simmer down, Claire," Denise says. "You sound like you're accusing Roberta of treason. What about it 'Berta? What do you know of this lawyer? How come you didn't bring it up before?"

"Yeah, it's not like she was hired yesterday," another says.

"So, Roberta?" Claire says with an imposed relaxed air and her hands woven together, resting on top of her head.

All the eyes in the room are on Roberta. She sniffles and jerks her head to the side before speaking. "I've known her since college. We're friends. She stares at my art every day in her living room. Every day that she's home that is, she works like a dog. What can I say? She's smart and sharp. Errigon chose well."

"Does she know you're one of us?"

"Of course not!"

"Never, in all these years, you never mentioned it. Are you sure?"

"No. Maria probably never even heard of us before we started to pursue Errigon. You know, I resent these accusations."

"What accusations?"

"Innuendo, then."

"Well, why didn't you bring this up before?"

"Just as I wouldn't betray our work, I also won't use my friendship with Maria. Even if I would, I can't see how it does us any good that I know Errigon's lawyer."

"It could do harm, though. What if she recognizes you somehow?"

"In a mask?" Roberta responds tersely.

"What about your voice?"

"So, I won't talk when she's around. Give me a break here, I'm not the enemy. I feel like I'm on trial."

"Hey, we're getting nowhere," Claire says. "I'm the divisiveness watchdog, 'member? Let's get back to the poster, as planned."

"Claire's right, let's create a good one and cool out."

"Can we work in another spoof on advertising?" someone buried at the back calls out. "I'm getting real sick of those ads with phallic lipsticks shooting towards luscious parted lips, or for that matter, if I see another ad of any kind with pouting, shiny, open lips, I'm going to puke."

"Yeah, or what about those damn cigarette ads aimed at girls? There's a lot of material there I bet we could work into our themes and hit a double blow."

"Wait, I don't see what shoddy advertising has to do with this. Let's get back on track and try to be methodical here. Who has the stats?" Denise asks.

"I do," Claire says waving some papers in the air. "The most striking numbers I came up with have to do with earnings."

"Ah, yes. We're back at the bottom line once again," Roberta says.

"Shh! Out with it, let's hear the good news."

"Well, everyone knows that women in the U.S. generally make two thirds of what men earn," Claire says glancing at her papers. "But the art world, you guessed it, is an entirely different story. Get this, women artists earn only one third of what men artists do. One third!"

They all pause on that one, as if slowly trying to digest a truck tire whole.

"That's a direct message if I ever heard one," Sandra says.

More upbeat, Roberta says: "And it bears on our lawsuit nicely. Frank'll be in even more of a sweat when he sees a poster about this."

"I still think we should have a poster aimed directly at Frank alone. Single him out. Make him jump all the way out of his skin."

"No! We're doing fine with him now. And let's face it, in the scheme of things, Frank Errigon is chicken feed. I don't want to have this debate every time we meet. We can't fuck up now. If we're too garish even our paltry support will jump ship."

"Yeah, and they're on the fence as it is, at best."

"Come on, since when have we even tried to pander to popular opinion polls?"

"Really, Luce, can it for now. Claire's dug up some great stats here, let's go with them. They're too good to waste. Frank's frying as it is. Our slow, torturous pressure is worth a thousand darts."

Through the bickering, a few side conversations blossom. It's getting late, and some of the Living Dolls crowded in off to the sides begin to trickle out.

Denise nudges Sandra's arm and gently remarks, "Cheer up Sandy, don't take the statistics so hard. At least you can put Leda in that fancy school of yours for free. In the high school years it'll be important, and it sure would take a chunk out of your operating budget if you had to pay for it."

"How?" Sandra asks with an open, hopeful face, while pivoting around to Denise.

"Very funny. You work there!"

"That and a token get me there all right. I'm part-time, a euphemism for low pay, overwork, and above all, no benefits."

"Hey, gals, let's get back to the poster, shall we? How are we going to get the facts across?"

"What about putting it down just the way Claire said it! Sentence one: 'Women earn 2/3 generally.' Boom. Sentence two: 'Women artists earn 1/3.' Boom. Simple. Wording more elegant, of course."

"Good, let's go with that, let's flesh out the phrasing though."

"And, I think we need something visual or spatial to go alongside this one. Maybe even bar diagrams. They're nice and straightforward. Anyone can read them."

"But they are a little boring, good for research papers and such. An image flashes before me of dusty old library tomes full of bar graphs. We want to catch people's eye. We need to wave money in people's faces."

"That would wake them up!"

"That would wake me up, I'm one of these underpaid, under represented artists," Roberta says.

"I don't think people will be alarmed enough by these figures." Leigh is speaking slowly as she is visualizing the poster. "After all, not too many people think that art takes time."

"That's true, no one thinks it's work."

"Just some drunken swipes on canvas."

"Maybe we can elaborate on the message?" Denise says.

"Like pie diagrams comparing hours spent at work, education, training, et cetera?"

"I think it's getting too convoluted now. Our hallmark, if nothing else, is crisp, clear messages."

"No, come on," Claire says. "Let's face it, anyone who's paying attention to our posters at all already has some respect for artists and knows we work hard."

"Or, they have financial investments in art."

"I think the original is good. It's stunning, in fact."

"So, wait, let's go back a step. You're saying, Claire, that we're preaching to the converted?"

Jokingly, Roberta pantomimes as she says: "That's it, I'm throwing in my towel as part of this poster campaign."

"Seriously, Dolls, let's get back to the two simple sentences and Sandra's thought. In other words, what about putting money on the poster?"

"Let's do a couple of mock ups."

"Maybe a bill torn in thirds?"

The Living Dolls all huddle around the coffee table while Claire draws some sketches of the ideas being tossed out.

"Or more to the point, what about a big, single dollar bill with a cut-off line at the one-third, two-thirds mark."

"So," Denise says, taking charge, "to sum up this idea, we have a long, sliced dollar bill, our two sentences above or below it whichever looks better, and our logo at the very bottom, right?"

"Try that one, Claire. Let's see."

Everyone pauses for Claire to do a sample poster. All eyes are on the page coming to life in blue Bic ink while Claire's mouth moves silently in jerking motions as she draws and writes. She looks just like a kid learning to use scissors for the first time.

"Let's see, Claire. Let's see," Roberta calls out impatiently.

"Just a sec. I've almost got it. I want you to be able to tell something from this, not just scratch a few incoherent scribbles."

After a few more moments of pen scrapings on paper in unison with Claire's mouth twitches, she pauses and then puts down her pen. Expectantly, she says: "There. What do you think?" as she turns the page around for all to see.

"That's it," Sandra says. "Do we like it?"

To this, they call out, "Yeah" in unison.

Sandra says, as if conducting: "Who's going to execute it. Not to put too fine a point, but I'm out. I did the last one."

"This one's on me, I can get it to print by Monday," Roberta says.

"Can we still talk about Errigon, or is everyone mentally out the door at this point?"

"Let's save it for our plastering party next week. Nothing's urgent."

CHAPTER FOURTEEN:

AT REST

S ANDRA LETS OUT A SCREECH as she stumbles over to the kitchen counter in her fuchsia colored, knee-length T-shirt night-gown. "Steve, what are you doing?"

"Good morning, Sandy! My cake's a hit with the toughest critic of all time!"

"Hi, Mom," Leda says with her mouth full of chocolate.

"Chocolate shortbread, chocolate génoise, chocolate filling, and chocolate shavings! You think that's an appropriate breakfast for a growing girl?" Sandra says, taking in the scene. "I hope you had something more substantial first!"

"More substantial! This is the most exquisite cake in the universe," Steve exclaims.

"Leda," Sandra addresses herself to her daughter, ignoring Steve's enthusiasm, "you know Daddy's desserts are for tasting later in the day. Where are your Oateos, or your Rice Krispies with yogurt? Or leftover pizza even?"

"You ate the rest of the pizza yesterday, Mom. I looked for some. The cake's good, try it. It's Daddy's best."

"See Sandy, I'm on to something here. This is big! How about calling it my Princess Sondra Cake?"

"*Sondra?*"

"Well, sounds more regal than Sandra. Okay, Princess Sandra Cake."

"Princess?"

"Too diminutive, you're right. Queen Sandra Cake."

"Forget it, Steve. And let's not have so much sugar displayed this early in the morning again." Just at that moment, Sandra hears a jingle come on from the television.

> *She brings home the bacon*
> *fries it in a pan*
> *and at night*
> *she lets hubby know he's a man.*

At this, Sandra marches over and crisply clicks off their tiny set saying: "Do we really have to be assaulted by that shit in the morning?" Sandra doesn't know why she's so grumpy. She wishes the day hadn't started off so poorly.

"Okay, Leda, now we know we'd better tread softly today." Steve gestures with his hands in a vertical motion, fingers splayed. "By the way," he says proudly and as though everything were quiet, calm, and amicable, "the filling is *mocha*, bittersweet mocha, not mere chocolate. Just so you know. I wish you'd try it, Sandy. I've got to know what you think."

Trying to regroup, Sandra switches to a calmer tone. "But not now, Steve. It's too early for my mouth to taste that stuff. Wait until lunch." She pulls on some purple leggings as she speaks. Suddenly, she remembers that she didn't use the test kit she bought and it works best with first of the morning urine. She shuffles off to the bathroom with Steve's voice trailing behind her.

"Stuff! Stuff! This is not stuff. It's food even heaven hasn't dreamt of. And I put a touch of pecan in with the hazelnut grinds. Just a tad. It's perfect. Try it now, just a nibble. You don't know what you're missing." Steve waves grandly in the air, trying to beckon Sandra to the plate.

Sandra returns four minutes later with a confused look on her face. She has added red socks cuffing the leggings and has put her fuchsia sneakers on. As she pulls a black tunic over her head, she finally capitulates. "Okay, a taste. A little one, and I'll have a real piece later, you maniac." Sandra moves across the room towards Steve who is holding out a fork with a generous bite on it. She teases him by dodging the fork for a while.

"Go on Mommy, hurry up. Eat it now, I have to go to school. Dad, did you make my lunch?" Leda talks as she tugs on Steve's shirt almost causing him to drop the fork and the cake altogether.

"Oh, I forgot! Here Sandy, take it," Steve says as he shoves the fork into Sandra's hand with the cake bite intact. "I'll do it in a sec. An egg and watercress delight on lightly toasted wheat germ bread."

"Yuck. I don't want that."

"You'll love it, wait and see. You like the cake don't you? Trust me."

"Well, put a banana in my box at least."

"And carrot and pepper sticks," Sandra says with her mouth full of cake. "It's good, Steve. Very good. I can see it with a short espresso and a Perrier on the side. With a slice of lemon hooked on the glass, after dinner. Anyone would be happy with it that way."

"Espresso, no! I mean, some people will do that of course, but that's not what it's intended for. It has espresso in it. To be perfectly balanced, one must eat this accompanied by a small glass of Gewürztraminer. That's how I designed it."

"Maybe you shouldn't push that wine when you're trying to sell it, Steve. Except at places like the Union Square Café where they could pull it off."

"Voila! Lunch is *prêt à porter*. Let's get you to school, Leda. Are you ready?"

"I need my red sneakers."

"Sweetie, you know those are too small. You picked out green ones this time. Put your greenies on." Sandra speaks plaintively. They had already been through this debate yesterday from which she walked away with a headache. Simultaneously, she's wondering how the baby talk came out of her mouth so facilely.

"Next time you need new ones you can get red again, okay?"

"Good idea, Mom. I'm ready, Dad. You carry my lunch and I'll carry my Susanne cat. Bye, Mom."

"Bye, Leda. Have a good time at school. See you later. Love you!"

Once the door is closed and locked after them, Sandra pours herself a cup of coffee and cuts a thin slice of cake. She eats and sips intermittently as she hunts around the apartment looking for her appointment book—her Big Task List, as she calls it. Sandra doesn't teach at Morningside today, so once she's done all the absolutely necessary phone calls and errands, and her forty-five minute therapy session, it's a studio day for her. Studio half-day, that is, since she has to pick up Leda at school at three o'clock.

On Tenth Street, on the fifth floor of an office building, filled largely with psychotherapists, Sandra sits still for a few moments while she is in the waiting area of her therapist's office—a glorified hallway actually. She's debating whether she should be using this time to think about herself, her pregnancy, or flip through one of the magazines on the side table. After tapping her feet on the floor and fidgeting a little, she opts for a recent, but not current, issue of *New York Magazine*. Something she wouldn't otherwise look at, except from a distance hanging on newsstand racks. The magazine normally infuriates her with its smug bourgeois glibness, but today it outdoes itself.

By accident, Sandra opens to a spread about hip New York artists, filled with glossy pictures of them in their studios. Not a single woman amongst them. "Shit," she says aloud in aggravation, unable to contain herself, flipping the page hastily only to find a Calvin Klein underwear ad featuring a pubescent girl clad solely in panties, masquerading as an androgynous yet mature woman. Disgusted, Sandra slaps the magazine back on the table and returns to her chair.

A few minutes later, a door opens and Sandra is beckoned by a woman in her sixties, who looks more suburban and wealthy than urban. Her office smells of leather and new carpeting and is decorated with books and small antiques. Her couch has an ambiguous, overstuffed shape which requires the user to make a conscious decision about how to use it. As Sandra crosses the threshold of the office, still hot with anger from the magazine, she blurts: "How do you expect me to relax and trust you and talk about what I'm feeling when you side with the aggressor?"

Without taking a breath, she continues: "What am I talking about? Your choice of magazines! They're horrible. And don't think I missed the issue of *Glamour* in the stack. The Pineapple Diet is in now, or so the cover relays. Don't you think that it's important to be more careful about what you're endorsing out there?"

"What does it mean to you that those publications are in my waiting area?"

"They're gross. No one should have to be exposed to them!"

"Do you feel you need me to protect you and I failed?" The therapist softly but firmly inquires.

"I'm pregnant," Sandra announces, changing the subject and her facial expression as well. She pauses, waiting to see if her therapist will react. When she doesn't, Sandra says: "Yeah, I know that I've been trying to get pregnant. But now that I am, I think that it's a crazy idea. I'm so nauseous, it's debilitating. I'm thirty-eight years old. I have a wonderful daughter who I adore. And I'm very busy. It's not like my career is flourishing. If I have to take more time out, I think I'll be finished. It's too demoralizing. I loved Leda when she was a baby and I loved having a baby. But I don't know if I need to do it again. I don't think I *want* to do it again. I doubt I could handle all the self-deprivation again. And the sleeplessness. I don't have enough energy for that.

"I mean, of course if it's born, I'll love it. But if I have an abortion, will I miss it or will I be relieved? I don't really know. I feel like I'm going in both directions at once. I just think if both options are okay, do the easier one, have an abortion and get on with my adult life. My career, so-called, needs a lot of energy yet before it will amount to anything. I don't feel like giving that up all over again, for who knows how long.

"You know, I calculated that I'd be fifty-seven before this one goes off to college, if it goes. I'll be in my fifties with teenagers! This whole business in my generation of waiting to have children was a big trick. It just means that you get a taste of a career before you have to throw it away, never be able to have a coherent thought again. Not that having kids young looks like a picnic. This whole deal is rotten, and will be until fathers learn how to become equal parents. That's a big problem.

"Yeah, I know what you're thinking: why can't I get back to work more quickly this time? Well, even if I force myself to be capable of that this time, how am I going to afford to pay someone to help me out? Steve can't take off any more time than he already does. And I don't make enough to break even if I have to pay somebody to take care of the baby."

Sandra pauses to reflect before she says: "I guess if I stopped coming to see you, it might be possible. But I can't imagine someone else being with my baby all day. I don't trust people that much.

"See what I mean? This whole project doesn't seem feasible. I'm not capable of taking care of two kids and myself at the same time. I've barely managed to do that with one kid, and she doesn't needs constant care at this point.

"In fact, though, the older Leda gets, the less well I do with her. I've gone from over-protectiveness to the other camp. For example, I completely lost it the other day—exploded. We were walking home and, as usual, there were a lot of creeps out there. I was doing all right ignoring them for Leda's sake and not doing my usual response routine when, all of a sudden, I couldn't take it anymore. I guess what got to me was that one of the perp's was a city official, and he was in uniform, a sanitation cop.

"But who knows if that's what did it, plenty of disgusting real cops have chooched me and I've been able to walk past. I'm afraid of their guns and sticks, and of the ones like the cop who hand-cuffed that woman to a banister in an abandoned building in the Bronx last week, stripped her, fondled her, and threatened the shit out of her. And they're supposed to be protecting us."

Sandra barely allows enough of a gap between words to breathe through all of this. She glances over at the clock to gauge her time and adds sarcastically: "I feel real safe when I'm the only one alone in a subway car late at night with a transit cop. The worst ones though are the private security guards hired for block patrol. They're totally menacing.

"Anyway, back to the incident. Basically, even though it wasn't my fault, it was my fault. It's bad enough Leda has to witness all the crap on the street every day as it is, but then I get her subjected to shit being hurled directly at her by a very threatening creep. I'm not teaching her how to deal with this stuff very well."

The therapist positions herself to squeeze in a question, "Why do you think what people do on the street bothers you so much? It's just my own association of course, but it calls to mind your memory of being out with your cousin Richard."

"Richard?" Sandra blanches.

"When the men or, actually, teenage boys came along, do you remember?"

"Yes." Sandra's voice is barely audible now and looks sullen. Sandra almost curls her back into the soft couch. And there is a long pause.

"Why?" Sandra suddenly exclaims. "Wait a minute, let's get back to what you started with. What do you mean, 'why does it bother me'?"

"Perhaps some of your current anger is related to the old

incident with Richard. Or, perhaps to the pattern of repressed childhood anger we've discussed before."

"Yeah, sure there's a pattern, and its ancient history, not just mine alone." Sandra's voice rises, becoming heated. "Abstractly put, our society is structured such that taunting women is a satisfying pastime for men. And don't tell me women provoke it! A man does, says, gestures, whatever, something in my direction and I become furious. *Justifiably* furious. Or, in any female's direction, a girl's, a woman's, for that matter, not only mine."

Speaking rapidly, Sandra says: "I actually did a mini-study once. I methodically wore all different styles of clothes, changed my demeanor, et cetera, on a rotated and measured basis to see if it would make any difference. I tried every possible combination and nuance, and guess what the only thing that stayed constant was? You guessed it, the harassment. And even though it is technically illegal, all we really have are paper rights to prosecute.

"Harassment is a part of the message that women, and girls, need men to keep them safe. And in return for that safety, we give up our real rights. Et cetera, you know and I know that I can go on like this forever. Maybe we should switch the topic, because I'm beginning to have visions dance before my eyes of my women's Broadway baseball bat battering brigade again."

The therapist opens her mouth to speak and reflexively juts her foot out at the same time. "Maybe we should, but let's try to stay with it this time and pursue your feelings further. I might be totally off here, but do you think that there is anything that you specifically, *not* women in general, do that provokes these kinds of street behavior?"

"Might be totally off? Might be? Sometimes I think you're from outer space! Don't you ever go outside?"

While Sandra fumes out of her therapist's office, the forty-five minute session having gone over, Maria is in her midtown office at the law firm, and uptown Claire is pacing the halls of the Metropolitan Museum. She has a map in hand and is going room to room methodically. The guards take her to be one of New York's crazies as she moves from painting to painting, scribbling on a homemade score card. She stops at each exhibit, and tallies the numbers out loud, "One M here, one F, one F," and other such outbursts as she makes pencil marks on her card. By the time she is on her last few rooms, Claire is rather agitated, making comments into the empty space between her and the paintings.

As Claire finishes her rounds of the museum, the intercom buzzes loudly next to Maria's ear.

"Yes?" she says gruffly into the telephone.

"A Roberta on the line for you, Ms. Jacobs."

"Put her through," Maria says eagerly.

"Maria? Good morning!"

"Hello, 'Berta. How are you?"

"Great! Your wish is about to come true. I'm going to the movies tonight with a friend, we're going to see some new Chinese movie that sounds interesting. You're coming. That's why I called. I think you and Peg will really hit it off."

"'Berta, what are you talking about?" Maria has an edge of fear lacing her words. "Is this because of our conversation that night?"

Sensing the panic, Roberta backpedals, "Oh, come on. No, honey, I'm not fixing you up with Peg. Don't be ridiculous. She's a lawyer, you're a lawyer. I like you both tons, so by transitivity, let's all go out! 'Member, you and I said we needed a movie fix. Here it is."

"Does it have to be tonight?" Maria asks as she's peering into her appointment book full of scribbles and notations She slams it shut instantly.

"Yup."

"'Berta—"

"Good, see you at seven at the Lincoln Plaza."

"Wait, 'Berta, don't hang up. I need to get your take on something."

"Can it wait until tonight?"

"No."

"So shoot then. What is it?"

"You were actually on my list to call this morning. I need the perspective of a New York artist. Are you aware of the posters plastered all over SoHo by the Living Dolls, Roberta?"

Roberta cringes inside, thinking about how to nix the conversation before she needs to lie. "Sure," she murmurs indistinctly.

"Are you also aware of the fingers found tacked to a couple of them?"

"Yup. What is this, Maria, an inquisition or twenty questions? I have to go, sweetie."

"Just one more question. Do you have any idea, have you heard any talk about, why this is happening?"

Relieved that she can answer truthfully, Roberta responds: "No, I don't, I haven't. I know it's making some people jittery about the art scene. Can't help you though, Maria. See you later." Roberta hangs up before Maria can stop her.

Unsatisfied, Maria reflects as she hangs up the telephone receiver. She immediately pushes the intercom button to beckon her secretary into her office.

"Yes, Ms. Jacobs?"

"Listen, I need to speak with a few people. The detective working on the SoHo fingers, a forensics specialist, and the head of an autopsy lab. In that order. Buzz me as soon as you have the detective."

The secretary vanishes through the door, and Maria begins to try to plot through the possibilities. "Fingers. Why fingers? Artists need their fingers, perhaps more than other people. Well, on the whole, not more than pianists or electricians. And why fingers on the posters? Okay, there's a connection being made between the finger warnings and the posters, or the contents of the posters, or the Living Dolls directly. I mean, twice can't be a mistake. Some guy, on two separate occasions, gets a finger and just happens to stick it to one of those posters both times, out of all the possible locations. Okay. But *why* is he putting fingers onto the Living Dolls messages?"

Just then Maria is jolted out of query by her secretary's buzz. Maria picks up her telephone with a, "Maria Jacobs here."

"Uh-huh."

"With whom am I speaking?"

"You called me, lady. Detective Lacy. I'm investigating the severed fingers. How can I help you?" His voice is gruff, but not offensive.

"I am working on a matter that may be related to your investigation. I am, however, unable to determine the precise relevance at this time. I'm hoping that you will be able to provide me with information I need."

"Such as?"

Taken aback by his directness, Maria stumbles and then recoups her equilibrium. "Well, I'm not sure. Whatever you have uncovered thus far. That is, I would like to know the status of your investigation."

The detective snorts out a guffaw. "The *status* of my investigation? Maybe you should come for a tour downtown and take a look at the caseload decorating my desk. The status is, we've opened a file for the case, a manila folder. We've had a few chuckles over what nut fairy is doing this."

"Excuse me?" Maria is unable to believe what she just heard. "Is it common to find severed limbs strung up all over town?" she asks facetiously, trying to match his rudeness.

"Yes, ma'am, it is. We find 'em every day, print 'em if we can, and chuck 'em. Nothing ever comes of this weirdo stuff. Too many crazies in this town."

"So, I take it that you have not cross-checked with the morgue or hospitals, looking for reports of missing fingers?"

"We'd turn up hundreds of them. What's news to you is old hat to us."

Realizing the futility of the conversation, Maria gives up. "I see. Thank you for your time, Detective Lacy." Maria holds the receiver a few seconds and then slams it onto the base.

Maria reflects for a minute, and then dials the main number at Mount Sinai Hospital, which she's had blazed into her memory ever since her father did time there last year. "Hello, transfer me to the head nurse in surgery, please."

This is the longest shot yet, Maria muses as she waits to be transferred to the right station. After three connections to the wrong department, Maria hangs up in disgust and decides that she needs to set a rational, step-by-step plan if she is going to pursue this. Imaginary unbillable hours march past her as she busily gets out a pen and pad.

Maria finds her mind wandering even from the Errigon file on her desk. She gets up and walks across her office to the mirror hanging above the couch and studies herself. Whereas she normally avoids her reflection, she now stares straight on as if noticing herself for the first time. She is not pleased with what she sees. All of a sudden, she is aware of wrinkles, gray hair, and flaws. She looks down at her dull blue Tahari suit and wants to rip it off, trade it for something more vibrant. She perceives herself as washed out, a middle-aged mess.

"Perhaps I should finally learn about makeup. How can I walk around like this day after day just smearing a few colors across my face? I can't meet 'Berta and her friend looking like this." She peers into the mirror a little longer before she exclaims: "Bullshit. What's the difference? We're just going to sit in a dark movie, and I'm only a person, not one of those computer altered models! Forget it, Maria. You're not going to a beauty contest. Get back to work."

At her desk a half an hour later, receiver at her ear, Maria has just gotten through to the Coroner's office. She has done her hair in a new style. She went into the ladies' lounge to fix it, having borrowed some clips and bobby pins from a secretary. She's finally speaking with the person in charge of the cut fingers.

"What's that? I'm sorry, it's very difficult to hear you, but I'm afraid if I try for a better connection I'll never get back to your extension again, this took several failed attempts as is." Maria's tone is completely exasperated.

"I said, ma'am, that all we've done is take the prints of the two severed fingers. That's it."

"What will you do with the prints?"

"Run 'em through the computer. See if anything pops out. Not likely, though, unless he was a well-documented criminal."

"Have you looked for characteristic marks, or whatever, that might determine the man who did this?" Maria feels she's groping in the dark for something to hold onto. Hope of any sort.

"No."

Taken aback by the answer, Maria dares to query further. "Why not? Isn't that sort of an obvious path to follow?"

"Yes, but it's not our department."

Maria strangles the receiver with her grip as she utters a polite "Thank you for your help," and hangs up.

Still displeased with her appearance, Maria dashes out of her office early to run to the Whitney Museum gift shop before meeting Roberta at the movies. She hurriedly picks out a brightly colored silk scarf and almost rips it at the corner getting the tag off before she's even paid for it.

Once on the street, Maria wraps the scarf around the back of her neck, either end hanging down, long over her suit. More content, inwardly Maria feels both ashamed and proud of herself at the same time. Running late, she doesn't stop to ponder the dichotomy. Automatically, she thrusts her right arm into the air, in search of a cab to take her across town.

CHAPTER FIFTEEN:

TO MARKET

IN MARIA'S APARTMENT, JACKIE'S DONE everything: cleaned the kitchen after dinner, gotten Bessy and Ricky into pajamas and changed herself into freshly ironed slacks. She's getting ready for a night out. Once set, she makes her way downstairs, to wait at the curb under the awning of the building entrance. She doesn't wait more than two minutes before her date appears.

"Hi, Jackie," Gregory says in his deeply resonant voice as he pushes the passenger door to his fire engine red Mazda open from the driver's side seat. "Hop in." Gregory is five foot, ten inches with broad shoulders and a solid build. He's cultivated the look of an athlete rather than the professor that he is. Tonight he's wearing a tan tailored shirt under a cobalt blue V-neck sweater and belted blue jeans. He feels twenty years younger than his chronological age.

Jackie gets in with a faint smile and shuts the door.

"Where're we going?"

"I discovered a terrific place on the edge of Little Italy called Frutte de Mare. It's great, a real old homestyle restaurant. You'll love it. The funny thing is, they're short on seafood. Their eggplant Parmigiana is out of this world. Not heavy at all."

"It's supposed to be heavy though, isn't that the point of it? This place sounds a little like the Bleecker Luncheonette, Italian Home Cooking. You know it, at the three-way intersection of Bleecker, Carmine, and Avenue of the Americas?" Mid-sentence, Jackie wants to swallow her words. She watches Gregory's face turn sour. She forgot for a moment that he doesn't like to be caught off guard with things he doesn't know.

They ride a little of the way after that in silence. Jackie leans back into the black mock leather seat and ponders how she met Gregory.

He had been recommended to her by her college advisor as someone who would be willing to sponsor an independent study. She had trotted immediately over to his office to inquire, and he told her to write up a short proposal and bring the books she was interested in covering to his office the following day at noon.

By noon the next day she was proud of herself and flying high. Jackie had actually managed to design her course of study on such incredibly short notice. After all, she is only a college student, he a professor. When Jackie arrived at Gregory's office it was exactly noon and he was on the telephone. Her clothing was disheveled and she had circles under her eyes, but her work was well thought out and organized. She had scoured both libraries and had consulted with a few people so as not to miss anything. She felt she came up with a comprehensive and creative plan. Gregory waved her in and gestured for her to sit at the chair in front of his desk.

"Okay, let me write this down. You want eggs, flour, and milk. You have everything else? Oh, right, the shrimp. Great, see you later, honey." Then, as he is about to hang up, both he and Jackie hear a voice from the receiver call his name. "Yes? Oh, of course, you know I do. Well, we'll go over this later, I have someone here, okay? Good, see you tonight. Bye." Gregory removes his glasses, clicking the arms folded and lays them on the desk with a clunk. He rubs his hand over his graying temples and on through his straight, short-cropped dark hair.

Jackie sits there without moving, embarrassed.

"Sorry, Jackie. Have you got everything?"

Jackie is beaming and just answers, "Yes," and nods to her pile of seventeen books on the floor next to her, topped with the outline she typed out at three in the morning.

"You know, I'm starving. Let's go over to the Faculty Club and talk this out over lunch." As he says this, Gregory rises from his chair and starts to come around the desk towards Jackie.

As a rule, Jackie doesn't eat lunch, and in fact doesn't eat much of anything these days. She's down to one hundred pounds on her five foot, six inch frame and would like to go lower. Jackie prickles at the image of having to sit there while he eats without any food in front of her. But the idea of actually eating lunch with him, something beyond her usual one and one quarter ounce bag of Planters' salted peanuts, makes her want to jump out of her skin. Her only thought is to somehow get out of this.

"I have a class at one, so I don't think I'll have enough time," she says, lying. "Why don't I come back later this afternoon to talk about my plans?"

"Nonsense, Jackie, everyone's got to make time for lunch. Food's one of the best things in life. Come on, let's go. We'll get you to your class on time."

With that, they were off. Down the century-old stone steps from the upper campus, past Alma Mater, and across campus walk. They walk along the bumpy but quaint cobblestone walkway that the Buildings and Grounds Department are forever repairing on a shoe string budget. For a passerby, it would be almost impossible to guess that Jackie and Gregory are together. Gregory walks out in front with his head up and a wide stride, engrossed in thought, and Jackie teeters four steps behind juggling all the books and her typed course description on top, flapping in the breeze. Even though the Columbia campus is compact, they walk on to a part of it that Jackie has never been to, over by the Engineering Tower. On the way, Henry, from Jackie's mathematical analysis class walks past and calls out: "Hey, Jackie d'you do the homework yet?"

"Yeah, it's not so bad," Jackie tries to scurry past before Henry realizes who she's with.

"Meet me in the lounge tomorrow before class to go over it, okay?"

"Sure." She'd agree to anything at this moment in order to get by quickly. Jackie loathes those last minute, panic get-togethers before the problem sets are due. If you're one of the ones who can't do the homework, the best you could hope for from these study groups is to become even more confused and to end up five minutes before class furiously copying down someone else's guesses.

As they brush by the tower to get to the worn marble stairs to the club, Jackie recalls her graduate student Teaching Assistant in Advanced Calculus class telling her that this corner of the campus was once all trees. She can't picture it covered over like a small forest and isn't sure she believes him. It hadn't occurred to her to wonder whether or why he had been around that long to have such memories.

Once inside the building, Gregory announces that he is going to wash his hands and instructs Jackie to do the same. Feeling confused and foggy already, Jackie doesn't understand what he is talking about and just stands there in the middle of the dingy foyer balancing her books.

Gregory guides her to the cafeteria-style part of the club rather than the more formal waitered room. Jackie takes in the typical food offerings with a predictable menu. Cheap, round Formica tables with plastic chairs cover the rest of the floor. All of the school lunch furniture and equipment is set in what was once a grand room. It may have been a ballroom, with its enormous expanse of hand-inlaid marble floor space. The vastly oversized windows afford a view that sweeps over the whole campus and lets in a drenching sunlight all year round. In keeping with the overall ambiance of the campus, the room has not been properly maintained and has been patched over here and there with inferior materials. It gives the impression of an empire in rapid decline.

Going down the food line, Gregory piles a corned beef sandwich on rye with Russian dressing and mustard, coleslaw, coffee, potato salad, and a slice of florescent red cherry cheesecake onto his tray. Jackie trails behind to the cash register with a quarter of a cantaloupe looking pathetically paltry and lonely on her orange plastic tray.

"At least top that with cottage cheese, why don't you?" Gregory says with a grin.

"No thanks, this'll be fine," Jackie says, staking her ground as if it were a point of battle.

Gregory places his tray on the nearby table, scoops up all seventeen books and plunks them down on a chair, leaving the three densely typed pages of outline to flutter slowly to the floor. He then arranges his food and Jackie's melon on the table and sits down to eat.

Halfway through his first bite of sandwich, Gregory nonchalantly asks: "So, Jackie, do you like to cook?"

"Hm? No," Jackie says, looking from Gregory to her books, to the pages she labored over, flopped now on the floor appearing wilted, and back to him. She is beginning to feel foggy again as though perhaps the ground and the air are becoming severed in some surreal fashion.

"Do you plan to get married?" Gregory asks while mopping a smear of dressing off his bearded mouth.

"No," she answers, still not paying full attention to the interrogation.

Sipping his coffee daintily, Gregory continues as if they are pleasantly discussing the weather: "To have children?"

"Definitely not!"

"What about boyfriends, do you have any?" he asks now diving happily into his potato salad.

Jackie glances around the room to see if any of her professors are there. She doesn't see a single familiar face. She doesn't know what is going on or why she is actually answering these crazy questions. She feels like grabbing her things and bolting.

She doesn't do it though. Her brain has the consistency of old rubber cement glue now. She just sits there politely and waits. Jackie has the claustrophobic sensation of being a deer trapped by hunters.

"You should learn to eat more Jackie. Come, let's get you to that class."

With that, Gregory bounces up, dabs his lower face with a napkin one last final time, and they are off. Jackie notices as she is being ushered out the door that it is one-thirty. She swears practically spitting fire, never to speak with the man again.

But that was a few months prior, before he began to hang around her geometry seminar. There, she began to see another side of him. His professional side. His brilliance shone through his every attempt to work through complex mathematical questions. He was witty and invested in work, immersed in abstract calculation. Jackie felt it an honor to be able to witness him exhibit his talents. And, slowly, bit by bit, Gregory began to chat with her afterwards. It was an evening seminar. He began to draw her out as they discussed proofs and theorems on short strolls.

Having arrived at their dinner spot, Gregory's car pulls into a parking space in Little Italy as he says: "Hop out, Jackie. We're here. Voila: Frutte de Mare!" Jackie takes less than a second to refocus and get out of the car.

As she steps onto the sidewalk she feels Gregory's arm rest on her shoulder and guide her into the restaurant. Inside the entryway there is a coarse fishnet, replete with authentic floaters and sea urchins, starfish, and plastic fish, draped over the double doorway that leads to the dining room. The maître d', dressed in slick black pants, a white shirt with pleats in the front, and cummerbund, comes to greet them.

"A table for two, sir?"

"Yes, two," Gregory says.

The restaurant is empty and he seats them at a choice table next to a water pool and fountain. In the water are pebbles in assorted neon colors, and live goldfish. Jackie picks a chair underneath a plastic grape arbor which sports plump green and purple grapes. As she's sitting down, she breaks out with a sly, warm smile.

"Greg, this is perfect! This restaurant is fantastic. You couldn't exaggerate a description and have it be kitschier than this."

"Shhh, Jackie, not so loud." Gregory gestures and his face turns red as he speaks.

The waiter comes by to ask if they'd like an aperitif. Gregory says no and orders some wine for the dinner. He already knows what he's having.

Uptown and in a yellow cab on the way to the movies, Maria feels that the ride across town is more than painfully slow. By the time she has paid and leapt out, she is feeling incredibly harried. Maria huffs up to the Lincoln Plaza movie theater at seven-fifteen, only to confront a mammoth sized line to buy tickets. It takes her two lengths of the line to find Roberta.

"Roberta! I'm here, sorry I'm late."

"Doesn't seem to matter, I was early, and look, we're still too far back to get in if you ask me."

"Well, I don't agree, we'll make it," Peg says, her green-blue eyes glinting under the florescent marquee lighting.

"Oh, sorry," Roberta says. "Maria, this is Peg. Peg, Maria. My only two lawyer friends. I hope you cover all the legal bases between you, in case I need help one day."

"Nice to meet you," Maria says over Roberta's chatter as she extends her hand to Peg.

"Likewise. Roberta, here, has mentioned you often."

Genuinely bewildered, Maria says: "I can't imagine what there is to report."

Just then a tough looking theater attendant marches down the line yelling out that the next show is sold out.

"That's that," Roberta says.

Maria looks relieved but foolish with her new scarf flapping out in the wind as if to mark her apprehension. As the roar of Broadway reaches a deafening pitch, she starts thinking about how close she is to her apartment, that she could be home, ensconced in her robe within fifteen minutes.

Peg, who is single and childless like Roberta, says into the din: "Say, let's not blow away the evening. We could at least go round the corner to La Fortuna and talk."

"Great idea, Peg," Roberta says. "But let's go somewhere that has a liquor license. I, personally, could go for an Irish Coffee at Teachers."

Not wanting to be a complete louse, Maria says: "Teachers Too is closer, let's go there."

As they walk up Broadway to the bar, it begins to drizzle, a slow, autumn rain. Peg moves over, closer to Maria and holds her jacket over the two of them as she speaks. "That suit of yours is too fantastic to ruin in the rain."

Maria sputters a bewildered: "Thank you," noticing that she likes the protection.

"I've read about your work on the Living Dolls case. I'm intrigued. Are there any new developments that you can reveal?"

Maria collects her thoughts, making an effort to separate the Errigon case from the fingers. She knows that Peg is referring to an interview of her in the *New York Times* about her inquiries into the fingers.

"No, not really." As Maria answers, she notices her official voice coming through. "I'm at a standstill at the moment."

"Such a desperate thing to do," Peg says. "I've been wondering if there's a connection between the gender of the perpetrator and the gender of the fingers, so to speak. In the paper, masculine pronouns are always used, but I can't figure out if that's generic usage, or if the fingers did really both belong to males."

Maria is shocked to realize that she never asked this question herself. Where is her mind? She wonders with a paranoid feeling whether she shouldn't just take down her shingle and stay home.

In a moment of uncharacteristically open-ended candor, Maria says: "You won't believe this probably, but that has never occurred to me."

"I did sort of gather that from what you said in the paper." Peg blushes as she speaks.

Maria observes Peg's face for the first time, and notices her flushed expression. A feeling of affinity stirs in Maria, just below the surface.

"My take on this thing," Peg says, and then draws back to a more hesitant tone, "based only on the *Times*, of course, is that it's a woman doing it."

In a leap of magical thinking, Maria hopes that Peg is correct. She wants Frank out of the picture. "Why do you say that?"

"Just based on the way women and men are socialized generally, nothing very deep, you understand. I mean, a man, even a desperate man wouldn't hang fingers out. He'd chop up a body, bag it, blow something up. But hang dainty fingers? No.

"Another thing, I bet the fingers are female. Am I right? See, I think it's a woman doing it, and part of the desperation is the macro self-hatred we all walk around with."

"Hey, Peg, lighten up." Roberta doesn't like where this conversation is going and she doesn't want to be forced to lie to her friends about her Living Dolls activities.

The mood is broken, and Maria feels cheated. As though she's missing a chance to crack the case. Ideas bounce around in her head at breakneck speed. She wants to shift gears and get herself home to throw these new pieces into the pot. Yet Maria is also pulled by a curiosity about Peg.

Roberta elbows around to Maria and exclaims in a low tone out of Peg's earshot: "Maria, have you lost a lot of weight lately?"

"Yeah, some," Maria responds as if she is an adolescent petulantly answering her mother.

"You don't look good, honey. Cut it out, you'll get sick."

As Roberta speaks, the three women find themselves at the entrance to the restaurant.

Seated in a booth, Roberta and Peg do most of the talking while Maria begins to confront a new set of feelings that are coursing through her. For a while, Maria watches Peg, Roberta and herself as if from a distant planet, until she realizes that Peg is looking directly into her face. To deflect the gaze, Maria shifts to Roberta saying: "Berta, I noticed on my way over that I have Ailey tickets for Tuesday. I have too much work to do, so why don't you take them. I have two. Ben won't go without me."

At Maria's mention of her husband, a twinge crosses Peg's face for an instant. Roberta, who has already picked up on the charged atmosphere, declines. "Thanks, Maria, I can't. You know, I bet you could find two teensy hours for the performance. Take Peg, she's a real Ailey buff."

Maria observes Peg blushing again, and her intrigue deepens. Forgetting that she and Ben ordered the tickets together, Maria shyly assents. "That would be nice …" Her voice peters out.

Peg musters a normal tone of voice to say: "You know, I could make it that night, and I'd love to. I read a review of their new pieces, and tried to buy tickets too late. They're at Lincoln Center, aren't they?"

"Yes. Meet me at seven-thirty at the box office, how about it?" As Maria utters the words, she feels a heaviness in the pit of her stomach. Jumbled and excited, but definitely a sensory overload shot through with trepidation. Maria can no longer fight the urge to leave. She rises abruptly, blurting: "I must go home now."

Surprised, Roberta and Peg look up at her. Peg suggests they exchange business cards in case anything comes up before the show.

Still downtown in Little Italy, Jackie has ordered a skimpy dinner, and is attempting to dance around what is on her plate through the meal to avoid actually eating it. She's never been good at passing up food. In order to keep herself hungry and under control, she has to order minimally. Tonight it's an arugula salad appetizer she works on. Accustomed and largely oblivious to Jackie's habits, Gregory eats heartily and is in a jovial mood.

"So, Jackie, how did your presentation go in Algebra?" he asks.

"Okay, I suppose. I kind of fumbled a bit over a proof because I didn't write out any notes."

"You did the whole hour from memory? That's incredible! I've only recently managed to do that, and I certainly know the material I teach inside out. I still need guideposts. I'm impressed."

"Fortunately it's fifty minutes. I don't think that I had even five more minutes' worth in me," Jackie says with a laugh and then cuts a leaf in quarters before putting a piece on her fork.

"You know, Jackie," Gregory says, striking a serious tone, "the department met yesterday and we feel that you should be the teaching assistant for Differential Equations next semester. What do you think?"

"That's ridiculous, I've never even taken the course myself." Jackie's tone is matter of fact.

"We know that." Gregory is beaming.

"So? I don't get it?" Jackie grabs for a piece of bread and nervously butters it.

"We think it would be good for you. Plus, you're so stubborn, we figure it's the only way to get you to learn the subject."

"But I won't be able to help the students." Finally, Jackie is happily flattered and has adopted the idea whole.

"Sure you will, just stay one week ahead of them. Solovitz'll be teaching, so it's not like people will be too baffled anyway. He gets consistently high student evaluations. You'll be fine."

The waiter comes and takes their dinner plates away and asks if they care for dessert or coffee.

"What do you have that's special?" Jackie asks, trying to participate.

"The cheesecake is out of this world, the cannoli are exceptional, and we have excellent spumoni and zabaglione. Espresso, American coffee or decaf—no tea. Grappa and anisette."

"I'll have the spumoni and an espresso laced with anisette. What about you, Jackie, your usual?"

"Yup."

"And one espresso, neat, no sugar, no nothing." Gregory gestures his hand slicing the air horizontally as he speaks.

As he is finishing his Spumoni, Gregory announces: "Jackie, I know we were going to see *Le Boucher* tonight, but if we get home early enough, you'll be able to meet my daughter Emily. She's coming by to pick up a few things she left over the weekend. I hope its okay with you. We've both seen that movie a few times over anyway." In almost continuous speech, he raises his hand and says: "Check, waiter."

"Okay, Greg, but first let's go take a peek at the festival on Carmine Street—Our Lady of the Holy something or other." Jackie looks almost childlike in her enthusiasm with her eyes wide in excitement.

"Sure, just so long as you can guarantee that we won't see any of those fingers everyone's talking about." Gregory grins as he speaks.

As she puts on her jacket, Jackie says: "I'll do my best. Not a legally binding commitment though, you understand."

Gregory pays the bill and leaves a medium-small tip. Greg and Jackie bundle up for the cold night air, and thrust themselves through the restaurant doors, outside, and onto the sidewalk. They can see the lit Ferris wheel and can hear the hurdy-gurdy music playing. As they walk down Grand Street in the direction of the fair, the wafting smells of the frying sausage and zeppoli approach them and beckon. The two blocks from the fair on either side are so packed with people and cars as to be almost impassable. Jackie becomes determined and fierce as she cuts a swath through the dense human soup. One block away, the fair noise is so loud as to make the other city streets seem calm by comparison.

"You're vicious tonight, Jackie. What's gotten into you?" Gregory says, panting as he strives to keep pace with her.

"I just love these fairs: the frying fat, the paintings on velvet, the gambling games in the church's basement. I don't know, the whole gestalt."

They wiggle their way onto the fair street. As in a jammed subway car, the center is empty and they are able to stroll. Most of the stalls are decorated with green, red, and white and a few sport both Italian and American flags. The hawkers call out their wares with impressively deep voices: "Calzone! Zeppoli! Sausage Grinders! Here, here, get a nice cold beer! Here, here, calamari!"

Jackie and Greg stop to watch a muscular young man mix up a huge vat of dough. He is stripped down to his white undershirt and has an apron over his white pants. A Marlboro cigarette with a long ash on it is hanging out the side of his mouth as he dives his fist and arm up to his elbow into the cauldron to knead.

Jackie decides to pass on that booth. By the time she reaches the next zeppoli stand, she can't contain herself any longer and blurts: "A double bag, please, and extra confectioners' sugar."

They both know their time is limited, but before they turn to go, Jackie tries her hand at the ring toss and wins a big blue bear. Gloating, and in partial jest, she immediately presents it to Gregory. He is taken aback, but takes the prize graciously.

After fighting their way out of the crowds, they hustle over to the car and split up efficiently so that Gregory ends up on the driver's side and Jackie on the sidewalk at the passenger door. Tucked into the outside of the window frame is a colorful business card. Jackie picks it up casually to toss, but the vermillion colored print catches her eye.

The card features a picture of a cream colored brunette nude woman lying down, seen from the waist up. It is a side shot with full view of a large white and pink breast. The woman's head is turned full front with a puckered, open mouth. Superimposed on the photo is print which reads:

HOT NEW SERIES!
"All My Women" "Genital Hospital" "21 Pump Street"
CHOOSE YOUR FAVORITE FANTASY
exclusively on 970-SOAP Afternoon Delight
starring the Slut Sisters

970-NINA:	Beautiful, but savage
970-GINA:	Always willing and accessible
plus 970-CANDY:	She'll Melt in your mouth
also 970-MOAN:	Hot, steamy sex
970-5367:	Hardcore, kinky excitement

Having wrangled their way through evening uptown traffic, and back at Gregory's apartment, he and Jackie have scarcely taken off their coats when Gregory telephones his daughter Emily to tell her that he is home. Emily lives downstairs with her younger brother, Michael, and her mother. She's a senior at Brierley, an exclusive Upper East Side high school for girls. When she comes up to her father's apartment, Emily is still wearing her pleated plaid skirt school uniform. This is the first Jackie has heard about the existence of any children, let alone from a divorce. And a daughter almost her age.

Jackie has maintained the assumption all along that Gregory is not married, but on the verge of it. From the first conversation she overheard in his office, to the woman's robe hanging on the back of the door in his bathroom. She's never asked, nor even been interested.

Somehow the similarity of Emily to herself and, nevertheless, the vast distance between them, keeps Jackie in a dazed silence during Emily's visit. After his daughter leaves, Gregory is more than perturbed.

"I mean, you didn't even talk to her. She's my daughter! What's the matter with you? Aren't you interested in me? My family is part of me too. The divorce has been very hard on us. You have to be understanding. Sensitive. I guess I never told you this, but when Pearl and I decided to divorce, I just broke down."

As Gregory is speaking, Jackie notices the blue bear smiling in the corner.

"I mean, I wanted the divorce as much as she did, but I fell apart once we made the final break. I locked myself in a hotel room for five days and cried.

"Cried and cried like a baby. I was fortunate to have found a great girl to be there and hold me through it. The funny thing was that she was just a kid, Emily's age. If you can imagine it, but so knowledgeable. Really comforting. When those five days were up I felt immensely better. Like I could really see the dawn of a new day coming, and it did.

"But you're going to have to help me out too. I feel twinges."

CHAPTER SIXTEEN:

AT WORK

A FEW DAYS LATER, JACKIE STEPS onto campus at nine-o-five, after dropping Bessy and Ricky off at the Morningside School. She is greeted by posters slapped across the entry gates. The first one reads:

**NOON RALLY
AGAINST CENSORSHIP IN THE ARTS.
LIVING DOLLS LECTURE AT ONE
IN DODGE HALL.**

All the way down College Walk, the trees are adorned with the past three years of posters from the Living Dolls campaign. The campus is flooded with extra security guards strewn about, waiting, with tension in the air. Already late for biology, Jackie hurries by the display barely noticing it.

Later on, as Jackie scurries across campus to her next class, she sees a tepid crowd gathered around three Living Dolls wearing mortarboards atop their masks. At twelve-ten, when Jackie arrives at room 301 Dodge for her Music Humanities course, she finds a sign on the door stating that the class is relocated to the rally on campus walk.

"Forget that," she says. "I've got work to do."

She decides to drop off a paper at a professor's office on her way over to the math library. To Jackie's chagrin, she bumps into Professor Sacks just as she's sliding the paper into her mailbox.

"Jackie, good to see you."

"Hi. How are you, Professor Sacks? I enjoyed your lecture last week. It was great for me because it was dead-on the topic I wrote about in this." Jackie taps on her paper as she speaks.

"Turning your paper in early, eh, Jackie? Great, I can spend more time on it. Would you like to come in?" Professor Sacks says as she is getting out her office key and unlocking her door.

Jackie edges back slightly, away from the now open office door. "Um, thanks. But I should really get to the library. Looks like it's going to be an unpredictable day with all that going on out there."

"The Living Dolls stuff, you mean? Pretty direct, huh? If anything can wake up a lot of the dusty old professors on this campus, they can. And I hope they do."

"Seems kind of ridiculous to me. Masks and posters. I thought that stuff went out of use with the floppy leather hats of the seventies."

"Oh, I don't know. In my day, Jackie, things were different, which is not to say better or worse. On the other hand, some things haven't changed much at all." After speaking, Professor Sacks slips into one of her characteristic pauses with a crinkled expression on her face which signals that deep inner thought is going on. Through the long pause she sweeps her stringy gray and brown hair backwards and down the back of her neck several times.

Jackie knows enough from class to keep silent through these moments. She is beginning to feel she's being held captive in the professor's office. The professor begins to break the silence with a change in facial expression. Then her eyes refocus and a deep, throaty sound erupts, signaling that she might continue.

"I'll never forget my first day as assistant professor at Princeton. I proudly opened the door to my office, as I did just now, not expecting anything. I had my shiny new key, glistening in the florescent light. I opened the door with it, so proud of myself, daughter of a farmer, teaching at the greatest university on the globe, and there it was. I found that the room had been filled with blood soiled tampax and pads. They had been thrown in the window of the office which was on the first floor. One of a series of subtle messages I received that year. I never did figure out if it was students or faculty who did that. Probably both. A colleague of mine at U.C. Berkeley found a dildo placed on her desk early on in her teaching career." Professor Sacks speaks as if she is recollecting commonplace events, without much emotion. Only the lines in her forehead crease in pain.

"Amazing. Nothing like that could ever happen now. And they'd get sued faster than superman can fly if they did," Jackie says, fiddling with the books on her lap as if she were getting ready to go. She is not at all interested in the topic, but is trying not to be too rude.

"I wish that were true, Jackie."

"I know. Feminists are making everyone angry. Now they're just man hating, like those crazy Living Dolls out there, what's the point? They're just making a joke out of the whole thing anyway." Jackie stands up, trying to be more definite about putting an end to this sermon on what she is sure is a dead issue.

"Oh, I don't know. I count myself as a feminist and I don't think I need to pass judgment on all men to do it. But anyway," Sacks says in summation, finally catching Jackie's drift, "I'm sure you have a class to go to. Come back any time, we can go over your paper if you have any questions after I'm done with it."

"Good bye, Professor Sacks. And thanks for your help."

"Good luck."

There is something eerie about the way she says Good luck, and it irritates Jackie. Five minutes out of the professor's office though, she forgets all about it. Jackie is rushing because she feels her study time eroding before her eyes.

She makes an abrupt about-face outside, away from her Professor's office, and marches over to the Mathematics Building to root out journal articles for her presentation next Monday in her Push-down Automata Theory course. Jackie's the only woman in the course, as is true for all but the general requirement courses that she's taking. So far, she's hardly noticed.

As Jackie steps into the math library she sees her friend Tom, who is the librarian and also a graduate student in philosophy.

"Hi, Tom. How's it going in here today? Any trouble from the restless computer science drones?"

"Oh, Jackie, hello. Not a peep today. I'm looking forward to the long weekend though."

"The library's not closed over Thanksgiving, is it?" Jackie proclaims more than asks with a sharp edge of anguish in her voice.

"Nope, but I am. Off skiing, finally. By the way," Tom says with a sly look on his face, "I was hoping you'd come in today. A book I ordered from Elsevier finally arrived. It's right up your alley, so to speak."

Gleefully, Jackie darts over to the new books shelves.

"No, smarty, you know where I keep those things," Tom says with a grin edging out of his generally somber, pouting face.

"Tom, you've got to stop doing this," Jackie says as she ducks under the checkout counter and walks back to Tom's desk. He has already pulled open the large, bottom desk drawer revealing that it is crammed full of spanking new books.

"You can't keep a private stash of math library books. These are great, and no one gets to read them."

"You do. I show you all of them."

"You're nuts. Let me see it. What'd you get in that's worth reading?"

Holding up a bright yellow, clothbound book, Tom exclaims as if he has written it himself: "The Foundations of Proof Theory!" Handing it to her he adds: "Here have a look see."

Jackie scoops it out of Tom's hands, swerves away from his

desk and under the counter disappearing into the stacks with an airy "Thanks" trailing behind her.

She is gone so quickly that Tom is only able to say, "Drinks tonight, on me," addressed to the empty entrance of the stacks. By the time his utterance is complete, Jackie is already seated at a dusty, graffiti carved desk devouring the table of contents of the new book.

Too soon for her taste, Jackie's study time is up. She tucks the new unmagnetized and uncatalogued book into her bag and gets up to leave. She has to rush to get to the Morningside School so that Bessy doesn't wait overly long for her. Fortunately, Ricky has a play date and is off to a friend's house through dinner. Ben will fetch him on his way home.

As it happens, Bessy arrived at the outer school steps a few minutes early, and sits alone waiting. While she is there daydreaming about nothing in particular, a white Lincoln Continental pulls up to the curb. Bessy half watches as the smoked glass window rolls down and an arm stretches out of it, clothed with an elegant pinstriped jacket and shiny gold cuff links on the shirt.

Bessy squints to see who it is in the car waving to her, but all she can see is a silhouette of a man with a stylish hat on. She notices that the pale white hand jutting out the window is offering her a thick fan of crisp bills. As Bessy sits there listlessly, the arm with the money retreats, the dark window zips closed, and the car slowly drives off.

More kids are ready for their pick up, but unlike Bessy, they are waiting inside because they recognize how cold it is. A few venture out and stand on the stairs stomping their feet to keep warm. By the time Jackie arrives, there is a small cluster of remaining kids, ready to go home.

"Hey, Bess, Bessy, here I am, over here," Jackie says waving as she bounds up the stoop to the school building.

"Uh huh."

"Hi, Bessy. How was school? You ready to go home?"

"Um."

"Buck up, Bess. I'm here. I'm just a little late. Ol' professor Slownik kept my class overtime. What could I do?"

"You don't have a class in the afternoon!"

"Oh, Bessy, you knew I'd be here, no?"

"I was worried about you."

"Why?"

"Maybe something happened."

"Bessy," Jackie says clasping Bessy's shoulders, one with each hand, "nothing's going to happen to me coming down eight blocks from my school to yours. Nothing's ever happened before and nothing will. Whatever 'happened' means."

"Like, maybe a car or bus hit you, or somebody hurt you, or your school caught on fire. Or maybe you decided not to come or to run away."

Seeing that Bessy is working herself into one of her froths, Jackie recoils and responds a little too crisply.

"Run away? I'd never do that and you know it. And anyway, I have nowhere to run to. I've got school to finish first and that's going to take a long, long time. Come on Bess, let's go home," Jackie says, placing an arm around Bessy's shoulders.

Together, they walk down Broadway towards the subway, Jackie carrying a load of books in one hand, and the other holding onto Bessy. Bessy's red Teenage Mutant Ninja Turtle backpack is flopping up and down as she strides on. Suddenly, she perks up a little. Just before they reach the station, Bessy halts and pulls Jackie to a full stop without warning.

"Let's take the 104 bus today. I want to tell you about the experiment we did today in science and the subway is too noisy."

"It'll take a lot longer, remember? You can become pretty impatient on the bus."

"I won't today, I promise."

"Okay," Jackie says knowing that Bessy will create a scene if she becomes antsy waiting for their stop. "Let's go."

They cross One-hundred-and-tenth Street away from the number one train stop and over towards the bus stop in front of Woolworth's.

"The experiment was about mold."

"Mold! Yuck." Jackie makes a face expressing mock revulsion.

At that moment a fire truck and ambulance whiz past, both with their loudest sirens on. Once they pass far enough down Broadway, Bessy says: "What did you say, Jackie?"

"All I said was—" Jackie pauses this time as an overly loud motorcycle goes by—"mold, yuck!"

"No, Jackie, it was fun. We were supposed to imagine how a scientist would go about discovering the best way to grow mold."

"Like, to make penicillin with?"

"Huh?"

"Never mind, Bessy. Sorry I interrupted you. Go on."

"Well, we had to—"

"Wait, hold on, Bess. Let's get on the bus and pay before we talk."

They climb onto the crowded southbound bus. Jackie throws a token into the hopper and flashes Bessy's bus pass as the driver gruffly tells them to move to the back. As they weasel their way to the rear which has some empty space, Jackie is pinched once on her ass and her right breast is brushed against a little too slowly to be a mistake.

"We were supposed to think like the scientist and figure out how she would do the experiment."

"She? Which one are you talking about, Marie Curie? Isn't this supposed to be about Pasteur? He's a man, Louis Pasteur."

"Huh?" Bessy looks confused again.

"The scientist, who is it?"

"Just anyone, it doesn't matter. One we think up in our heads. So we needed to grow mold and I remembered that moldy bread we have in the fridge. I can use that." Bessy is clearly proud of herself.

Jackie takes pause for a moment, and doesn't hear the rest of Bessy's story, noting that she would never say "she" for a scientist in general. She wonders where Bessy got that form of speech. It's not correct English, after all.

"So how come you said 'she'?" Jackie interrupts Bessy in the middle of her explanation.

"Huh?"

"You said 'she' for the scientist." Jackie notices that she is overly exasperated at this point and sorry she raised it.

"Oh." Bessy pauses with a grin. "In science class and art class we say 'she' and 'her' a lot. We're supposed to."

"Why?"

"I don't know. Let me tell you what we saw in the microscope, Jackie!" With that Bessy tugs at Jackie's sleeve in brief annoyance, and then continues on with her story.

Midtown, in the up elevator of her office building, Maria is pondering a real life story herself, engrossed in thought about the appearance of the third finger. Floating around the back and sides of her mind are Peg's comments. Maria tries to imagine the person who could tie someone's hand down and brutally ax off a finger. Three fingers total now. Hard as she tries, Maria can't see a woman doing it. She notices that it's easier to imagine that the mutilated hand is attached to a female. A silent female, at first. Maria then envisions her horror, her scream into the silence of the act. Maybe the woman doesn't scream. She sits and watches, in disbelief, unfeeling. Numbed from the shock of the experience.

Maria practically runs to her desk from the elevator, tossing words over her shoulder at her secretary. "Get me the Coroner. Now!"

"Hello. Maria Jacobs, attorney at law. I'm calling about the new finger, the third. Have you tested it yet?"

"So to speak," comes the reply.

"And?" Maria hates the way he's making her beg.

"And, nothing. We took the print, ran it. Zip. Didn't find him. Big surprise."

"Listen, please can the sarcasm. I've had it with no one treating this case with the seriousness it deserves."

Maria continues in a tone which suggests that they're having an argument, "And, another thing. The three fingers, are they all from different people, can you tell?"

"Yup." He'll torture her now.

"Yes, what?" They *are* from different people? Let's make this conservation easy, not hard."

"No. Yes, we can tell. No, they're not from different people. All from the same right hand, as a matter of fact."

"So you knew that with the first two fingers?"

"No, could have, but didn't think of it."

Taking a breath to try to calm herself, on the exhale she begins to speak in measured syllables. "And this way of talking that the fingers came from a man might be misleading?"

"Got that right, lady lawyer. They're off a woman, like yourself."

Maria shudders with his crudeness. "Any clue of her identity, then?"

"Nope."

"What's the investigation turned up so far?"

"Zilch."

"What've you explored? How are you looking for her?" Maria is doing her best to keep her voice contained, but her emotions are getting away from her. She feels strangely close to this unknown female.

"We're not actually pursuing that line. Not within our jurisdiction, and probably a hopeless search. Could be anyone. Could be off a stiff. Could be, could be. Don't have that kind of manpower."

Maria hangs up the phone in disgust. She glances at her watch, and then to her calendar, and notes that she has to scurry to a staff meeting which has just begun. She stays put, immobilized by the turmoil brewing within her. For a brief moment she feels the mutilated woman's scream well up from the pit of her stomach and rise to her larynx. Maria tries to stifle it and tamp it down, but too late. She feels her person undergo an ill-defined paradigm shift. As if she was one with this woman, this person who is characterized only by her sex.

Sitting in the meeting, Maria is distracted by a couple of senior partners' comments about a client of the firm. Because of the client's choice of clothing, two lawyers draw elaborate conclusions about her guilt. For Maria, listening to these pronouncements is like being slapped in the face with a cold, wet towel. In a split second, many past incidents and remarks made to Maria by lawyers about herself and about women, comes into focus. Suddenly a context opens up for the events to fit into, where none had existed before in Maria's mind. It is as if a cell of her brain drained to make room for information that had been lingering in the waiting room for years. She wishes that she could run back to her office to process what she senses is a very climactic moment for her.

Lost in personal reflection, the time comes quickly for Maria to describe the progress of the Errigon case. She has a hard time establishing a link between the fingers and the case to the satisfaction of the most powerful of the senior partners at her firm. Maria is so far beyond pondering that question, that she cannot muster the enthusiasm to try to convince them of the connection, even though she knows she should. She does not want to be moved off the case under any circumstances. Her turn in the spotlight finally over, Maria begins to jot down colleagues' remarks that may open new paths of promise to find the identity of the woman.

Back behind her desk, the meeting over, Maria resolves to call the Living Dolls directly. She is becoming convinced that they may be the target of the threats underlying the hung fingers. Hoping to reach a person, instead, Maria listens to the witty outgoing message of the Dolls' answering machine and leaves her name and number into the recording tape.

Just as Maria replaces the receiver with a sigh of disappointment, Claire begins her routine afternoon scan of the Dolls' messages. Breathing irregularly when she hears that Maria is on the case of the fingers, Claire calls her back immediately.

"Living Dolls, here. Returning your call."

Surprised by the rapid response, Maria stumbles out: "Yes. Hello. Thank you for returning my call so promptly."

Maria pauses, and Claire makes no move to speak. Maria presses forward. "I'm calling because, as you may know, I am Frank Errigon's lawyer and I have been investigating the three fingers hung on your posters in SoHo."

After another pause of silence, Maria resumes. "I have become concerned that the Living Dolls may be the target of the underlying threats from the actions. I was hoping that perhaps your group has been making inquiries, that we might be able to share information, as it were." Maria hastily adds: "Please be clear, I am not, under any circumstances, soliciting information that directly pertains to your lawsuit, your campaign, that is, against the Errigon Gallery itself. This is a friendly call, directly relating to the fingers only."

Claire's continued silence pushes Maria to babble, spilling the little that she has learned or inferred about the case.

Finally, Claire speaks, with relief in her voice. "Thank you very much for your call. I can't tell you what it means to me. I have been trying, unsuccessfully mind you, to convince my colleagues of the seriousness of the recent events. Events? Crimes! So far, I am truly sorry to report, we have done nothing. Sitting idly by while the threats pass unheeded. Perhaps your call will function as the impetus we need."

"So, you can't help me at this point? No clue as to who the fingers may have come from? Or what the overall message is about? Anything?"

"Who the fingers belong to? I never thought of that question."

"I thought maybe an artist was assaulted in that way recently, and maybe you'd be privy to that." Maria is rubbing her mole as she speaks, trying to contain her anxiety.

"No." Claire is taken aback. "How could I know any more than you? You have the whole police squad at your disposal, I assume."

"That and a token, as the saying goes." Maria's frustration is building to a fervor. She wonders, as though she is shrieking the words internally, how can *no one* be doing anything about this?

When the conversation is over, Maria sits back in her chair, drained. She desperately tries to feel some circulation in her body as her hands move from her forehead to the leather arm rests. Questions course through her veins as she tries to stir herself. "Who is this fingerless woman? An artist the art community doesn't know? A mother with desperate, small children in search of her? A loner? Where is she?"

Maria rises to her feet feeling that it is up to her to find the identity of the lost woman. She exits her office and heads for the ladies' lounge for a change of atmosphere. Finding it full of word processing staff chatting on break, Maria reluctantly returns to her desk as if she is being forced to look herself full in the face. She feels as though there are mirrors at every turn of her life, and knowing that she's meeting Peg later only adds to her agitation and a sense of pressure to find a solution to the case.

A couple of hours later, both Peg and Maria, each in her own office, are preparing simultaneously to meet at Lincoln Center. Peg has already freshened up in the bathroom, and is now changing out of her corporate attire into a sporty jumpsuit that shows off her best features. Consciously admitting that she won't work tonight, she leaves all her files on her desk, grabs her purse and jacket, and heads out.

Maria is sitting at her desk, appointment book open and spread out before her. She's going over her workload for the long

Thanksgiving weekend. Trying to squeeze in as much work time as possible in and around the turkey, Maria also earmarks Sunday as the day she will finally construct the monster Lego kit with Bessy and Ricky that they've had sitting around waiting for assembly for months, writing simply, "LEGO" in the small weekend day box in her book. She outlines this notation in red, and laces the border with green exclamation marks.

As an afterthought, Maria pens in "jog" under Saturday morning, not feeling even slightly committed to its execution. She glances at the clock and realizes that she needs to leave in ten minutes at the most. Maria picks up her telephone to call home to Bessy before her bedtime. Maria hesitates, thinking that her presence is ephemeral enough as is. They need real time together, not "Good night" and "I love you" coming out of a piece of white plastic. What *is* she doing, Maria wonders frantically, going with a stranger to a dance show, when she could be home with the most important people in the world to her?

Maria packs her briefcase, propelled on her way to meet Peg. She hadn't reflected on what she is doing even for a second, until now. All of a sudden, the impact comes crashing in around her and Maria runs to the bathroom with diarrhea.

Having arrived too early, Peg wanders around the fountain in the middle of the Lincoln Center plaza, staring into the splashing bits of recycled water. Some minutes later she spots Maria dashing up the steps from the curb. Still dressed in business clothes, Peg notes, feeling a tinge out of place in her casual togs.

"Maria! Over here," Peg calls as she advances toward Maria. A beautiful grin breaks out across Peg's face as they near each other.

"Hello, Peg. I hope I'm not late." Maria keeps moving as she speaks to steer Peg and herself over to the box office to pick up the tickets. Maria notes that she automatically feels familiar and comfortable with Peg.

On the way in, Maria and Peg chat about office politics, and their caseloads. They have more than one chuckle over some of the antics of the law partners they each work with.

Joking, Maria asks: "How is it that you've come away unscathed, Peg? Not married, right?"

Peg laughs uneasily and responds: "Hardly, Maria. I was sure the gossip in Roberta already told you that I'm gay."

A silence washes over Maria. Implicitly, she knew this, of course, but she had not let it enter the upper level of her consciousness. She pulls herself in to ask: "Live with someone, then? No, I'm sorry. I have no idea why I'm being so nosey. This is none of my business. I just often think back to the days when not every second has been accounted for in advance."

Peg touches Maria's hand on the theater armrest briefly in order to emphasize her words. "No, it's okay. I consider this girl talk. I love it. Once in a while, that is.

"And no, I don't live with anyone. I haven't since my law school days, many moons ago. I'm not suited to long term co-habitation, it seems."

With a laugh, Maria throws in, "I don't think our species is!"

"I've got to say, though, Maria. I don't exactly go spreading the rumor about my sexual preference in professional circles. I'm not entirely sure, if you don't mind my saying, why I told you so easily."

"You ever dated a lawyer?"

"You kidding? No. We're all in the closet."

"That's not true," Maria says, not feeling entirely at ease with the conversation. "There seem to be lots of gay lawyers who are pretty damn vocal about it."

"Do I detect a hint of bitterness in your voice, Maria?" Peg says lightly. "Most of the lawyers you're thinking of are men, and many of them work on gay rights issues. They're not in the rigid world of corporate law like we are."

Just then, the theater lights begin to dim, as the chandeliers are pulled upwards, towards the ceiling. The theater warning bells bing softly, and the rustling, chatting, and coughing die down to naught. During the performance, Peg glances over to Maria, and studies her face while she is captivated by the movements on stage.

At intermission, Peg and Maria wander out to the mezzanine, chatting and comparing notes on the dance. They sip Champagne cocktails and share a sandwich, the only dinner either of them will have that night. As they make their way back to their seats, Peg's voice sounds a serious note.

"Maria," Peg says, turning to face her as they walk down the darkened hall, "I made a couple of rules for myself a long time ago."

She pauses, Maria turns to face Peg, curious to know what is coming. She feels relaxed around Peg, and is enjoying this moment which promises to prove intimate.

"What, Peg?"

"My first rule is, no marriage to anyone of any gender."

"And rule number two?" Maria doesn't yet see where this is heading.

"Rule number two is, no dating married women. They're too fucked up, generally." Peg stops talking as they take their seats. Once ensconced, Peg looks at Maria. "I know this is totally brazen, Maria, but I feel very warmly towards you. We're alike in so many ways, we travel in the same crazy legal world of midtown, and you're gorgeous, intelligent." Pulling back enough to regain her composure, Peg adds: "If you ever thought you might be interested in me, I'd love to make an exception to the rule."

Maria doesn't know what to say, and so remains silent, thinking that the saying is true, she really should be careful of what she wishes for.

Eventually, the curtain goes up, and the remaining piece plays. For Maria it begins to feel interminable. She is prickling all over, with a hot and itchy body becoming unbearable half way through.

She feels better once the show is over, and they are out in the cool night air of the plaza. "I'm going to walk home, Peg. I'm just a few blocks north. What about you?" Maria is speaking uneasily now.

Sensing the tension, Peg takes a stab at shifting the venue. "I'll walk you a ways, I live downtown, so I need to get into the express at some point. Maria, have you heard of the League of Women Lawyers, or whatever the exact name is? It's a new group forming in Manhattan. You might be interested in it."

"Yes, yes. I know. I've heard of it. In fact, an old school chum has been after me about it."

"After you?" Peg says incredulous. "You should check it out, I think it might be useful for you."

"Why? You think I don't have enough to do?" Maria says with a smirk. "I don't have time for anyone's special interests, not even those of my own kids." Maria knows she's too shrill and she wonders about it.

"Sorry." Peg clasps and pats one of Maria's hands for a split second as they walk. "I wasn't trying to force anything on you."

Feeling like an oaf, Maria walks on in silence, wanting to burst. After two blocks, she looks into Peg's face. When Peg catches on, she looks back. With slowed pace, the two smile at each other. Maria slowly slips her left hand into Peg's right. They continue on walking in that fashion, past where Maria should turn off for her apartment, and on to the Seventy-second Street subway station. At the entry way, as they are looking squarely at each other, Peg breaks the silence. "See you soon, Maria. I enjoyed every minute."

"Yes. Me, too. Goodbye, Peg."

Having prepared Bessy's dinner earlier that night, Jackie readies herself for this evening's installment of rape prevention karate instruction. As she rushes out the door to her class, the phone rings.

"Jacobs' residence!" she blurts abruptly, getting a subway token out of her purse with the other hand at the same time.

"Jackie?" a female voice whispers.

"Who's this?"

"It's Jan, I—"

"Jan, what're you calling me for?" Jackie demands, irritated. "I'll see you in a few minutes if we hang up now. Otherwise we'll both be late for class. That is, if you're coming. I haven't seen you there in a while."

"No, Jackie. We're having a separate class today. Just you, me, Gloria, and Sarah. We hope it's not going to attract too much attention, four of us gone at once."

"Hold on a minute here. What are you talking about? Start at the beginning. And please stop whispering!" In her mind, Jackie still has one foot out the door to class. She never wanted to be too friendly with Jan but they had exchanged phone numbers one day.

Jackie had had a feeling when they were alone in the gym early in the semester that Jan was coming on to her. It was before class and they were both early and sitting on the gym floor waiting for class to begin.

Jan broke the silence. "Maybe everyone else is late and we're on time." She was sitting cross-legged, clad in her off-white karate suit and white belt. She is lanky and has short cropped mouse brown hair. Her features are plain except for her remarkably thin, straight nose.

"Hmm?" Jackie was thinking about a paper she was writing for her epistemology course. "Yeah, I can't believe I got here early. Everything went wrong on the way. Even my token was warped and wouldn't go down the turnstile slot."

"How do you like this course?" Jan prodded, sensing that she was losing Jackie's attention.

"It's okay. My knees hurt too much between classes though. I usually debate before class whether I'm going and then end up coming every time anyway."

"I don't think a man should be teaching it," Jan said definitively. "This is a course for women. I think it's nerve for a man to teach rape prevention. It's men who invented the damn crime."

No sooner had Jan uttered those last words than Jackie discounted her as a viable ally. She started to daydream through the rest of their conversation until class started. Out of politeness and cowardice she ended up exchanging phone numbers just before Norris had them begin punching the air.

"It's about Norris. No, it's about Gloria, Lisa, and Amy. I can't tell you over the phone, there's no time. You can stop debating this time and come to Sarah's apartment. 32 King Street, ground level 1-G. Just take the One train to Houston and get out at the south exit, that's King Street, and walk half a block east. Leave now. Got it, okay?" Jan's voice distills into a bit of a plea by the end.

"Okay," Jackie knows she is acting totally out of character, but something in the urgency of Jan's voice compels her and also piques her curiosity. "I'll be there as soon as I can. I'm outta here now. Bye."

Jan says "Goodbye" into the phone as she hears Jackie slam down the receiver.

Jackie rushes to the subway without knowing why she is doing so. She curses the day she joined the damn class. "This is all I need. papers to write, presentations to give, kids to usher back and forth, Maria to deal with, and now this: intrigue in my rape prevention class! Definitely yoga or even the track team would have been simpler than this. And only three weeks until finals. Thank God, it's Thanksgiving tomorrow and I'll have a few days to breathe. I just wish they'd go away for the weekend and I could have the apartment to myself."

Jackie scurries, muttering through the tunnel entrance to the train. A homeless woman with cellophane bound feet held together with string, swats Jackie's back. "Good work, honey, you're one of us now."

Sarah's apartment turns out to be one room with the kitchen forced into a small accordion door closet. The square footage of each wall is larger than the floor area because the ceilings are so high and the floor space so small. It gives one the impression of being squashed into a vertical vault.

Everyone else is there by the time Jackie arrives. Sarah and Gloria are sitting on the single bed covered with a colorful sheet to make it look more couch-like. Jan is sitting in the only chair, which leaves the floor or a plastic blue milk crate for Jackie. She chooses the floor.

"I have a folding chair if you want," Sarah says.

"No, I'm fine, thanks."

"We didn't start because we wanted all of us to hear the whole thing together," Jan says. "Jackie, you're the only one who doesn't have a clue though. It's going to be a shock—I'll just say it quickly. Norris has been raping his students. Gloria's told some of it to Sarah, but now the three of us will hear it." As Jan is talking, Gloria starts to cry and Sarah's eyes fill.

Jackie feels a chill and immediately thinks of Norris's flirtations with her.

"Why us?" she asks. "I mean, why are the four of us gathered here?"

"Gloria spoke to Sarah," Jan says, "and they picked you and me as two reliable people to tell. Maybe partly because we're in college and older than the rest of the students. I don't know. At this point it might not matter anymore. We have to do something about this to make sure Norris goes behind bars and stays there."

"After we at least get to shoot his kneecaps off," Sarah says with burning venom.

Jackie is still wondering why she's involved in this group and whether she hadn't better walk out now rather than get in deeper. Once Gloria starts to talk it's too late. Jackie's eyes are welling up a few sentences into the story. In empathy, but also from her own fears she constantly tries to keep at bay.

"He told me that it was part of the training, that I should try to resist," Gloria says suddenly, pulling herself together. Gloria has a husky build, dark blond, long, straight hair and a sweet face. The usual serenity on her face is now hauntingly askew. Her eyes are puffy, but beginning to clear as Gloria allows her anger to build.

"I can't believe I could be so stupid as to believe him. He said he wanted to give me private lessons because of my natural ability for karate. That he could see me as a black belt in short order." Gloria is pulling at the bedspread now.

"I even had a crush on him—I can't imagine it. My whole self has been turned inside out. I can still feel him all over me and inside." She stops picking at the cover and is sitting stiffly still now. "I'm never going to get rid of this feeling. Never."

Sarah tries to give Gloria a hug, but fails because it's too much like trying to squeeze a wall of cinder block.

"Why aren't Lisa and Amy here?" Jackie asks so meekly it is barely audible.

"At the last minute, Amy decided to come, so she's on her way," Sarah says mechanically in her deep voice. Sarah has wavy, chestnut colored hair and a freckled complexion. She's almost six feet tall and usually wears loose-fitting brightly colored pants and tunics.

"Lisa's not ready to meet in a group like this, and her parents aren't letting her out of their sight anyway. She just needs more time."

"I've spoken to her on the phone a few times," Gloria says. "She's not in good shape."

Jackie is afraid of hearing too much, so she tries to impose some order on the meeting. And, hopefully, some distance. "What should we be trying to accomplish with this meeting? I feel in the dark here. Is it for strategy? Has anyone called the police?"

With this last question, Gloria bursts into tears afresh. Somehow the image of a uniformed officer brings home the gravity of what has happened to her, and the concrete reality of her rape becomes inescapable.

A frozen quality glazes over the room, as if everyone is struck without being able to move or speak. For a few moments, the only sounds are the outside traffic and Gloria's gulping, muted sobs, until the doorbell buzzes with its harsh rasping ring.

Gratefully, Jan shoots up. "That's got to be Amy." Jan takes a couple of steps and pulls open the door without looking through the peephole. This doesn't go unnoticed, and a piercing sting goes through everyone. There is a collective sigh of relief when Jan cries, "Amy!" and Amy comes into the room with a half-smile on her face.

She takes off her green wool pea coat and reveals brown corduroy pants topped by a loose fitting purple sweater. Amy is slender, of medium height, with below-the-ear-length beaded and cornrowed hair and clear, dark brown eyes.

"How're you doing, Amy?" Jan asks as she clasps a hand around her back.

As a built-in reflex to the how-are-you question, Amy replies: "Oh, fine," and then catches herself in the actual present. "I'm doing all right, I mean. I got my HIV results today. Negative. I'd be more relieved if I felt confident that they knew what to look for with AIDS. At least if they were sure that HIV is the determining factor. Who knows what that shitface Norris has brewing around in his body. My anger boils over all the time. I'm ready to get the fucker. I'm torn between wanting to prosecute and wanting to hire the mob to slowly torture him and then cut him into small pieces."

"He really did his worst, or at least the worst," Sarah says. "I can't even imagine how you must feel."

"No, that's just the thing," Amy says, hesitantly. "This is going to sound strange, but, it turns out, being raped really isn't the worst thing. I mean, I don't know how you feel Gloria, but to me, what Norris did was hideous and horrible and I still can't close my eyes without it all playing before me again, but it was *concrete*. I can feel angry, and I know why very clearly. Rape's not the ultimate crime against women it's billed to be. I think that's men's prurient invention. To me, the ultimate crimes are the more amorphous, gray ones that keep us guessing and personalizing."

"Maybe that's because you don't think you had a hand in it," Gloria says quietly.

"Do I think that it was my fault? No. Do I think that I had a hand in it at all? Yes, of course. I was definitely foolish enough to agree to a solo lesson, foolish enough to think that I had been singled out for some reason. Yes to all of that."

"See," Gloria says hesitantly, "I take it to mean that I was responsible too, not just Norris. I played along. I feel really guilty. I can't totally blame him, however disgusting he is, because I helped bring it on myself."

"I just think that it's comforting for you to feel that way, Gloria." As Amy speaks these words, Gloria visibly tenses from head to foot. Everyone else stays put and tries to avoid getting tangled into what they all simultaneously fear will brew into an acrimonious argument.

"I mean, it's a way of making order to pose it in those terms. If it's your fault, then you were and still are in control of yourself, your body, your world. If that's so, then you can stop it, or something like it, from happening again. It's, in this way of thinking, just a mistake that you made. But if you see the rape as a crime committed by Norris, a rapist, a criminal, against you and against your will and power, then it is a scarier thing. There was virtually nothing you could have done to stop him once you were alone in the room with him."

Amy's visibly shaken now; to conclude her train of thought, she repeats: "Nothing."

After a long pause, Gloria slowly says: "I don't know."

Jackie is feeling more uncomfortable than ever, not having an opinion one way or the other about this debate, and not feeling motivated to form one. She still feels that there should be some forward movement. "Can we try to plan some action?"

As if she didn't hear Jackie speak, Amy says: "I mean, I'm not trying to be hard on you, Gloria. I was raped by Norris too. But I just think, or hope, that it might help you to hear how I see it.

I'm working very hard to keep this perspective and not become paralyzed by the whole thing."

While Amy and Gloria are locked in a mutual gaze, the others shuffle their arms and legs a bit, and Jan tries to pick up Jackie's thread. "Maybe this is a good moment to think about the future. About preventing Norris from committing more rapes. If we are organized, we have a better chance."

By the end of the meeting, the group decides that the first step should be for Jackie to get legal advice from Maria. They are hoping Maria will volunteer her services—even Jackie who deep down knows she won't—is caught up in this idea.

When Jackie arrives home, Maria is already in bed asleep. Jackie writes her an urgent note on yellow stick-it paper and puts it on Maria's briefcase. This way, even if Maria sneaks out early, they will have had some form of contact.

Maria had been worn out from the day, but mostly from the explosive experience of being with Peg. When she arrived back in her apartment, she was ready to crawl into bed instantly. Ben was waiting for her, though, with other plans. He fixed a snack and a drink for Maria, and placed them on the coffee table, announcing authoritatively that she must come over and sit with him on the couch. Maria hadn't even gotten her coat off. She rubs her mole, standing motionless in the foyer as she feels her mind go to mush.

Seated on their living room couch, arm's length apart, Maria and Ben chat for a few moments before he made it clear that he wants to talk about their marriage counseling. It had been an assignment from the therapist, and Ben has been feeling the days slipping by without anything happening. He is determined tonight. In fact, he knows that it is too late an hour for this discussion, but that it won't happen any other way. Maria is slouched, her body sunk into one end of the couch with her head crooked back resting over the wide edge. Ben, at the other end, is sitting upright, alert.

"You know, Maria, I was wrong after all. We both need to want to go for this to work. I mean, how can we get anywhere if you barely speak? It's not like you're a shy person."

Maria looks at Ben. "Maybe I am in this kind of situation, Ben. It's not that I don't approve of psychotherapy, you know, but you have to remember a little bit how I was brought up. Therapy was considered shameful. It's hard to buck sentiments that were instilled so young and for so long. Even if I don't agree. Maybe you can't understand this.

"Also, I rush over there from my office, rush back to my office when we're done. It's hard to move in and out of these completely different mental frames. Especially when I have so little time. To me, this is not the best way to spend it right now. When I feel like things might begin to shake out on their own. The kids are well taken care of, we're settled in this apartment for as long as we want, and I finally feel like my work is falling into place. I guess I think we just need to give ourselves time."

"Oh, come on, Maria. Can't you hear how you sound? How much more time, and for how much longer will it continue to slip over the horizon? Why not *now*? What's wrong with a jump start?"

"Nothing, Ben. Nothing. There are just so many directions that I can invest my energy and remain, at least minimally effective."

"Is it so hard for you to talk in there? I mean, you must have opinions about all of this. This is your life, too."

"Of course I do. But I can't turn it off and on. It's not how I operate, you know that."

Ben leans forward on the couch towards Maria and extends his hands to hers. As he clasps her hands, he speaks in soft tones. "Maria, please. Do this for us. Do this for me. I need you. I love you. I want us to continue to build our life together. With every millimeter we move apart, a piece of me shrivels. Try."

Maria melts at Ben's expression. She squeezes his hands in response. "Ben, listen. This is what I *can* do. I'll set aside time before each session, to reflect before I walk in. Maybe that will help lessen this feeling I have of being a chicken running amok with my head cut off. Maybe I'll be able to ease into this and participate."

CHAPTER SEVENTEEN:

IN HIDING

W ANTING TO MAKE UP FOR some of the lost time due to Thanksgiving that afternoon, Maria rises at six the next morning, slips quickly into her clothes, and breezes past the bathroom mirror slapping on a minimum of makeup without pausing. She is out the door by six-twenty without so much as a sip of orange juice. Maria doesn't see Jackie's message until she is storming down the steps to the subway and begins unzipping a small inner pocket in her briefcase where she keeps tokens. With a half-quizzical, half-annoyed expression Maria lifts the note to eye level and reads it, without slowing the pace of her march towards the turnstile. It reads:

> *MARIA—NEED HELP DESPERATELY!*
> *AM IN TROUBLE.*
>
> > *—JACKIE*

"Shit!" Maria mutters. "What can it be now? I hope she's not pregnant, I can't handle that. I'm too busy."

The trains are running well and she makes it to her office before seven. Irritated that her secretary isn't in yet, Maria buzzes someone from the night shift.

A hopped up voice spouting a "Yes, Ms. Jacobs?" booms over her office intercom.

"Suzie, bring me a large black coffee, as fast as you can, please." Maria's voice crackles and snaps too much.

The note from Jackie together with developments in the Errigon case have unnerved her beyond her usual level of agitation. In fact, she is in early today to prepare for a meeting Friday morning with Frank at his gallery before it opens at ten. She and Frank, they had decided, need to speak privately before Kim or anyone else is around.

As she gets out the Errigon file, her breakfast is brought in.

Absentmindedly, Maria says, "Thanks, Suzie," without looking to see that it is actually someone else who brings it in and silently leaves.

Maria's intercom buzzes, and a female voice blurts through the static: "Susan Lieberman on the line for you."

"Tell her I'm not here," Maria says while glancing at her clock. Then, in a fast change of heart: "No. Wait. I'll take the call. Put her through."

"Susan, hello. I'm glad you called."

Surprised, Susan responds: "Really? Great, Maria—"

Before she can finish her sentence, Maria cuts in: "Yes. Susan, you see," Maria's voice has a sheepish quality creeping in now, "I … I never received those brochures you mentioned when we last spoke." She knows full well that she tossed the entire, unopened package in her trash basket straight from the mail pile one day.

"No? You should have. I'll send out another batch today. In the meantime, perhaps you'd like to attend our meeting next week? Wednesday night, nine o'clock, the Shaker Meeting House on the west side of Gramercy Park. It won't be boring, I can promise you that."

"Thanks, Susan." Maria's voice sounds relieved. "I'll try to make it. Really."

Practically before the line is disconnected, Maria nervously punches in Roberta's number. "Hello?" Roberta's voice on the other end is groggy.

"'Berta, it's Maria. I'm sorry to call so early. I thought you'd be up, though."

"No, I am, Maria. I was just lying here, but I'm awake. What's up?"

"Well, I'm sort of calling to say hello. I think it's my turn for a check-in call."

"Check-in call?"

"You know, a sort of what-am-I-doing kind of call. Like yours."

"Uh-oh."

"How are you, by the way?"

"No, no, no. Maybe we'll get to that later. How are *you*, is the question. Or, what are you?"

"You mean, animal, vegetable, mineral?"

"Maria, don't make me pull teeth. You called me. So, talk. What's going on, you and Ben still seeing the shrink?"

"No. I mean, yes. But I'm not calling about that. Or not directly any way."

A few moments of silence later Roberta explodes. "Maria! Come on. You're baiting me now. Don't do this to yourself." And then more calmly: "I'm listening."

In a wobbly voice, uncharacteristic of Maria, she says: "I'm just confused, shall we say. That's all. I thought I knew something, anything, the basics, about myself. Now I find that I don't, that I didn't." Maria's voice trails off.

"With regard to what, Maria?"

"'Berta, please don't become impatient with me. Please. Anyway, you started this. You knew what would happen, didn't you?"

"I started *what*?"

"If not for that purported movie date—"

"Ohh. Peg?"

"Yes, Peg," Maria says, as if for her own information as much as Roberta's.

Roberta props herself upright, intrigued. Amused, she asks: "You mean to tell me that you and Peg—? So fast?"

"Don't start racing away. I'm talking about *me*. About how I feel. You're the one who's been so insistent about introspection. Well, I'm trying, but I'm not finding anything there that I can hold on to. I feel like my whole person is a jumble where order once was."

"Looked like internal chaos to me, to be honest, sweetie."

"Yes, you're probably right, but I didn't know it."

"So, what *happened*?" Roberta asks as someone who enjoys gossiping.

After an embarrassed silence, Maria responds: "Well, on the surface, not much at all. But first of all, I'm married and I like to think that means something. Second of all, I've never been anything if not traditional and definitely heterosexual. I mean, as you know, nothing else even occurred to me. For me, anyway. And so then, I already feel like my life is unraveling at the edges, like all its edges, as it is, and *then* you fix me up with Peg. I just met her that night, and I'm already captivated. She made me feel different, almost inside out, or something emotionally equivalent.

"At the dance performance she had the nerve, or courage, or whatever, to tell me she'd be interested in seeing me again, and my whole being sighed a gasp of relief and passion. And horror, at the same time. And I keep repeating in my head something that you said to me about it's the person that matters, not their sex. I think, fine, but I'm also married and have kids and a life, and I've got to be out of my mind. Then I start to think I must be having a nervous breakdown."

"Oh, Maria. Sounds like you think you need to make a decision. But listen, sounds like you actually need some space."

"Yes, I guess that's true. I think I must. But I have no idea how, or even what I'm deciding about."

"Well, that's precisely the point, isn't it? It's not like there's some task you must accomplish that you're at a fork about. Can't you just have a wait-and-see kind of approach?"

"How, Roberta? I can either pursue this, or run from it. That's a decision. Each step is a decision."

"But pursuing it, as you say, isn't a global decision, it could be a series of small steps in which you can stop at any time."

"Yes, of course. But in reality, I think taking the next couple of steps will be tantamount to a more global decision. At least in certain respects."

"Like?" Roberta asks perplexed.

"Well, my marriage, for one. Even meekly inquiring into another relationship does make a rather strong comment on how I view my marriage."

"Does it have to?"

"Yes."

"Then you've got yourself sort of boxed in, don't you? Why not concentrate on loosening things up?"

"Because, 'Berta dear, in my mind I've already gone further than I admit. It was happening before I met Peg. I'm not saying she's a vehicle, but I think that things have been moving around for a while.

"Peg seems quite unique. It's like she was the missing piece."

"She is unique. So, don't joke around with her."

"Territorial with your friends, eh? She strikes me as someone who can take care of herself. Probably better than most."

"There's a tone in your voice I recognize, Maria. Even though I can't see you, the sparks are palpable. Funny how the world works. You're going to be the one of us to end up with a woman, and me a man, of all things. I guess the laws of physics *are* false!"

"Hey," Maria says jokingly, breaking her mood, "don't seal my fate so quickly. I may really surprise you and leave things the way they are after all this.

"Speaking of you, 'Berta dear, how are you doing?"

"I have less of an idea than when we last spoke. I got myself in shape mentally, rehearsed, and confronted him. Calmly, with logic and reasoning, I set out the situation as I see it."

"And?"

"Ffft—he just agreed. Again. Said he loved me, that our relationship is the most important thing to him. That he was going to get moving. He set up an appointment to talk business with his wife. The whole time the evening they were supposed to talk, I found myself really sweating it. I was nervous, anxious, elated. I couldn't concentrate on anything else. And then he didn't call me. I thought I was going to burst.

"When we spoke the next morning and I asked how it went, he told me calmly that they didn't get a chance to talk because they spent the time having a petty argument over bullshit."

"Huh?"

"Yup. Yup. They argued over whether to go view a broken down piece of junk piano that someone was giving away free."

"Oh, god!"

"You got that right. And then he blamed her. *She* started it, *she* wouldn't stop. She, she, she. Again.

"So I explained to him, you know, elementary stuff, like how, from my point of view, inaction is a form of action and a choice. That if he got caught up in her crap, don't blame her. I was a wreck, though. It was like someone came and drained all my blood. And like an idiot, I had spent the night worrying for him."

"Letdown number what, Roberta?"

"I don't know, but I think I should take this as my exit cue."

"Will you?"

"I *should*. I just don't know if I can. Maybe. It would definitely be by the brute force method. For all of this, I love him too much. Love is a ridiculous word in this case. It's like saying 'blue' when I mean cobalt.

"But, it's like there are two of him. The one I know, and this other limp flower he describes through his behavior and inaction.

It is very, very confusing, I don't know which to look at. I don't know which to count. So, that's where my story stands at the moment. Fortunately, I am working along all right. Otherwise I'd be institutionalizable right now, I'm sure."

"'Berta, I'm really sorry. I'd hope for more for you. Maybe you should just take a break from each other. Give him some time to clarify his situation, and you a little distance."

"Yeah, it's what I said to him. The problem is I don't want distance from him. I can't tolerate it. Neither can he. I think he lets our time together override and erase his marriage, so he doesn't get anything accomplished. We said we'd try a week of silence and broke it the next day. It was like we could each breathe again."

"At this rate then, you two are stuck in this position for the long run, sounds like."

"I hope not," Roberta says despondently.

"'Berta, I've got to go. Please, next time let's really try to talk in person."

"Great. I'm all for it. Bye, Maria."

Having hung up, Maria turns to the folders on her desk and tries to refocus her mind.

At the front of the file is the Living Dolls' most recent poster, a report card for the galleries. Frank Errigon was pointedly left off the list. He thinks it's because they're designing a special one just about him next. This thought alone has him sweating it out in a panic. Frank now emphatically wants to offer a settlement in exchange for the Living Dolls dropping both the legal suit and the heat focused on him. Maria's not so sure that's the best move. At their meeting they'll have to reach a decision.

Thanksgiving Day at Maria's apartment, Jackie is trying to shut out the commotion going on around her in order to study. Ben is making his special spiced cranberry sauce in a huge soup kettle while Bessy and Ricky assist him by sucking on cinnamon sticks at the kitchen counter.

Ben is loudly reminding himself of the recipe he devised years ago when Bessy says: "Dad, could I have some cocoa?"

"Do we have marshmallows?" Ricky asks. "I want a cocoa too, with marshmallows!"

Ben is engrossed in his concoction and doesn't hear the kids' requests until their second utterance.

"Cocoa? Yeah, sure. Just let me get through this tricky part and then I'll make you some." All the while, Ben is shaking assorted powders into the pot and stirring methodically. The aroma of cooking cranberries and cinnamon permeates the whole apartment.

First Ricky, then Bessy, becomes impatient waiting for some action on their demands. After a few minutes, they signal each other and get up to make the cocoa themselves. Ben is oblivious while the kids squabble over proportions of milk to cocoa.

By the time Bessy and Ricky are resettled at the counter with melting multi-colored marshmallows in their hot drinks, Ben is finished with the cranberry sauce but has forgotten his promise. More as a rehearsal for himself, Ben recites the plans for the day to his kids. "So, once this stuff's cool enough, I'll pack it in jars. Meanwhile, we'll change and get ready to go. Then, we'll swing by D'Ambrose and pick up the pies on the way to get your mom. Then, then, then, we'll be off! Off to Grandma's and the great, stuffed turkey that's sizzling already."

Taking all this in, Bessy climbs down from her high counter chair and quickly wanders into Jackie's room. "Jackie, we're almost ready to go."

Startled, Jackie looks up from her books to see Bessy standing at her side, with a chocolate-y brown mouth and chin. "Great, sweetie. I hope you have a good time at your grandmother's while I'm here working away."

"You could come, too!" Bessy looks hopeful and puts on her best beckoning expression.

"No, Bessy, you know I really can't. I love Thanksgiving, but I've got to study. I'll be here when you get back and you can tell me all about it. I want to know how the cranberries come out, their smell is driving me nuts it's so good! Play a few rounds of cards for me with your cousins."

Bessy is disappointed but tries to weather it gracefully. "I will, Jackie. See you later."

The two hug, and Bessy goes off to change into her party dress for the event.

Downtown, Steve is smoothing a yellow tablecloth over the opened card table and wondering, as he has many times before, if they can seat seven people at it. He's excited, and loves hosting dinner parties, especially since they have the occasion to do it so rarely. He spent the last three days concocting the perfect dessert for this Thanksgiving meal. Steve also invented a new kind of stuffing this year.

Sandra and Leda are in the kitchen preparing greens for the salad. Leda is sporting a multi-colored leotard and purple tights because she has been practicing some moves from the dance class she recently began attending.

"Mom, is Kayla coming tonight or not?"

"You know she is. We bumped into her and Linda in the lobby last week and they said so. Remember?"

"Oh, yeah. So it's me, you and Dad, and Kayla, Linda and Ruth, and Jackson? That's it?"

"That's the list. Sounds like enough to me. You think we should put out some games for you and Kayla to play tonight?"

"No, Mom. I've got some other ideas."

Sandra and Steve didn't plan it, but they're both wearing blue jeans, basketball sneakers, and T-shirts with the sleeve cuffs rolled up. When Steve comes in the kitchen for cutlery, Sandra takes note of their uniforms and hopes to get a chance to change before any of their friends arrive.

At that moment, Sandra's telephone rings with surprising loudness. Sandra strains to get to the receiver before the second ring. "Hello," she says quickly with a touch of annoyance, thinking of what still remains further to do.

"Hi," comes a hesitant female voice through the line. "This is Aviva Stern, Claire's daughter. We met once a while ago."

"Oh, hello. How are you?" Sandra asks curiously but cognizant of wanting to get off as soon as possible.

"I'm fine except that I'm concerned about my mother. I'm very sorry to call you on Thanksgiving, but I'm about to go over to Claire's, and I wanted to try to get some information beforehand, if possible. My shifts at the hospital aren't conducive to having phone conversations at normal hours."

"Don't worry about it, Aviva."

Aviva continues, reassured. "Thanks. I didn't know who to call. My mother's always spoken very highly of you. It seems you two see each other frequently. Then tonight, I remembered that we'd met. So I'm hoping its okay to call you."

"Sure, Aviva. Your mother and I are fairly good friends. But what can I do for you?" Sandra says, resigning herself to the conversation.

"She seems agitated lately. Like she doesn't know what to do with herself. I'm so busy at the hospital that I feel I've lost touch with her to too great an extent. She's even come clear over to root me out while I'm still on a shift. Anyway, one of the things she's been talking a lot about is some fingers. She says there's been real, severed fingers found in SoHo, attached to some kind of posters. Is this true?"

Sandra gives an internal sigh of relief to hear that this naive young woman knows nothing of the Living Dolls, or her mother's activities in the group. "Yes, it is. In fact, I just spoke with Claire yesterday afternoon. Apparently a third finger was found. They've each had cryptic notes attached, this one just said: 'It's hopeless.'"

In the back of Sandra's mind, she is recalling her conversation with Claire. Claire had wanted to call a special meeting of the Dolls in light of the third finger, but no one was enthusiastic.

Claire was incensed. Sandra had tried to mollify her, but ultimately had to cap it in order to go pick up Leda from a play date.

"What has all this got to do with my mother?" Aviva sounds anxious now in her lack of understanding.

"I don't know, Aviva. I really don't know what to tell you." Sandra has also become concerned about Claire, but she doesn't think it appropriate to add fuel to Aviva's fire. She's can't think of anything concrete to point to, nor something practical to do.

"Well, thank you for talking to me." Aviva is dejected.

"Sorry I can't be of much help. I look forward to seeing you again. Congratulations on your M.D."

"Oh, thanks. Good bye."

They both hang up with heaviness in the air. In Sandra's apartment, at least, it dissipates quickly as she busies herself with the rest of her party preparations.

Aviva proceeds to Claire's immediately, with many jumbled thoughts about her mother swirling loose in her mind. Claire had already made the stuffing, and once Aviva arrives, the two put the finishing touches on a humongous turkey they are roasting for the homeless shelter down the street. As has been their established tradition, once they deliver the bird, the two buy the *New York Post* for the movie clock and go to a double feature, with all the trimmings of popcorn, Coke, hot dogs, and Milk Duds.

They are standing in Claire's kitchen scooping stuffing into a container. Aviva looks as though she is concentrating all her energies on the task. The kitchen has a small window which looks out over upper Broadway. A red, Chinese-lettered neon sign for a restaurant below blares in and washes half the room with its color.

"Mom, what do you say we change the routine this time? Maybe we could go out to eat and talk or something."

Claire seals the lid onto the bulging opaque plastic cylinder and doesn't respond.

Aviva pokes her with the wooden spoon and smiles. "Hey, you, dreamer. Come back to earth, it's Thanksgiving. Live it up. Let your daughter buy you dinner. Marvin Gardens, maybe?"

"Hey, Viv, what's up? You have something on your mind?"

"No," Aviva says lying. "I just thought that maybe we're getting too pat in our old age."

"Don't you start talking like that or I really will begin to feel old. If it's all right with you, I think I'd rather stick with the routine tonight. I could really use some distracting entertainment."

"The movie you picked can hardly be described that way. It looks like another depressing one."

"Well, those are the kind I like. They make me feel good. We can go out after if you want, though."

Ben, Bessy, and Ricky are cruising down Fifth Avenue packed into the car, having said their final goodbyes to Jackie, sauce and pies in the trunk. They are hoping that Maria will be ready to go when they get to her office. Ben had called her from the bakery to let her know that she should make her way to the lobby.

Miraculously from Ben's point of view, Maria is out front at the curb as the car pulls up.

"Hi, Ben, kids," Maria says in a chipper voice as she pops into the front passenger seat. "Want me to drive, Ben?"

"No, thanks, Maria. We're set. We're off in the express car to Mount Vernon. To Grandma's house we go. Hi ho the derry-o."

Ricky rolls his eyes to Bessy, and then they continue their game of blackjack in the back seat.

By the time the four pull up to the stucco house on Elm Street where Maria spent her high school years, Ricky and Bessy have begun fidgeting and bickering and Maria and Ben in the front have fallen into a relaxed silence.

Just as Ben launches his "We're here," Maria's mother appears at the front door, waving. She's not dressed for the cold, clad only in a cotton knit dress, covered by a flower print apron. She bounds down the front steps and approaches the car as the kids are piling out and Ben is delving into the trunk for the food.

"Pies from D'Ambrose, Mom. And sauce, from Ben, of course."

"You shouldn't have. What did you throw away so much money for on that fancy-schmancy bakery? Party Cake is just as good, if you weren't going to make them. Speaking of which, I bet I know where you were already today, Maria, for at least seven or ten hours."

Bessy and Ricky are inside, and Ben is passing his mother-in-law on the steps just then. She pokes him in the arm with her elbow. "Am I right, Ben? I am. I know it. What's all the silence about, you two?"

Ben pecks her on the cheek. "Happy Thanksgiving. How's Pop doing?"

Maria snorts past her mother, trying not to let her ruin Thanksgiving by going into her "you work too much" routine. Maria's heard it at least ten thousand times, and is almost immune to it. The part of it she can't ignore is the comment on her lack of mothering.

When Maria gets inside, she sees her kids already conspiring with their cousins. She hugs her father hello and passes the more comfortable living room, to make a beeline, out of reflexive habit from her adolescence, for the round kitchen table. She finds her sister Trudy has already followed the well-worn track.

As Maria plunks down into her seat, she says: "Trudy, hi. How's your trip up?"

"We came last night so there'd be no problem."

Maria feels a twinge of primitive sibling jealousy at her sister's words even though she knows in her conscious mind that she would not have wanted nor needed to sleep over.

"We're like two old horses on a beaten path ending up at this table in our designated seats," Maria says with a wry laugh trying to dispel her unease with being face to face with her older sister.

"Yeah, next we'll announce we're going out back to play and end up at the candy store. Hey! I wonder if our kids have figured that one out yet."

Maria is beginning to remember what she forgets time after time, that it takes her well into the evening to adjust to being with her family all together, especially with Trudy. At a loss for conversation, Maria brings their younger brother up. "Jack's not coming, huh?"

"From California, Maria? With an infant? You know he's not. You can't have your head that far stuck into client dossiers."

Trudy speaks in a light tone, but Maria takes offense all the same. She's never figured out how Trudy keeps a full-time job and manages to spend so much time with her family.

At this juncture, their mother comes in, turns off the oven, and lifts a huge, well browned and glistening turkey out. Trudy gets up with a "Let me help you, Mom" while Maria stays seated and silent.

"No, thanks, dear. You two sit and chat. You see each other little enough. I don't know why. Forty-five minutes from one door to the other isn't so much. After we moved here and my sisters were still in Brooklyn, we got together every week."

Trudy cuts into the commentary by declaring: "I'll scoop out the stuffing, you sit." She gets up and takes the spoon out of her mother's hand, rests it in the roasting pan, and guides her mother to a chair.

At the same time, in lower Manhattan, Sandra plops onto the couch with Jackson, Steve's old school chum from their days growing up in the Bronx. He has just arrived with a bottle of wine in hand.

"It's one of the first Beaujolais Nouveau's out this season, I hope it's good."

"Even if it isn't, I love the decorations," Sandra says in high spirits. Jackson had placed one of those colored, paper dressings for the end of turkey legs on the top and had stuck kids' Thanksgiving stickers all around the wide part of the wine bottle.

Steve comes barreling out of the kitchen sporting a white apron splattered with grease and food bits. "Jackson! Glad you could come, old buddy." The two men bear-hug and then stand back to admire each other.

"You know, Steve," Jackson says, chuckling, "we let too much time go by. I'm only over in Queens, I think we could manage more than our regular twice a year. We could build up slowly. Next year, let's try for three. You look great, though. In fact, you look the way you did in high school. I can just picture you walking out of chem lab like that, test tubes in hand, instead of that spatula."

"Chem lab, kitchen lab. Maybe it's the same thing," Sandra says.

"No, no, no. We can eat what I concoct in the kitchen, and that's the difference," Steve answers with a wide grin.

"Not always, Daddy. Remember that green thing last week? Couldn't eat that at all."

Just then the four of them hear two distinct knocks on the door and Steve goes to open it. "Well, hello, Kayla. Hi, Linda, Ruth."

"Hey, Steve, how're you doing? Been standing over a cauldron all day, I hope," Ruth says handing Steve a large bowl filled with sliced beets. Linda hands him a small jar of sauce while she kisses him hello and whispers: "Secret ingredients, don't ask for the recipe".

Leda makes a beeline for Kayla. "Want to come in my room? I've got something to show you." She takes Kayla's arm and swiftly whisks her down the hall and into her bedroom. The door shuts firmly behind them.

Observing, Sandra remarks: "That was fast work. I wonder if they'll come out for dinner."

"It's great how they get along, since we're all in the same building," Linda says.

"And, no one seems to be going anywhere too fast," Ruth says.

CHAPTER EIGHTEEN:

AT SCHOOL

THE NEXT MORNING, THE MOST heavily trafficked day in the year, Maria manages to eat breakfast with her kids before finding her way to the Errigon Gallery to meet with Frank. On the ride downtown, Maria can't get it out of her mind that Peg's apartment is just three blocks from Errigon's. By the time she hits the Spring Street station Maria has the irresistible urge to talk to Peg. On the subway platform, she finds a working pay phone and dials Peg's number, after sparring with directory assistance.

"Hi, Peg. It's Maria. I'm on my way to an appointment near you. If you're not busy, I thought I could stop by for a minute."

"Great to hear your voice, Maria. I would love it."

Three minutes later, Peg holds her apartment door open, smiling. Maria enters nervously. "Hi, Peg. Good to see you so soon again."

The two of them sit on Peg's Moderne styled couch she bought over at Depression Moderne on Sullivan. Looking for quick conversation, Maria remarks: "Not very comfortable, this couch. You could hardly curl up and read here."

Peg laughs. "I don't have time to anyway." She looks into Maria's eyes and says: "Hello, Maria."

"Listen, Peg. About the other night. I didn't really mean anything, I mean, I did, of course, but—"

Peg briefly takes Maria's hand. "I know. You're feeling a little confused."

"Yes." Maria feels as if a lingering heaviness has lifted off her chest.

"In fact, I don't want to put words in your mouth, but *very* confused, or very ambivalent, might even be more accurate."

"Yes," Maria says.

"You're intrigued, shall we say, by me."

Trying to maintain some composure, resisting the feeling that she is ten years old, Maria says: "Yes, but not the way you think. I'm a pretty settled, boring person, you know."

"Maria, this is probably too bold, but I'm going to venture to say that until the moment you arrived here, you were feeling highly charged by the other evening. And now you're confronting the actual, living and breathing me and you find that I'm still a woman. Another man would rattle your existence enough, but *this* is unfathomable."

A slow "yes" comes quietly out of Maria's mouth. She pauses for a few moments before asking: "How did you know?"

After taking a deep breath, Peg responds. "Because. Because I don't think the kind of energy, shall I say, that I'm feeling between us could only go one way. From my perspective it became intense very quickly. And because, although not in the same way, I've been there, as the saying goes."

"Energy. That's an excellent word! I've expended a good deal of it thinking about you. I just don't have anywhere for it to go."

Peg takes Maria's hand as she says: "Except here." With that she tries to put her arms around Maria's shoulders for a light hug.

Maria retracts her body with a pained expression on her face.

Peg returns to her original position. "I probably should keep my mouth shut, but I can't. Apart from the fact that you've fashioned your adult life to date around a traditional family, you've got another dimension that I didn't, I suspect." Peg stops talking abruptly.

"What is that?"

"I don't like this role I'm putting myself in of purported knower, but it seems to me that you haven't accepted yourself much. You don't seem to embrace either your being or your female identity. Looking at me, you're forced to in an immediate kind of way that you're perhaps not ready for. Nothing has prepared you for it. You know, nothing in my life has prepared me for feeling what I'm feeling about you right now."

Maria is excruciatingly uncomfortable, as if she's onstage with no words. She just says: "I do need to go to my appointment, Peg. I shouldn't have come to breeze out."

Rising off the sofa, Peg says: "I'm glad you did."

"You are?"

Peg looks directly into Maria's eyes. "Yes, I am."

Maria gets up and reaches for her coat silently. She turns to face Peg, and slowly reaches a hand out to Peg's shoulder, and then hesitates. Peg assists by moving closer so that Maria's hand reaches over her shoulder. The two of them hug for a few seconds before Maria pulls away.

"Peg. I can't. I mean, I just don't know how to—"

"Shh," Peg whispers as she regains their embrace. "Touching you is like playing with electricity, Maria. You must feel this also."

Standing awkwardly Maria barely utters: "I do." And then: "I really must go, Peg."

Maria thrusts herself out of doors, into the cold air, and tries to re-balance. She tries to fit herself back into her old, usual frame of mind, but the attempt is as fruitless as trying to put an appliance back into its original packaging. Yet, somehow, in transit to a familiar world a scant ten minutes later, Maria is composed and ensconced in Frank's office.

"Frank, I'm your lawyer. I'm the one with the experience in these matters. As you know, I think we should lay low and let them play out before we make a move. You haven't been hurt yet, just a little embarrassed."

"A little embarrassed! How about humiliated? Wiped out? Chapter Eleven even! And experience? What experience? This case is unique and you know it." Frank waves his arms as he speaks.

"An important question is, where are the Dolls getting their information? I mean it does look like they are zeroing in on you, I'm beginning to agree with you. How did they get records of your sales with clients' names?"

"Kim's the only one who's been around here consistently. I guess it's got to be her. I find it hard to believe though. She seems too sweet and, I thought, happy here. Why would she do this to me?"

"Well, the Dolls do claim they have spies everywhere. You never know, it could be at least partly true. In fact, they could've picked you to hit because they had Kim on board. We need to find out. When does she get in today?"

"She should be here momentarily." As Frank is saying this they both hear the door to the gallery open and close.

"Frank, you talk to her now, out there, and I'm going to make a phone call from your desk."

Alone in the office, Maria dials her own telephone number.

"Hello? Jacobs'."

"Jackie, it's me, Maria. What's going on? You're not pregnant are you?" Maria can't stop herself, having held a potential fiasco with Jackie at the back of her mind since she read the note yesterday.

"Me? No, hardly. Too far from it, in fact." Jackie chuckles as she speaks. "But listen Maria, this is serious. You know my rape prevention class?" Jackie pauses.

"You know I know it. What's up, Jackie? I'm at a meeting and I don't have time to play Twenty Questions! Out with it."

Back to cat and mouse, Jackie once again plays it calm against Maria's hysteria.

"Well, you were right," she says with nonchalant ease. "Norris, the teacher, has been putting the moves on his students. Moves called rape and sodomy, to be precise. He picks the younger ones and gives them free private lessons, so-called. Once they're there he rapes them, telling them they have to get used to having their bodies, particularly the sexual parts of their bodies, manipulated in order to learn to defend themselves."

"That's gruesome, Jackie, but what's this got to do with you, or me? I mean, you'll drop the class now, obviously. Finally. It was only making your knees hurt anyway."

"Well, a bunch of us have gotten together to plan strategy to put him behind bars. So the first step we figure is advice from a lawyer. That's you. Hence my note."

Maria stops listening with full attention and starts to half-daydream as soon as she assesses that Jackie isn't in any sort of trouble at all.

"Maria, are you there? Hello?"

"Huh? Oh, sorry, Jackie. You know that sexual assault isn't my field so I won't really be able to help your friends. Why don't you call the NYU Law Clinic? They're good at this sort of case."

Deflated, Jackie is virtually pleading and doesn't like the feel of it: "Can't anyone in your firm help us? Or can't you recommend someone you know? I mean, really Maria, these girls don't have any money to pay for a big case. With your recommendation maybe they could get someone pro bono?"

"That's asking a lot for such a small case, Jackie. I'll think about it. I have to go now. Bye." She hangs up without waiting for a response.

Jackie holds the buzzing receiver on her end and feels both flattened and furious. She has a physical sensation that she has a heavy metal slab leaning on her body. She has an image of flicking her arms and springing the slab off of herself, releasing it to fly through the air on a wide trajectory, thumping to the ground a good distance off. Jackie privately resolves to get back, not only at the rapist, but at Maria too.

Frank almost shuffles back into his office looking despondent. With a flap of his hands he says: "I don't know. Maybe, maybe not. I tried to be subtle, but I think it backfired. She acted as if she couldn't believe what I was asking her. But if she did it, she would have rehearsed these answers long ago. She's a bit inscrutable, you know."

"Hmm." Maria taps on his desk. "It might have been a mistake to tip our hand to her, to let them know just how ignorant we are."

On the other side of the office wall, Kim is seething. She has had it lately with all the tension in the gallery and all the wild goose chases she is sent on over nothing. Just because of the Living Dolls. Who cares about them anyway?

"Well." She sits tapping her thumb and index finger with chewed off nails against her Vladimir Kagan desk. "Maybe I do. Maybe they have a point in picking out Errigon to sue. He is a pig if he could accuse me like that. The creep."

As she mumbles, Kim pushes her black hair to one side and takes out a sheet of blank paper, looks at it, puts it back. She then takes out some gallery letterhead. She rolls a piece through the typewriter and composes:

> **Dear Living Dolls:**
> **Keep up the good work, you've got him where**
> **you want him.**
> **Best wishes,**
>
> **Your new friend**

Kim types their address, which she knows too well from staring at their posters, on an envelope and puts the folded letter inside. She stamps it, and walks straight out the door to a mailbox.

Uptown, Jackie is still smoldering at Maria and finishes the breakfast dishes and heads for her room to get dressed.

"Hi, Bessy. What's up?" Jackie chirps from the hallway at Bessy's bedroom door, managing to alter her mood for Bessy's sake.

"I'm writing," Bessy says earnestly. She's sitting in a corner of her room on a little mat with her stuffed pony, Greta, at her side and a pad of paper on her lap, pencil in hand.

"Wow! That's terrific. Is it for school?"

"No. It's a poem, but I can't think of the rhymes."

"Can I read it?" With this Jackie approaches Bessy and catches a glimpse of the first two lines:

> *Maria, my mother*
> *doesn't know to bother*

"No. I mean, maybe, when I'm done." Bessy puts her hand over the page as she speaks.

"Okay. I'm going to get dressed now. See you later."

Bessy scraps her poem and goes over to a baby doll on the other side of the room.

"Hello, my baby. It's time for your breakfast. I'm going to feed you in eensy-weensy bites, just the right size for your mouth."

Bessy picks up the doll and cradles it in her left arm, while feeding her from a pretend spoon in her right hand. She wipes the doll's mouth saying "all done" in a sing-song tone and gives her a kiss on the cheek.

"It's time to get you dressed, and then we can play all day long together." Suddenly, Bessy's eyes sparkle and she adds excitedly: "Maybe we can even take you to the park!"

Bessy pops up and scampers into Jackie's room, doll in tow. Tugging on the purple shirt Jackie has just slipped over her head, she asks breathlessly: "Can I take my baby to the park today Jackie? Ple-ase!"

"Oh, I don't know, sweetie. Ricky would have to come with us, and it could only be for a little bit because you're going to the movies with your daddy today, remember?"

"I don't want Ricky to come. I want to go alone with my doll and you. Maybe Ricky can go to the movies and we could go to the park?"

Jackie bends down on one knee to Bessy's eye level now that she's done dressing. "Maybe we could go to the boat pond and Ricky could play with his new boat in the water while we have a tea party with your doll. How's that sound?"

"Okay," Bessy answers hesitantly unsure if she's being tricked into something she doesn't want.

"Ricky!" Jackie calls, "Get ready. Pack your boat, we're going to the park until show time."

Ricky sticks his head out of his room. "Can I bring two boats? My new one and the small sail boat?"

"Sure, just keep track of them. Both of you get ready while I pack a snack for us."

About twenty minutes after they leave, Ben comes home to surprise the kids with lunch out before the movies.

"Hmm." He looks around into the silence, deflated. "Well, if they come home soon we can still make it."

As Ben mutters this under his breath he's mechanically walking over to the bar. He puts some ice in a glass and begins to pour out some scotch when he catches himself.

"No, this is ridiculous, it isn't even noon."

He throws the contents of the glass into the sink. He walks toward the kitchen, gets about two-thirds of the way there, stops, turns around and seats himself on a couch in the living room and stares out the window a while. All of a sudden he gets up energetically and goes over to the telephone and dials.

After several attempts, Ben finally gets through to Maria's office. "Hi, Sharon, it's Ben. Can I speak to my wife?" Ben almost hums into the phone.

"She's on another line, but she should be off in a minute. Will you hold?"

"Sure." He remains upbeat and optimistic.

Maria is in her office, taking fifteen minutes out to arrange a few events for herself for the week. She is on the telephone scheduling a haircut and coloring session for the end of the week, as she's making notes in the evening slots in her appointment book. Under next Friday, she enters: Call Peg, and then she scratches it out, knowing she doesn't need to be reminded of that.

She's sewing with Bessy on Tuesday: Bessy: sewing, getting a massage after work Wednesday: Shantara: 8 pm and is planning on working out at the gym at least three of the days: GYM, GYM, GYM. Suddenly, Maria puts her pen down and steps outside her frenzied planning to notice how hollow she feels. As the impact wafts through Maria's core, her intercom buzzes afresh.

Through all of this, Ben is still on hold. At first he waits almost cheerfully. Then, after about three minutes he begins to become impatient, and after a few more he's tapping on the chair between his spread legs.

At her desk, trying to assimilate her self-revelation, Maria reluctantly puts an incoming call on hold. It's Ben's call she picks up.

"Ben? Is everything okay? I thought you'd be at the movies by now." Maria is functioning on overload and is apprehensive about what this call will bring.

"No, it's not time yet and Jackie's flown the coop with the kids anyway. No note, so I guess they'll be back soon." Ben is trying to sound lighthearted.

"Oh. So, what's up?" Maria has more than a touch of wary indifference in her voice. She wants to be alone with her thoughts for a little longer. She knows that something important is shifting in her psyche.

"Well, I thought, it's a nice day, why not take the kids to lunch first and then the movies." He pauses.

"And?" By now, Maria knows where the conversation is headed.

"I thought it would be great if the four of us could go together. How about it, Maria? It'll be fun." Ben tries not to plead. In spite of himself, he says: "Remember, in our last session we agreed to try more family outings, Maria. This is a good opportunity."

"Ben, not that again," she responds agitated. "Anyway, you know how much work I have. I can't."

"But you can. It'll be okay. Work tomorrow. Work this evening. Come on, we'll have a good time."

"I may work tonight and tomorrow in any case, I'm swamped here. Sorry, Ben, it's just out of the question today."

"Maria," he says angrily, "how much longer is this going to go on?"

"Ben, please, I can't stay on the line blabbing with you. I have several important cases to attend today." Maria toys with the idea of speaking more softly, but doesn't do it.

With anger now rapidly turning to bitterness, Ben answers: "Of course. Okay. Whatever. See you when I see you." He hangs up the phone slowly enough to hear Maria's phone click by the time his receiver was back on the phone base, without her even having said goodbye.

"All efficiency, that woman."

Silence falls around Maria as she revels in a new sensation coursing through her body, having already forgotten her jousting match with Ben. She utters a few random words out into the open space of her office. She hears the difference. The words move from the inside out. Not vice versa. She knows that her gaze is different also. That when she looks, it is seeing from inside out, not a kind of vision that seeks her own reflection from an external point. Maria knows that she is transforming into an integrated person. That she will no longer move about in the world feeling that constant, yet indeterminate, lack. She feels herself, as if it emanates from the lower center of the trunk of her body, lodged there as a fixture.

Maria's fatigue lifts. In its place, she meets a sensation of amazement and relief. She walks over to the decorative antique mirror hanging on the opposite wall and stares straight into it. For once, she just looks, without wincing, without picking out flaws in her visage. She looks herself in the eye and smiles.

CHAPTER NINETEEN:

IN PLAIN SIGHT

AT THE SAME TIME THAT Maria is staring straight-on at herself, Claire hurriedly leaves her studio on Sullivan Street. She turns the corner at Prince, oblivious to the crowd huddled at the sidewalk service window of the pizzeria. She wades through swarms of people, some on in-line skates, eating pizza and smoking cigarettes. Walking at a fast pace, Claire is breathing heavily and sweat beads form above her lip. Pedestrians begin to step out of her way by the time she crosses Wooster Street a few blocks down. She looks like a powerhouse rolling down the street with her strong arms pumping back and forth to the rhythm of her step. Her blue Sears overalls splattered with clay lend to her imposing image on the slick streets of SoHo. Wooden and wire tools jut out from Claire's upper pockets. As she passes the packed Dean and Deluca Cafe, eyes follow her down the block.

The street becomes increasingly grimier as the SoHo galleries recede and the borders of Little Italy and Chinatown approach. Claire continues past an Italian men's club with a blackened storefront and three men sitting on chairs, each with demitasse cups in their hands. The men nod to each other silently as Claire storms past. The smells on her journey alternate between rancid grease, coffee, garbage, and cat litter as Claire nears her destination.

Still on her march down Prince Street and panting, Claire reaches Mulberry Street and steps up the three outer cracked, marble stairs of the corner building at once to reach the intercom system. Her finger immediately goes for the button of 3-A of this six story walk-up tenement.

"Hello. Hello, who's there?" a voice crackles through the grated circle next to the buttons. It is Karen.

"It's Claire, buzz me in," Claire says. She is already pushing on the door handle when the catch is released with a grating sound. She rushes past an elderly Italian woman holding a rickety walker and struggling with her mailbox, and practically runs up the three flights of stairs in one leap. She resembles a quarterback on a college team working out by running up the bleachers at the stadium.

Intrigued by the surprise visitor, Karen unbolts and throws open her metal apartment door while Claire has a flight to go.

"Claire, what brings you to this edge of town?" Karen says cheerfully. Her face changes to concern as she notes the look of prickly needles in Claire's eyes.

"Karen, we've got to talk," Claire blurts, breathing heavily.

Karen ushers Claire inside her small apartment without another word and gets her seated with a glass of water before she asks: "Is your daughter, Aviva, all right?"

Claire nods while she's catching her breath and sipping. Sweat is pouring down the sides of her face. She takes in Karen's apartment as if seeing it for the first time. There are wedge-shaped door stops pitched into the left side of all the furniture and lamps. The floor tilts so steeply that, otherwise, everything would gravitate to the downhill walls. Hanging here and there about the main room of the four-room railroad apartment are awards Karen has won for her painting, and photographs of some of her better shows. The unmistakable smell of an old, unkempt apartment building wafts in the windows from the air shaft.

Relaxed and slumped, Claire looks as though she is in a stupor.

"Talk to me, Claire. If it's not Aviva, what is it?"

Slowly, Claire looks up at Karen who is standing over her with a worried expression on her face. She casts her gaze down again and holds her silence a moment longer. "I can't do it anymore," finally comes out in a halting voice with choked words.

Karen waits to see if more is to come before she pulls a chair up next to Claire and takes her hand. "Honey, I've seen you depressed before, I've seen you dejected, but this takes the cake. What, are we going to law school or medical school or business school again? I'll apply with you, but you know we'll withdraw the applications before a week's out. Or are you discovering computers this time? A little passé, but anything for an ounce of respectability, eh?"

Claire cracks a weak smile.

"Let me trash your water and I'll make us some hot toddies. What do you say?" Karen moves to take Claire's glass.

"No," Claire says harshly, like an explosion. "Any alcohol and I'll completely crack. Have any herbal tea?"

"Cinnamon rose, and peppermint. Either of those okay?"

"Yeah, great. Peppermint. I can make it." Claire rises and goes into the kitchen. She's fumbling with getting the gas range top lit by turning one gas jet on after another, waiting while unlighted gas spews out long enough that the entire room smells highly flammable and noxious. Karen enters with wooden matches and turns all the jets off. She waits a few moments, goes to open every window in the adjacent room, there being none in the kitchen, before lighting a flame with her matches. Claire stands stark still, watching the blue-orange flame, as one might, mesmerized at a camp fire.

Observing her friend, Karen fills a kettle with water and sets it on the stove. Claire makes no move to reseat herself, and remains in place gazing with a tense daze in her eyes. Karen watches her watching the flame as the water heats to a boil. Both women remain locked in their stance as the kettle begins to buzz and then, finally, shriek with the mounting steam pressure inside. Claire blinks as if she has a facial tic, which causes Karen to awaken to the noise. Karen pours water into two mugs and plops a tea bag in each.

"Sugar, Claire?"

Karen receives no response.

"I don't remember how you take your tea." With still no response, Karen pushes on trying to remain sympathetic and concerned, rather than annoyed. "Okay, let's bring our cups inside, and I'll pull out all the options." She nudges Claire with her shoulder while holding a mug in each hand. "Come on, sweetie. Let's go. We'll sit and maybe I'll find out what's doing."

Both of them resettled in their seats, steaming tea mugs in hand, Karen asks: "So, now, maybe you can tell me what this is about?"

After more silence, Claire's face looks as though she's trying to express something and keep herself contained at the same time. "I just can't take the whole thing anymore."

Claire reverts to silence, and Karen waits.

"The up and down of it."

Silence again, and Claire breaks out into a visible sweat.

"A little success, and I think, great, now things'll happen. And they don't."

Claire's speech alternates from rapid to snail-pace slow, down to virtually four words per minute. Karen feels like she wants to jump out of her skin in frustration.

"I mean, you know, I've done pretty well. But I've got this vagina that seems to be a brand of some sort. Like the title 'persons of color,' I'm a person-with-vagina. Like that defines something. And I really hate the victimology side of feminism, but sometimes it's true."

Claire rises, spilling hot tea on her knee without flinching. She walks about the perimeter of the room as if in a trance. Then stops in a corner. "I don't know. The Swanson affair got to me. He was a nobody. He's murdered, and he's somebody. A great artist somebody. But he wasn't great." Claire's voice rises to a pitch and then trails off. "I don't know. I'm just worn down."

Karen stays stone-still in her chair but feels like squirming and fidgeting. She knows she has no answer to Claire's funk. What she's saying is all too true, but doesn't seem to warrant this sudden and severe agitation. Karen knows that Claire knows that none of this is news. Trying a new tack, Karen says: "What do you say you let me cheer you up with an outing? Dinner? Dancing?"

Claire responds while reseating herself in measured, careful motions, "With what riches that you've mustered without my knowing? No, thanks, Karen. Sweet offer, though." Claire's voice doesn't sound like she believes it to be a sweet suggestion.

As if switching to another foot, Karen tries a different strategy. "Well, that's what the Living Dolls are all about, isn't it? That's why we spend a good deal of time plotting, meeting, planning, and pasting. It's our way of empowering ourselves individually and collectively. And it's working. We're going to be in *Vogue* magazine, of all places!"

"Whoopie, co-opted before we're even finished." Claire's voice is grim and sarcastic. "Wonderful. And, great, we get to spend the meager hours we all have in between shit jobs banging our heads against iron gates that won't let us in. Ever."

Claire is silent again. This time her eyes fix on and bring slowly into focus the awards of artistic achievement Karen has received that are hanging in front of her. Inaudibly she mumbles a few words, very slowly.

"What, Claire? You're not coherent now. Maybe you should go home and get some rest." Karen rises hoping Claire will follow suit and leave.

"I said, you'd be perfect." Claire's words come out like a revelation, in measured intervals. She's still staring at the wall as she speaks.

Sensing the gravity without grasping it, Karen sits back down as if obediently following a command. She's got an eerie feeling prickling her spine now. Intuitively she knows to wait quietly even though she feels like bolting to get help for Claire. Running through her mind is the simple question of which emergency room to take her to. She settles on Saint Vincent's for its relative proximity but also because one doesn't always need to wait hours there. Maybe they'll get lucky there. The last time, they waited forever at Beth Israel.

"It would be a kind of test," Claire says, speaking aloud to herself, as if figuring out the steps of a construction project. "On the one hand, we have Swanson who became an overnight success, made it into every corner of the media. On the other hand, we'd have you. Just to see. In contrast to Swanson, you've actually been successful while living. But you're female.

"We'd see how much attention the whole thing would get. The fingers weren't really a good test. No one cared. No one even noticed that they were female fingers." Claire wipes her sweaty brow with the back of her hand. As the hand begins to fall back to its resting place on her lap, it bumps into a wooden knob jutting out from her bib pocket. The hand, almost disembodied from Claire's volition, grabs the knob and pulls out the ceramic tool. It is a nylon cord of about sixteen inches with wooden handles at either end. Claire uses it to cut her sculptures away from the plaster bats she works on. Tool in hand, the hand continues its descent to Claire's lap.

Anxiety is welling up in Karen in equal proportion to the undercurrent of agitation in Claire's stupefied facade. Karen rises once again, this time with more determination. "Come, Claire. Let's go for a walk. We could both use the air." She's still thinking of maneuvering them both over to the hospital.

To Karen's surprise, Claire rises as well, looking docile. She now has both hands limply holding the ceramic tool and she moves toward the door without a sound. Just as Karen reaches to unbolt the top lock, Claire rapidly wraps the cord around Karen's neck from behind and pulls with a swift slicing action.

At the same moment, Aviva looks up from her late night shift of rounds at Beth Israel Hospital with alarming recognition.

a sudden flash, she pieces together some of her mother's visits to her in the hospital with the posted fingers. Aviva drops her next patient's chart and quickly leaves the room.

Karen's body bounces to the floor and has a final spasm as it hits the rough wood planks. Her head falls faster with a thud. Because of their relative positions, none of the splattering blood lands on Claire.

"Now we'll see, Karen. Now we'll know. We had to find out." Claire's profuse sweating has stopped. She is standing stark still [h]ave her mouth, bending over Karen's head with her arms crooked [a]t an angle. "Finally there's an end to the doubt. All the years of [su]ffering, of wondering. Of walking around slumped. Being invis- [ible] in a visible world. How many times have I had to wear heavy [jew]elry to make sure I'm here? That I'm real. Well, no more. How [man]y times have I bumped and banged against that wall they [said] isn't there and thought it was my own failing? That it was [re]al.

[H]ow often have I wished that at least it was personal? That [if it were] personal, I'd be a person. And that's a start. I rarely had [that opti]on. We rarely had that option, Karen. But you're the lucky [one]. You can stop now. You're done. I'll let you know what

[Claire] winds her now bloody tool into a ball, tucks it back [in her over]all pocket and wipes her hands on her pant legs. She [leaves the apar]tment and calmly walks back down the three flights, [feeling as though] a great burden has just been lifted from her being. [Outside, on the] Street, Claire confronts the still darkness of the [night and] a dampness hanging in the air. No one is out and [nothing is] aire. She strolls home with a vague hum emanat- [ing out] of her mouth.

CHAPTER TWENTY:

AT PLAY

TUESDAY EVENING, STILL IN HER office, Maria decides to take a break from her work to read the untouched *New York Times* that was left in her office at six that morning. She walks to the coffee room, only to find both pots empty.

"Damn," Maria mutters under her breath. She shrugs. "Well, I guess I don't really need it. I can't schlep up to the cafeteria—I don't have *that* much time."

She trots back to her office and plops herself on the couch. She spreads out the paper on the coffee table in front of her. Impatient and annoyed at herself for taking a break at all, she whizzes through the paper, only reading what is of utmost interest to her. She moves the quickest through the Metro section, almost missing a small article tucked in the lower corner of one of the end pages.

Painter Slain
Karen Apfelbaum, 43, was found dead in her apartment Monday afternoon. The superintendent of her apartment building on Prince Street found her partially decomposed and garroted body near …

Maria's knuckles blanch as she reads through the article. "Could there be …? Karen Apfelbaum, I don't think I know that name. It could be a mere coincidence. People *are* murdered in this city. And *garroted*? That's not what happened to Swanson.

"Wouldn't it say if she were missing fingers?

"Damn! I need to get a hold of the Coroner, now!"

Maria paces her office frenetically, throwing questions and remarks at herself. She stops near her desk. "I've got to find out what Frank knows about this painter." She juts a finger towards the telephone hook button and pushes it. As the dial tone blares, Maria exclaims: "And what his connection to her is!"

Her mind buzzes as she reconsiders. Picturing Frank's hysterics, Maria resolves to hold that call until she knows more. Instead, she punches in Roberta's number. Roberta's outgoing message and beep come through the office speakerphone, loud and agitated. Maria disconnects without leaving a message. She quickly pushes the hook button once again and then punches in simply the number two key.

A "Hello?" comes through the speaker.

"Peg? I'm so glad you're home. What a miracle!"

"Maria." Peg has alarm in her voice "You okay?"

"Yes. Yes. I'm fine," Maria responds automatically. "No! I mean, I'm not at all fine. Can I come over, now?" Maria asks more as a statement than a question.

"Get here as soon as you can." As Peg says this she glances around her apartment, mortified by the mess and clutter she has accumulated. She calculates that in the time it will take Maria to get there, she can fix most of it.

Half an hour later, as Peg is preparing a platter of finger food, wondering if it'll be appropriate to the occasion, her apartment buzzer sounds. Virtually no sooner than she's released her finger from the lobby button, Maria is at her apartment threshold.

"Peg, I'm really sorry. I'm not sure what's possessed me to ge in on you like this. I just—I just don't know what to do. I 'd to talk to someone."

2

Calm, Peg says: "I'm someone. Come in, Maria. Don't apologize any further." She gestures to the couch. "Sit, please."

Maria sits awkwardly as if out of sync with her body.

"Well, you *could* take off your coat, first. Stay a few minutes." Peg smiles as she speaks.

As she's sliding out of her coat, Maria asks: "Peg, did you see the paper today?"

"The *Times*? Yes, sure."

"Then you saw that another artist was killed? In her apartment, just like Swanson." Maria's breathe is irregular as she speaks. She chokes out the words as if it were her own neck that was sliced off.

"Not really, Maria. Not *just* like Swanson. The method was different, I'm sure a lot of things were different." Peg pauses. "Maria, do you know more than was in that little article? Otherwise, I don't understand hitting the panic button now."

"No, that's it. It got through to me, I guess, that I might be out of my league here. Maybe Frank's correct that all of the SoHo incidents—the murders, the fingers—" Maria rubs her left index and middle fingers and then brushes past her mole as if for reassurance. "The posters—they all tie together."

Maria stops to take in the white oatmeal colors of her surroundings. She observes the impersonal tone of Peg's living room, the not-too-comfortable couch, the glass and chrome coffee table with the untouched metal food platter Peg stocked for them, and she feels an urge to flee it to a safe haven.

"Where's your bathroom, Peg?" Maria gasps out the words.

Taken aback by the urgency, Peg reflects and then responds: "Use the one through that door there, inside it's the second door on the left. The first is a closet." Peg gets up and leads Maria to the door with her pointed finger.

Maria passes through the door to be stunned by the contra of decor in what turns out to be Peg's bedroom. Centered on t back wall is a large mattress and box spring which sit on a c peted platform. The carpet is in burgundies, sea-purples, and e greens, and continues across the floor. The entire room is lush d womb-like, outfitted with Mediterranean reds, burnt oranges, and earth tones. The light is muted, and there are heavy drapes in folds and tiebacks along the wall adjacent to the bed. Above the bed is a richly colored, wool hanging. Pillows of different shapes and textured coverings line the head of the bed and spill out onto the floor. The room has the feel of a warm, slow organism.

Maria is in sensory overload, and stumbles, her mind reeling, into the bathroom. Not actually needing to use the toilet, Maria washes her hands in the tepid water that emerges from the cold tap and then sprinkles her temples and neck to rouse herself. She slowly emerges from the bathroom to find Peg seated on the edge of her bed, both hands sinking into a woven throw behind her.

A surge of terror passes over Maria's face, and then her visage relaxes. The two women reflect each other's gaze as if sharing one set of sight beams. Gaze intact, Peg rises to move toward Maria. They kiss, and then embrace and kiss. They lock hands and move together toward the bed. At first they sit on the bed, side by side, and turn to face each other, twisted at the waist and torso, to kiss. Peg, arms around Maria's back, pulls her in closer, and down, so that Peg is underneath with their lower legs dangling off the bed. Peg's hands slide down to Maria's buttocks and she rolls the two of them as a unit so that now it is Peg on top. As Peg unbuttons Maria's blouse, she kisses every new inch of flesh as it becomes exposed. They undress each other, slowly, kissing and caressing each other. By the time they are both naked, their bodies are prepared and bursting with sexual energy.

Maria lies on top of Peg and kisses her, their breasts kissing as are their bellies, vulvas, thighs. Maria turns Peg on her back, kissing her mouth with a hot, wet tongue moving and exploring the possibilities of oral sensation. Maria places a hand on Peg's belly and applies circular pressure. At the same time, she moves her mouth to Peg's breasts and licks them, from the underside up to the nipple, around the bottom and across the areole. Maria's body is heated and moist. It is as if she is finally utilizing decades of stored sexual energy. Peg lets out a groan of mounting pressure.

Maria places a hand on Peg's vulva and sighs a sigh of excitement and bodily tension. As Maria's mouth finds its way to Peg's clitoris and envelopes it, her fingers penetrate Peg's body every which way they can, in her vagina, her anus, and simultaneously, as Maria's sucking becomes rhythmic and wet. Peg's clitoris expands and vibrates until she reaches a point of saturation and her vaginal walls pulse and contract. Maria slows until Peg whispers: "Don't stop." Maria brings Peg to another climax and a third, each with mounting intensity until Peg pulls Maria up to her embrace.

As they lie together, Maria reflects on the sounds that she has never before this day heard emanate from her own body. She realizes that, until this moment, she has not experienced a genuinely pleasurable, mutual, and love-filled sexual encounter. Feeling vertigo over her past, Maria's mind wanders over diverse, nonspecific thoughts. Reluctantly, Maria eventually rises to dress and go home.

On Wednesday morning in the art room, Sandra is in a chipper mood. Standing near the sunlight-drenched, black-barred, school windows, she speaks crisply. "Class, we're lucky again. Today we're going to have a model pose for us, so get your sketch pads ready."

Bessy is beaming as she removes her tools from the boxes on the shelves and hoists down an oversized newsprint pad bearing her name. This is her favorite class. She loves to watch Sandra, that's the best part. In fact, Bessy loves Sandra. She has a running story in her head in which Sandra is her real mother and takes care of her much the same way Bessy treats her favorite doll.

The class is working away with their sketching pencils. Sandra paces slowly around the room commenting on sketches, occasionally stopping to demonstrate a way of drawing a curve or shading.

The room is usually quiet when they have a model, but now it is stone silent.

The room is so quiet that when Isabel from the office downstairs makes a faint knocking noise at the classroom door, everyone, including the model, jumps. Sandra walks over to the door and steps outside for a moment, long enough for Isabel to hand her a telephone message marked *URGENT*, but sufficient for Bessy to furrow her brow and conclude that something terrible is happening to Sandra. She scrutinizes Sandra's expression as she reads the pink slip of memo pad paper. Finally, after Bessy sees a fleeting smile cross Sandra's face, she relaxes.

Sandra has to read the note a second time to make sure she has seen correctly.

MEETING ON THIS EVENING WITH FRANK, 5 PM SHARP!

The Living Dolls had shot for next week, but Frank Errigon was so crazed that Maria pushed the meeting forward. Sandra glances nervously at her watch trying to figure out how she is going to retrieve Leda from school, bring her home, make sure Steve is there on time, and get to the meeting all by five o'clock.

"It's definitely impossible," Sandra whispers to herself. "He's just going to have to get Leda himself for once."

As soon as the class ends, Sandra runs to the office phone and dials Steve's bakery.

"But Sandra, I can't keep leaving early for your cockamamie meetings, I have work to do!"

"What do you mean 'keep leaving'? When have I ever asked you to before?"

"Last Wednesday."

"But you didn't do it and I was an hour late for an hour-and-a-half-long meeting! You really *have* to today, Steve. This meeting could be the culmination of our work. There's no question here, don't prolong this, okay?"

"Oi, Sandra, we've got to do something about our lifestyle. This isn't working."

"Is that a yes?" Sandra silently notes to make an appointment for an abortion. Simultaneously, she hurls questions at herself. "Why the hell don't we have health insurance that would pay for this? And why don't we have that fucking RU486 in this backwards country yet? Why do I have to go through surgery when I could swallow pills instead?" Sandra screams this inside her head. "If I can't afford an abortion, how am I going to afford a child?" Sandra shrugs her shoulders in dismay and continues her internal discussion. "Anyway, it's all moot since we couldn't possibly fit another child into this ridiculous set-up we have," she argues as if against herself. "So Leda won't have a sibling, is that so bad?" Sandra ponders all of this feeling unconvinced either way, until Steve's voice breaks in.

"For now, it's a yes."

"Great, but you've got to be there no later than three or Leda'll feel rejected and stranded. She'll worry."

"Uh-huh."

"And make her a decent dinner, not one of your experimental concoctions. You know, protein, vegetables, grain. No sugar. Okay?"

"Anything else you want to add, Sandra? I *have* cooked a meal before."

"You'll get her to bed by nine, right?"

"Nine? Your meeting is going to go from five till past nine? No, that's impossible! I'll have to get back to my kitchen."

"I'm just talking about an outside chance, that's all. It'll probably take about two hours, that's my guess. You'll be at her school by three, right?"

"Bye, Sandra."

Sandra hangs up and immediately calls Leda's school to let them know that her father will be picking her up.

"Thanks, Isabel." She waves as she sails out to her next class where she is going to introduce the kindergartners to collage.

"Ben? It's Maria." Her voice is defensive from the start.

"Hi, how're you doing?" Ben is delighted, hoping for the best.

"Fine, Ben. I'm calling to say that one of my meetings was moved to today at five o'clock, downtown. I don't know how long it will be, but I'll come home from there."

"Oh, great. The kids'll be fast asleep again by then, I'm sure. What's this very important pow-wow about?" Ben knows he shouldn't pursue this tack, but he can't stop himself.

"You know I don't discuss my cases, Ben." Maria's voice sounds distant and she sighs before pushing through what she feels is unnecessary tedium. She's long forgotten the days when tables were turned and she used to ask Ben the same kind of questions he now asks her. So has Ben.

"The meeting may only take an hour, or it may take four. There's no way of telling, the opposition is very stubborn and powerful. This is a settlement meeting, we hope."

"We have to talk, Maria." Ben is squeezing the telephone handle with all his might, as though the extra effort might help change things.

"Not now Ben." Maria's voice is softer. She's gripping the edge of her desk with her right hand. "I have to go."

They both click down their phone receivers simultaneously this time.

Maria punches in Roberta's number with agitation coursing through her fingers.

"Berta?"

"Hello, Maria," Roberta almost sings out.

"Want to meet for a quick coffee this afternoon? Maybe Borgia at three, three-thirty?"

"Sure, Maria. Great. See you then."

Back at the Morningside School, Bessy is in her gym class. The class is playing Capture the Flag. As she vies on the outer edges, she admires the sweat dripping down Scott, the teacher's, face. It makes his skin look so shiny and alive. Some of the boys in the class sweat copiously also, with wet triangular spots emerging on the front of their t-shirts or with drips hanging from the tips of their noses. Bessy wants to learn how to sweat like that.

She is wearing her red and white striped, hand-me-down, sailor T-shirt and black Levi cut-offs. She had gone to great lengths to achieve just the right amount of tightness for these shorts. It takes her a good ten minutes just to get into them in the morning and zip them up. Nevertheless, she's not so sure that she likes the appreciation when a classmate comes and stands at the sidelines with her briefly.

"Look how Reva's fat thighs bulge out at the bottom of her shorts," Paul says nodding with disdain in Reva's direction as he gently bounces his back on the matted padding of the gym walls.

Bessy thinks about how his swaying makes him look sophisticated. She can't find a response to his remark so she stays silent. Reva's almost her best friend, so Bessy feels caught, and like she's betraying her by not protesting.

"Not like yours, Bess," Paul says. "Your legs just go smooth all the way, no bumps. Reva needs a diet or something."

Bessy, feeling hotly ambivalent, is still quiet. She likes the compliment but feels guilty about being the one to be compared favorably up against Reva.

"My mother's always on a diet." Paul continues oblivious to Bessy's silence. "But she's got the wrong strategy. She doesn't eat anything all day long and she eats a big dinner at night. Then she watches television and goes to sleep. So she stays fat."

Bessy searches her memory, trying to recall any signs of excess weight on Paul's mother. Bessy herself knows the amount of calories, fat, and sugar in every kind of food she eats and has been on a diet for some years, but she's not about to admit this to Paul.

At the end of the period, the girls' cubby room door cracks open while Bessy's class is changing. Marc's head pokes in, and he whispers: "Hey, psst! Dominique, Mary, Bessy—you ready for the club? All's clear on our side. Come on."

The three girls hustle to finish dressing and start for the boys' changing room. They are tingling with a mixture of apprehension and excitement: this is to be their first Playboy Club meeting.

"Caleb's going to keep watch at the door," Marc announces and gives Caleb a gentle shove in that direction. Caleb's expression demonstrates that that was not a planned announcement.

"Okay, like we decided yesterday, Dominique, Sean and Stuart are going to strip," Mary says.

The three of them start to take off the clothes that they had just put on. Dominique, who is in the middle, finishes first with her clothes heaped in a pile at her feet. Only her waist length, carrot red hair trickles over her shoulders. She stands, somehow, tentatively, like a young Botticelli figure. When Sean and Stuart are nude too, they give each other a subtle nod.

The girls didn't notice the signal until they thought about it afterwards. It was the planned indication for the two boys to open fire and pee on Dominique. They spray her from top to bottom. Even her beautiful hair is dripping in urine. Dominique turns pale and is so surprised, she doesn't utter a peep. She just stands in her spot, frozen, with her arms limply dangling, plastered with wet strands of red hair.

Mary and Bessy run to collect Dominique's soggy clothes and whisk her, still nude and wet, back to the girls' room. Mary helps Dominique clean off in the shower while Bessy rinses out her clothes. Dominique sobs quietly. Mary is chipper, and Bessy is stunned.

Midtown, at quarter to three, Maria dashes out of her office. Roberta is already ensconced in the café with a latte in hand.

"Maria, hi." She rises to greet her friend.

"Roberta, you look fantastic. What's different?"

The two of them stand face to face, examining Roberta.

"I don't know. Nothing physical." Roberta beams. "Well, that's not quite true. I had quite an unusual experience the other day."

Roberta pauses, and Maria becomes eager and impatient. "Tell me!" she prods.

"I've been such a drag lately. I really apologize, Maria. I mean all this murky depression. I was really stuck. Stuck because *he* was stuck. Like I absorbed all his grief, his ambivalence, his anxiety. *I* owned it and started to feel claustrophobic. I couldn't see how to get out of it, I sort of lost myself, in retrospect.

"Then, I don't really know what happened. The other day I went to a friend's opening. I dragged myself there, actually. I almost couldn't face anyone. I just felt obligated to make a showing.

"But I went. A lot of friends were there and I was talking and talking. I viewed the paintings—it was a group show. And all of a sudden, I was in the middle of it. I was inspired by the work, the people, the enthusiasm, you know?

"Then, as I was walking out, chatting with someone about what I'm working on now, this *thing* happened. It was physical and mental at the same time. I had this uncanny bodily sensation and I just felt my own presence. I remember I said, 'I'm back!' I've never felt anything like it. I just knew that I was in my own body once again. I was me again. And it felt good. Really special."

"Huh," Maria said thoughtfully, astounded at her lack of understanding. "Sounds like good news Roberta, even if I don't have a clue about what the experience was like. It's lasted then?"

"Yes, it has. I *am* here. I wouldn't have grasped it either until then, but at the time, it was obvious what was happening."

"And what's with the relationship, are you two taking a break from each other?"

"Not officially, no. But in effect, I think so. You know, I'm really heartbroken over it because we never would or even could have gone without each other before. And I don't really think the part of him that I knew and fell in love with is going to come back. Or at least not in time for me. I just feel I've already over-dosed on the destructive side of him.

"But there's nothing I can do about it."

"Except," Maria says, "take care of yourself."

"Right, it's depressing to me that it's come to this. That I need to defend myself from him. It would have been totally inconceivable a few short weeks ago.

"But at least I've regained some balance, if not perspective. I know I can survive whatever happens. I've got the rest of my life back, and *that* doesn't depend on him."

"Good, 'Berta. I'm glad to see you like this, I was beginning to feel seriously concerned for you."

"Thanks, Maria. You know, it's funny. In the meantime, I've come to some kind of terms with my sexuality. Or, I don't know, maybe I'm rationalizing an imminent break-up." Roberta pauses to reflect.

"What, 'Berta?"

"Well, don't misunderstand me—what I've said before, I still know. I mean, sex with him was incredible, this amazing, explosive experience. *But* there's some kind of limitation I didn't figure my way around. He just doesn't fully grasp my body—nor me, his. Women and men just seem to have different nerve structures, you know? So it just seems like there's a limited amount of pleasure I can give him, bounded by my handle on the workings of his sensory experience. If I were a man, it would be simple, obvious."

Maria looks skeptically at Roberta. "So? I'm missing something here, I think."

"Well, so," Roberta sayss, pondering, as if she were running her hands over the chest of her lover, "I mean, reproduction is one thing, but for real, deep, vast, primordial pleasure, perhaps like needs to stay with like. It's a kind of knowledge that doesn't fully translate into language or any rational, didactic type of framework.

"You know, I can utter wishes, saying 'here, touch me here,' 'rub this,' 'slower,' 'faster,' 'stop,' 'continue,' but then the flow is lost.

I'm in the realm of words, not sensation, and the whole-body continuity is broken."

"But, 'Berta, don't you think, there is something wonderful about body difference and the surprise of that difference?"

"On the other hand, there is something more powerfully erotic about sameness. While giving pleasure, one knows what the sensation is like, and thus doubles the pleasure by directing it to someone else, together with the self-arousing, homo-erotic component, simultaneously. Not really an option when you don't have any real knowledge of what one's actions feel like on the other end. Then, I feel thrown back on words and dispositions—wondering, guessing, hoping."

"What's the real point, 'Berta? I mean, if you're in love with him, part of that must be sexual, no? And, if you're not—"

"Always practical, Maria. Yes, you're right. I was talking on a more theoretical plane, about what's even *possible* sexually with mixed sex partners."

"I'm always a few steps behind you, Roberta. I always was. I'm still hanging on your pronouncement that the other person's sex is immaterial—'people are people', if I can paraphrase your words."

"I don't know who's behind who here, since I've arrived at your original observation that the consequences of the other's physical *shape*, shall we say, play a role in the initial attraction.

"Tell me, though, what's up with you?"

"I have a lot going on right now. Most of all, a case here in SoHo. Tonight's going to be pivotal. I hope I'm ready for it."

Knowing that Maria is referring to the Errigon meeting, she becomes nervous. "Maria, you haven't even ordered anything. Let's get you, what, a cappuccino?"

Looking at her watch, Maria jolts as she begins to speak quickly. "Oh, you know what, 'Berta, I should skip it and get going. I ought to run along and prepare my client. He's a wreck. I'm sorry, 'Berta. I'm the one that dragged you here for nothing."

Relieved, Roberta responds: "No, no, go, Maria. It's fine. I have plenty to do. See you soon."

"Great, bye Roberta."

"Maria," Roberta calls after her. When Maria turns towards her, Roberta exclaims: "Good luck! Call me soon. Bye!"

Maria heads quickly over to the Errigon Gallery.

"Ach, Maria, you're here," Frank says as he comes to greet her at the gallery door. He's been pacing up and down the length of his cavernous front room, peering out at the street each time before turning about face at the window to march back to the whitewashed rear wall.

Maria takes Frank in in one long look and says: "The single most important thing for you tonight is to look composed. Do you have any other clothes here? You look disheveled and at least as on edge as you are."

"Clothes, who cares about clothes when my business, the empire I built up from scratch, is about to go down the drain?"

"You do, for one. I do, for two. And for tonight, let's try to coolly stick to the facts. Your business is actually doing quite well lately, Frank. You're going to have to simmer down now, we have a half-hour until the meeting and we must go over a few points."

Maria walks to Frank's office door, lets herself in, sits on the couch and opens up the Errigon file. She doesn't need to review anything for herself but she is hoping that a little paper shuffling will calm Frank down. It's also what people expect from lawyers. He is the weak link in the whole case. Maria's convinced that the Dolls know this and that's why they picked his gallery to target.

By five-fifteen everyone is assembled at the gallery. Maria, Frank, Sandra, Denise, Claire, and Roberta. Maria places Frank behind his desk to give him some stature and to make him feel more in control, having put his chair on a high setting for added emphasis. She sits in one of the leather chairs in front of the desk, and four Living Dolls, donning their masks, are dispersed onto the couch and remaining chair.

One of the Dolls on the couch has a cigar sticking out of her mask and below the mask wears only a skimpy camouflage colored Lycra mini tank dress, fuchsia fishnet stockings and black high heels. Another has a white button-down shirt adorned with a slender mocha brown tie, and tailored khaki army trousers. The third wears similar khaki pants, combat boots, and an embroidered peasant shirt. The one on the chair has the most elaborate and large mask which tops a lavender and pink camouflage style print dress with a flair skirt. None of them have notes, papers or anything other than small, non-descript carrying bags. Nothing to identify any one of the Dolls. They have agreed that Roberta will not speak since Maria could easily recognize her voice. They estimated that one of them being completely silent would be intimidating.

For a moment there is silence while everyone gets used to the idea that the meeting is about to take place. The masks drive Frank crazy, he breaks out in a sweat just looking at the Dolls. Through most of the meeting he keeps his gaze down at his desk and this gives him a doped look. Even Maria's cool demeanor is set back, although not perceptibly to anyone else. Within thirty seconds she regains her internal balance, her adrenaline stores ready for a fight.

Sandra and the other Living Dolls are thrilled and confident. They know that to be poised in the inner office of Errigon's with him proposing, if not yet begging for, a settlement is already a victory.

"The rest will be the icing," Denise had said as they opened the gallery door to enter.

Once everyone settles down and the edge of anxiety in the air has peaked, Maria begins to formally commence the meeting. Denise has the same impulse, and beats her to it.

She begins a little too loudly at first. "I think we all know why we're here. On behalf of the art community, we Dolls have made some specific requests of Mr. Errigon regarding the practices of this gallery. While these suggestions have been set to writing previously, we thought that for clarity's sake we would bring a fresh declaration of essentially the same concerns to this meeting."

With the word "essentially," a nerve vibrates visibly through Maria's body and face. Frank is in such a panic already that his mind is clouded as if it were balled up with cotton puffs. He does not pick up on the significance of what Denise has said. The only time he gets up his nerve to look at the other Dolls, he thinks he sees one of them sitting at what looks to him to be a military regulation attention pose as if she has a weapon pointed directly at him. He closes his eyes and when he looks back he just sees four masked women normally seated.

Meanwhile, Denise drones on in a calm, businesslike fashion. She moves papers around and sports mannerisms as though she were leading a high powered executive board meeting at a Fortune 500 company. All she lacks are transparencies.

Denise continues on without break for at least fifteen minutes, trying Maria's patience. Maria, of course, had assumed that she would conduct the meeting, giving her the upper hand. Usually while others are speaking, Maria can plan her strategy. She finds with Denise that she needs to devote her full attention to the words, and the nuances, being spoken. Maria's position weakens as the minutes pass and she is struggling mentally to regain her ground. The internal battle being waged inside Maria gives her face a peculiar expression which she can't entirely control. Normally she has an excellent poker face that baffles people and irks her opponent, but now she looks as though she has mistakenly taken in a mouthful of strong horseradish.

Sensing that Maria is about to cut her off, Denise takes some charts out of her bag. Standing, in a court room drama voice, she says: "Here are some facts and figures we're all familiar with. I've taken the liberty of bringing enough copies to pass around so that we all have the same documents in front of us."

Denise takes her time handing out the collections of charts. She is intentionally striking an officious air, nodding her masked head occasionally for punctuation. On the spot, Denise has the flash of recognition that she has missed her calling as an actor. Something perhaps on the order of the Squat Theater Company would be just right for her. This thought sends her mind reeling back to one of their many storefront performances, interacting with the actual downtown street life as part of the show. A vision flashes across her mind of the time a fire truck came barreling down the street replete with a fire squad, hose, and sirens, that was folded into the show as the firefighters wound their way in and out of the building.

Denise is emboldened by these images and she pushes on with an even more authoritative voice, pacing like Perry Mason as she goes through the documented evidence. The other Dolls are enraptured by the show and manage to support her by affecting poses of calm attention and concentration.

Maria has by now made three unsuccessful attempts to gain the floor. She is so frustrated that she uncharacteristically bolts up and grabs Denise's wrist. "Enough!"

Denise reclaims her arm with a touch of prudery. Remaining seated, she bows slightly with elegance and cedes the right of way to Maria.

The Dolls know they have won. Roberta is taken aback by Maria's demeanor, and makes a mental note to find a way to discuss it with her.

At one point while listening to Maria ramble on shuffling her papers, Frank looks as though he is recovering his composure. Picking up on this, the three Dolls on the couch strike the hear-, see-, and speak-no-evil poses. It works on Frank and he's thrown back over the edge once again. Angered by the prank, Maria's voice gains force. She's moving at a good clip in spite of the fact that she has little to say. She's trying to get better terms for Frank.

While the meeting is in progress, Jackie is uptown in Maria's apartment and ought to be studying for finals. She dials Jan's number instead.

"Jan?"

Dreamily, as if still asleep, Jan manages a groggy: "Yes?"

"It's me, Jackie. Maria was a washout, but I've found us a good lawyer. I like her. She'll be very sensitive and she's sharp. And she's going to charge us as minimally as she can. It's not pro bono, but it's as close as we'll get, I think." Jackie's panting with enthusiasm.

"I tried to reach you last night, they're dropping the whole thing now." Jan's voice is dull and flat.

"Huh?"

"Gloria, Lisa, and Amy, all of them, decided not to press charges."

"They what? What happened, are they crazy?" Jackie sounds angry but she's really just shocked.

"Don't argue with me, I'm just as upset as you are." Jan's speaking rapidly, firing out her words one after the other. "They're afraid to go through the whole legal shtick: investigations of their character, prodding their vaginas, and so on. T.V.'s done a pretty good job of showing how seamy and humiliating the whole process can be. Not to mention the real case where the victim was asked to reenact the rape right in court. How much worse can it be, to keep being forced to relive the rape in public? And it seems, none of them saw the *Cagney & Lacey* where Christine wins her acquaintance rape case against her superior. It might help if we could find a rerun of it, but I doubt it. They're petrified. Plus, they think Norris'll come after them if they talk."

"I can't believe this." Jackie's exasperated and incredulous. "I spend the whole last week chasing lawyers for them, three girls have been raped and we know who and where the pervert is, and they're not going to put him away! He'll keep doing it. Have they thought about that?"

"Jackie, stop yelling at me. It's not my fault. I tried talking to them, Sarah spoke to Gloria, but it's no go. I mean, we might not like it, but it is their choice. And they do have a point of sorts. Not only have they been raped, but their life will be dragged through muck and torture for maybe a year while they're supposed to be punishing Mr. Karate. We can't force them."

"But did they think about the sense of power of putting him away? Of security? Of revenge, even? The lawyer said this is as clear-cut and simple as a rape case can come. Would they come talk to Phyllis—that's the lawyer's name—just once to hear her explain the process? She won't whitewash it, but at least she'll give them the upside that their case is an easy win."

"Jackie, if she said that she's lying and you know it. Nothing's an easy win when it comes to rape. And plus, what's the best we can hope for? A revolving door sentence? Chemical castration? What's any of that going to solve?" Jan's voice rises to a squeaky pitch as she talks.

"So." Jackie speaks haltingly now, the gears in her mind finally clicking and turning. She's measuring her words. "It was you who put fear in them, Jan. Why?" Jackie's trembling now.

"I just wanted them to know what they're getting themselves into. They're only kids. The court could ruin their lives even further. Maybe the best thing is to put it all behind them." Jan's own fear is coming across clearly.

Sounding calm, Jackie asserts: "Jan, I have a question for you and I want an honest answer."

"Um?" Jan starts to make spit-greased circles with her index finger on the white and gold flecked Formica tabletop where she sits.

"Norris did his number on you also, didn't he?"

"Uh, what?"

"You heard me, Jan. Talk. That's why you stopped showing up for class."

"Well—"

"Jan!" Jackie screeches, cutting her off. "This is incredible! Do the others know this? The case is tremendous with four of you testifying. Jan, you're the most mature of them, you have to be a role model. Don't teach them to fink out."

Jackie is grasping for an inspirational voice. "They'll never forgive themselves later, and you'll never forgive yourself. You're practicing and teaching passivity! That's what we've been taught from birth. Raise yourself up Jan, take a little control. The ball's in your hands. Don't let yourself and the other girls down. Don't give in to victimization. That's another thing we've been taught: how to be good victims. Break out of it now Jan, before it is too late!" Jackie's shocked, she didn't know that she had that speech in her.

"Jackie, I never figured you for a feminist."

"Feminist, shmeminist. Don't give me that jargon, give me action. We'll get him and have him locked away where he can never do this again."

"At least until he walks out on good behavior, that is." Jan's voice exhibits the hopelessness she feels.

"Come on, Jan. That's not for rape cases."

"I don't know. I'll have to think it over. Let me talk with the others."

"No," Jackie says with determination, "let *me* talk to the others. You're the one who is scared. Better yet, let Phyllis talk to all of you. Okay?"

"Yeah, okay. Just talk though, no promises."

"Just a talk, Jan, no promises."

Jackie hangs up the phone and immediately calls the lawyer for an appointment the following day. She'll have to cut review classes to make it. After a brief pause to ponder about Jan, Jackie goes to Bessy's room to check up on her.

Bessy is in her room quietly preparing her Barbie doll. The doll is nude down to her bare feet permanently molded for high spike heeled shoes. Bessy has her in the middle of her room, lying on top of a large serving platter from the kitchen. There's a box of Diamond wooden matches to the right side of the platter. Bessy has a lit match in her hand that she's applying to Barbie's breasts alternately, one after the other. There's a horrible smell of burning plastic filling up the room. Trails of charcoal colored smoke emanate from the blackened breasts. Bessy lights match after match and doesn't stop until Barbie's once bulbous chest is completely flat.

CHAPTER TWENTY-ONE:

ON RELIEF

ORTUNATELY FOR FRANK, THERE ARE no customers in his still open gallery when the Living Dolls march out triumphantly. Only Kim sitting at her desk watches the single file parade across the floor to the front door. Denise, who comes out of the office last, intends to close Frank's office door but her hand slips. The door, after clicking shut, springs ajar three or four inches. No one notices.

The four Living Dolls representatives decide to chuck their masks and go to Googie's Bar on Thompson to celebrate. Once nestled in a semi-private wooden booth with their drinks—three beers, one dark and two light, and a club soda with lime—they toast and clink glasses a few times over.

"We did it!"

"We got pretty much everything we wanted out of them."

"And we really didn't give in much. Drop the suit, which is a load off our backs too, and a non-disclosure agreement. Not bad, not fucking bad. Let's toast again."

"To our just rewards!"

"To Denise, you were fantastic in there!"

Another round of clinks circle the table, with elated smiles and hugs on either side of the booth.

"And the show. The show! Karen deserves it, we all do," Claire says.

"That's right, Claire. That was all thanks to your stroke of genius at the end. I can see our scorecard now: Errigon Gallery, triple check. Exhibit featuring Karen Apfelbaum, and Living Dolls retrospective."

"Yeah, we'll need to give this a lot of thought," Sandra says.

"You all see I was right, don't you?" Claire says.

"Not really, Claire—" Denise says.

"Not really, what?" Claire says before Denise can get the rest of her words out. "Not really, what? Look at the difference, not much stirred up by Karen. *Nothing.*"

"Claire, Claire," Sandra says, trying to reach for Claire's hand. "Cool it. We're all upset about Karen. I'm mortified."

"Of course," Denise says. "But let's not undermine her dignity wishing her death was being splashed across the tabloids. I don't think I could handle that. I don't want to be confronted with the murder on every corner. It's in the front of my mind every second as it is."

"Really." Claire is snide. "What about the rest of us? What about *me?*" Claire's look is mean, and her eyes appear to be red as laser beams. "As if I needed to wake you all up, you're so naive, posting—" The beams go dead and Claire's voice cracks to a stop.

Roberta and Sandra compare notes with their eyes, as if to say: "Stay around, we'll deal with this after."

"You know," Denise says, "we've got to do the watchdog bit. Errigon has a lot to live up to. We have to find ways to police him. For example, we're going to have to make sure he keeps one and the same pay scale for women and men alike. That's going to be tricky. I don't know how we'll do it without the inside help which we don't have."

"Well, at least watching his exhibit ratio for women will be simple, we just have to count, multiply, and divide," Claire says, having shifted into a brightened façade.

"Not so. He can always cry submission imbalance or something. We need an angle on this, too."

"Let's plan a later meeting and just be happy now. What do you say, Dolls?"

"I don't know," Sandra says. "We've got serious business here. We need insurance against his reneging."

"But Sandy, not here," Claire says. "This is a public bar. We can't be overheard. It would finish us. We've got to be cautious, protect ourselves. We've never met out in the open like this. We just can't risk it."

"I think we can. It's early, it's empty in here and we'll speak softly. Let's just get it over with," Roberta says all in one gulp and with an indisputable edginess.

The table's gaiety droops to a standstill and the four Living Dolls each begin to fidget with their glasses and napkins. With a blank expression, Claire toys with the pink and white sugar packets in a dish next to the salt and pepper shakers.

"We need two things. One, a method for checking on him, and two, a weapon which will either keep Errigon from going back on the agreement or at least make him very sorry after the fact."

Sandra raises her hand in the air perpendicular to the table and palm out. "The first can be my department. After all, Errigon's assistant wrote us a piece of fan mail. I'll contact her."

"Be discreet, you never know."

"I think there's something," Roberta slowly says, "we can do with the nondisclosure clause if he reneges."

"Another poster?" Claire asks perking up and dropping the pink and white packets.

"Ah! We're still in the poster business, thank god."

"What about a simple poster stating the terms of our out-of-court settlement, with names and dates, et cetera?"

"Roberta, why don't you lay it out and do a small printing. Meanwhile, if we feel a whiff of a hint that he's up to anything at all, our first step will be to mail Errigon a copy of the poster. That ought to stop him in his tracks."

"If it doesn't, we'll have to think again. For now let's have another round of piss water from the keg and be happy. We've had our first really clear-cut, solid as concrete, victory since our beginning three and a half years ago. Waiter!"

While the Living Dolls plot through their second round of drinks, Maria and Frank chew over the meeting and the settlement. They end up convincing themselves that they won and Frank is his old, cocky self. The charges are to be formally dropped and the heat off him.

"Hah! I'm even going to be put on their Best Hits list. What a laugh. Rags to riches all over again."

"It's not quite such a joke, Frank. You don't go on Best Hits until you follow through with the exhibit. And we have to be careful about your record keeping from now on. You'll have to be able to demonstrate that you're living up to your end of the deal."

"Yes, yes, yes. Let's worry about that when we worry about it. I haven't felt this good in months, maybe years. Can I buy you a drink somewhere, Maria? Dinner maybe? You name the place. You did a stupendous job!"

Maria speaks as she rises from the sofa. She's beginning to feel uneasy seated in Frank's office while he prances about.

"Thank you, Frank," Maria says in a dry but friendly tone, "and thank you for the offer, but I must be going now. Why don't you call my secretary for an appointment within a week or two so we can go over the implications of the agreement."

When she's finished, Maria extends her hand for a shake, but Frank cuts her off. In his elation he is oblivious to the fact that she's trying to say goodbye and leave.

"Implications, schmimplications. Don't bug me about that. I won't worry about them, if you won't. Ha Har!"

Walking over to her and taking her hand and patting it, Frank speaks softly. "Maria, you're my lawyer and my friend. I can speak openly with you. We got the suit dropped, we got a non-disclosure agreement. That's all I wanted. If I don't stick to the exact letter of this private law, who's to know? I can't really sit around calculating every penny I pay an artist and then matching it with the pennies I've paid other artists. Business doesn't work that way.

"Nor can it revolve around keeping a gender score card. Art has to remain unfettered and unshackled. I'm sure the way we've got it now is just fine. The Dolls can stop their pranks and save face at the same time. I mean, really, that must be what they wanted. Who would want to have to keep spending their time pasting posters all over town wearing Halloween costumes? No one. So we took the thorn out of my side and relieved them of the hole they dug for themselves, in one blow.

"Unknit that brow, Maria. Everything will be fine. I promise." With that Frank kisses the hand he is still holding in a clasp.

"All the same, Frank, make that appointment and we'll review. See you then." Maria turns the clasp into a handshake, gathers up her briefcase and coat and leaves out the crooked door trailing two "Goodbyes" behind her, one for Frank and one for Kim.

Maria heads straight for a telephone to call Peg.

"Peg, you free? Can I drop by in a few minutes?"

"Sure, Maria, but I don't think that I can handle another one of our twenty minute sessions. You make me completely crazy, and then you're gone. I'm left with dreams."

"Peg, Peggy. I'm sorry. I know what you mean, my dreams—fantasies—are so real, and then in a split second, they're gone. I'd have about an hour if I come by now."

"Come! See you soon."

Reclining, entwined, on Peg's oversized couch, Peg and Maria are nude. Maria says: "Twenty short minutes ago I was in a settlement meeting. Now, I'm here. Talk about transitions." As if defending what she just said, she adds: "And, you know"—Maria turns to look directly into Peg's eyes, and kisses her gently—"I had no idea how easy this could be."

Peg squeezes her tighter. "Am I a 'this' now?"

"No, really, Peg. I feel so comfortable with you, and excited at the same time. It's like puppy love all over again, but better."

"But you know, honey, you can't go tell the world. You can't go tell anyone."

"I haven't, but you're acting a little melodramatic, aren't you?"

Speaking in a somber, and crisp, voice, Peg says: "No. I am not. You're a mother, you're a lawyer. You're a woman. You can't lose everything just because you're happy to be sleeping with me."

"I don't recall any sleeping," Maria says with a smile, placing slow, wet kisses across Peg's shoulders.

"Maria, I know that you're naive about this aspect of the world. You've never confronted it. Listen to me, though. You need to just take my word for it, before you learn the hard way. You think you don't have a hard enough time as a woman lawyer? Try telling people in our professional circle that you're having an affair with a woman.

"You want Ben to find out? He'll have a divorce and custody inside of ten seconds. For the best interests of the children. You might not even get visitation rights. Don't gamble, Maria. You have no idea."

"Come on, Peg. Ben might be upset, breach of trust and all. But he's not an idiot."

"Precisely, he's no idiot."

Maria stops protesting long enough to begin to fathom the enormity of the repercussions of her actions. She has a strange sensation of being trapped in her female body, as if she just noticed the limitations of it.

"Particularly, don't get any wild ideas while I'm away next week. No solo actions, agreed?"

"I forgot that you were going. I'll miss you terribly."

"Me, too. I wish you could come, even for a day."

"A night would be better," Maria says as she kisses Peg's arm, holding it in her hands. "Imagine, a whole night together, dusk to dawn, as they say."

"Sounds great. Maybe one day you'll be able to swing it. You do have an au pair, you know. And a husband. That's already one adult per kid. It's enough, no?" Peg's voice has a strained quality to it that she tries to conceal.

"Peg," Maria says, beginning to feel defensive, "you know it's not just that. I have work to do, just like you. Every day, and many nights. On top of that, I have a family, four other personalities to deal with. I don't think you get it."

"Stop, Maria," Peg says as she cups Maria's face gently in her hands. As Peg brings her head to Maria's, her breasts brush past Maria's chest, and she kisses Maria's eyes, slowly, each in turn. Peg lowers herself and caresses Maria's abdomen, and begins to feel a heating sensation wash over her body.

A few moments later, Peg and Maria make love with a hunger palpable in the surrounding air. In their passionate, driven motions, they achieve a depth of sensuality that neither of them had previously known.

Meanwhile, Roberta and Sandra have hung back at the corner outside of Googies after the others finally went home. Claire's mis-speech alerted them both to recognize that it is Claire who is responsible for the fingers.

"You know," Sandra offers, "her daughter Aviva contacted me. She wanted to know if I knew what was up with Claire. I couldn't help her at the time, but now maybe we should fill her in."

"Does she know about us?"

"Uh-uh. No. Definitely not."

"Well," Roberta says thoughtfully, "do we want to let her in on all of this? I mean, if she'd be a help, but otherwise—"

"But it's her *mother* we're talking about. And all of this is going to come out now anyway."

"Maybe not, Sandra. Let's think this through. Want to walk up to Washington Square Park and sit?"

"It's freezing out here! How about going in to Cafe Reggio— it's so noisy in there, no one'll overhear us."

"Yeah, but we won't be able to hear each other. No, let's go to Mamoons. It's not so cozy, but it'll be empty and if we order a couple of falafels, no one will bother us."

Walking over to MacDougal and Third Street to the Middle Eastern fast food store outfitted with orange and yellow plastic benches and glaring fluorescent lights, Roberta and Sandra decide to call upon Aviva for assistance. They use a pay telephone in the store while waiting for their orders.

Aviva is sitting in the hospital cafeteria on a break when she hears herself being paged to the nurses' station. She has a blue plastic tray in front of her scattered with a sampling of the institutional fare. So far, she's only nibbled lightly. She's reading the evening edition of The *New York Times*. Aviva is almost done with the second section when a small article catches her attention. It is about Karen's decapitation. The article mentions that there are no leads except for some earthen dust found mixed with Karen's blood.

As Aviva rises she whispers: "I was right."

After a brief discussion with Sandra on the telephone, she leaves the hospital with the desk nurse trailing after her, asking who will be her cover.

"Find someone," Aviva says as she's hailing a cab.

It's not until Maria is seated in a cab heading home that she feels the familiar hollowness of a case that has ended. It is so strong this time that she has to practically muzzle herself in order to restrain the impulse to tell the driver to take her to the office instead. When Maria enters her apartment, she sees Ben loading the dinner dishes into the dishwasher and her kids playing Monopoly on the living room floor.

"Where's Jackie?" she says to Ben first thing, and that's when her kids see she's back.

"Hi, Mom," Ricky says, absorbed.

"Hi, Mom," Bessy chimes, also distracted.

In a resigned but irritated voice, Ben says: "She has a lot of studying to do. It's almost finals time for her. I told her to go to the library."

"But this is what we pay her for, Ben."

"Take a bath, Maria. Try to relax, see if you can come out and talk to your kids, if not to me, in a normal tone of voice. When you're done I'll give you some dinner."

Uncharacteristically, Maria does what Ben said without a single remark. She walks over to the fridge and takes out some cheese, and grabs a small plate and some crackers from the cupboards. Maria reaches for the raisins and a box of cookies. She pauses to stare at the assembly before her, and realizes that she's reacting out of habit, not current need. She puts it all away and heads toward the bathroom. On her way, Maria swerves into the living room to duck down and peck her kids on the head. They are still concentrating on their game and barely look up.

When Ben sees Maria fixing a Scotch, he calls over: "Not tonight, Maria. I bought ice cream instead. You can have it after your dinner."

Maria realizes that Ben is right and puts the glass down. She walks to the bathroom feeling strong. Bessy gets up and pours the Scotch from the glass down the drain and follows her mother to the tub.

"I have some new jasmine bubble bath, Mom. Want to try it?" Bessy puts her hand on Maria's back as she slumps over the tub, rinsing it out.

Without turning around, Maria answers: "No thanks, honey." Just then Maria feels a surge of guilt and love, mixed, for Bessy and wants to give her a huge bear hug and kisses.

She holds it in for a second while she gets someone's pubic hair to go down the drain, and the feeling passes. Instead, once she has the water temperature adjusted and flowing in, she faces Bessy, cups her hands on her shoulders and says: "Let me take this bath alone sweetie, and then I'll come out and we'll do something together. Okay?"

"Sure, Mom. It's almost my bedtime though. Maybe you could tuck me in tonight and read me a story?" Bessy is unsure if this request is going a step too far.

"You've got it, Bess," Maria says reaching out to Bessy for an embrace.

Bessy leaves glowing, closing the door behind her.

As Maria undresses, she reconsiders, puts on her pajamas and robe and trots purposefully to Bessy's room. As she is reading to Bessy, she yearns for the Scotch she left behind. She recognizes the benefit of her now old habits. Her mind aches to be dulled enough to not experience the emptiness she feels at home. Maria fails in her attempt to divert her craving to the ice cream. As she mouths the words of a book she's read at least one thousand times, she has a running internal monologue. She gets hung up on the fact that she forgot to ask what flavor is in the freezer. Ben has a nasty habit of buying Butter Pecan. Maria can't stand that one. She's eaten it, too much in fact, but she can't stand it.

Swathed in her sky blue, terry-cloth robe as she emerges from Bessy's darkened bedroom, Maria hears Jackie's voice coming from the kitchen. "I thought she was supposed to be studying, but she's just yapping on the phone. Ben's such a dolt," she thinks.

"Gloria, explain this to me again, why can't you come to the meeting tomorrow with Phyllis?" Jackie is perched on a stool at the kitchen counter with her sneakered feet perpendicular to the floor, wedged up against the white wall.

"Uh huh, and you decided all of this today at lunch. The lunch Jan bought you? Don't you see what's going on, Gloria? Jan is scared and she's trying to talk all of you out of prosecuting. Haven't you ever asked yourself, why?

"I was hoping Jan would reveal this to you herself, but now I have no choice. I can't stand by and watch all of you lock this inside while Norris walks free to commit rape after rape." Jackie pauses for emphasis before continuing on to the punch line.

"He raped Jan too. Get it? He scared her the best of all. She's petrified, but if you're strong, she can be too. I'll help you, and we have Phyllis to fight for us. She's got a good track record. We have to give her a try. We can stop at any time, but I promise you, we won't want or need to. Sleep on it and come to the meeting. No strings attached. Just show up. No, better yet, I'll come get you and we'll go together. Deal?"

Jackie hangs up the phone with a loud groan.

"What's up Jackie, I thought you were studying in the library tonight?" Maria asks.

"I was, but then I got wind that one of the rape victims from the class is still trying to sabotage my efforts to help them file suit. One down. Now I have to call the other two and reconvince them to come meet the lawyer I found. Just to listen to her assessment of their case, not sign their lives away. I can see already that I'll have to get up at the crack of dawn tomorrow just to be able to go door to door and round them up to take them by the hand."

"You know, I think you always make sure to distract yourself at finals time."

"Thanks, Maria."

Maria walks off to her bedroom. She doesn't feel like listening to the blabber of Jackie's voice tonight.

Ben is reading *The Financial Times* on the living room couch.

"Pay no attention to her tonight, Jackie. It's her end-of-the-case mood. We've seen it before, and we'll see it again. You've set yourself a pretty tough task. I hope you don't get burned." Ben tries to sound encouraging but it doesn't come out quite the way he intended it to.

"Thanks, Ben. If my talking is disturbing you, I can do it later."

"No, not at all. I'm going to join Maria anyway. I've just been waiting for her to finish putting Bessy to sleep. They needed some time alone together."

Ben finds Maria stretched out on their king size bed face up.

"Maria?"

"Yes, Ben," she says without moving or even shifting her gaze from the ceiling.

"Would you like something for dinner now? You must be famished."

"No. Thanks."

"Maybe something simple but warm, like an omelet?"

"No."

"Or a pâté sandwich, the way you like it?"

"No, thanks."

"Some fruit and nuts?"

"No, really, Ben. Please don't keep on listing food." She still hasn't moved, although she has now bent her neck in order to look at Ben. As if for the first time, she sees that she's not the only one in the house to use food as the locus for a power struggle.

"Well, how about just some ice cream then?"

"Is it Butter Pecan? I forgot to ask?" Maria says with a touch of annoyance. She feels she's weakening under Ben's entreaties.

"I bought French Vanilla, Heath Bar Crunch, and Coffee. What do you say to a small combo of all three? Huh?"

"Maybe just some vanilla, thanks."

By the time Ben comes back with two bowls of ice cream, Maria has fallen asleep. He loosens her robe belt, covers her, and gives her a kiss on the forehead. Ben plops the ice cream from one bowl into the other and leaves the empty bowl and spoon in the kitchen sink. He takes the other one, now overflowing, back to the couch to eat while gazing out at the Manhattan skyline. He barely listens to Jackie in the background.

Fifteen minutes later, Maria is roused from her light sleep.

"No. I'm not going to do this anymore, I don't need to."

She lifts herself out of bed, slowly and deliberately, as if conscious of waking to the persona that she has become. Maria slips her arms out of her Saks robe and lays it carefully on the foot of the bed. As she moves across the room to the bathroom, Maria experiences an inner feeling of solidity. As if symbolically in order to restructure herself, she takes her evening bath on her own terms.

As the hot bath water is pouring in, Maria slowly undresses in front of the mirror. She meets her own eyes, head on, and feels each button as she opens it. Pajama top off, she then bends slightly to pull down the pants, still observing her movements in the full-length mirror. She runs her hands down her nude legs and around the circumference of her waist, belly and buttocks.

Washing her face, hair pulled back by a headband, Maria looks at herself in the mirror in between splashes of water. She is processing new information about herself wordlessly, with curiosity and excitement.

Once immersed in the steaming liquid, Maria enjoys the multiple sensations of her body. She lies there, acknowledging every part of herself. The water ripples in response to movements of her hands, her toes, her knees. Maria allows herself to appreciate the warmth and freedom of the bath as if it were a new experience with infinite possibilities.

When she is ready to let the water drain, Maria gently and lovingly caresses each part of her body. Indulging fully in her aroused state, she recognizes a new level of connection with herself that she knows is hers for keeps. Standing, Maria selects a clean towel from the shelf above and to the side of the tub. She dries herself with careful, deliberate motions. She balls her pajamas and dumps them into the laundry basket, and nestles herself in bed like a curled lion cub, nude. She drifts into a deep sleep, her chest heaving rhythmically under the covers.

Later that night, Jackie sits at one of the center tables of the crowded and dark Gold Rail Restaurant on Broadway near Columbia. Halfway through one of their humongous hamburger specials, she speaks with her mouth full of French fries: "I'm really glad you hadn't eaten yet either, Gregory. The only people I get to talk to lately have to do with this rape case."

"Me too. I'm glad, I mean. I've been staring at a theorem all day. I think I've got it beat though. When I went for a jog this afternoon, the solution came to me. I think I'm going to be able to present it to the department at the Colloquium this week."

"That's great. I wish a solution would come to me. It's much worse than pulling teeth to get these girls to press charges against the creep."

"Jackie, haven't you thought of the possibility that they're backing out now because they lied?"

"Huh?" Jackie stops eating at this remark while Gregory continues on to mop up his entire plate. An almost unheard of feat at the Rail.

"Well, I mean, when you're a teacher, students throw themselves at you, as I well know. There's not much you can do about it. You can resist and resist, but it's inevitable that one day, feeling a little lonely, you give in. I mean, it is consensual and everything. It happens. It's not a big deal, and generally, everybody's happy. Who knows, maybe he broke it off quickly with some of your friends and now it's just sour grapes."

"But Gregory, only one of them is even in college yet, what do they know? He's their teacher. He's in a position of authority vis-à-vis these girls. He abused that power. He told them it was in the name of rape prevention. The most you can blame them for is naiveté, and that's not a crime."

"But let's say they each had a crush on him. Let's say the idea for a private lesson was initiated by one of them. It's a little late to say 'no' when he's got your breasts in his hands. It looks to me like they all asked for it, and got what they wanted."

"All four of them? And those are only the ones I personally know about. You don't even know any details of the case and you've already pronounced sentence." Jackie's voice trails off.

She feels sick to her stomach, having a sudden sensation of disembodiment She is being treated differently because of the shape of her genitals. In a flash she sees the world divided into two classes with her on one side. A side she wasn't previously aware of.

The feeling passes and she remarks in a matter-of-fact tone: "Norris crossed a line no teacher should cross, nor anyone else. It was rape."

Gregory's face darkens, and noting it, Jackie continues without letting him get a word in. "Anyway, let's change the subject. I want to get married," she says, lying. As she utters the words, she pinches her right thigh.

Gregory's face eases and he relaxes. "Married, Jackie? No." Then he pauses for a moment before continuing: "I mean, not now. I couldn't. You see, I spent most of my youth being shy and studying mathematics. I proved some great theorems quite young. I didn't date at all. I met Pearl, we got married, et cetera. But now I've blossomed, and women are something I'm very good at. I don't know what happened, but I'm really good at it, and I'm having a ball. So, I'm really flattered, but I just couldn't commit to that at this point."

"I didn't mean to you. I just meant that I want to get married, kind of an abstract thing I've been tossing about. Maybe to my friend Kevin. You've met him, I think?" Wiping her mouth ostentatiously, Jackie casually adds: "Well, I'm done. I should go study now, Greg. Thanks for meeting me."

Jackie stands up with the bill in hand. Before she turns to pay and go she looks into Gregory's crimsoned face. For a fleeting moment Jackie feels she has equalized the two of them.

A cab pulls up on a nearby street. Aviva rushes out with a white pharmacy bag in hand, leaving the driver too big a tip. She goes straight up to Claire's apartment and unlocks the door with her set of keys that she's kept since she lived there herself.

Once inside, Aviva finds Claire seated in the living room on the couch. Claire is still. Aviva enters the room with the words: "Mom, I know."

Claire looks up at her daughter, and Aviva slides down to sit on the side cushion of the couch. The apartment is silent save the outside city noise of sirens and traffic. A plane flies low overhead and sounds as if it is going through the apartment. Aviva puts her arm across her mother's shoulders, and, after a moment, Claire rests her head on her.

An hour later, Aviva, Sandra, and Roberta are standing in Claire's kitchen, deep in discussion, as Claire slumbers in her bed, sedated.

"I feel like I should have done something sooner." Aviva's pained words flow as the red neon sign from the building exterior flashes across her face.

"Me, too," Sandra says into the night sounds of upper Manhattan.

"We didn't and now we need to be practical and move quickly," Roberta says, speaking firmly. "We're talking murder, at least one, and possibly assault or theft for the fingers."

Aviva blanches listening to Roberta. "I know about the fingers. They must've come from the hospital. It explains all those surprise visits. She never did that before. Explains a lot, really."

"Well," Sandra says, "we know the steps. First, we need to get legal advice about how to proceed. And it seems to me, we need to approach someone, keeping Claire's name out of it at first. We'll probably need second and third opinions before we know what we're doing."

"I think I can make a stab at the first round and be sure to keep it confidential," Roberta says.

"And anonymous." Aviva is emphatic.

The three women linger, partly going over their plans, but also because Sandra and Roberta feel uneasy leaving Aviva, who they both perceive as a naive child, solely responsible for Claire. Both write down their telephone numbers in clear block print for Aviva and make sure that she feels free to call upon them at any time.

"I'll call you in the morning to check in," Sandra says to Aviva as she is leaving.

"And," Roberta says, "we'll meet as soon as I have something to report. Hopefully by tomorrow afternoon."

The following day in school, Bessy yells down the corridor as she gallops towards the teacher: "Sandra! Sandra, hold on."

Sandra turns to see who it is. Pleasantly surprised, she says cheerfully: "Good morning, Bessy. What's up?"

"Are you on your way to a class now?"

"No, I have a break for a period. But come to think of it, where are you supposed to be?"

"Gym. I can't go today." Bessy looks at the floor as she speaks.

"Why not? You look fine to me. What's the problem?"

Bessy looks into Sandra's face, considers for a moment and then just mumbles: "Nothing. Just can't."

Anyone can see that there is more to the story. Sandra takes Bessy gently by the hand. "Come with me, Bessy. The art room is empty now. Let's see if we can get to the bottom of this."

No sooner have they entered the room when the whole Playboy Club story comes gushing uncontrollably out of Bessy's mouth. She herself doesn't know what's come over her.

"How did it make you feel, Bess?" Sandra asks, not knowing what to say.

"Horrible." Bessy shifts her position and says: "And scared. I wasn't scared they'd turn and do that to me, but just scared. An inside kind of scared. You know what I mean?"

"Uh huh. Yes, I do." Sandra decides to go for it even though she isn't sure it is the right thing to say to a kid. With Leda she speaks often enough about hard issues; she does so more subtly to have an accumulative effect. Here she might only have this one shot, and Sandra can't imagine Bessy's parents helping her sort through this stuff.

"You see Bessy, sometimes boys do things like that to put you on notice. To remind you that they think they're tougher and better than you. Some of them grow out of it, but a lot of them don't.

"You have to keep remembering not to let them tell you who you are, no matter how many of them are bugging you. They're a pain, but they can't control your life unless you let them." Sandra knows that what she is saying is scant, even a half-truth, but it is about as far as she thinks it is appropriate to go. She gropes for something at least faintly positive and strengthening to say.

"I guess that club of yours won't have any more meetings, will it?"

"No way!"

"How are the other girls who went? Who was it, Dominique and—?"

"Mary. Dominique was really upset. She didn't say anything. And I haven't seen her much since. But Mary, she seemed kind of happy. I didn't ask her anything, she looked so weird."

"Well, maybe you and Dominique could get together, with or without Mary, and talk about the whole thing. It might help."

"Maybe. I guess." Bessy is unconvinced.

"Just try it. It certainly can't hurt, right?"

"Right. I guess not."

"You know, Bessy, it's almost time for my next class and I have to make a phone call first. I'd better get to it. Anytime you want to talk though, come find me. I'll make time."

As Sandra says this, Bessy imagines herself hurled cat-like with paws splayed into position on either side of the art room door frame so that no one can get her out. But all she actually says is a dutiful and muted, "Thanks."

They both gather up their things and start to leave. Piercing into the background noise of the school corridor, Bessy shrieks with a hint of alarm in her voice: "Sandra?"

"Yes, Bessy?"

"Could I do my Winter project with you?" she asks.

"Sure thing, Bessy. When you come in for art next, let's figure out what you'll do. Deal?"

"Deal! See you." Bessy scoots out the door and down the hall.

As Sandra walks in the opposite direction, she ponders what to do about this kids' club. On the one hand, she hasn't asked Bessy if she can take some action on it, like speaking with Calley. And if she had, Sandra knows very well that Bessy would have said no out of fear of being branded a tattletale. On the other hand, Sandra doesn't have much confidence that Calley could be effective with the issue anyway. She wonders if she could speak with the kids involved on her own. She rules the latter out also as a bad idea on all scores.

As she is debating, Sandra makes her way to Martin's office where she knows she can use the phone in private. Why a math teacher needs an office and a phone when she has neither, is a mystery she unfortunately knows the answer to.

Sandra dials the number and clears her throat.

"Errigon Gallery," Kim answers as cheerfully as she can. Just then she was looking through a printout from N.Y.U.'s student placement office of job openings.

"Are you relatively alone?" Sandra says, muting her voice.

"Huh?"

"Don't hang up. This is a friend. I'm a Living Doll. Are you who I should speak with?"

"I sent you the letter, if that's what you mean." Kim sounds irritated. "Why are you calling?"

"We need to know if we can count on you."

"For?"

"We have to keep tabs on compliance with our settlement. Can you help? Do you have access to that sort of information?"

"Yes, but for starters, I can give you a lead. After your meeting, the last one of you out left the door open. Here's what Errigon said afterwards."

As Kim speaks with the receiver crooked between her shoulder and her cheek, she tears up the want ad listings she had pored over just moments ago, and throws them in the garbage can below her desk.

At her own desk, Maria tears up a reminder note she wrote to herself the day before and taped to her desk lamp. As she's putting it into the trash, she reflects on the fact that she feels lonely knowing that Peg is out of town, and attributes her hollow sensation to this.

"It's fine to miss her. It's fine to feel lonely without Peg. I've gotten used to her, maybe a little dependent on her even," Maria thinks. She knows there's more to it though as she observes the fact that she's been imagining Peg's eyes on her, watching her, even when she's alone. Maria begins to admit, that she even talks about herself, to herself, in the third person, as if Peg were speaking.

She realizes that she has been attempting to prepare for Peg's return. For Maria's own return, through Peg. Maria begins to sense that she has never existed except through someone else's eyes. As if she couldn't validate herself, as if she had no internal self-perception. She feels very tired. The image of herself as a hard, hollow shell becomes more and more pronounced in her mind. She wonders how this crept up on her so suddenly, since it's obviously been part of her constitution for some time.

As if reviewing her life, Maria thinks of all the times Peg gazed warmly into her eyes and Maria was compelled to deflect her eyes downwards, sideways, unable to meet the look. She felt a sham, self-conscious. Maria also knows that Peg is not the first person this has happened with. In fact, it has occurred the least with Peg. Maria is amazed by how centered she feels around Peg, as if her eyes, her self-image, do come from within at least some of the time. That she can render herself up to Peg, on occasion, because there is a self there. Not often enough, as is graphically evident to Maria now in Peg's absence.

Just as she's feeling particularly empty, Maria's phone lights up. She grabs for the receiver, fleeing her observations with haste.

"Maria?"

"Peg! I'm so glad to hear your voice."

Laughing, Peg asks: "You are?"

"Yes. How are you?"

"Great. Except that I'm here and you're there, and there are one thousand miles in between. How did that happen?"

"I don't know. Ask your client out there." Maria is smiling as she speaks.

They chat about work for a few minutes, and crisscross over other subjects, as if tipsy with the sound of each other's voices. They make plans to see each other as soon as Peg returns.

Peg says wistfully, laced with hope: "We need a fat, solid week together. Every day, every night."

Joking, Maria responds: "Then what, we'll be done? You think that'll be enough to keep us into our next lives?"

"Of course not! Then we'll need another week, and another, and so on. I've tried to avoid these words, Maria, but I won't anymore. I love you. Je t'aime. Ich liebe dich. Te y'amo. I love you."

Maria's silence burns. She feels thrown back on herself, only to find the hollowness gaping open. She doesn't feel she has a comparable I to balance Peg. To say I—a full, real I love you, too. Instead, she squeaks out a "Me, too," feeling shriveled.

"You know, sweetie," Peg says as if she doesn't notice Maria's hesitance, (although she does, and makes a mental note to deal with it head-on in person), "I should click off now. I'll call again. Maybe tomorrow."

Maria feels a wrenching sensation, as if to hang up would

be painful. Lingeringly, she says: "Okay. Keep up the good work. Come home now."

"Bye." Maria hears Peg's voice utter kindly before hanging up.

Deflated, Maria cradles the receiver on its base. She moves slowly pondering her historical difficulty with separation. It dawns on her what the problem is with letting go of someone, even if only temporarily. If the person, like Peg, has become the thread of Maria's very existence, it's as though Maria loses her eye. Her *I*. As if struck over the shoulder, Maria suddenly recognizes that it's her very self she's parting with.

"How have I gotten by all these years without realizing?" Maria wonders. She's completely bowled over by this new insight. Her mind is racing, trying to somehow incorporate this new piece of information.

Just then her interoffice line buzzes and startles her out of her thoughts.

"Jacobs, here."

"Ms. Jacobs, your four o'clock meeting has been changed to four-thirty. Is that convenient for you?"

"No, but it's fine, Susie. Thanks."

As Maria responds, she is glancing at the late afternoon portion of the day in her appointment book. Her vision broadens to take in the whole week on paper. She sees a maze of exclamation points, green asterisks, and other forms of highlighting scribbled across the page, jutting out at all angles.

In recognition, she exclaims: "This isn't a calendar, this is a jail of failure. The clients, okay, but the rest of this takes up eighty percent, and I don't do half of it. Or even a quarter! If I want to go on an outing with Bessy, or jog, or starve myself, can't I just do it? All these imperatives are a lame attempt at mind control. A kind of self-imposed terrorism of demands and threats. Why do I need to be both bully and victim?"

Maria closes the book and her eyes and quietly resolves: "I don't." She takes a bottle of white-out from her top desk drawer and spends the remainder of the unbillable quarter of an hour deleting everything from her book except for client dates and times.

Relieved, Maria pushes the leather bound and monogrammed book to a far corner of her desk. "And I don't need to carry this around everywhere. It stays put. No longer. No longer will I use directives on paper to define who I am. *It* is just what it is, an appointment book, and *I* am me. I will learn how to make decisions for the moment, in the moment. The I-am-here-now paradox of linguistics can become my truism."

Feeling like she's finally situated herself, Maria sets about her work with vigor. Every now and then throughout the day, she checks herself, as if to say: "I *can* do this. It's working. I *am* me."

Just as Maria utters these words, her telephone buzzes. She picks up the receiver with a new sense of authenticity, "Yes? Jacobs."

"Maria?" It is Roberta, calling about Claire.

"Berta, how are you?"

"Fine, Maria, good. Listen—"

"Roberta, you don't sound fine. What's the news on the romance front?" Maria's voice is chipper.

Roberta doesn't have the patience to discuss her love life, but responds to Maria's question, not wanting to launch straight into the tricky task ahead of her. "Actually, not a lot of romance is in my life at the moment. I finally came to some decisive conclusions."

"A-ha! Tell me."

"Well, after getting depressed for a while, feeling like I was sinking into a morass of skewed compromises, me putting up with too much of his baggage, really, I felt compelled to action. No matter how much in love I feel, I had to confront the reality that I don't want to call something love that is so lopsided, so unequal. I don't care if men are trained to take certain things for granted and feel free to, in effect, take advantage of our upbringing, and I don't care if no one has ever called on him to hold up his half of the responsibility for a relationship. I will. And I am. That's what *I* need. I need to feel like we can be partners, and be solid together, and not have me turn into the police officer, coach, and mediator for our relationship.

"The more I thought about it, the more I realized how strongly I feel about it."

"That's a hard decision to come to, isn't it, 'Berta? I don't know if I'd have the strength, or if I'd just keep hoping that eventually it would work out."

"Yes, I know. But even though I feel sad knowing that maybe he can't *or won't* meet me on this, I feel firm on this. It makes me more secure in myself, that I can take care of myself and not get lost yet again.

"I just can't sign up for yet another relationship that is going to help my psyche deteriorate any further. I have enough of that in other corners of my life."

"You sound resolved, 'Berta. I'm glad. Listen, I really should get back to work, can we make a date?"

"Maria, I was actually calling on your professional expertise, can I keep you a little longer?"

Roberta relates as much as she thinks Maria needs to know about Claire in order to be able to provide some useful advice. The conversation continues for some time, until Maria is summoned urgently to a meeting in a conference room down the hall.

The morning of Peg's return, Maria finds it difficult to contain herself. She ordered a special cake from the Cupcake Cafe, sporting their signature exuberant wild flower icing decoration with "Welcome home" written on top. Maria dashes over to the café on Ninth Avenue after work and then zooms downtown to Peg's apartment. Maria's head a jumble, she's hoping that Peg has already arrived home. Maria has been waiting for this, anticipating the new experience of being able to look straight into Peg's eyes, from her own. On the way over, Maria feels a tinge of fear mixed in with her excitement. She believes this to be the acid test of her transformation. She does not want to fail. She reminds herself many times over to concentrate, not to fall into old habits. The words feel empty though. She can't even mentally reconstruct what her old self-less self was like anymore.

Her first second with Peg tells Maria everything she needs to know. She feels her own weight, as if, for the first time, Maria can hold down her own half of a relationship.

Seated on Peg's couch, drink in hand, Maria goes over her week in complete detail, and the two of them hash over the ups and downs of Peg's trip. Peg shifts her position to change the subject.

"Maria, I don't want you to get the wrong impression, because I enjoy your company immensely. But an aspect of how our relationship is evolving doesn't sit well with me."

"What are you getting at, Peg?" Maria says tenderly, but hoping, at the back of her mind, that they're not about to have a scene. She's had enough upheaval for the moment.

"There's not too much we can do about it, I suppose. Not a lot of options, anyway. But I'm not really enjoying being the other woman, so to speak. I mean, I can't call you too much. Our time together has to be finely in tune with your work schedule, not to mention mine. I'm just feeling too confined, I think. Too restricted, is more accurate."

"What do you want me to do, Peg?" Maria brushes her hand across Peg's cheek.

Peg tingles and blushes at Maria's caress. "I don't know. Maybe I need to know where this is headed. Is this, in fact, an affair, as you once called it?"

"I don't know what an affair amounts to to you."

"Well, to me it sounds packaged. Like it's already happened. It's definite and finite. A summer fling sort of event."

"It's not summer, and this isn't a fling to me. I love you, Peggy. But, I don't know if I do know what this is to me yet. I feel like it's still evolving. Like I might still be evolving, I feel as though I'm just beginning to find my authentic self. I have to do that. I can't give you an answer. I'm sorry."

"Don't be." Peg draws Maria to her, and kisses her with more passion then she knew she had. Their tongues meet, meld together and part.

"No, listen, Peg. I have more to say. While you were away, a lot of issues fell into perspective for me. I mean, you know that emotionally, on a circumstantial level, this relationship has been difficult for me. I spent a lot of time worrying about many things—my old life, my marriage, my kids—"

"Maria, don't. It's all right. You don't need to render an accounting to me." Peg says the words feeling guilty for trying to put pressure on her.

"I *want* to continue, Peg. Really. Especially my kids were on my mind. I kept thinking, how could I do this to them? Ideas like that floated around in my head. And I sort of had myself convinced that I could hide our relationship from them, from the world."

Defensively, Peg speaks up. "But, that can't last, you know."

"I'm not finished. A few days ago a different perspective flashed across my mind. Ben and I were on the couch in the living room doing our usual emotional avoidance and the kids were on the floor playing a board game. All of a sudden, I realized that the model we're presenting to them is sterile. Sterile, at best. And I saw how horrible that was.

"I felt relieved and ridiculous at the same time. I had been so hung up about the lesbian aspect, about what that might do to the kids, that I forsook the human element. That you and I are in love."

"Passionately," Peg says, kissing Maria's fingers one by one.

"That we have a chance for a mutually respectful, affectionate relationship. What better model could there be of an adult relationship for kids? It completely bowled me over when I saw it this way."

"I like your thinking, Maria. I should go away more often."

Maria moves closer to Peg so that their bodies are touching. As she positions to hug Peg, Maria murmurs: "Don't you dare." Maria slides a hand up and then down Peg's back, and their bodies fuse for a long, slow kiss. Maria kisses both of Peg's eyelids and wraps herself around her, radiating heat from her rising body temperature.

Slowly, Maria gets up, and says in a quiet, whispered voice: "I need to go now, Peg." Her breathing is irregular. She beckons Peg with her hands, and they hug once again, standing with their feet woven in between each other's. Peg runs a hand through Maria hair, and whispers: "Maria, you drive me totally wild."

"Great," Maria says as a low groan of pleasure emanates from her throat. They finish their embrace, and Maria grabs for her coat and bag and slides out the outer door of Peg's apartment.

CHAPTER TWENTY-TWO:

WOMEN FROM
THE DOLLS

THE ERRIGON GALLERY IS LIT brightly on the darkening SoHo streets. This warm spring evening is opening night of a heavily advertised and already celebrated show. The reception is set for six o'clock and Frank and Kim are inside attending to last minute details.

Kim stands at the center of the main exhibit room, simultaneously observing how the paintings are hung and going over the brochure. "Nice. Nice," she says to herself, and then to Frank: "Thank you, Mr. Errigon. I like how this looks: Ms. Kim Chew, Assistant Curator, exclusively representing the work of the late artist, Karen Apfelbaum."

"You've earned it, my dear," Frank Errigon exclaims in a light, offhand tone. "You handled the whole Living Dolls affair marvelously. A woman's touch was just what we needed to pull this off to advantage. And look, the show's been splashed across the media. We're champions—what a coup! The only gallery known to man to profit from feminist art.

"It'll be packed in here tonight. Remember: sell, sell, SELL! I'm counting on you, Kim. Now, let's go over everything one more time. Where are those artist's statements?"

Frank darts around the gallery running through a mental checklist. He pats each item as he surveys its placement. Kim, fashionably clothed in a black sheath dress, fishnet stockings, and platform shoes made out of clear plastic over her pedicured feet, remains calm. She surveys the set-up remaining in place. She walks to the main table to adjust the fragrant, multi-colored freesia.

"Good job, Kim," she murmurs under her breath with a sense of confidence. Kim is momentarily blinded when she looks through the storefront windows to the sidewalk outside. She is struck by camera flashbulbs and fixed lights on tripods for the filming underway. When she regains her vision, she fusses with the daffodil and tulip planters that line the interior of the over-sized windows.

On the exterior façade of the gallery building, four Living Dolls in full costume are plastering posters. They are lining the block with a complete retrospective of their poster campaign as well as eight copies spread on either side of the doors of their most recent addition touting the Errigon show as a tribute to Karen's achievement and the future advancement of women in the art world generally.

The entire street is littered with paste buckets, brushes, and scrolled posters. Several reporters are covering the event, and a New York University political science student is filming the Dolls for a documentary on contemporary women's activism. To the glee of the student, a crowd has gathered and has engaged the Dolls in back-and-forth banter about their work.

A few blocks from the gallery, Maria is at Peg's apartment. The two sit, partially dressed, on pillows taken from the bedroom and placed around the coffee table. They've set out an opulently colored and varied meal, held in the white box and plastic containers of take-out stores—roast chicken in tomato-eggplant sauce, squid in cilantro and ginger, and an arugula and beet salad that Maria purchased at Citarella on her way downtown. They have an oversized bottle of Evian on the table as well as a fragrant sauterne that Peg ran out to Sherry Lehman to buy the day before.

Swallowing a particularly satisfying morsel of delicate squid while spooning extra sauce over her chicken, Maria declares: "Thank god we had the sense to cancel our reservation at Chanterelle."

"Definitely," Peg says, emphatically. "I love their food, but who needs to sit rigid and upright for four hours while the courses are doled out? This, right here, is heaven, if you ask me." Peg pours herself some wine, sips, and then dives into the savory beets on her plate.

"And," Maria says, continuing Peg's thought, "we would've missed the reception for sure!"

"Not on your life, my love. Nothing could keep me from that. Is Bessy coming? I have a gift for her."

"Peg, you're amazing." Maria leans over for a long, slow kiss. When their lips part, mingling flavors and spices, she says: "Yes, Jackie is bringing Bessy and then the three of us will go home together."

"Where's Ricky tonight, with Ben?"

"No. Nope. I wish. Ben's retreated from them. It's sad, but there's not much I can do about it, at least not more than I already have. Ricky's having a sleep over."

"I'm sorry, Maria. He'll come out of it, hopefully." Peg speaks softly, not knowing quite how to soothe Maria's agitation. "I mean, the one thing it sounds like Ben has been consistent about over the years is that he's a really caring father who Bessy and Ricky can count on."

"That's true, but I'm realizing that, contrary to the popular picture presented, I did a lot to hold things together. And then, later, it was me and Jackie who carried the brunt of the burden, separately—always butting heads—and that Ben sort of dashed around doing cosmetic stuff.

"Amazing how different the picture he painted, and I believed, was from reality. I used to feel like you can't know someone until you live with them, and now I see that you still don't know them until you divorce them, if then." Maria's voice hits low, somber tones as she speaks. In moments when such thoughts swirl around, any vestige of lingering ambivalence evaporates.

"And, amazing," she says, lost in a rehashing she's gone through multiple times, "how he's flipped one hundred and eighty degrees. I say the divorce word, and he's crying, he loves me, he doesn't understand. Ten minutes later, he's working out at the gym, going out, joking. Happy, happy, happy—"

"You don't prefer he'd stay miserable, do you, Maria? I mean, you don't want him to fight this tooth and nail."

"No, of course not." Maria runs a hand down Peg's arm and ends in a caress. "But still. You know, if he'd done half of what he's doing now—being a person, a *mensch*—maybe we'd still be married."

Maria perceives a cold chill run through Peg, and tempers her remark. "Peg, don't misunderstand me. I *love* you. I wouldn't be in love with Ben, I'm just saying that we could've been more functional and gotten a little enjoyment out of our family life. Instead, I retreated further and further away, and sacrificed my kids' happiness in the process."

Shrinking visibly, Peg says: "Well, maybe you shouldn't be getting divorced. Maybe you just need a good marriage counselor, and save everyone a lot of trouble."

"No. No, Ben's gung-ho on this now." Maria pauses. "But beyond that, I *need* this. Even apart from you, I need this. This is hard work, emotionally difficult. It's an identity crisis of large proportions. I mean, I've spent my entire adult life with Ben. You may not be able to appreciate this, but I've evolved in this process. I feel like I'm circling back to who I am rather than living as the person I had become in that marriage. I'm centering on a norm, a standard, an inner structure and strength that's been dormant and waiting. No, this is definitely good, but it's going to take time.

"That's why I want you and I to go slowly. Deliberately and consciously to fashion the life, the relationship that we both want and can share. Also, I have to think about my kids. They adore you, but I don't want them to become any more dependent on your presence than they already are until you and I are sure we have a solid foundation together."

"I know," Peg whispers, looking directly into Maria's eyes.

"I love you, Peg."

"I love you, too, Maria."

Breaking the mood, Maria shifts and says: "You know, we should get moving if we don't want to miss the party!"

As they begin to clear the remains of their meal, the two women bump against each other and fold into a sensuous embrace.

Releasing her hold on Maria, Peg asks with a cynical chuckle: "So, how's ol' Frank taking this show?"

Maria laughs. "Oh, he's in seventh heaven. Just to have the pressure off probably would've been enough, but then he caught a whiff of profit and ran with it. When the show started to get attention, Frank started to promote it heavily, touting himself as sole champion of women's art. He gave his receptionist a fancy title, and a lot more work."

"A raise, by any chance?" Peg asks, waving her wine glass elegantly in the air.

"Of course not, what could you be thinking, Peg, fairness?"

"*This* is progress, Maria?" Peg crinkles her forehead.

"I don't really know. Actually," Maria says, "I think that it is. The work of Karen Apfelbaum gets deserved recognition. The Living Dolls succeed in their mission and receive substantial media attention. Kim, the receptionist, gets a title and status elevation. Eventually, she can parlay that into something elsewhere."

"And," Peg says, "Frank Errigon benefits the most. I don't know why I'm surprised."

"The pathetic thing is that he doesn't have a clue about how transparent his opportunism is. Frank thinks he's sly and clever. But who cares, really? He wasn't going to lose out either way."

Unconvinced, Peg moves over to Maria for a kiss as she whispers: "I suppose ..."

Maria and Peg dress for the opening and exit the apartment arm in arm.

At barely six o'clock, a crowd has formed outside the Errigon Gallery, waiting impatiently to be let in. As Kim opens the doors with a broad, inviting smile, people jostle one another to pass through. Masked Living Dolls are intermingled with the others. Only Roberta, because of her connection to Maria, is in plain clothes, her face open to view. It was decided that she would not in any way acknowledge her acquaintance with the Dolls, nor they with her.

The film crew and equipment move inside as well, and set up to continue the documentation. The flowers have all been adjusted and readjusted several times as have the price lists and brochures. The central table is copiously decked with food, sporting a spring motif. Frank is once again elegantly outfitted, and flutters cheerfully to and fro, dropping in on conversations and chuckling gaily. In so doing, he is making mental notes about the diverse populations that are represented in this set of viewers. People seem to have travelled from far and wide to come to this opening.

Predictably, the academics stand huddled around the food, holding glasses full to the brim with alcohol in various forms. The urban professionals form clumps around Karen's major works, discussing the politics of her death and posthumous celebrity, and those from the suburbs are comparing notes on the best routes to avoid in- and out-going traffic. The Lycra-clad twenty-somethings are grouped in a corner, intently following the banter of a male, thirty-something SoHo sculptor. And a collection of thirty- and forty-something women have engaged Claire, in costume, in a serious discussion about artistic expression.

Sandra catches a glimpse of Aviva standing alone, looking out of place, in the back exhibit room. She is staring at one of Karen's starker works.

Sandra taps Aviva's shoulder gently as she quietly greets her: "Hey, Aviva." She looks into Aviva's eyes. "How is it going? We haven't spoken in a couple of weeks. Are things settling back to routine at all for you?"

Aviva looks tired, and visibly older than just months before. "No, I can't say that they are. Not yet."

"Are the arrangements made?"

"Yes, I think they finally are," Aviva answers slowly. "The up-state facility has signed all the documents, and Claire's to start there June 1st."

"God, that seems so far away," Sandra responds, sad and exasperated.

"Yes, I know. But, there was a lot of red tape to wade through. You know, it's a state institution, a girls' correction facility, no less. And from this point of view, what's the big deal, what's the hurry? For them, they're just getting a wood shop instructor. A luxury, really, that they don't feel any urgency about."

"I hope we've made the right choice, Aviva."

"Well, I think that we have. What could we do, we're not going to turn her in—" Aviva's voice trails off as she shudders internally at that prospect and her face blanches. "At least this way, she's heavily monitored and in a position to use her skills encouraging sorely disadvantaged teenage girls. Claire could really throw herself into that, I think."

"Let's hope so, Aviva." Sandra smiles a serious, warm smile and embraces Aviva.

Jackie enters with Bessy at six-thirty, just minutes after Peg and Maria arrive.

"Mommy!" Bessy screeches across the room, and gallops into Maria's open arms.

"Hi, sweetheart," Maria exclaims, scooping Bessy up.

Peg and Bessy exchange smiles, and Bessy says: "Hi, Peg-gy!" as she gropes at Peg's shoulder.

Jackie walks over to Maria at a more regular pace. "Hello, Maria, Peg."

"How's it going, Jackie?" Peg asks in a light tone.

"Good. Finals are closer than I like to think, but I'm hanging in."

"Ricky got packed and off all right?" Maria asks.

"Oh, sure. He was thrilled. Had visions of playing chess and Battleship all night with Calvin. What could be better, huh?" Jackie's eyes twinkle as she responds. "Hey, Bessy, want to go over and raid the food table? It looks pretty yummy over there."

"Hey, wait. Not so fast, buster," Roberta says. "How's my best pal, huh?" Roberta gives Bessy a squeeze.

Bessy smiles up at Roberta and hugs her around the waist before skipping off to meet Jackie in front of the strawberry tarts.

Turning to Maria and Peg, Roberta says: "Hello, strangers."

"Come on, 'Berta. You're the one that's been too busy for us, domesticated as you are now. How's it going?"

"Great, but I am *not* too busy! Come over! How about, we'll make you two dinner this weekend, what do you say?"

"Thanks, 'Berta," Maria says, "but we're *four* this weekend. I have the kids. I doubt you want to contend with that."

"Don't be ridiculous. I'd love to. How about Saturday, five or six-ish? You probably won't want to get home too late with Bessy and Ricky, right?"

"Okay," Maria says in mock resignation.

"What can we bring? Dessert?" Peg asks.

Roberta smiles. "How about the main course? Ha, just joking, don't look so rattled, you two. What're you, going totally serious on me? No, dessert would be great. Any recent food restrictions or animosities I should be aware of?"

"Nope, none," Maria says, "except Bessy, who'll only eat pasta these days. And drink chocolate milk, of course."

As the reception bubbles along, upbeat, a young couple begins to argue petulantly in the doorway. Just as they move their discussion to the stoop, a middle-aged couple emerges from the commotion and begins to find their way down the street. The man is dressed in ordinary, brown male business attire. The woman is wearing a silk Eileen Fisher ensemble in lush purples and mauves. She has a fashionable haircut and walks in shoes from the latest Sacco spring collection.

The woman pauses to read one of the plastered posters and chuckles softly. She takes the arm of her husband as she speaks, in an amused tone: "Remember the last time? Seems pretty funny to think about that now, huh?"

The man reacts with a gesture, as if unsure how to respond.

"Say, Milton, let me take you to a new restaurant that opened down the street. Sounds like the food's great and the atmosphere's hip."

With no answer, Mabel nudges her husband. "Come on, let's try it. It's just two blocks down and around the corner."

The two make their way down the street with Mabel leading the way.

"Hey, Milton. It is going to be a great spring this year, I can tell."

ABOUT THE AUTHOR

MONTANA KATZ is a psychoanalyst. She has written two other novels (*Clytemnestra's Last Day* and *Side Effects: A Footloose Journey to the Apocalypse*), a play (adapted from *Clytemnestra's Last Day* by the same name), books on psychoanalysis (*Contemporary Psychoanalytic Field Theory: Stories, Dreams and Metaphor* and *Metaphor and Fields: Common Ground, Common Language, and the Future of Psychoanalysis*), and two award-winning books on gender bias (*The Gender Bias Prevention Book* and, with co-author Veronica Vieland, *Get Smart: What You Need To Know But Won't Learn In Class About Sexual Harassment And Sex Discrimination*). Her writing is situated at the confluence of fact, history and the unconscious.